LOYALTY DEFILED

It is 1906 and Tanya Summersfield finds it hard to tolerate her manipulative Aunt Stella. The return of her autocratic father does not improve things, for despite their respectable façade the family is not without its dark secrets. Although the Summersfield wealth has gone and their home, close to St Paul's, is decaying, Tanya's father refuses to allow her to continue teaching in the East End. As the undercurrents of obsession and revenge in the Summersfield household enmesh Tanya in their web, she is forced to fight – not only for the man she loves, but also for life itself...

LOYALTY DEFILED

Loyalty Defiled

by

Alison Stuart

Magna Large Print Books
Long Preston, North Yorkshire,
BD23 4ND, England.

British Library Cataloguing in Publication Data.

Stuart, Alison
Loyalty defiled.

A catalogue record of this book is
available from the British Library

ISBN 0-7505-1829-4

First published in Great Britain in 1996
by Headline Book Publishing PLC

Published in Large Print 2002 by arrangement with
Darley Anderson

Magna Large Print is an imprint of Library Magna Books Ltd.

Printed and bound in Great Britain by
T.J. (International) Ltd., Cornwall, PL28 8RW

This book is dedicated to Jasmine April – the new star in our lives who has stolen all our hearts.

ACKNOWLEDGEMENTS

Darley Anderson for your wisdom, guidance and faith in me. And for making dreams come true.

Jane Morpeth for your encouragement and support.

To my special friends for just being there: Karen Vincent, Carol Townend and Verity Reynolds.

And, of course, Chris – for being himself.

Who can be wise, amazed, temperate and
  furious,
Loyal and neutral, in a moment? No man.

Shakespeare

Chapter One

'Nothing is as it seems. Remember that, Tanya. It will protect you from the blows this world so frequently delivers us.' Aunt Maude regarded Tanya with unusual severity. 'I worry about you. You've led too sheltered a life.'

'And who is to blame for that? For years Papa has chosen to forget my existence.' Tanya flicked back her long amber-gold hair where it cascaded over her shoulders, her face set with indignation.

'That will change once he returns to England.'

'I doubt it will change for the better.' Tanya's green eyes sparked with anger. 'Papa cannot forget that he is a brigadier. I will not be drilled into submission like one of his troopers. He ordered me to stop teaching as I wished, disregarding that my school fees had not been paid for the last year. How else could I repay Miss Stockwell for allowing me to complete my education?'

'Of course you could not teach, my dear.' Aunt Maude shuddered and picked up her embroidery but was too agitated to resume sewing. 'The very idea is unthinkable. As a Summersfield you have a position to uphold.'

Tanya jumped up from her chair as though fired from a cannon and paced the room. 'When we had money that was so.' With difficulty she checked her anger. It wasn't her aunt's fault that she had been ordered to return to London. 'Our circumstances have changed, Aunt Maude. And you're right that nothing is as it seems. For years Aunt Stella has striven to maintain the façade that our family has both position and wealth. There is little money now. Instead of wise investments it was used to maintain Papa's and my brothers' lifestyles in the officers' mess. I haven't received my allowance for two years. How does Papa expect me to live if I do not work? I suppose it was Aunt Stella who informed him that I was teaching. What right has he to interfere in my life?'

'Stella was concerned for the good name of our family. She saw it as her duty.' Maude regarded Tanya over the top of her pince-nez and frowned. Her marriage to Bernard had never been blessed with children and she loved Tanya like a daughter. She could feel the energy in the young, vibrant woman. Tanya was a vivacious beauty with her oval face, high cheekbones and small, upturned nose. She was no peaches and cream doll. Her beauty came from her spirit within, the joy of life in her almond-shaped eyes and her irrepressible smile. The luxuriant amber hair pulled up on her head and flowing in natural curls between her shoulder blades added to the untamable essence she exuded. Such spirit was not the stuff of teachers. That was not the way for one such as Tayna to be independent as she desired. She had the courage, tenacity and determination of a pioneer. And that's what frightened Maude. Tanya was seventeen and too innocent and vulnerable for such a wicked city as London.

Maude was worried about the recent disasters reported in the papers. She saw them as portents of troubles to come. 'Heed my words, Tanya,' she persisted. 'The very world we live upon is unstable this April. First the top of Mount Vesuvius is blown off in an eruption like something out of Dante's Inferno. A huge sulphurous cloud and lightning flashes accompanied the lava pouring down the mountainside. It is a warning, I tell you. An omen.'

Used to her aunt's eccentricities, Tanya smiled indulgently. Aunt Maude's small face was unlined despite her fifty years.

'If it is not God's warning,' Maude went on, 'why was it that eleven days later San Francisco had that fearful earthquake? All those people killed and thousands were made homeless. What will be next?'

Tanya didn't want her kindly aunt upsetting herself. 'They were terrible tragedies, but there have always been volcanic eruptions and earthquakes.'

Aunt Maude shook her head. Her long grey hair was neatly plaited in a coil on top of her head and she picked at a lace ruffle on the bodice of her cornflower-blue blouse. Maude always wore shades of blue. It had been her late husband's favourite colour and she wore it in tribute to him although he had been dead for fifteen years. She sighed. 'I have this feeling that something dreadful is about to happen to us. I can't shake it. Mark my words, nineteen hundred and six will be a bad year for us.'

'Those events happened in Italy and America,'

Tanya tried to reassure her.

'Exactly. And where is London if not smack bang in the middle of the two,' Maude groaned.

Tanya did not laugh at her aunt's absurd reasoning. Maude did have premonitions of family disasters though not how they would happen. The last time was just before Tanya's two brothers were killed. Maude had seen each of them in a dream, their image fading until it vanished. Within a month of the dream, each had been killed in battle. 'I'm sure you are worrying needlessly,' Tanya said. 'The only volcano around here is Aunt Stella when she's in one of her moods.'

Maude laughed and held out a hand for her niece to take. 'You're always a comfort, my dear. Unlike Stella who can be such a trial. It's regrettable that your father has served so long in India and before that a decade in Africa.' She halted her embroidery, the needle resting in the incomplete petal of a scarlet poppy. 'The Summersfields can be a headstrong brood. It comes from raising generations of army officers. But as women we must conform to convention.'

Tanya fingered a tassel on the maroon velvet cloth covering the mantel of the black marble fireplace. Clearly Aunt Maude was distressed by her outburst, but then she hated any dissent within the family.

'Aunt Stella takes too much upon herself,' Tanya declared. 'I'm no longer a child and can manage my own life. I refuse to live by her outmoded Victorian ideals. We are part of the Edwardian age – an age of progress, of women demanding their rights.'

'Don't let your father hear you speak like that. It was Victorian ideals that built the Empire he has been proud to defend for the last thirty years. And I'm sure that Stella meant to do what was best.' Maude set aside her work. 'Stella can be dogmatic at times. It's a family trait.'

'I enjoyed teaching.' Tanya's voice rose with passion. 'I've been home for over three months now and I'm bored with nothing worthwhile to occupy my mind.'

'You must consider your position as a brigadier's daughter. Our family is an old and revered one. We have served the regiment and our country for generations, a proud heritage which cannot lightly be dismissed. It simply isn't done for a gentlewoman to take employment. That is for the lower orders, the poor.'

Tanya had heard enough. She resumed her restless pacing of the sitting room which was cluttered with furniture. When Maude was widowed and had returned to her brother's house she had refused to part with any of her possessions and had been give a bedroom and sitting room on the second floor.

'We cannot live today on the glories of the past,' Tanya answered. 'We are close to ruin.'

Aunt Maude looked shocked. 'That is speculation. Neither my father nor Reginald would have lived beyond their means.'

'Then why has the house been left to rot around us? For years repairs have been needed to the roof, but nothing has been done,' Tanya reasoned. 'And it's not speculation. I've seen the household accounts. We've bills outstanding to all the shopkeepers.'

'A gentlewoman does not trouble herself over money.' Maude's fingers twitched at the rope of pearls hanging to her waist. 'It's not a polite subject to be discussed. I'm sure it's an oversight on Reginald's part. He's been abroad for so long. Once he returns everything will be as once it was. This will be his home now that he is retiring from the army.'

'Papa's retirement will mean many changes. I remember his rages when his orders were not obeyed. And how are we to live on just his army pension?'

'Reginald will find a means to support his family,' Maude said loyally. 'There will be many opportunities for a man with his connections. You do not know your father as I do. He can appear tyrannical when displeased, but then you must remember that he expects his men to obey his orders without question. I've never known him to be unreasonable if matters are explained fully to him. Unless, when without his permission, you began teaching; then he would feel that you were lowering the standards expected of this family. He is a proud man, with integrity and honour.'

She leaned forward, her eyes pleading with Tanya to understand. 'If you do not cross your father, you will find that he is not as hard-hearted as he makes out. Reginald was always kind and protective towards me. Stella may have her nose put out of joint by his return. Their personalities always clashed.'

Tanya did not comment. It was obvious that Maude respected her brother and was grateful that he had allowed her to live here when she was widowed. Hating conflict of any kind, Maude would never have disobeyed her brother's wishes. But she was fortunate that she had some independence, her own income paying for her requirements. Her husband's estate was managed by a competent solicitor.

'If you're bored,' Maude continued, reverting back to their earlier conversation, 'then help Stella with her charity work. She's on so many committees, she'll find you plenty to do.'

Frustration, pent up in Tanya for months, found its voice. 'I can do so much more for the poor than serving in a soup kitchen. I could teach them to read and write.'

'Nonsense, my dear.' Maude put her hand over her heart, her expression appalled. 'Reginald will not hear of it. It would be most improper. And you have to think of your future. How would a husband view such conduct?'

Tanya looked at her aunt incredulously. 'Any man I marry will take me as I am.'

Maude stared at her in speechless shock for several moments, then sighing, declared, 'Where do you get these ideas, child? A man expects a wife to be meek and compliant. It is Reginald's fault you're so headstrong. Why he did not insist that you went to India and found yourself a husband there, I don't know.'

Tanya's eyes flashed with affront. 'I may be his only surviving child, but Papa conveniently forgot my existence in the years he's been in India. That suited me. He only had time for my older brothers who joined his precious army. Their lives were sacrificed to family tradition, as were the lives of so many other Summersfield men, on the battlefield. Harry in India and Ben killed by the Boers. I will not be sacrificed to the marriage market.'

'Marriage is not a sacrifice,' Aunt Maude retorted. 'Your Uncle Bernard and I were very happy for the ten years we were together.'

Sadness filmed her aunt's eyes and Tanya's defiance lost its edge. She was angry with her father and Aunt Stella for interfering. The last thing she wanted was to make Maude unhappy. Her older aunt had loved Uncle Bernard. He had drowned when he tried to save a young boy swept away in a river current. Both had been dragged under, their bodies found a mile downstream at the next low tide. Maude had moved back to Pilgrim's Crescent to share the house with her spinster sister, even though the two of them did not get on.

'Do you want to end up like Stella?' Maude asked caustically. 'Spinsterhood has robbed her of her joy in life. She's embittered. Yet once she was different. As a young woman she was so passionate, so full of life.' Maude broke off, her gaze distant as she became absorbed in her thoughts.

Tanya bit her lip to stop her amusement showing. It was difficult to imagine the disapproving harridan as young and passionate. She watched Maude return from her reverie and said, 'Aunt Stella is passionate about respectability and what the neighbours may think.'

'Indeed, Stella was once very different,' Aunt Maude repeated; she spoke more to herself than to her niece. She stared into the fire burning in the grate, the brass firedogs and surround reflecting the yellow flames like a hundred eyes in the darkening room. Even with the chill April winds, this was the only fire in the cold house; no other was lit before they dined in the evening. Maude paid for the luxury herself. 'Bernard came to me last evening when I visited Mrs Rivers,' she continued absently. 'He spoke of danger to us both. That we must be on our guard.'

A shiver made Tanya clutch her hands to her arms. She wished Maude would not talk of her husband like that, or visit Mrs Rivers who held seances and spoke to the spirits of the dead. Tanya couldn't see that what Maude did was wrong, especially if it brought her comfort, but Stella would not speak to her sister for weeks if she learned she had visited Mrs Rivers. On more than one occasion Stella had threatened to have Maude committed to an asylum for the insane for such unholy ravings. So much for Christian charity and understanding, thought Tanya. For an ardent churchgoer and pious woman, Stella was intolerant and bigoted.

'Aunt Maude, there is no danger to you here,' Tanya soothed.

Her aunt's gaze remained distant. 'I worry about you, Tanya. You are too eager for independence. You must be guided by your father. I would hate to see your life ruined like Stella's was. I have some capital, as you know. If ever you need money, I will help you.'

'It's very kind of you to offer, Aunt Maude, but that is your security for the future.'

They heard the front door bang shut, blown by a gust of wind. Stella had returned from her committee meeting. Tanya put her arms round Maude's shoulders and kissed her cheek. 'You've given me the only love I've known in this house since my brothers joined the army. Mother was always so remote when she was here. She seemed to care more for attending balls than me.'

Maude sighed. 'Your mother, God rest her soul, thought her child-bearing days long past when you arrived as something of a surprise after twelve years. She was an only child. Babies unnerved her. She was uncomfortable with them and took little interest in your brothers until they were ten. She could be frivolous but she was the wittiest woman I knew. India takes its toll on so many officers' wives and cholera is no respecter of class. Although it's been five years since she died, I still miss her monthly letters. They were always so entertaining.'

An impatient voice called from below. 'Tanya, we have a guest. Where are you?'

'Coming, Aunt Stella.' She rolled her eyes to the scrolled plasterwork round the ceiling. 'It can't be anyone important. Aunt Stella never invites people to the house, she's too much of a snob to allow them to see how dilapidated it has become.'

Maude picked up her embroidery and began stitching, prompting Tanya to ask, 'Aren't you coming down to meet our guest?'

'I've met enough of Stella's do-gooders to last me a lifetime. Don't let Stella see that her interference angers you. She will not tolerate having her will thwarted and she can make life very difficult if she wishes.'

'It's time she learned that I'm no longer a child,' Tanya said firmly. 'I will decide my own life. I've had enough of Aunt Stella curbing my freedom. She disapproves of any friends I bring home. If I go out in the evening she insists I'm home by nine thirty. I will not live like a nun or a recluse. And if Papa proves just as autocratic, I'll tell him the same.'

Maude studied her with concern. 'I admire your spirit, but Stella has your welfare at heart. The young always want to break with convention. If Stella is protective, she has her reasons. She, too, used to rebel against our father's strictness – oh, the heartache her conduct caused!'

'What did she do?' Tanya was intrigued. Stella was as strait-laced as the whalebone corsets that confined her stout figure and creaked with every movement. It seemed impossible that the humourless and puritanical woman could have experienced the same rebellious feelings as herself. 'I can't imagine Aunt Stella as other than a sharp-tongued spinster who regards any form of pleasure as sinful,' she said. 'Did she ever have a man pay court to her?'

The serene face which was as smooth as a woman's half her aunt's age became pinched with sadness. 'Didn't I just tell you that nothing was as it seems? Stella was as frivolous and romantically inclined as every young woman. Then life went sour for her. It changed her.'

'Did she fall in love, but the man never married her? Was she jilted like Miss Haversham in *Great Expectations?* Only instead of pining away in her wedding gown, she became a martyr to charity work.'

She wasn't jilted. The man was unsuitable – a penniless artist. But it was a long time ago,' Maude answered vaguely. 'There's no point in raking up the past with its painful memories.'

'Tanya!' Aunt Stella called. 'Our guest is being kept waiting.'

Tanya checked her curiosity about her younger aunt. 'I have to go. If Aunt Stella felt as I do, then she should understand that I want to be free to live my own life.'

'While you live under this roof and are supported by your father, you must obey his will,' Maude warned.

At the door, Tanya paused. 'Then I shall go out to work and support myself. I'm a good teacher. Miss Stockwell was impressed with my work.'

As Maude watched her niece leave, heaviness settled over her heart. At seventeen Tanya was so like Stella had been at that age. Defiance against convention had only brought harm to her sister. The same must not happen to Tanya.

As Tanya descended the stairs, she regarded the faded gold wallpaper which must have been elegant when it was hung forty years ago. It had turned bronze with age, darkened by the coal fire and the flames of thousands of candles and oil lamps over the years. Gas lights had never been installed in this large Georgian house, and the only running water was a cold tap in the servants' scullery. Not that they could afford proper servants now. There was only Ginny who was maid of all work and Olive Stoat who cooked for them. Both came in daily and left after the evening meal. Aunt Maude paid the salary of her own personal maid Millie. There was also Parkins the gardener who worked two days a week. Once, this four-storey house had been a grand establishment, dominating Pilgrim's Crescent which was over-shadowed by the great dome of St Paul's Cathedral. Now the outside stonework was black from the London smog, and the leaking roof and broken gutters made the upper floor uninhabitable from the damp and mildew. The window frames had rotted, and they rattled against their sash cords, creating perpetual draughts along the dingy corridors.

'At last! I expect better manners from you when a guest calls,' Aunt Stella declared as Tanya reached the bottom of the stairs. Dressed in grey taffeta, her huge bosom heaving with indignation, her aunt's short, plump figure reminded Tanya of one of the city pigeons.

Behind Stella, Ginny's thin, gangling frame was sagging under the weight of a silver tray. To Tanya's surprise it held two crystal decanters filled with sherry and brandy. Occasionally a glass of sherry was offered to the Reverend Hargreaves if he called, but Stella did not approve of strong spirits. For her to have decanted one of Papa's brandies stored in the cellar must mean that this was a special guest. Her aunt surveyed Tanya's appearance with a tut of annoyance. 'I suppose it's too late to do something with your hair. You must take time to dress it more demurely. Only common women wear their hair down.'

'I prefer it this way.'

'You mortify me at times, Tanya. I've never heard such nonsense. What has preference to do with decorum? You must dress as befits our standing in the community.'

Stella was four years younger than Maude but the lines of dissatisfaction about her mouth and eyes made her look older than her forty-six years. Her white hair was frizzed at the front and her thinning locks concealed under a triangle of heavy white lace.

On entering the withdrawing room, Tanya's glance fell upon a tall, slim man dressed in a black suit, standing by the fireplace. His back was to her and she saw him check his appearance in the mirror and adjust the line of his necktie before he turned to face her. Tanya guessed he was in his late twenties, but his smooth, rather boyish face defied age and he could easily have been several years older. His thick dark hair waved back from a wide brow and the blackest eyes she had ever seen. No imperfection marred his features. Long side whiskers framed a refined jaw and a narrow moustache emphasised his full lips. He was an exceptionally handsome man.

'Ginny, why is this fire not lit?' Stella demanded.

Ginny blushed and mumbled an apology. The

decanters on the tray rattled as she plopped it down on the Sheraton sideboard. Tanya felt sorry for the maid. It was unfair of Stella to try and impress their guest at Ginny's expense.

'And light the oil lamps, Ginny,' Aunt Stella ordered. She smiled at their guest. 'My brother, the brigadier, would never have gas in the house. He declared it was too dangerous.'

The three oil lamps cast the room in a favourable light, giving it an air of elegance and a hint of its past glory. Most of the furniture was Georgian in origin, though the blue brocade on the chairs was worn and fading when seen in daylight. When Ginny drew the navy velvet curtains, she was careful to conceal the darned holes where the fabric had rotted with age.

The fire lit, Ginny departed, her gaze lingering on the handsome stranger.

'Mr Tilbury, may I present my niece, Tanya,' Stella said with a softness to her voice which Tanya rarely heard. 'Tanya, Mr Tilbury has donated a substantial fee to the church poor fund. He has recently returned to London from abroad.'

'A pleasure to make your acquaintance, Miss Tanya.' He inclined his head in an informal bow, his voice deep and attractive. Eyes blacker than midnight appraised her in a way she found unsettling.

Unused to the attention of any man, Tanya blushed. Since her aunt was seated and showed no signs of serving the drinks, she poured them. Mr Tilbury politely waited to sit on the settee until she was seated. She chose an armchair on the far side of the room.

'Tanya, don't sit over there,' Stella objected. 'I hate to twist from side to side to talk to you both. Please sit next to Mr Tilbury.'

An uncomfortable feeling that her aunt was intent on matchmaking aroused Tanya's resentment. Changing seats, she held Mr Tilbury's worldly and disturbing stare. A smile tilted the corner of his mouth in a disarming manner. It was difficult not to be affected by his good looks.

'Miss Summersfield, you did not tell me that your niece was so beautiful.' He raised his glass to Tanya, his expression admiring. 'But many men must have told you that.'

'My niece was at boarding school until Christmas,' Stella interjected before Tanya could answer. 'With her father away and her brothers killed in action, we have no male escort within the family. It has been some years since we have socialised.'

Tanya was surprised at the way her aunt appeared to hold Mr Tilbury in awe. Stella never usually viewed her fellow committee workers or their patrons favourably. She regarded herself as the most diligent worker of the group. Mr Tilbury must be someone important.

Unexpectedly, her aunt stood up. 'You will excuse me, I have remembered something important which I must attend to.'

She hurried out of the room leaving Tanya disconcerted that she must entertain their guest. 'Where did you make my aunt's acquaintance, Mr Tilbury?'

'Through her work with the poor. She is a

remarkable woman.'

'Do you serve on the same committees?'

He laughed. 'I've no patience for such work. I merely offered a modest donation to provide medication and clothing for those in need.'

'That is very commendable, Mr Tilbury. Have you visited the homes of these people and seen the conditions in which they are forced to live?'

'You cannot enter London from Essex, where I was brought up, without passing the slums of the East End. Seeing ragged toddlers going barefoot in the middle of winter, their tiny legs often bowed by rickets, is not a sight easily forgotten.'

The harshness in his voice surprised Tanya. She leaned forward, sensing a sympathetic listener. 'It is not just clothing they need, but the chance for a better education, or even any education.' She warmed to her subject. 'Many of the children play truant from school because they are needed at home. They have to look after younger brothers or sisters while their mothers work. Others from the age of ten work in back-street illegal sweatshops. As a consequence they cannot read or write. I'd like to work with the illiterate adults to give them the opportunity to better themselves. Unfortunately, my aunt is against the idea.'

A brow arched as he regarded her. The intensity of his stare caused her heartbeat to quicken. He was not deriding her but taking her seriously. 'Your aunt is right. A gentlewoman would be at risk working in the slums. You seem very knowledgeable about the poor. Yet I cannot believe that you have been allowed to visit their homes.'

'I have not. But I've spoken to some of them

when I've served at the soup kitchen.' The passion rose in her voice as she responded to the keen interest in his gaze. 'Their plight cannot be ignored. Somehow I'll find a way to hold classes.'

'It would be dangerous without a male escort to protect you. There are people within those rookeries who'd set upon you for the price of the clothes that you wear.'

Her chin lifted with defiance. Too often she'd had this conversation with Stella who was horrified at the idea. She would not tolerate any interference from a stranger. 'I will find a way.'

He adjusted a gold cufflink in his immaculate starched cuff so that its engraving sparkled in the oil light. 'Would you think me presumptuous if I offered to escort you? I could spare two hours in the early evening twice a week.'

Dumbfounded, Tanya stared at him. She didn't know what to say. It was the answer to her prayers, but she did not know the man. And Stella would never agree. Finally she found her voice. 'Your offer is most generous, but…'

He waved aside her protest, his smile assured. 'I will speak to your aunt.'

'What would speak to me about, Mr Tilbury?' Stella asked from the door.

'Your niece has told me of her wish to teach in the East End. I have offered to escort her to ensure that she is not molested.'

Tanya waited for her aunt's outrage to surface. To her amazement, she seemed unwilling to displease her guest. His donation to the poor must have been extremely large to have so impressed her.

‘My niece could have no better protector, Mr Tilbury. But the location must be chosen with care.’ There was a disapproving tightening of her lips as she added, ‘Stepney and Whitechapel are dangerous places once night falls. The inhabitants are scoundrels, thieves and worse. As for the women, they are no better than–’

‘Aunt Stella, they are the people who need help the most,’ Tanya interrupted. ‘Without education they are trapped by the circumstances of their birth, with no chance of bettering themselves.’

‘At least work with the children,’ her aunt declared. ‘They have a hope of redemption. You cannot get a leopard to change its spots. It’s a hopeless case to teach adults.’

Tanya’s gaze beseeched Mr Tilbury to support her as she answered, ‘No case is hopeless. The children have school to attend and truant officers to try and ensure that they do. But how can the adults learn if I do not offer to help?’

‘Your niece is right, Miss Summersfield,’ he said. ‘But if you refuse your permission, I shall quite understand.’ He smiled at Stella, his lips parting to reveal white, even teeth.

‘Please, Aunt, you must agree,’ Tanya burst out.

Stella did not look at Tanya, her gaze was scrutinising their visitor. The usual stern lines mellowed about her eyes and mouth, and there was respect in her gaze. Tanya had felt the pull of Mr Tilbury’s easy charm and it amused her to see her staid aunt similarly affected.

‘Could these classes not be held somewhere more respectable – like Cheapside?’ Stella asked.

‘Naturally, your niece could not be subjected to

the notorious rookeries of Whitechapel.' His voice was smooth and conciliatory. Again a smile tilted his mouth, its power beguiling.

'I would work where I'm most needed,' Tanya insisted. 'Please, Mr Tilbury. My aunt is over-anxious as to my safety, but I have no such fears.'

He inclined his head to her. 'I'd be honoured to help you in any way that I can. But not without your aunt's approval. We must bow to her judgement.'

Tanya held her breath as Stella's expression changed from disapproval to a thin smile of acceptance. She had never known her aunt succumb to the charm of any man, but Mr Tilbury appeared to have won her over. 'I will place the welfare of my niece in your hands, sir. Can I also persuade you to join us for supper this evening?'

'With regret I must decline. I have a prior engagement. Perhaps some other time.'

Bright coins of colour appeared on Aunt Stella's cheeks at his refusal. Why was her aunt so indignant that he was leaving?

When Mr Tilbury had departed, she regained her composure. 'Mr Tilbury is an estimable gentleman, Tanya. Though how upon such short acquaintance you came to be speaking of your wish to teach I can't imagine. It is most improper. But since he approves and is prepared to escort you, it would be churlish of me to deny you. He is a man of means and position in the city. A generous man and most charming. I am sure your father would approve of him, which is why I agreed to this venture.'

Tanya sighed. 'Mr Tilbury has the welfare of the poor at heart by offering to escort me. He is not paying court to me.'

'Well, I trust that if he did, you would not be so foolish as to repudiate him. Surely you find him handsome.'

'He is very handsome.' She did not add that now he had left she was puzzled by his willingness to assist her. There had been calculation in his ebony gaze as he made his farewells, and something more. It was as though he expected her to fall for his charm, as no doubt many women must have done. Instead she went on, 'I do not know him well enough to have any thoughts on the matter as yet.'

Stella was contemplative as Tanya rang the bell cord to summon Ginny to collect the glasses. She wanted Archie Tilbury to court Tanya. Reginald would be furious if his daughter became engaged without his consent. It would be the first step towards revenging herself on her brother for his part in stopping her marriage to the man she loved.

Chapter Two

Three days later Tanya's childhood schoolfriend Clare Grosvenor called on her and was shown into the conservatory adjoining the family parlour. Tanya put down her sketchpad. She'd been drawing Buster, the scarred, feral tom cat who liked to sun himself in their garden.

'Clare, how lovely to see you.' She embraced her friend. 'I've missed you.'

Clare had married last September and now lived in Tunbridge Wells. She was short, dark and vivacious with the largest, bluest eyes Tanya had ever seen. Her only imperfection was protruding teeth revealed whenever she smiled, which she did constantly. She had been the most generous-hearted and unaffected girl in the Ladies Academy. Tanya had known her for several months before she discovered that Clare was the daughter of Tobias Havistock the millionaire shipping magnate.

'I see that you're still scribbling away.' Clare picked up the pad and studied it. 'What an ugly cat but it's a brilliant likeness.'

Tanya ignored the praise. 'What are you doing in London? I thought you were staying in Kent until the end of May. And how is Simon? Does marriage to him still agree with you?'

'Simon is well and I couldn't be happier.' Clare kissed her cheek. 'He had some urgent business in town. But we're only here a day or two. You know how he hates the city. He thrives in his life as a country squire.'

'It isn't doing you any harm. You look radiant.' Tanya held her friend at arm's length and surveyed her. Her dark hair was swept up under a large cream picture hat and she wore a rose-pink tea gown which emphasised her glowing complexion.

'It must be all that fresh country air and married life. Get yourself married, Tanya. You don't know what you're missing – *really* missing.' She grinned, as saucy as ever. Clare had inherited her father's blunt speech and never troubled to hide her fascination with men and sex.

'Marriage certainly suits you. How does it feel to be a respectable matron? You used to be such a tomboy.'

'You and me both. We did get into some scrapes,' Clare giggled. 'Do you remember the time old Stockwell caught us climbing trees with our skirts hitched up about our knees and showing our bloomers? It was a dare who could go the highest. You won, of course. You always did. I thought Stockwell was going to have a seizure.'

'And what about that May Day,' Tanya reminded her, 'when you decided you wanted to go to the old woodland spring which was out of bounds? We got up before dawn so we could stare into the waters. It was a local suspicion that you would see the image of your future husband on May Day morning.'

Clare put a hand to her mouth. 'I'd forgotten that. And all we saw was that dirty old tramp who came out of the bushes with his trousers round his ankles and his willy sticking out. God, how I screamed. I'd never seen one before. And it was such a disappointment. You were so calm. I couldn't believe it when you told him to put it away, since it was such a puny little thing and nothing to show off.'

Tanya blushed. 'I never said that.'

'You did. You said you'd seen your brother walking naked from the bathroom and his was much larger.'

'Harry liked to walk about as nature created him, but I was only nine at the time.' An impish grin belied her prim tone. 'It's a relief to know that you weren't fated to marry a tramp. Or die a virgin, which was your worst nightmare.'

'Thank God for that!' Clare winked. 'And what have you been up to while I've been revelling in decadent bliss at Oaklands?'

Tanya shrugged and sat down on the window seat. 'Not much. You know how Stella is. She won't allow us to accept any invitations as we cannot return them. It's because she's ashamed that the house has not been redecorated for years. Though she did bring a gentleman home last week. And you'll never guess, he agreed to escort me into the East End so that I could teach.'

'And the old bat agreed?' Clare said, astounded.

'Yes. I'm still stunned. I've been thinking about teaching all winter. I need to do something useful to occupy my time.'

'I was hoping you would return with me to Oaklands. You need to meet people your own age and Simon has some very charming friends.' Her stare was knowing. 'Charlie Rothwell will be there. I declare the poor man has lost a stone in weight pining for a chance to meet you again after the wedding. Aren't you tempted?'

'Charlie was rather sweet. A week ago I would have jumped at the chance but I must teach if I get the opportunity. It's only a month before papa's ship docks at Tilbury.' Tanya jumped up, too excited to sit still. 'Teaching is important to me.'

‘I can see that,’ Clare teased.

Ginny bobbed a curtsy from the doorway. ‘Miss Tanya, Mr Tilbury has called and asks if you’re at home.’

‘Show him in here, Ginny.’ Tanya smiled at Clare. ‘He’s the one who’s helping me to teach. He was going to make the arrangements for the use of a church hall.’ She saw Clare’s eyes widen with surprise and interest.

Mr Tilbury stepped into the conservatory. The weather was sunny and he was dressed in a fawn suit which accentuated his dark skin and hair. Tanya had forgotten how handsome he was. He favoured both women with a devastating smile which revealed his perfect teeth. ‘Perhaps I intrude, Miss Summersfield.’

‘Not at all, Mr Tilbury. May I introduce Mrs Grosvenor. Clare is my dearest friend. She is not often in London since her marriage.’

He bowed to Clare who was unable to take her eyes off his tall, slim figure. His smile broadened as he bowed to Tanya. ‘I will not stay long. I’ve arranged with Reverend Carver for the use of a hall. It’s between the Tower of London and Aldgate Station. We have it Tuesday and Thursday evenings until eight thirty. I’ll call for you next Tuesday at six o’clock, if that is convenient. I took the liberty of having three dozen posters printed advertising your class. They will be put up in public houses in the East End.’

Impulsively Tanya took his hand, her eyes glowing with happiness. ‘I cannot thank you enough for all you have done.’

He bowed and raised her fingers to his lips. ‘It

is my pleasure, Miss Summersfield. Now, if you will excuse me, I'll leave you to enjoy the company of your friend.'

'Oh no, Mr Tilbury,' Clare interrupted. 'You must stay. Please don't leave on my account.'

His smile was ravishing as he regarded Clare. 'You are kind, but I have a business appointment in Cheapside in half an hour.' His dark stare flickered admiringly over Tanya. 'I'm delighted to have been of service to you.'

When he left, Clare let out a soft sigh. 'He's gorgeous. No wonder you're excited about working with him. Poor old Charlie Rothwell can't hold a candle to him. And it's obvious he's interested in you.'

Knowing Clare's fascination for romantic attachments, Tanya heatedly denied it. 'Don't be silly. This is only the second time we've met.' To her consternation she felt her cheeks grow hot.

'I knew it. You like him. You're blushing. A man like that doesn't put himself out for a woman unless he's interested. Snap him up quick, Tanya. He's a real catch. No wonder you don't want to come to Oaklands.'

'That's not fair.' Tanya rose to her friend's baiting. 'I'd love to visit you. It's the teaching I'm interested in, not Mr Tilbury.'

Clare grinned wickedly. 'Don't tell me you don't find him attractive?'

Tanya laughed. 'He is, but–'

'I'd make a play for him myself if I wasn't happily married. What a pity I'm only in London for another day. Just you keep me informed about the delectable Mr Tilbury in your letters.'

Raising her hands in mock horror, Tanya groaned. 'Don't you start trying to marry me off. I've enough trouble with Stella.'

Tonight was Tanya's first class and she was nervous. Fearing that she looked too young and the men and women would be uncomfortable being taught by someone of her age, she dressed her hair in a severe coil at the nape of her neck, holding it in place with a black crocheted net. Sensitive to her pupils' poverty, she chose a plain navy suit and navy straw boater. She also decided to wear no jewellery except a marcasite watch brooch which had been her grandmother's.

A quarter of an hour before Mr Tilbury was expected, she entered the withdrawing room anxious for her aunts' approval of her appearance.

Aunt Maude smiled and nodded in satisfaction. Stella looked displeased. 'What have you done to your hair? It may be more demure, but it makes you look old maidish. Mr Tilbury will be mortified to accompany such a drab companion.'

'I wish to gain the confidence of my pupils, not encourage Mr Tilbury's attentions,' Tanya retorted.

Stella tutted with annoyance. Halting her work on the table centre she was crocheting in cream silk, she pursed her lips. 'You're an attractive woman. You should make the most of your looks, not appear in public as a dowd.'

Maude intervened. 'Tanya is right. An East End classroom is not a place to flaunt her feminine charms. And you're unfair to call her dowdy,

Stella. She looks smart. Tanya is pretty enough without elaborate curls. Any man should be proud to escort her.'

Stella sniffed. 'Tanya should be trying to impress a man of Mr Tilbury's standing, not some illiterate villains from the East End.'

'Just because they are poor doesn't make them dishonest,' Tanya protested.

'This Mr Tilbury seems to have made quite an impression on you, Stella,' Maude commented.

The silver crochet hook stopped its rapid flashing in and out of the intricate work as Stella regarded her sister with a cool stare. 'No more than anyone who generously donates to the poor. I agreed to indulge this whim of Tanya's because Mr Tilbury is prepared to escort her. It may get this foolishness out of her system before her father returns. Reginald will never condone his daughter taking paid employment, or hobnobbing with the lower orders. What would the officers at his club say?'

'Those men resent any woman asserting her rights,' Tanya declared, growing angry at Stella's criticism. 'But women will no longer be silent and shackled to a life dictated by men. The suffragettes have shown us that we have a voice. Brave women are imprisoned every day and suffer starvation to uphold their fight for women's rights.'

'They bring shame to our sex by their disgraceful conduct,' Stella snapped. 'Chaining themselves to railings and leaving themselves open to be reviled and molested by any passer-by is disgraceful conduct.'

'Come now, Stella,' Maude interceded. 'What have the suffragettes to do with Tanya wishing to educate the poor?'

Tanya bit her lip to prevent an outburst to defend the women she admired. She had attended three of their meetings but had been disturbed by the militant action now governing their campaign. For the moment she was more concerned with the poor than the women's movement.

Her visits to the soup kitchen had shown her girls barely in their teens who were heavy with child. She had been appalled at the poverty and by the bruised faces of women who endured the drunken brutality of their partners. She had seen women of thirty as wizened as ancient crones, their bodies abused by constant childbirth and worn out by the slave labour of the sweatshops where they worked for a pittance. There were women who owned nothing but the grimy rags they stood up in. They had sold everything to stay alive until they only had their bodies left to sell to provide them with a morsel of food and a tot of gin. Often drunkenness was their only escape from the misery of their lives. She had also witnessed the camaraderie of these women when they banded together, supporting each other in adversity. She had been moved by their courage and strength, their ability to laugh and make merry when there was little to rejoice over. Fate had decreed that they be born in poverty, but lack of education kept them trapped there.

Maude picked up a parcel from the floor at her

feet. 'Tanya, these are for you. I hope they'll be of use.'

Unwrapping them, Tanya gasped. There were a dozen early reader books and several writing slates. Without an allowance she had been unable to afford more than six slates and chalk. 'Thank you, Aunt Maude. You're very generous.'

'I know how important teaching is to you,' Maude continued. 'I want it to be a success. But mind you collect them at the end of each lesson, or those ragamuffins will be pawning the books and slates come tomorrow.'

The doorbell rang, halting the conversation. Since Ginny had already left for the day, Tanya answered it. On leaving the parlour she heard Maude say sharply, 'Stella, it's not like you to go against Reginald's wishes. Are you sure that we can trust this Mr Tilbury?'

'Tanya is headstrong. There are a few weeks before Reginald returns. By then she'll be disgusted by the uncouth habits of the creatures she teaches and will listen to reason. This is just a way to show her independence. Next month it will be something different. Young women are capricious. If I try to stop her, it will only make her all the more determined. Of course I trust Mr Tilbury. I would not be allowing him to escort her if I did not.'

Stella's words stiffened Tanya's spine. So her aunt thought she was capricious and that her desire to teach the poor was just a whim. She'd show them otherwise. If they thought her stomach would turn at foul language or shoddy manners they were wrong. She was made of sterner stuff. If it was possible for her to help those less fortunate than herself, nothing would stop her.

On entering the hall Mr Tilbury removed his homburg which had been tipped at a debonair angle. Not a hair was out of place. He wore a dark grey suit and waistcoat, an expensive hunter watch and chain draped across his taut stomach. His pale blue cravat was intricately folded and held in place by a plain gold pin.

'I thought we'd take a taxi-cab as far as Aldgate pump and walk from there to the church hall. To arrive in too grand a style, when your pupils are in rags, would not be appropriate.'

Her estimation of him rose. 'Few people who work with the poor take the trouble to consider their feelings.'

'The hall is in the proximity of the rookery known as the Courtyard. It has an unsavoury reputation as a haunt of cutthroats and prostitutes. I hope you don't get any of the inhabitants in the class, but it was the only hall I could find.'

'I won't be offended by their bad language or rough manners, if that is what you're thinking. And surely they are the very people who I can help the most, if they are prepared to learn.'

She picked up her black cape. He took it from her to place it over her shoulders and she was aware of his breath on the back of her head. The masculine scent of Macassar oil from his hair and the spicy cologne he used was pleasant to her senses. As she turned to face him she was struck by the enigmatic gleam in his obsidian eyes. He appeared the perfect gentleman, but that look disturbed her. He was her sole escort to one of the most perilous districts in London.

Through the lace curtains in the dining room, Maude studied Tanya and Mr Tilbury as they walked to the end of the crescent to hail a cab. She was surprised that the gentleman was so young. Stella had no time for youth, she cultivated the wealthy matriarchs of the community. Perhaps he was related to one of them. He was exceedingly handsome. They made a very fetching couple. How romantic if Tanya married him. He looked such a respectable and presentable man.

As she watched them walking, her brows drew together. There was something vaguely familiar about Mr Tilbury. He reminded her of someone. She shook her head and sighed. All too often she saw similarities in a stranger to someone she had known in the past. Sometimes a man in a crowd would remind her of Bernard, or James her elder brother who had been killed with General Gordon defending Khartoum in the Sudan in 1885. Frequently the sight of a young gentleman laughing and leaping into a hansom cab would make her heart clench with sadness at his likeness to her dead nephews Harry and Ben. They had been so full of life. She was getting old and fanciful, conjuring living ghosts to replace loved relatives.

Returning to the withdrawing room, she addressed her sister peevishly. 'Why didn't you introduce me to Mr Tilbury?'

'They were in a hurry.'

'They make a striking couple. He must be interested in Tanya to take so much trouble.'

Stella fidgeted with her crochet pattern, making a great fuss of studying the instructions. She was up to something. Maude knew her sister too well to be taken in by her feigned disinterest.

Undeterred, Maude chuckled. 'Surely you have considered the possibility of a match between them.'

'Have you forgotten that Tanya is dowerless?' Stella prevaricated. 'She'll have no money of her own while her father is alive.'

'A man of Mr Tilbury's standing will not require a dowry if he loves Tanya,' Maude said dreamily. 'But then, Tanya will not go to her marriage penniless.'

'I'm afraid that she will,' Stella remarked tersely. 'Unless Reginald reinvests what capital is left, all she will inherit on his death is a ruin of a house and a pile of debts.'

Maude shook her head. 'Tanya will be provided for. She's so like you were at her age, Stella. I don't want her to suffer as you did.'

Stella whitened. 'I do not wish to talk of the past. I was young and foolish.'

'Nevertheless,' Maude persisted, 'Tanya is headstrong. When she marries she'll get her dowry. I've also changed my will in her favour.'

'That's very generous of you, Maude,' Stella was unimpressed, 'but for years you've been living on the money from Bernard's estate. It couldn't have been much to start with or you'd not have scurried back here to live. I doubt you got much for Bernard's bottling factory when you sold it.

Your capital must be almost gone by now. You've made some extravagant purchases recently, including new curtains and a carpet, and rarely a month goes by when you do not buy a new hat. It will take a fortune to maintain this house.'

Maude looked at her sister in amazement. 'My capital remains at over five thousand pounds. I had intended to give Tanya one thousand on her marriage to enable her to buy her own property and to live comfortably. Whatever gave you the idea that my capital was so small?' Her tone became indignant. 'And I didn't scurry back here. I came to keep you company while Reginald was abroad. Also, I did very well from selling Bernard's business. It had always been a profitable concern, although you chose to deride it. I resent the way you treat me as though I'm simple-minded, Stella. I receive an adequate income each month from the capital for my needs. I never wanted to profit by Bernard's death. It would be like desecrating his memory. All I ever wanted was him. No amount of money can replace my husband. Tanya will inherit it all.'

Stella's lips curled back into a snarl. 'You mean all the time you've lived here, I've scrimped and saved to buy essentials and lost sleep worrying over the neglect of this house and you are *rich*?' She glared at her sister, hating her for all the needless hardship they had endured. 'When you moved back, I assumed it was because you were almost destitute. Why didn't you tell me you had a fortune at your disposal?'

'It is not a polite subject for conversation,' Maude said primly.

'How could you be so selfish?' Stella accused, the bitter lines on her face snaking together as her anger mounted. 'You could have paid for the repairs to the roof. We needn't have sold those paintings three years ago to pay the tradesmen's bills.'

Maude stood up, unwilling to listen to her sister's spiteful tirade. 'Reginald never said that he needed money. I thought he was being mean not paying for the repairs. He has spent most of the last thirty years abroad.' She walked sedately to the door. 'I'm surprised at your attitude, Stella. Didn't Papa instil in us that a woman should never trouble her head over money or matters of business?' The cold glitter in Stella's eyes offended Maude and she added, tartly, 'I'm sorry that you feel as you do. But Tanya will have her dowry. The rest she will inherit as my heir.'

Stella flung aside her crochet work, heaved her large bulk out of the armchair and advanced on her sister. She waved her fist menacingly. 'You're a selfish old woman. We need that money to repair the roof. This is your home. It's your duty to see that it does not become a ruin.'

Maude had never been able to stand up to Stella's bullying, but in this she would not defile Bernard's memory. 'The money is for Tanya. I will not touch it.'

'And what if she does not survive you?' Stella taunted. 'Must we continue to live like paupers? You could live another thirty years.'

'You're obsessed with this house and maintaining our position in society. That's why I never mentioned my money.' Maude backed away from her sister's fury. 'The house is Reginald's responsibility, not mine. If Tanya dies before me without a child to survive her, then my money will go to Barnardo's orphanage. Tanya is the last of our family line. What use is this house once we are all gone? It has always been a great sadness to me that I never had a child. This way at least the orphans will benefit.'

'A plague on the damned orphans,' Stella spat.

Maude's face paled with shock and she hastily left the room.

Stella clenched her fists and paced the floor to control her anger. Tears filled her eyes as she regarded the faded and torn velvet curtains, the threadbare carpet and the three pale squares on the wall paper where oil paintings had hung. Once this room had been elegant and beautiful, like all the rooms in the house. Now they were all dingy and forlorn and unfit for visitors. She had made an exception with Archie Tilbury.

A sinister smile played on her thin lips. Tanya could be as stubborn as her father. She had the same strength of character. If she came to care for Archie, she would marry him, and Archie with his good looks and charm could not fail to win Tanya's love. Stella had felt the potency of that charm; had he not allayed her suspicions and doubts? Unless Reginald had changed, he would be furious. He would see Archie Tilbury partly for what he was, *Nouveau riche*. Her brother despised any man who did not come from an old family. He would never consider Archie Tilbury good enough for his daughter.

Reginald had been wild as a young man. And

being a man, he had got away with it, had been applauded by their father, the colonel, for his high spirits. Bitterness rose in Stella's throat. That same trait in herself had been beaten out of her. For a glorious week after running away with her lover she had tasted the power of indcpendence. Then Reginald and her brother James had found them.

Her eyes hardened, hatred channelling through her. She had never forgiven them for destroying her chance of happiness.

Archie Tilbury would not be weak. He was an opportunist. She had explained the neglect of the house to him as the act of a wealthy miser and he had believed her. Once Tanya married Archie he had promised Stella that she would always be mistress here, even when Tanya inherited the house. Strong-willed as Tanya was, Stella had never yet failed to manipulate another woman to her will.

She paused in her pacing to run a hand caressingly along the back of a Chippendale chair. This was her domain; she would never relinquish her power in this house. Reginald's wife had never wrested the reins from her and she would not allow Tanya to either. Her mouth hardened into an uncompromising line. Tanya would not be so easy to subdue. She was already showing an independence and rebellion against her dominance. The sooner she was married to Archie the better. He would know how to keep her in her place. He could be as devious as herself in getting what he wanted. His marriage in to the Summersfield family would introduce him to the higher echelons of society to which he aspired.

Through tear-glazed eyes, she saw this room as it had been when she was a child. And would be again, if she had her way. Denied her lover, the house had become her obsession. With Reginald abroad she was its mistress. She had mourned its neglect as though it had been her own child ailing. Archie had promised to restore the house once Tanya inherited it. Although he always evaded her questions on his business dealings, she never doubted that he possessed the means to fulfil his promise.

A scream of frustration was blocked in her throat at remembering how Maude had kept secret the money she had received on her husband's death. Stella regarded that as a form of betrayal. Maude's miserliness had denied the house its glory all these years. Only her sister, the dreamer, could regard spending Bernard's money as a desecration of his memory. They could have lived in comfort and style.

She wouldn't get away with this. Maude, too, would pay for forcing her to live in humiliation for so many years.

Chapter Three

Tanya alighted from the taxi at Aldgate pump on to a packed pavement. Couples strolled arm in arm, pausing to inspect the wares on the costers' stalls set up along the roadway, the naphtha lamps hanging on the stalls brightening the night.

Sailors from the docks gabbled in a foreign tongue as they swayed towards the open doorways of the noisy pubs. Irish navvies, working on the construction of the underground train tunnels beneath the city, shouted bawdy comments at the street women. Tanya was shocked by the number of these women. They paraded in their gaudy, grimy clothes blatantly offering their bodies to every passing man.

Averting her gaze from them and the customers who mauled them in public, Tanya's cheeks singed with embarrassment. She was unable to close her ears to the obscene suggestions shouted after a man who refused a woman's custom.

'Perhaps your aunt was right. This district is no place for a gentlewoman,' Archie Tilbury said heavily and drew Tanya's arm through his. 'I should have taken longer to find a room closer to St Paul's.'

She shook her head. 'I must work where my pupils live. The attraction of the public houses or penny gaffs will be hard enough to combat. If they must add a half-hour walk to their classes at the end of a long working day they may not come.'

'You speak so passionately about teaching. Is it really that important to you?'

'I enjoyed assisting at the Ladies Academy. Did my aunt tell you that I disgraced the family by staying on an extra year to take some of the classes?'

'She mentioned that your sense of duty made

you offer your services. What subjects did you teach?'

'Art mostly. A gentlewoman should be accomplished with her watercolours as well as her embroidery.' Irony entered her voice. 'Not that my love of art is confined to such genteel pursuits. I enjoy sketching ideas for altering and redecorating rooms. When we put on a school play I painted all the scenery and designed the costumes. It was great fun.'

'Perhaps at heart you're an artist, not a teacher,' he teased.

'In Father's eyes that would be even more disreputable. At least I can help others with my teaching skills. I want my life to have purpose. Is that so wrong?'

His eyes were shaded by the brim of his homburg but his smile dazzled her. 'It is extremely commendable.'

They turned off the main thoroughfare into a narrow, cobbled side street lined with three-storey warehouses. There was no pavement and only a single hissing gas lamp lit the gloom. Tanya shivered with unease. There were iron bars on the warehouse windows and the place had a sinister air of decay. Rotting vegetables and broken crates had been tossed here by the high-street costers. A rat, as large as a tom cat, reared up twittering on a pile of rancid eel heads.

A gang of youths came running pell-mell through the pedestrians towards them and Tanya stepped closer to Mr Tilbury. The youths jeered and pushed against the elderly or a woman alone. A brassy-haired street walker dealt one of the boys a punch to the shoulder which sent him stumbling into the gutter. As nimble as an acrobat, he sprang to his feet to thumb his nose at the woman shouting abuse after him.

Archie Tilbury tucked the parcel of slates and books he was carrying more firmly under his arm. 'Hold tight to your bag, or you'll find yourself lighter of a purse.'

He put his free arm protectively round Tanya's shoulders. Its warmth and strength were reassuring. She could smell the youths' mud-slimed clothing from a dozen feet away. They reeked of foul water and rotten cabbages. Scarcely an inch of colour showed through the brownish-grey which covered both skin and garments.

'Those gangs of mudlarks are a disgrace,' Mr Tilbury murmured against her ear. 'They make their living sifting through the debris at the sewer outlets on the river.'

Tanya gagged from the stench of the sewers on them and was glad of Mr Tilbury's nearness.

'Bleeding toffs out slumming,' one jeered as he attempted to elbow Tanya in the ribs.

Another urchin, the shortest of the group with legs bowed with rickets, whistled coarsely and thrust a filthy hand close to her face. 'Give us a tanner, missus. Ain't eaten fer two days.'

Mr Tilbury kept his arm round Tanya and increased his pace. 'If you want food, come to the mission tonight. The Reverend Carver supplies soup for the needy every evening in the church hall. Miss Summersfield is teaching there tonight. Come and learn how to read and write.'

'What do I need with schooling?' The urchin cuffed the mucus from his nose. 'Me and me mates got better things to do. Keep your bleeding soup and you know where you can stuff it an' all.'

Tanya was not easily frightened, but the boy's belligerence set the fine hairs at the nape of her neck prickling with awareness of danger. The air crackled with menace. These youths might have the faces of children, but there was no mercy in their gaunt, haggard faces. Their eyes were as worldly and ruthless as grown men's.

Suddenly one drew a thin blade from his coat sleeve. Tanya gasped. She felt Archie tense. A glance showed him ashen-faced. It was not unusual for people to be attacked and robbed in this area in daylight.

Several passers-by turned to watch the disturbance, but no one moved to offer assistance. There was not a policeman in sight.

Tanya's blood curdled with terror. She gripped her hands together, knowing that any sign of weakness would be fatal.

Mr Tilbury rapped out a word she did not understand and the boys fell back. Their gazes were still suspicious but no longer antagonistic.

'Quickly, my dear,' he ordered. 'The church hall is just ahead. We're in no danger but youths of that age can be unpredictable.'

Tanya's heart clattered against the restrictions of her corseted ribs. Those few paces stretched like a mile. Each step brought the fear that the youths would surround them again.

'What was that you said to them?'

He hesitated before replying and dropped his

arm from her shoulders. 'It was cant. A code of these parts. I heard it shouted once and saw that the bullies respected it.' Again the disarming smile. It warmed her after her fear. 'It was fortunate I remembered it,' he added. 'I'm sorry you were subjected to that, Miss Summersfield. You were very brave.'

'To show fear would only have encouraged them. Actually, I was quaking in my shoes.'

'Are you sure that you want to teach tonight?'

'I knew it would not be easy. I don't run away from a commitment.'

He chuckled and tipped his homburg back on his dark hair, his handsome, boyish countenance snatching at her heart. 'So speaks a brigadier's daughter. Stiff upper lip in the face of adversity and all that.'

She was struck again by the dangerous aura he exuded. Yet his pallor, when the mudlarks surrounded them, had made her suspect that he was as alarmed as herself. Would he have fought to defend her? She dismissed the thought as uncharitable. He had defused the situation without violence.

'You have many admirable qualities, Tanya.' He smiled engagingly. 'I hope that I may call you Tanya. Miss Summersfield is so formal.'

She nodded. They stopped outside the redbrick structure of the church hall. Archie Tilbury paused on the top of the steps leading to the basement. 'We're down there. Take care with the steps, Tanya.'

He went first and held out a hand to assist her to descend the narrow steps. Passing through the door, she hid her dismay that the room was gloomy and lit by two inadequate gas lamps hanging from the ceiling. There were no desks, but she had not expected them in a church hall. Four trestle tables and accompanying benches had been lined up.

'You look disappointed,' he said, censure creeping into his tone.

'Not at all.' She had already decided to make the best of it. 'None of this would be possible without you. I'm very grateful, Mr Tilbury.'

His expression brightened at her appreciation, his gaze an admiring caress as he smiled at her. 'I did little but I would prefer you to call me Archie. I'll inform Reverend Carver you're here.'

Tanya laid out the slates and chalk and looked up to see a short, stout man in a black cassock waddling towards her. He was bald with a thick cinnamon coloured moustache covering his lips.

'How do you like your schoolroom?' he asked as he shook her hand. 'We serve soup upstairs from seven thirty, but you may prefer your students to wait until the end of the class if they are hungry.'

'Hunger destroys concentration. They will learn better on a full stomach. Seven thirty will be fine.'

He looked at Archie. 'That all right with you, sir, since you agreed to provide the soup on the evenings of the class?'

Archie waved his hand dismissively. 'Miss Summersfield is in charge of all aspects of the class.'

Reverend Carver departed and Tanya, now flustered, turned to Archie. 'I never expected you to do so much when I spoke of my desire to teach.'

'It was the agreement I negotiated to obtain the room,' he clipped out. His back was rigid as he paced from her. 'You do not seem pleased. I thought this was what you wanted.'

She put a hand to her temple. She felt a fool and embarrassed. Much as she was beginning to like Archie Tilbury, she did not relish being in anyone's debt. But was it right to allow her pride to stop her helping the illiterate?

'Forgive me, Archie. I'm nervous at meeting my pupils.' She forced a smile. 'Thank you. You've been extremely generous.'

The stiffness left his shoulders and taking her hand he smiled deep into her eyes. 'Your pupils will adore you.'

'What if I fail?' The possibility had not occurred to her before; now it seemed frighteningly real.

'You will not fail.' He tipped up her chin with his forefinger, his nearness invading her senses and making her strangely breathless. 'I have every faith that you will live up to my expectations, Tanya.'

There was a gleam in his eye which spoke of something other than her qualifications as a teacher. She wasn't sure whether she was pleased or dismayed. It was impossible to be in Archie's company for long and not be affected by his charm. And she was too much of a woman not to be flattered that such a handsome man had taken so much trouble to help her to achieve her ambition.

The clatter of heavy boots on the stairs made

them draw apart. Two men ambled into the classroom. Both were in their early twenties. They whipped off their caps displaying greasy, unkempt hair which hung over their ragged shirt collars. They brought with them the rank smell of fish and stale beer.

'Hadn't reckoned the teacher would be a woman, let alone one that's a looker,' the shorter of the two said with a grin. 'I'm Dave Fisher. I'm a porter down Billingsgate. Reckon to get meself 'itched to a shop girl come September, but she won't 'ave nothing to do with a bloke what can't read. This is me mate Joe Lang.'

'Welcome to my class.' Tanya held out her hand to Joe who looked ill at ease. He had a round freckled face and the saddest brown eyes she had ever seen. His hands were jammed firmly in his pockets and he made no move to take her hand in greeting.

'Don't mind 'im, ma'am,' Dave chirped. 'Shy, 'e is. And 'e's got a mangled 'and. Ain't so sure 'e should be 'ere. But like I told 'im, what's 'e got to lose? Ain't no one gonna give 'im labouring work with 'is 'and all buggered. 'Appen he can learn to write with 'is left 'and.'

'With practice and patience I am sure that Mr Lang will learn to write with his left hand.'

Joe shuffled self-consciously. 'Always 'ad trouble with joined-up writing anyways, miss. Though I reckoned it were because me knuckles got rapped bloody by the teacher's ruler if I used me left 'and which felt more natural like,' he mumbled. 'Got a wife and four nippers to feed. I can add up any amount of figures in me head but can't get them down on paper. Do you reckon a bit of learning will 'elp me get a job? All I know is being a porter at Billingsgate. If it weren't for me missus out scrubbing floors until 'er back is fit to break, we'd be in the workhouse.'

'Education is never wasted, Mr Lang.'

As they took their seats, three other men arrived separately, two were Polish and spoke only broken English and the third, an Irish navvy, reeked of rum. In the next quarter of an hour four other men arrived and a waif-like young woman far advanced in pregnancy slid onto the bench nearest the door as though she would bolt at any second. Holding her hand was a girl of about fourteen. Tanya guessed they were sisters.

When she approached them, the older of the sisters looked nervous. There was no wedding band on her slender and surprisingly clean hands. Her clothes, although rusty with age, were darned with neat patches and a clever gusset had been inserted in her bodice to accommodate her expanding waistline.

'Would you be taking the likes of me in your class, ma'am?'

'It's open to everyone who is willing to learn. What's your name?'

'Polly, ma'am. Polly Wilkins. This is me sister Sal. She ain't had no schooling since she were ten. Afore that she were sickly every winter with 'er chest. I don't want 'er to end up ignorant like me. And she won't do no learning 'less I come with 'er.'

Tanya smiled at Sal. Her face was gaunt and

her body underdeveloped from malnutrition. 'Are you willing to work, Sal?'

The girl nodded but didn't meet Tanya's friendly gaze. She was shivering in her thin cotton dress and on her bare arms were several bruises which could only have come from a beating.

During the next few minutes several others arrived and finally a middle-aged woman hobbled in leaning heavily on a walking stick fashioned from a tree branch.

'Beg your pardon for being so late, miss,' she wheezed. ''Ad to walk from Bow and me knees ain't so good with the rheumatism now. I'm Mrs Rudge. Most call me Widow Nan Rudge.' She smiled, revealing several gaps in her teeth, as she eased herself down onto a bench on the front row. There was a glow of warmth and serenity in her grey eyes and Tanya instantly liked the woman.

Widow Rudge untied her moth-eaten black shawl, her movements weary from her exertion but her eyes bright and eager. 'I ain't 'ad above six months' schooling in me life. Me mam had a dozen kids and I were the eldest. She needed me help with 'em. Now me own boy, Johnnie, 'as gone to make a new life in America. Said 'e'd write to me regular. Johnnie's all I got in the world. It ain't likely I'll see 'im again. So I wanna learn to write me own letters and read Johnnie's whenever I've a mind, without being beholden to anyone.'

A lump of emotion rose in Tanya's throat. There was a quiet dignity about the widow that she admired. With relief she noted that Archie had taken a seat at the back of the class and had opened a newspaper to read while the lesson was in progress. She was nervous enough on her first night without having him watching her.

Discovering that only half of thcm could even write as much as their name, Tanya called each one in turn to one side and asked them questions about their previous education. Each pupil's needs appeared to be different. Since the class was so small, she decided that she would give them individual tuition. For the first hour she gave each an exercise to do on their slates. A couple of the men lost interest and began to chatter.

'Is there a problem, Mr Baker?' she enquired.

'No. I'm just having a word with me mate 'ere,' the thickset bearded man snarled.

'You're disturbing the others. Could you not keep your conversation until the break?'

'I talk when I please.' Wilf Baker slammed a burly fist down onto the trestle table making the slates leap into the air. 'There ain't no woman gonna tell me when I can and can't speak.'

Tanya saw Archie fold his paper and begin to rise. With a slight shake of her head, she gestured for him not to interfere. 'Mr Baker, there is more to education than learning the three Rs. Manners also maketh man. Courtesy costs nothing.'

Wilf stood up, his vast bulk emanating menace. He was used to throwing his weight around the chemical factory where he worked. 'I ain't come 'ere to be insulted by a stuck-up bitch.'

Tanya faced him without flinching. 'You told

me that you came here because you were angry at the working conditions in your factory. You said you wanted to be able to fight for the rights of your fellow workers. The owners of your factory look down on the workers because of their rough ways. To bargain with these people you have to win their respect. There's nothing subservient about good manners. Every pupil must respect the others' wish to learn. If anyone does not agree with those terms they are free to leave.'

'Sit down, Baker,' the Irishman grunted. 'Miss Summersfield didn't insult you.'

Wilf gave a noncommittal grunt.

Archie leaned back in his chair. 'Baker, an apology is in order to Miss Summersfield.'

Seeing Wilf's face flush with angry colour, Tanya hastily intervened. 'I need no apology on this occasion. I prefer to see results in your learning, Mr Baker.'

There was a tense moment as the man hesitated, his eyes slitted as he regarded Tanya. Then his large shoulders relaxed and he sat down, saying, 'I were out of order, Miss Summersfield.'

It was the nearest the surly man would come to an apology and Tanya accepted it gracefully. The other men were watching her and there was acceptance and approval in their eyes. Tanya felt her stomach unclench as the tense atmosphere dispersed. It was a good time to call a break for them to enjoy the bread and soup.

When the pupils returned ten minutes later, two men were missing. Tanya tried not to be disappointed. She still had eleven pupils, including Wilfred Baker.

It was nine o'clock when she arrived back at Pilgrim's Crescent. Her mind was racing with excitement at having completed her first class. Each of the remaining pupils had promised to return on Thursday.

'You must be proud of your achievements, Tanya,' Archie praised. 'You won the class over. You never judged them, even that pregnant woman who was clearly unmarried.'

'Who am I to judge her. I know nothing of the circumstances which brought her to that fate.'

He studied her intently. 'You're a remarkable woman. Too many men and women of our class make an issue of morality. Perhaps because often they have clawed their way to so-called respectability. There are no greater hypocrites than the *nouveau riche*, whereas the nobility have always lived scandalous lives and are masters of discretion; they hide the skeletons in their cupboards well. The lower orders have too hard a time surviving to worry about morals.'

Realising that he may have misinterpreted her meaning, she amended, 'That does not mean that I hold virtue in light regard.'

'I did not think that you did.'

The light from the gas lamp a few yards away reflected in the darkness of his eyes as he gazed down at her. Tanya's heart began to pound uncomfortably fast. She owed this man so much. Ill at ease beneath his stare, she backed towards the door. 'Thank you again for all that you've done.'

'It has been my pleasure.'

She opened the door and stood in the hallway which was illuminated by a three-sconced candelabra. He lifted her hand and kissed the pulse at her wrist above her glove. The warmth of his lips tingled upon her flesh. The gaslight caught the large garnet ring he wore on his little finger and she noticed how fine and slender his hands were. A musician's hands.

'Goodnight, Tanya. I will call at the same time on Thursday.' His voice was velvety with sultry promise.

'Goodnight, Archie.' Her voice was husky.

She watched him step back into the taxi-cab without glancing in her direction. It left her feeling hollow, abandoned. Unaccountably, she shivered. Archie intrigued and excited her. She was already looking forward to their next meeting.

Archie had long ago perfected his exits and his entrances. He knew how to create the impression he desired. He laughed into the darkness of the cab and rubbed a finger reflectively along his moustache. The Summersfield woman was falling under his spell. The old charm never failed.

He alighted at his rooms. His lodgings were in Garrard Street in the heart of the theatre district of West End London.

'Did the old biddy come up trumps for you, my boy?'

Granville Ingram was sprawled on the crumpled bed, the *Sporting Life* discarded at his side. His evening shirt was open to the waist displaying a chest bare of body hair. The black trousers encased his hips and thighs like a second skin and his slender waist was encircled by a scarlet cummerbund. On the bedside cabinet was a gold hunter and chain. Granville had risen from the gutter, as his speech betrayed, to be one of the top comedians on the music hall circuit.

'Everything is going to plan,' Archie replied.

'You got it made there!' Granville eyed him covetously. 'Must be worth a bob or two, that old girl.'

'Why aren't you working?' Archie stared round in disgust at the bottles of drink and plates of uneaten food on the floor.

'Had a few mates in for a drink,' Granville cooed. 'I were lonely.'

'The curtain went up half an hour ago. That's the third performance you've missed this month.' Archie regarded the once handsome face of his companion. It was becoming ravaged by drink. The bright blond hair now owed its colour to hair dye which masked the encroaching grey. Granville was forty-two and deep lines of debauchery furrowed from his nostrils to below his mouth.

Archie sneered. 'The old girl doesn't interest me as much as the niece. She's the one who will inherit now that her brothers are dead. Could be I'll marry her.'

Granville drew up one leg to regard Archie sardonically. 'Marriage ain't for you. No more than it is for me.'

'What's marriage got to do with us, Granville? It's not as though it will change anything.' Archie was staring at his reflection in the fly-specked mirror. He turned his head from side to side studying the perfect features. A bluish line of beard was beginning to show. He'd have to shave again if he went out.

Granville pouted and swung his legs from the bed. 'Don't you get lippy with me. Where would you be if I hadn't looked after you these last years? I've kept you in style and don't you forget it.'

'Are you threatening me?' Archie moved quickly and pushed the comedian down onto the bed. His eyes darkened menacingly as he caught up the cords secured to the brass bedhead and tied them round Granville's wrists. 'I've paid my way. Recently I've earned more than you and taken greater risks.'

'You could be one of the best forgers in the business. But it's dangerous work on your own.'

'I can look after myself.'

Already Granville was panting, his eyes heavy-lidded with excitement. His mouth was slack with desire when Archie straddled him to secure his other wrist. Then sitting back on his heels, Archie removed his jacket and braces, flicking the leather tabs so that they lashed across Granville's bare chest. 'You aren't keeping to our arrangement, Granville. Perhaps it's time I moved on.'

'I've always been good to you,' Granville whined. 'You can have me gold cigar case. You always fancied it.'

Archie grinned. 'That's more like the old Granville.' There was no tenderness in his eyes as he continued to lightly flay his partner with the braces. Each stroke became harder but he never broke the skin. Granville's eyes were rolling back in his head as he groaned in agonised pleasure. When Archie ripped open the comedian's trousers to expose the engorged erection, Granville arched upwards, his breathing laboured. Abruptly Archie moved away from the bed.

'Don't stop.'

'You can still make the second house at the theatre,' Archie scowled. 'Look at the state of you. The great Laughing Granville Ingram – there's been precious little to laugh about recently with you drunk so often.'

'C'mon, me boy. You never used to be so mean,' Granville wheedled.

Archie grinned darkly. 'Time you learnt a few lessons. I ain't your boy and I don't like threats.'

'You ain't gonna leave me.' Fear contorted Granville's face. His erection withered. 'We've been together a long time. Ain't I seen you all right in the past? We're good together. We don't want no woman spoiling it. And there's more than one way I can earn me bread. 'Ow about a night down the Dilly later?'

Archie basked in Granville's fear that he would leave him. He knew that with his looks he could have more influential male lovers. Power over others had always excited him. Fear and power were weapons to use mercilessly when charm failed.

His mood changed as he untied the cords with a salacious smile. 'I'm not in the mood to go thieving down the Dilly tonight. I'm putting that behind me to concentrate on the real money that comes with forging. I don't need you no more to pick a drunk's pocket. That's a mug's game.'

'You can't leave me. Not after all we've been through together.' Granville's eyes glinted craftily. ''Sides, happen I knows too much about you, Arnie Potter. You wouldn't want the old biddy to learn the truth, would you?'

'What could you tell her other than that I've used an alias from time to time to protect my true identity? Moving in our circles, that makes sense. I don't reckon on being locked in prison like Oscar Wilde for doing what comes natural to me. Do you?' he scoffed, but even so his stomach twisted with alarm. Granville did know too much. A disarming smile flashed. 'We go back a long way, but things have changed between us, Granville. I'm the master now.'

'I'll do anything. Anything.' Granville's eyes were again glazing with passion. 'Only don't leave me, Arnie.'

Archie decided to be magnanimous. He loved the power of being adored by men and women. He used his looks ruthlessly, expert in the nuances conveyed by every practised smile or expression. For the moment Granville still had his uses.

'Show me how good you can be, Granville. Did I say I was leaving you? Just because I aim to marry Miss schoolmarm Tanya Summersfield don't mean you have to stop paying my rent on this place. Where else can we meet so conveniently?' He picked up his jacket. 'I'm off to a club.'

Granville's face puckered. 'I can't bear it when you're like this. I'll lay off the bottle. Work more.

I can still draw the crowds, but I can't do it wivout you. Old fool that I am, I luv you.'

Archie carefully folded his jacket and lay down on the bed. 'Then show your master what a good servant you are. Show me that you're better than any woman.'

Chapter Four

During the next three weeks several more pupils joined the evening classes, encouraged by those already attending. Tanya also discovered Archie to be an amusing and charming companion. When he invited her to attend a performance of Oscar Wilde's *The Importance of Being Earnest* in the West End, she happily accepted. It was her first visit to the theatre and she loved every second of it. She was captivated by the atmosphere of the theatre and the production. As they emerged into the night air, they were hemmed in by men in top hats and evening cloaks, the women at their sides sparkling with diamonds and trailing mink and white fox fur stoles. The road was jammed with taxi-cabs and hansoms.

'The evening is so warm, could we walk for a while?' Tanya asked.

'If you do not mind being jostled by the crowd. The streets can be unruly at this time of night.' Archie smiled at her indulgently.

'Are they any worse than Aldgate or Whitechapel?'

'You get a better class of drunk in the West End.'

She laughed at his wry humour and he drew her arm through his as they sauntered amidst the milling populace towards Leicester Square. The clamour of chestnut, seafood, and sweet sellers rose above the sound of music from public houses and restaurants. A band in an upper floor dance hall was playing the cakewalk and energetic cheering accompanied the dancers' strutting steps. In the centre of the square were trees and roosting starlings clackered incessantly. The occasional whine of a beggar was discordant and Tanya noticed that Archie was careful to steer her away from any vagabonds or street-walkers. They turned a corner and ahead of them was the stage door of a variety theatre. Several young men in evening dress clutched bouquets of flowers. Some were openly drinking from a champagne bottle, their comments ribald as they assessed the merits of the showgirls.

'What are they waiting for? Surely the show is finished.'

'They're known as Stagedoor Johnnies,' Archie said dismissively. 'Men with money to burn and the morals of alley cats who flock around the highest priced whores in London.' He guided Tanya back to the main thoroughfare. 'It's best if we take a cab from here. These streets are no place for a gentlewoman at night.'

She readily agreed. There had been occasions when she had been shocked by the scenes of drunkenness and debauchery she had witnessed in the East End. It made her realise how dangerous the streets were and that it would be impossible to teach in the evenings without the protection of a man to escort her. Yet it angered her that a woman could not walk out unescorted and not fear molestation.

Archie hailed a passing hansom to take them home. These vehicles were becoming less popular with the rise of the motor taxi-cab. Yet Tanya enjoyed the horse's slower pace and the rhythmic swaying of the carriage. On a moonlight night such as this, it was romantic. When Archie took her hand she did not pull away.

'Your father's ship is overdue in docking, isn't it?'

'They were expected two days ago.' Her voice lost its lightness. 'It was in the newspapers that it was delayed after docking in Gibraltar.'

'His arrival does not seem to be filling you with joy.'

She hesitated, unwilling to sound disloyal. 'Papa is almost a stranger to me. He has always served abroad, in India mostly and a few years in Africa. Even when he was on leave I was away at school and sometimes only Mama would visit me. It's not that I don't want to get to know him better, but I wish he would not run our household like a regimental parade ground. He will be against my teaching.'

'Not when I explain the good you are doing.'

She shook her head. 'He will not approve of his daughter working in any form. What would the officers at his club say?'

His hands squeezed hers. 'But your father need not control your future. A husband may be more understanding. As I would be.'

His words surprised her.

'Can it be that you are unaware of the affection in which I hold you?' he chided gently.

Tanya studied his handsome features in the pale moonlight. She did enjoy his company and when he stared at her in that bold way, her heart always missed a beat. Sometimes it was difficult to breathe when he smiled so disarmingly. Was this what it felt like to be in love? Marriage was such a big step. It would enclose her in another kind of captivity, where a wife must be subservient to her husband. A part of her craved freedom – independence. She wanted to be her own woman.

'We have known each other such a short time, Archie.'

'Long enough for me to know that you are the only woman for me.'

He raised her hand to his lips and through the lace of her evening gloves their warmth caused a tingle of pleasure to speed along her arm. His fingers were tender as they caressed her cheek and gently touched the corner of her mouth. For a heart-stopping moment she thought he was going to kiss her. She held her breath but he drew back from her with a smile, plunging her into confusion.

The tilted smile was coercing and beguiling. 'I adore you, Tanya.'

When he looked at her that way, she felt all resistance melting. Yet something held her back. She wanted Archie to kiss her. Respect for her may have stopped him until now, but perversely that irritated her. Sometimes Archie was too correct, too charming. The romantic in her wanted to be swept off her feet by an ardent kiss, not placed on a pedestal as he seemed to do. 'Please, Archie, give me more time before I give you my answer. I do care for you.'

'One can care for a puppy,' he said stiffly. He turned away and she saw the tendons in his neck tense and knew that her answer had displeased him. He had been kind to her and tonight had been wonderful and exciting. Was she being foolish not to accept him? His handsome profile remained brooding when she did not capitulate. She wavered. Her heart beat rapidly whenever she was with him and his handsome looks often made her catch her breath. But was it love she felt or just physical attraction? She didn't want to lose his friendship and she was attracted to him.

When they halted outside her home, she was startled to see so many lights on in the house. A glance at the marcasite watch brooch pinned to her evening gown made her gasp. 'I hadn't realised it was so late. We said we would be home an hour before this.'

The front door was thrown open as they climbed the cracked steps.

'So this is how my daughter deports herself,' Brigadier Summersfield bellowed. 'Go to your room at once. No lady stays out until this hour. And certainly not in the company of a man without a chaperon to safeguard her reputation.'

Tanya was shocked. How could her father talk to her like that? With not even a word of greeting after ten years away. 'My reputation is in no danger with Mr Tilbury,' she returned, echoing his censure.

Her father's bulbous eyes glittered with scorn. For a man nearing sixty his figure was trim and athletic. What remained of his hair was grey and cropped short to the sides of his head, the bald dome now stained with the angry colour which suffused his face. He had grown a handlebar moustache which gave his face an arrogant sneer. He might not have been wearing his regimental scarlet but he was as pompous and bombastic as she remembered.

'Insolent chit! Get to your room. And as for you, sir!' He glowered at Archie. 'You will have no further communication with my daughter.'

'You wrong us both, sir,' Archie responded stiffly. 'I hold Miss Summersfield's reputation in the highest regard. Miss Stella Summersfield knows that my intentions towards your daughter are honourable.'

The brigadier regarded his coldly. 'You took advantage of an old woman's gullibility. Did you seek to compromise my daughter's reputation so that she could be forced to marry you?'

'Papa, that's outrageous!' Tanya faced him, her eyes dangerously dark, matching his contempt. She had listened to enough. She had done nothing wrong and neither had Archie. How dare he judge them unheard.

Father's and daughter's glares locked in combat, each delivering a warning salvo. Neither surrendered and battle commenced.

'It is not seemly to harangue us on the doorstep for all the neighbours to hear. The play finished later than we anticipated. I think you owe Mr Tilbury an apology.'

'Apology be damned!'

Archie held out a business card, his usually smooth voice rasping like waves crashing over shingle. 'I regret that wc havc mct in thcsc circumstances, sir. You're obviously tired from your weeks of travelling and were worried for your daughter's safety. I'll return tomorrow when you're rested. Goodnight, Brigadier Summersfield. Miss Summersfield.' He raised his top hat to Tanya and leapt into the hansom, rapping his walking cane on the roof of the cabin for the driver to proceed.

The brigadier followed Tanya into the house, slamming the front door behind him, the verbal bombardment recommencing with the velocity of a battle cry delivered at full charge. 'That upstart will not set foot in this house again. Damned philanderer. And as for you, my girl, go to your room. You'll stay there until you learn to deport yourself as a gentlewoman. I'll not have our family shamed in this way.'

Tanya counterattacked. 'I'm not a child, Papa. And I know how to behave. It was not my conduct which was at fault this night.'

He lifted his monocle to his eye, his belligerent stare scrutinising her from head to toe. 'Looks like I've returned just in time to stop you going the same bad way as Stella did at your age.' Rage made his words as staccato as musket fire. 'I put an end to her antics. And, by God, I'll do the same to you.'

'I will not be bullied, Papa.' Too angry to reason

with him, she ascended the stairs. She glimpsed Aunt Stella hovering in the shadows at the end of the hall. A hand was held to her mouth as she viewed the scene with horror. Then Tanya's arm was grabbed and she was spun round.

The red and yellow weave of the stair carpet blurred. Pain flared in her cheek as her father struck her, the force of the blow pitching her full length on the stairs. Levering herself up on a bruised elbow, her voice was scathing. 'Behold the glory of the British Army. Whatever happened to diplomacy? Is this how officers train their men? By teaching them to strike women when they lose an argument?'

He staggered back as though she had spat upon him. 'How dare you speak to me like that. You goaded me too far, child. I have never struck a woman before.' He was breathing heavily. 'I had not expected to return to discover that my daughter has lost all sense of decency and respect.'

Tanya stood up and without a backward glance proceeded to her room. Rage simmered at her father's treatment. What had she done that was so terrible? She was appalled at the way he had treated Archie, a man who had behaved impeccably towards her. After a dozen meetings he had not even kissed her yet.

Obstinately, now that her father had banned her from seeing Archie, her attraction to him was strengthened. Her father would not stop her meeting him. She would not be dictated to.

After Tanya rose and dressed the next morning,

she was furious to discover that her bedroom door was locked. She was a prisoner in her room. Instantly she raised a fist to demand to be released. It halted before it hit the door. She would not give her father the satisfaction of witnessing her frustration. Crossing to the window she surveyed the garden below. The gnarled branches of an ancient wisteria reached past her window. The fragrant scent from the mauve flowers which hung like bunches of grapes on a vine filled her room. As a child she had often climbed down it to escape after being shut in her room by Stella for some misdemeanour. She decided against using it to escape now. It would prove nothing.

'Damn him,' she fumed as she paced the floor between the brass bedstead and the marble-topped washstand with its flowered china jug and bowl. 'How dare he treat me like this?'

A tap at the door was followed by Aunt Maude whispering, 'Tanya, are you all right? Answer softly. Reginald is asleep along the corridor.'

'How could Papa lock me up? He's acting like some medieval despot.'

'You shouldn't have angered him last night. He was worried about your safety. He never could tolerate anyone thwarting his wishes. Learn to guard your tongue, my dear. At least appear to be meek and submissive to his demands. I'm sure he'll reconsider his opinion of Mr Tilbury. He's such a presentable gentleman and clearly enamoured of you.'

Before Tanya could answer, her father bellowed, 'Maude, I forbade you to speak to Tanya.'

There was a yelp of fear from her aunt and Tanya heard the rustle of her skirts as she fled back to her own room. It increased her anger towards her father. Maude was a gentle woman and easily upset. The brigadier may think he could tyrannise his womenfolk, but she had no intention of submitting to his bullying tactics.

An hour later Tanya's temper continued to boil. No food had been brought to her. If her father thought to break her spirit by starving her, he was mistaken. Yet the time she had spent alone had made her consider the need for diplomacy when dealing with him. Maude was right. Direct confrontation would only make him more stubborn.

To pass the time, she picked up a sketchpad. Her watercolours were in the room at the top of the house where she had created a studio. There the natural light from the fanlight window was excellent for her painting. Her pencil flew across the paper as she sketched a plan of the dining room. It was her favourite pastime to plan how she would redecorate each room if the family's fortunes were restored. The elegant Chippendale table and chairs she would keep, but the cumbersome Victorian dresser could go into the kitchen. Instead of the maroon wallpaper, she would have the walls pale green, and a cream Indian carpet would replace the heavily patterned carpet which had worn threadbare at its centre. The dark drapes round the windows would go. Also the potted palms which shut out much of the light. She drew a crystal chandelier hanging from the ceiling and subdued gas lighting in the alcoves.

So absorbed had she become in her creation that she jumped at hearing the key in her lock. Stella slid inside, a finger to her lips to warn Tanya to keep silent. Her aunt was white-faced.

'I mustn't be found here. Reginald has forbidden anyone to speak to you. He's furious that I allowed Mr Tilbury to take you to the theatre. I dared not mention the teaching. And you must not. It will rebound on me.'

Tanya chewed her lower lip in agitation. 'I don't want Papa blaming you but I don't want to give up teaching. Papa is being unjust.'

'Ask his forgiveness for last night,' Stella urged. 'Then everything will work out. But for the next few days you must be careful.'

'Where is Papa now?' Tanya demanded.

'He's checking the wines in the cellar. He's in a foul mood that stocks are so low.' Stella placed a covered plate on the dressing table. 'Eat that, it's only cold meat and cheese. Then hide the plate in case he comes in here. He forbade food to be brought to you.'

Why had Stella risked her brother's wrath for her? Tanya wondered. Who was she trying to protect? Herself or Archie Tilbury? And why?

'Has there been word from Mr Tilbury?' she asked. 'He said he would call today to explain to Papa.'

Stella looked distraught. 'Reginald refused to see him. Fortunately Ginny smuggled a note to him for me. I had to ensure that he did not mention the teaching. Your father may yet accept him once he learns that he became acquainted with you through my committee work.'

'It's outrageous to treat Mr Tilbury in such a manner.'

'Reginald is stubborn. He wouldn't listen when I explained that Mr Tilbury is a man of position and wealth.'

It was unlike her aunt to be so vehement in defending anyone. Or was she defending her own position by supporting Archie? Tanya had never seen her aunt so taken by any man. Archie's charm had certainly won her round. Tanya hoped it would work as efficiently on her father.

'Mr Tilbury has been so generous. I'm embarrassed at the way Papa behaved.' She hesitated a moment, wondering if she should confide in her aunt. Then she decided to. 'Mr Tilbury asked me to marry him last night.'

'Did you accept?'

'I said it was too soon.'

'Then you'll regret it.' Stella's face was taut, her expression unfathomable. There was sadness, anger and hardness meshed into the lines around her eyes and mouth. 'Reginald will put an end to it if he can,' she said harshly. 'My father would not permit me to marry the man I loved. Don't let that happen to you.'

'Was there nothing you could do?'

Her aunt's eyes were hostile as she snapped, 'My father ordered me beaten for loving a man they considered beneath me. He then ordered Geoffrey thrashed. Reginald, our elder brother James, and some of their fellow officers found him. Someone stamped on his fingers, splintering the bones. Geoffrey committed suicide by throwing himself under a train. Father said it proved that he was unsuitable as a husband. They were responsible for his death. He was a gifted painter. With his hands broken, his livelihood was taken from him.'

'Aunt Stella, I am so sorry.'

'My father died not long after from perforated stomach ulcers. It was a fitting end for an evil man.' Her aunt squared her shoulders and a blank mask slid over her features. 'It was a long time ago. I prefer not to speak of it. I wanted you to understand. Don't throw away your chance of happiness. Mr Tilbury is an excellent match.' Stella's voice became impassioned. 'Don't let Reginald ruin your life as he did mine. Look at me. A spinster – an unpaid housekeeper. Reginald spoke to me as though I was the most lowly of servants when he learned you were out with a man last night. All I've done for him over the years means nothing.'

She frowned as she noticed the sketchpad on the coverlet. 'That looks like our dining room, without the grand lighting, of course.'

'I was just passing the time. Sometimes it's nice to pretend what this house could be like if we still had money.'

'It's a wicked sin the way it's been left to go to ruin.' Stella's eyes grew misty as she studied the drawing. 'Once this house was beautiful. You have a knack with that pencil of yours. Little good it does us. Reginald contacted a broker to sell more of his shares to settle his mess bills before leaving the army.'

'Are things so bad?'

'Any financial problems he is experiencing are

of his own making. Now he is talking about selling the Elizabethan and Stuart miniature portraits. Soon we shall have nothing.' Her lips set into a bitter line. 'I must go. Eat your food. At least Reginald has not banned me from continuing my church duties. I will send word to Mr Tilbury apologising for my brother's behaviour and beseeching him to be patient.' She stared at Tanya long and hard. 'You do mean to marry Mr Tilbury, don't you?'

'I don't know. But I don't want Papa telling me who I can't marry.'

Stella smiled bleakly. 'It would give me great satisfaction to best Reginald in this and see you happily married.'

The key turned in the lock and Tanya was again alone. Stella was the last person she had expected to champion her cause.

She pressed a hand to her temple. She took a deep breath to calm her anger. She needed to think clearly. Events were moving rapidly – too rapidly. She no longer felt in control.

She frowned, realising how little she knew about Archie. He never spoke of his life or family. She did not know how he earned his living, or whether his income came from private means. He had skilfully avoided answering any questions about himself.

One thing was certain, she was not going to marry Archie Tilbury just to be free of her father's tyranny. Archie was something of an enigma. And that intrigued and fascinated her. Was part of her attraction to him due to the mystery surrounding him? It was time she found out more about Archie before she committed herself further.

To calm her anger Stella had gone into the garden and was busy tending the flowers she loved. She was fuming at the way Reginald had returned and in his usual autocratic way treated his family as though they were men under his command. She had always hated that characteristic in her father and brothers. Women to them were nonentities, mindless servants to obey their wills. Well, no more. She had suffered enough at her family's hands. She was no longer a naïve young girl who could be manipulated. Now it was her turn to dictate the terms of the future.

Her face was set and her lips pursed with bitterness as she cut some lilies for the dining room. The resentment which had festered over the years was throbbing like a boil needing lancing. The painful memories brought a rush of tears to her eyes. Why had her brothers and father been so cruel?

She would never forgive them. After Geoffrey's death she had discovered that she was pregnant. Great-Aunt Geraldine had taken charge. She was a formidable woman in her sixties who through her charity work had discovered a family in Tilbury who would care for Stella until after the birth.

Great-Aunt Geraldine had taken her to Fenchurch Street Station and at Tilbury Riverside they were met by Jerome and Priscilla Whitchurch, middle-aged, childless, religious bigots.

Great-Aunt Geraldine had handed her over like so much unwanted luggage and returned to London on the next train. The Whitchurches had made her walk two miles across the marshes to their isolated farmhouse. She had endured four months of humiliation at their hands. On arrival she had been stripped of her fine clothes and made to wear sackcloth and never allowed out of the house.

Her spirit had rebelled and she raged at them. 'How dare you treat me like this. My lover would have married me but Papa forbade it.'

Husband and wife had stood side by side, their expressions condemning. The man topped his wife's five feet by only two inches and they were both railing thin, with boy, cadaverous faces.

'You're a wicked sinner,' Jerome Whitchurch shouted. 'You must repent.'

They tied her to a wooden chair and washed her mouth out with carbolic soap. Then they knelt on the floor and prayed for her to repent her sins. Every evening they subjected her to this ritual. When she refused to repent, they left her tied and without food.

For four days she endured the misery. Her legs and arms were constantly cramped. It was midwinter and she was half-frozen, for no fire had been lit. She was left to sit in her own urine and excrement and still she refused to submit.

'Are you prepared to be reasonable?' Jerome demanded.

She did not look at him, but she was becoming frightened. The baby's movements had become weaker.

'You will have to submit in the end,' Jerome announced. 'This stubbornness is the work of the Devil and God will always triumph. Repent of your sins.'

At her silence, Jerome Whitchurch thrust his ascetic face into hers. He constantly sucked a lavender lozenge to sweeten his breath, but it could not disguise the smell of his decayed teeth.

'We have our instructions,' he declared, 'and they will be obeyed. Sinners such as yourself taint society. They must repent or be locked away where they can no longer bring shame to their family or corrupt others with their wantonness.'

Did her father intend to lock her into an asylum for bearing an illegitimate child? She was appalled and suddenly very frightened. Her head reeled and her stomach cramped. Her father had ordered this. He did not care that her heart was broken. He wanted to break her spirit and if she and the baby died in the process, she doubted he would mourn her. It would be a convenient solution. Colonel Summersfield was only interested in his sons who would rise in the army and bring further glory to the family name.

She hung her head, gathering her thoughts and her strength. The child was all she had left of her lover. For the sake of the baby she must swallow her pride and be compliant. She would triumph over her father by surviving. And then one day … one day he would pay for all she had endured. As would her brothers.

'I repent of my sin,' she said heavily.

Jerome Whitchurch raised his hands to the ceiling. 'Praise the Lord, this sinner will return to the fold.' He looked at her with a fanatical brightness in his pale grey eyes. 'You must do penance to redeem your soul. But you will leave here cleansed, not only of your sinful burden, but of your wickedness.'

Each day of humiliation only served to nurture her hatred for her father and brothers. When the pains started, no midwife was called. For two days and nights she screamed in agony until her son spilled onto the fouled bedclothes with a lusty cry. She was close to death.

Priscilla Whitchurch stood over her, her thin face without compassion. 'Reckon the family will deem it fitting enough should she die after the disgrace she's brought them. As for the little bastard, he'll live to carry his mother's shame throughout life.'

'Please let me see him,' she begged, fighting to stay conscious.

'That's not wise,' Priscilla insisted. 'A wetnurse will be found for him and your father will pay for a foster family to raise him.'

Stella stared at the tiny bundle wrapped in linen and still bloodied from the birth. 'One look, please. So that I may know him when we meet again in heaven.'

The torment in her eyes must have momentarily touched a maternal chord in Priscilla. She held the baby stiffly in front of Stella's eyes then with an impatient tut jerked him away. 'Sleep. You must forget him. He will be looked after.'

Stella had seen enough. The boy had a shock of dark hair and even wrinkled from birth he was the shrunken image of his father. From that moment she began to fight for her life. Her baby needed her to protect him. She must survive.

Her strong will saved her, but it was four days before she was well enough to ask, 'Where's my baby?'

'He died,' Priscilla Whitchurch announced.

'But he was strong,' she protested. 'I heard his cry.'

'He lived two days. Took a fit in the night and I found him dead in his crib.'

For a second Stella had been about to scream out that she had murdered him, but there was a light in the woman's eyes which told Stella that she was lying. Her son was alive. She would have felt it if he had died.

'He isn't dead,' she declared. 'What have you done with him?'

Priscilla Whitchurch shook her head sadly. 'Mothers find it hard to accept the death of a child. But if it is God's will…' She knelt at the bed and prayed for the baby's soul and the mother's redemption. When she rose, she informed Stella, 'Your great-aunt is to arrive in a few days to take you to Chalkwell where you can recover by the sea. You are fortunate that your family are so understanding. Many a daughter fallen from grace has been cast out onto the streets where she belongs.' She glared sternly at Stella. 'You will pray with me.'

She waited for Stella to place her hands together and assume a pious expression. She knew then that being parted from her baby was not God's will but her family's. She was seething with unanswered questions. Where was her son?

She had to find him. She would find him.

Priscilla Whitchurch's shrill voice rose with passion. 'Forgive this poor sinner, Lord. Let her not slip back into evil. Let her find salvation and not fall into wickedness and end her days with the ungodly souls sent to find absolution within an asylum.'

The warning was clear: she must submit totally to her father's will or be locked away. Ever since, she had been obsessed with the need for revenge. She had bided her time. After her father had died from perforated stomach ulcers and her brother James of battle wounds, Reginald became the focus of her bitter hatred. He had spent most of the intervening years abroad, but now he was back. He would not escape her again.

Chapter Five

Archie shrunk back into the shadows of the unlit alleyway and watched his accomplice at work twenty yards away. The figure waited under a gas lamp on a corner opposite the steps of Piccadilly's Eros statue. Flowersellers, usually women too old to continue in their sisters' more lucrative trade, waved a bunch of violets or sweet peas, their thin voices whining, 'Penny for a posy for your sweet'eart, sir. Tuppence for a bookay.'

It was fitting that the women of the night should ply their trade under the eye of the tall bronze Cupid, expectantly poised on tiptoe, his bow raised to launch its arrow of love. Many women paraded in their gaudy finery, but the one he watched was different from the rest.

Archie suppressed a grin. No one would recognise Laughing Granville Ingram dressed as a Daughter of Eros. It was the comedian's favourite and most secret role. And he played it to perfection. His painted face and long blond hair was framed by a large picture hat adorned with red silk flowers. The sapphire satin dress was tight-fitting and padded to display an hour-glass figure. He sashayed enticingly, his skirts lifted as he traversed a puddle to display high-heeled shoes, black stockings and a red garter. A white feather boa draped from shoulder to ankle was swished from hand to hand, drawing speculative looks. Every sultry glance from the heavily made-up eyes was an invitation to a top-hatted gentleman who had been dining at the Carlton or Imperial, or was strolling back to his club.

Archie had changed from a suit to old black trousers and a brown jacket with the sleeves patched at the elbows. His large cap with its torn peak was pulled down low over his eyes. He eased his weight from one foot to the other, becoming impatient at the delay. A church clock had already struck midnight. Granville was not usually this slow in attracting a victim. He sniffed. The sour smell of his old clothing offended his nostrils. He was now accustomed to wearing fresh linen and expensive cologne. Once he would not have known any better. But he needed to continue his old exploits in order to support his grander lifestyle. During the four years he had been with Granville this had provided them with a steady income. Their partnership was profitable and they were masters of their game.

He leaned back against the soot-blackened wall of a tobacconist's shop which had closed for the night and blew into his hands to warm them. He'd love a smoke, but the smell and gleam of the ash could give him away. The alleyway was small, providing a delivery entrance for the shops in his block of buildings. His gaze surveyed the pavements of Piccadilly Circus. It would not do for him to be spotted by a member of the Gilbert gang. The Gilbert brothers took exception to any man working their patch without paying them a percentage of their pickings. And word was out that the Gilbert brothers were looking for him. So far he'd evaded Slasher Gilbert's detection and he intended to keep it that way. His life would be in danger if they caught him. Thank God for Granville's disguises. But how long would his luck hold out?

In the next street he could hear the shrill voices of Bess Golightly's whores from the open windows of the brothel. Then his sharp ears detected the unsteady tread of a drunk approaching. He grinned in the darkness at hearing Granville croon seductively, his voice pitched to a low feminine drawl. 'You're a fine-looking gentleman. I bet you know how to give a woman a good time.'

'I haven't had any complaints.' The man's voice was cultured which meant he was probably loaded.

Granville giggled throatily, and drew the man

into a darkened doorway a few feet away from Archie.

'I thought we were going back to your room,' the man objected.

'Just like to give my friends a taste of the pleasure yet to come,' Granville chuckled, his fingers already loosening the man's trousers and working on his thrusting flesh. He went down on his knees, his mouth closing over him. The man groaned. His head was thrown back and his eyes were closed tight with passion.

Archie sprang forward. His cudgel connected twice with the back of his victim's skull, then as Granville leapt away, he jabbed it hard into the man's gut. He crumpled to the flagstones without a sound. Seconds later a bulging wallet, gold hunter and sapphire tie pin were hidden in Archie's jacket. Granville had removed the pearl shirt studs and gold cufflinks. They both took to their heels through the side streets.

Twenty minutes later the booty was hidden in a secret cache beneath the floorboards of their bedroom.

'There was fifty quid in the wallet,' Archie chuckled. 'The man must have more money than sense to carry that much cash. It was a good night's work.'

Granville pulled off his wig and sitting in front of the dressing-table mirror began to wipe off the make-up. 'Even if the damned Hippodrome 'adn't replaced me act because I ain't turned up for two nights, I couldn't 'ave earned this much. And it were more fun. Though he was a disappointing choice. His wallet may have been fat and bulging but everything else was very lean and unexciting.'

'You always did prefer them young and vigorous, Granville,' Archie grinned. 'I'm off down the pub. There's a cock fight on tonight in the cellar.'

'I thought we'd stay in,' Granville pouted. ''Sides, I don't like leaving the goods here. Ain't there a fence at this pub?'

'That's quality stuff. I always take the good stuff over to Joe Strong at the Britannia near the Tower. He gives the best price. I'm not going that far tonight.'

Granville grimaced. 'Joe Strong is also known as Strongarm, ain't he? He were a boxer.'

'That's right. Knows how to look after himself.'

'He'll need to. 'E deals with the Jew Goldstein, don't 'e? Couple of the girls down the Dilly were saying that Slasher and Fancy Gilbert are out to get Goldstein. Reckon 'e were trying to move in on their opium racket. And speaking of the Gilbert brothers, we gotta be careful. Those brothers are maniacs if they find someone's been working their manor without using them to fence the goods. There were another lad with his throat cut found washed up by Westminster Steps last night. That's how Slasher kills those who cross 'im.' Granville snatched up a whisky bottle and swigged several mouthfuls.

Archie felt his insides turn to water. 'They haven't caught us yet,' he blustered. 'And they won't. You coming down the pub or not?' His voice was neutral, uncaring whether Granville joined him or not.

For three days Tanya had been locked in her room, fed only bread and water. She was supposed to be teaching tonight and she was becoming frantic at having to let her pupils down. At midday the bedroom door opened and Ginny grinned at her as she entered.

'The brigadier's summoned you to 'is study, Miss Tanya. I'm sorry 'e took it so bad you seeing Mr Tilbury.' Ginny toyed with a strand of black hair which had escaped her cap. 'I don't mean to talk out of turn, but reckon you should know 'is mood. Nothing pleases 'im. Reckon 'e's missing the army 'E's like a bull with toothache. Go careful, Miss Tanya. 'E's bin drinkin' since Mr Tilbury called earlier. The gentleman refused to leave until the brigadier heard 'im out.'

Tanya did not admonish Ginny for her forwardness. She was fond of the maid and knew that she was only trying to help her.

Ginny rushed on, 'Bit of a to-do, there were, and Mr Tilbury stalked out real angry like.'

'Thank you, Ginny. This wasn't quite the reunion I was hoping for with my father.'

She was angry that her father might have insulted Archie. Clearly their interview had not gone well. When she entered the study, she kept her eyes averted from the mounted trophies. Boars' heads and those of deer, leopards, tigers and other wild animals covered the walls, all shot by her ancestors while on service abroad. She had always hated this room with its display of beautiful animals that had been shot for sport.

A glance at her father, who was standing by the

window, halted her intended reproach. She was shocked by his appearance. Beneath the tan he had acquired in India his complexion was blotchy and deep lines channelled the flesh between his mouth and jaw. The handlebar moustache, although waxed, drooped forlornly. It was also glistening with sweat, as was his wide forehead.

'Papa, are you unwell?' Her antagonism faded at seeing a shiver grip his body.

Picking up a cup of tea on the desk he laced it liberally with whisky before drinking it down. He clasped his hands behind his back. 'Damned English weather. The cold eats into your bones.'

Tanya frowned. Dust motes danced in a ray of sunlight from the window. There was not a cloud in the sky.

Spearing Tanya with a fierce glare, he continued, 'Mr Tilbury called upon me and asked for permission to court you. I have yet to give him my answer. Can't say I trust the fellow.'

'He's a good man,' Tanya said softly, having decided that confrontation with her father would only make matters worse. 'I know we returned late, but I was enjoying myself so much that I did not want the evening to end. I had never been to the play before.'

He put a hand to his sweating brow and massaged his temples as though his head pained him. 'Tilbury will take tea with us next Sunday, but you'll not be gallivanting around town with him until I'm convinced that he's a worthy suitor for my daughter.'

Tanya refrained from informing him that she

was uncertain whether she regarded Archie as a suitor; unless her father believed that he was, he would not permit her to see him again. How could she then continue to teach?

Frustration gnawed at her. Papa had been out of England for so long, why did he have to return now, just as she had found something exciting and useful to do with her life? She disliked deception but there was no other choice. She would be letting her pupils down if she did not attend the class tonight.

'I had agreed to visit an exhibition of paintings at a gallery in Westminster with Mr Tilbury this evening. We would be home by nine.'

'I have not forgotten your insolence, Tanya. You are confined to your room until Sunday. By then you may have learned to conduct yourself in a manner befitting a Summersfield and my daughter.' Reginald was frowning as he stared out of the window. 'Who's that man working in the garden? Stella seems to be having a lot to say to him. Don't recognise him as one of the usual servants.'

'That's Parkins. He's been our gardener for about a year. Old Billings died. He comes twice a week. Aunt Stella has always taken an interest in the garden. She insists we only use fresh herbs for cooking. She changed the formal rosebeds to a cottage garden some years ago. I think the hollyhocks, delphiniums, foxgloves and lilies are attractive,' Tanya answered abstractedly. She was concentrating on finding a way to get to her class tonight.

Her father rocked back on his heels, hands

locked behind his back. He did not look at her. 'Maude informs me that I should be considering a husband for you. I'm not so sure Tilbury is the right man. There's something about him...'

'I will not be told who I will marry, Papa,' Tanya flared.

He whirled round to glare at her. 'I don't know what that damned Ladies Academy taught you, but it wasn't respect for your parents. You do not come of age for another four years. While you live under this roof, you will do as you are told.'

Tanya battled to control her temper. He was acting like a despot. It was better to appear meek and subservient, but that did not stop her rebelling at his attitude.

'I'm sorry, Papa. I'm sure you know best.'

His manner relaxed and he nodded for her to sit down. He moved to the desk. When he lowered himself heavily into the chair, his movements were like an old man's. He did not look well and that would not be improving his temper.

There was a knock on the door and Ginny entered and curtsied. 'Brigadier, there's a gentleman to see you. A Captain Hawkes.'

The ill humour left her father's face. 'Splendid. Show him into the library.'

He actually smiled at Tanya as he continued, 'I've a business proposition to discuss with Captain Hawkes. I also hope I'll be able to persuade him to stay here as a guest. But he can be somewhat sensitive...' He hesitated. 'He's a good chap but was a non-commissioned officer. He was my aide-de-camp in India. An injury to his knee during a skirmish up in the hills with brigands meant he was invalided out of the army. He worked his way up through the ranks and was rewarded for his bravery and courage.'

He wiped a hand across his moustache and grimaced. He was beginning to look extremely ill. There was a blueish tinge around his mouth which worried Tanya and his breathing was heavy.

'Good man, Hawkes,' he continued. 'Trust him with my life. Indeed he saved it once when my horse was shot from under me on patrol. Like to help him out. But he's proud and stubborn. He refused to be my manservant when I offered him the position.' He rubbed his chest as though it pained him. 'Hawkes had the effrontery to say he'd take orders from no man now that he was out of the army. He's a bit of a rough diamond.'

'Papa, are you sure you're not ill?' Tanya's anxiety rose.

'Nothing wrong with me,' he snapped. 'I've never had a day's illness in my life. Damned weather, that's all it is.' He fixed her with a stare that warned her not to contradict him. He cleared his throat and went on, 'I've told Stella that Hawkes will be my guest. I don't want her haughty ways offending him. I expect you to make him feel welcome. You may find he can be a bit touchy if he thinks there's any charity involved. Bit too much of his own man considering his background...'

It appeared to take a great deal of effort for him to lift himself out of the chair and his hand shook as he poured more whisky into his cup and drained it. 'I hadn't expected Hawkes to arrive until the weekend. Since he's here, I'll no longer confine you to your room for your insolence. But you will not leave the house.'

Tanya inwardly groaned. This officer's arrival would complicate getting out of the house to teach tonight. The last thing she needed was some old starch-necked officer from her father's regiment staying here.

'But, Papa…' Her protest was cut short as her father staggered. He clutched at his chest and fell to the floor. 'Papa!'

Tanya ran to his side. His face was screwed up with pain. Sweat glistened on his face and she could see the perspiration drenching his white shirt front.

She ran to the door shouting, 'Aunt Stella, come quickly! Ginny, fetch Dr Garrett. The brigadier has been taken ill.'

The maid appeared first with her coat in her hand.

'Papa has collapsed. Summon Parkins to carry him up to his room.'

Stella had entered the study and peered down at her brother. 'Looks like his heart to me,' she declared.

A man stepped past Tanya to kneel at her father's side. 'Brigadier! Sir!' There was no response.

Tanya noted the man's slim figure in a black suit and his wheat-gold hair which flopped forward over his brow. He put two fingers to the pulse point on her father's throat. 'His heartbeat is erratic and slow. He never had heart trouble in India.'

'His temper has been choleric since his return,' Aunt Stella stated. 'There you are, Parkins. Carry the brigadier up to his room.'

The gardener shuffled into the study in his patched corduroy trousers and grimy waistcoat. He had removed his muddy boots and there was a hole in the toes of each thick woollen sock.

'I'll carry the brigadier,' the man Tanya assumed must be Captain Hawkes said. He heaved her father up and over his shoulder. Tawny eyes were turned upon Tanya. 'Which is his room?'

'Are you sure you can manage? It's up two flights of stairs.' She had noticed that he limped and her father had mentioned a knee wound.

'I'll manage. Just get the doctor here without delay.' The limp was more apparent as he walked to the door.

Tanya led the way and, entering her father's room, turned down the bedclothes. There was reverence in the way the captain gently lowered the unconscious figure onto the mattress.

'He's not going to die, is he?' Tanya asked, suddenly fearful.

Captain Hawkes stepped back from the bed, his gaze remaining on the brigadier. 'He's a tough old buzzard.' There was respect in his voice and a faint trace of the flat vowels of a Cockney were apparent in his speech.

'You would know that better than I, sir. I hardly know my father.'

He turned to regard her. She again found herself subjected to a tawny golden stare, his eyes ringed by darker lashes the colour of wet sand.

There were fine white lines at the corner of his eyes in an otherwise tanned, cleanshaven face. His countenance was rugged, not unhandsome, and rather commanding in appearance. The broken aquiline nose added to the impression that this was a man who probably had not followed orders with blind submission. And he was much younger than she had expected. He looked no older than his mid-twenties.

'You must be Tanya. I mean Miss Summersfield. I'm Sam Hawkes.'

'Papa told me he had invited you to stay as our guest, Captain.'

'Plain Sam Hawkes suits me fine, miss. I won't trouble you by staying. Though I'd like to call and learn how the brigadier is.'

There was a tap on the door and Dr Garrett strode in. Stout, red-faced and bewhiskered, he was panting as he stooped over the bed. Stella was behind him. She stood at the foot of the bed like a sentinel as the doctor made his examination.

'It's his heart, I'm afraid,' he announced, taking the stethoscope out of his ears and straightening. 'The blueness about his lips is fading. That's a good sign. Complete rest and no untoward excitement.'

'Will he recover?' Tanya asked.

Dr Garrett paused in scribbling out a prescription. 'Always difficult to say with the heart. Unpredictable organ.' He handed Tanya the prescription. 'Make sure he takes a few drops of that night and morning. I'll have some pills made up and sent round.' He snapped his black bag shut. 'I'll come back this evening to see how he is. Complete rest, remember.'

'I shall be attending him personally,' Stella declared.

'And I'll help,' Tanya offered.

Stella looked displeased. 'Indeed you shall not. A man's sickroom is no place for a young unmarried woman.'

Tanya walked with Dr Garrett to the door. 'Thank you for coming so promptly.'

The portly man smiled kindly at her. 'Your father's not much more than fifty, is he?'

'He's almost sixty,' Tanya corrected.

'He looks strong enough. He should pull through, but as I said, with afflictions of the heart you can never be entirely certain.'

Stella was fussing and straightening the bedclothes. Sam Hawkes addressed Tanya. 'I'll call tomorrow to see how he is.'

'Complete rest, the doctor said,' Aunt Stella announced. 'That means no visitors.'

Tanya glared at her. The captain's genuine concern for her father touched her and Stella was being deliberately abrasive. 'That does not apply to Mr Hawkes. Papa insisted that he be made welcome.' She escorted the captain to the front door, concerned to make amends for Stella's rudeness. 'Are you sure you'll not stay as our guest?'

He looked around at the wide hall with doorways leading off into five rooms. 'It wouldn't be right with the brigadier ill. I've lodgings anyways off London Wall.'

'Please, feel free to visit Papa whenever you

wish. I'm sure your company will cheer him. He spoke highly of you, Mr Hawkes. Perhaps I should take your address in case Papa wishes to contact you.' She fetched a pen and paper from the study and wrote it down.

'I'll be off then, Miss Summersfield.' He tugged his cap onto his head and smiled at her. It transformed his rugged face into a striking countenance. There was a masculine magnetism about him which Tanya had always felt in her brothers' company. 'Pleased to make your acquaintance, Miss Summersfield. I'm sure the brigadier will be fine. He's tough as old boots.'

As Tanya closed the door behind him, Stella appeared at the foot of the stairs. 'At least we'll be spared that common little man from being our guest.'

'He didn't seem that common to me, Aunt. Obviously Papa regards him highly. He mentioned some business venture they planned together.'

Stella's disdainful sniff dismissed Sam Hawkes as a person of no consequence. 'Have you seen Maude? She's not in her room. If she's gone out without telling me, it means she's visiting that Rivers woman. No good will come of her consorting with dead spirits. It's all trickery and nonsense. Hocus-pocus and the Devil's work.'

'Don't be so narrow-minded,' Tanya returned. 'Mrs Rivers gives Aunt Maude comfort. It has nothing to do with the Devil.'

'Takes her for a ride, along with her money,' Stella scoffed. 'A fool and their money are soon parted.'

Tanya glanced up the stairs, worried for her

father's health. He had been a trial to her since his return but seeing him so ill had roused her daughterly affection for him. If a man like Sam Hawkes held him in esteem, then he must have qualities she had yet to discover. Indeed, there was so much about her father which was unknown to her. She was suddenly frightened that he would die and that she would never come to know him. Guilt smote her that her wilfulness might have caused his illness.

'I want to sit with Papa and help in any way I can, Aunt.'

'It is best if I nurse him. I've more experience. Didn't I attend upon you and your brothers when you were ill?' Stella's stare was steely. 'You can sit with Reginald while I attend a meeting this afternoon with Mr Tilbury. I was mortified by the way Reginald treated him. And he implied that I had failed in my duty by allowing him to call upon you. I resent that. I've run this household for thirty years without a word of gratitude and I will not have my judgement criticised.'

Tanya seized her chance. 'I'm meant to be teaching tonight. If you are seeing Mr Tilbury, do you think I could still go with him? I could then explain to my class that I may not be able to teach them in future.'

Stella considered her request. 'It would lessen any humiliation that he may feel at your father's attitude if he escorts you tonight.'

Tanya's spirits rose, but her relief that she would not have to disappoint her pupils were tempered by unease. For some reason her aunt was determined to press Archie's suit. This disturbed Tanya. She should be delighted Stella was supporting her, yet it made her uncomfortable. Clearly Stella took pleasure in thwarting her brother's orders.

It wasn't until Tanya was with Archie that another disquieting thought occurred to her. If Archie truly was a gentleman, he would surely never have agreed to disregard her father's wishes.

Archie laughed when she questioned him. 'The brigadier was being unreasonable. And I know how important it is for you to explain matters to your pupils. Besides, I don't like disappointing you.' He lifted her hand to his lips and smiled into her eyes. The warmth in his voice allayed her misgivings. 'I also wanted to see you.'

She returned his smile. A clandestine meeting was romantic and she felt very daring for having defied her father, even if he was in his sickbed. If he ever found out, all hell would break loose. He would certainly forbid her to see Archie again. Archie was not all that a gentleman should be, to have arranged to meet her this evening. That excited her. It made him more fascinating. She had always hated the strict conventions which governed their middle-class lives.

What then did that make her? Reckless. Disobedient. Wilful. She was resolved that her father's return was not going to stop her leading her life as she decreed.

Chapter Six

When Sam Hawkes called the next morning, Tanya answered the door as Ginny was out shopping in Leadenhall Street market. She took him to her father's bedchamber and gestured for him to remain outside. 'I'll just check that Papa is not sleeping.'

As she approached the bed with its high carved mahogany headboard, her father opened his eyes. The whites were yellow and bloodshot, his complexion an unhealthy grey and his moustache drooped over his upper lip.

'How are you feeling, Papa?'

He grunted in reply. 'Your damned aunt's been in here fussing all morning.' He pushed back the bedclothes. 'I'm getting up. Can't abide being in bed.'

'No, Papa. You could have a relapse. You must stay in bed. Mr Hawkes is here to see you.'

The door opened and Stella breezed in with a cup of tea. 'You must drink this, Reginald. I've put in some whisky as I know you won't drink tea without it.'

The brigadier glowered. 'What else have you put in it, you old witch?'

'Just a few drops of your medication as Dr Garrett ordered.' She puffed up his pillows and straightened the sheet. 'Drink it down. Then you can see your visitor.'

'Send him in, woman.' He wearily waved her away. 'Don't keep him waiting.'

Stella folded her arms across her large bosom. 'Not until you've drunk your tea.'

He downed it and grimaced. 'I'm sick of being surrounded by women. Send Hawkes in.'

Tanya left the room. She sighed as she gazed up at Sam Hawkes. 'As you can hear, Papa is being difficult. Perhaps you can make him see reason. He must stay in bed and rest.'

He nodded, his expression concerned. 'I'll try. But with respect, the brigadier can be stubborn.'

'I'd call it pig-headed,' she corrected with a smile. 'But he may listen to a man.'

There was more irritable shouting from within the bedchamber and Stella flounced out. Her stare was hostile as she addressed Sam Hawkes. 'The brigadier is far too excitable to have visitors. You'll have to call back another day.'

'No,' Tanya intervened. 'I think Mr Hawkes should see Papa. Papa will listen to him. He resents being fussed over by women.'

'When do men ever appreciate the sacrifices we make for them?' Stella bristled. 'Does he think I have nothing better to do than wear myself out looking after him?'

'Get in here, Hawkes,' Reginald ordered, his voice without its former vitality. 'Stella, bring us some whisky. Be quick about it.'

Stella paled at the rudeness of the command. Ignoring Sam Hawkes, she vented her resentment on Tanya. 'The old fool will have a relapse carrying on like that. He doesn't need visitors. He needs laudanum to sedate him.' She waddled along the landing, her voice strident and condemning. 'I won't be responsible for any repercussions. If he receives visitors, the consequences will be on your head.'

Tanya curbed the impulse to retaliate and instead smiled at their guest. 'I apologise for my aunt's rudeness, Mr Hawkes.'

'There's no need.' There was a bold scrutiny in his searching stare which was almost predatory. It wasn't just his dark blond hair and unusual tawny-gold eyes which reminded her of a lion. There was strength and an animal power emanating from him. A natural leadership.

'Hawkes, where the devil are you, man?' the brigadier demanded.

'He's getting impatient,' Tanya commented.

They both laughed as Sam Hawkes strode into her father's room.

'Hawkes, it's good to see you.'

The affectionate tone might have belonged to a stranger, Tanya thought. Her father had never addressed her with such affection.

'Families!' the brigadier informed Sam. 'You're lucky not to have the responsibility of them burdening you, Hawkes.'

'If you say so. Yet having been taken so bad, you're fortunate to have them to care for you. Your daughter says that you're thinking of leaving your bed. Reckon on speeding your journey to your grave, do you?'

'Not you as well, Hawkes. Those damned women have been at you to say that. Confound you all!'

'I'll not stand your nonsense, sir. So you can

put your feet back in bed this instant. Or I'm out of here.' Sam turned to close the door. Before he shut it he grinned at Tanya who was looking distressed by her father's outburst. The answering smile of relief transformed her drawn features into striking beauty.

The brigadier sighed and rubbed a shaky hand across his brow. 'Truth is I feel weak as a babe and I don't like it. We had such plans, didn't we? And now this has happened.'

'You'll soon be better.' Sam attempted to rally his spirits.

'Not with all those damned women fussing round me. Tanya said you refused to stay here yesterday. I need you, Sam. Never was much of a ladies' man, even with the wife. God rest her gentle soul.'

Feeling pressurised, Sam answered stiffly, 'I'm content where I am. I'll call in every day. But I've me future to settle.'

'Dammit man! I thought we'd agreed,' the brigadier punched out through laboured breath. 'I was to buy a racing car and you were to race and maintain it. There wasn't a driver in the army could come close to you for skill and daring.'

Sam put up a hand to stop him. 'It was a good dream around a camp fire of an evening, sir. But it ain't practical and we both know it. I've enough money put by to set meself up in a garage. If you want in on that, there'll be a profit, I promise you. Racing is for rich playboys. I intend to work hard for me living.'

'But the excitement of it, Sam,' the brigadier urged. 'The thrill of the race. The money we can make on wagers.'

Sam eyed him sternly. 'Excitement is just what you don't need at the moment. Didn't you say you needed a sound investment to secure your future? The motor car is the transport of the future. It needs petrol and it needs regular servicing. There's also a growing market for second-hand cars. That's how we shall make our fortune. Trust me.'

'Has civilian life robbed you of your sense of fun?' The brigadier answered moodily. 'What better advertisement for the garage than having a race winner as the owner?'

'Whoa.' Sam chuckled. 'I ain't in the league of the gentleman drivers. And to tell the truth, I'm sick of the snobbery involved. I had enough of that in the army. I don't need to prove I'm anybody's equal.' He frowned. The brigadier had that nasty blueish tinge around his lips again and he was breathing erratically. What had happened to the robust man of a couple of months ago? He looked ill – ill enough to die.

The brigadier looked at him with eyes which no longer held the vibrant fire Sam admired. 'You don't need to prove anything. I'm an old fool daydreaming. But stay here, Sam. Am I really asking too much?'

It was rare that the brigadier used his first name. And he was too proud to plead for anything. He was clearly troubled.

When Sam didn't reply, he added, each word laboured, 'I'd be indebted to you, Sam. Would you have me at the mercy of these damned women?'

'They are your family.'
'Truth is, I'm worried about Tanya. Too headstrong by far. She was seeing some fellow. He struck me as a bit of a bounder. You can tell it in their eyes.'
'Isn't that always the opinion of fathers?' Sam replied.
'There was something about the fellow I didn't like. I'd intended to make some enquiries about him. Do that for me, would you?'
'That isn't my place.' Sam was adamant. 'I'm sure you're worrying unnecessarily. From the short meetings I've had with your daughter, she seemed a level-headed woman.'
'She's not much more than a girl. She's seventeen and has been away at boarding school until a few months ago. She knows nothing of men. And it's not just this fellow she's seeing. She's up to something. She's disobedient, headstrong and stubborn. Dangerous traits. The girl's got the same way of holding her head when disobeying me that her brother Harry had. I don't want her hurt. Or worse–'
A tap on the door stopped the conversation, to Sam's relief. He was worried about the brigadier's health, but he had no intention of becoming caught up in any family intrigue.
The brigadier lay back gasping. 'Help me, Sam.' It wasn't just a plea for medication.
Tanya entered the bedroom carrying a meal for both men of braised chicken and duchess potatoes. Sam Hawkes was bending over her father holding a spoon of medicine to his mouth.
Seeing her approach, her father groaned. 'Take

that away. I couldn't eat it.'

'You must eat, sir,' Sam Hawkes said firmly.

'I don't want it.'

'It will give you strength,' Tanya persisted.

'Take it away. Are you deaf? I don't want it.'

She put the tray on a table and rounded on him, her eyes blazing dangerously. 'You can bully Aunt Stella with your rudeness. It won't work with me. You sound like a petulant child. Will you eat your lunch?'

'No.'

Sam moved to the door. 'Then I'm leaving.'

Tanya looked at him. 'Mr Hawkes, Cook has prepared a meal for both of you. If you stay, perhaps you can persuade my father to eat.'

Sam returned to the bed. 'Will you eat if I stay, sir?'

The brigadier pouted but nodded.

'Good.' The young soldier lifted the covers off the food. 'If we're to go into business together, I shall need a strong, healthy partner.'

'Then move in here, man,' Reginald Summersfield gasped. 'You're a better tonic than any medication. You don't want to be wasting your savings on lodgings until we get our business started. Tell him he's welcome to stay, Tanya.'

'Of course you are, Mr Hawkes. You can have one of my brother's rooms.'

'No. I–'

'Sam,' her father croaked, his face again dewed with sweat. His face was screwed up with pain as he clutched at his heart. 'Don't desert me now, man.'

'Papa!' Tanya ran to the bedside. His eyes were

closed and sunken. She cast a desperate glance at Sam Hawkes. 'Please agree to what he says. Anything to make him rest easy.' She had no wish for this man to live with them, but her father clearly needed him. If it gave him peace of mind he would have more chance of recovery.

Tanya saw Sam struggling with his emotions. Finally, with obvious reluctance, he said, 'I'll stay for a few days.'

Her father nodded. Gradually the pain engraved in creases about his mouth lessened and his body relaxed. 'Perhaps I'll try some of that food now.'

Tanya smiled with relief at their visitor. 'I'll return after you have eaten and show you your room.'

Half an hour later, her father was dozing and Tanya led the captain to a door at the far end of the first-floor landing. The room smelt musty and Ginny was halfway through removing the dustsheets from the furniture. Tanya nodded for the maid to continue.

'This room hasn't been used for several years,' she explained to their guest. 'By the time you return with your things we'll have a fire to air the room and it will be properly prepared for you.'

'I'm putting you to a lot of trouble.'

'Not at all. Papa's health is what is important. I'll show you the other rooms so that you are familiar with the house.'

She led him to the black and white tiled bathroom and separate water closet. 'Papa had these installed when he married Mama. The hot water comes from a boiler which needs an hour to heat up, so let Ginny know when you want a bath. It's usually kept on all day on Fridays for the family bathing and on Monday when Sarah comes in to do the laundry.'

On the second floor she opened the door of a room dominated by a large bay window. In it was a grand piano draped with a white silk Indian shawl, its tassels reaching almost to the floor. There was a chaise longue and several faded armchairs. In one corner a cello was propped on its stand. 'This is the music room. When Mama was alive and in residence we often had musical evenings. And this door leads to the games room,' she said, opening it and brushing aside a cobweb which had formed inside the door. 'It hasn't been used since my brothers were alive. We used to play battledore and that's a ping-pong table folded up against the wall. And of course there's the billiards table and darts board should you wish to play. Papa often played with my brothers.' She stared at the dark green flock wallpaper which was peeling away from the wall by the window. 'Like the rest of the house, it has seen better days.'

Moving to the stairs, she pointed up at the next floor. 'All except one of the rooms on the third floor aren't used. Damp has got into them. I have a studio up there.'

She led the way down to the ground-floor family parlour which gave on to a conservatory, dining room and withdrawing room. 'The kitchen is in the basement. You have only to ring and Ginny will bring you any refreshments you require. Breakfast is usually at nine. Dinner in the evening is rather early at six. My aunts prefer not to dine late and Mrs Stoat, our cook, leaves at seven. If those times are not convenient, she will leave you a meal which could be heated up. You must treat this house as you would your own home, Mr Hawkes.'

He shifted uncomfortably. 'It isn't like any house I've lived in, Miss Tanya. And I don't think your aunt would approve of my sitting at your table to eat. Your father seemed set on the idea of me being a guest here, but I've no intention of imposing on anyone. Anything I can do to help the brigadier, I will.' He regarded her with piercing intensity. 'I owe him a great deal. But I know my place. I'd rather eat out. Thank you all the same.'

'While you are our guest, we would expect you to treat this as your home, but you must do whatever you wish.'

Sam Hawkes was a singularly self-possessed man, but there was nothing arrogant or staid about him as Tanya had feared. Unfortunately, his presence in the house would mean further deception on her part. If he learned that she was going out twice a week to teach, he might inform her father. From his accent she guessed that Sam Hawkes came from the East End. Maybe he could become an ally not an enemy if he learned of her work. But she would have to be careful. This was not a man who would be easily duped and his loyalty would be wholly to her father.

Archie Tilbury whistled as he left the Britannia pub. Joe Strong had paid generously for the four gold watches he had stolen in the last month. He'd do all his future business with the ex-boxer. He turned immediately towards the Tower of London. The nearby district known as the Courtyard was not one he'd venture into with thirty pounds in his pocket. To his mind those back alleys were worse than the slums of Whitechapel. They were not a place for a stranger to venture into alone, even in daylight.

He took the tuppenny Tube train from Tower Hill to the West End. As the train rattled through the underground tunnels, he patted the money in his pocket. It would enable him to live in style for a few more weeks while he paid court to Tanya Summersfield. It was costing him a small fortune in fancy clothing and paying out for the church hall mission and soup but it would be worth it to win a wealthy heiress as his bride. He hungered for a position in society to get away as far as possible from the poverty of his childhood. He had been shocked at the dilapidated state of Stella's home, but if her miserly brother kept his money stashed away in a bank that suited him better. He was interested in cash not bricks and mortar. The brigadier was unlikely to live long and Tanya would inherit all his hoarded wealth. He rubbed his hands gleefully.

The edge was wearing off the double life he was leading. There were too many risks involved. At least Granville was generous with his money – when he had it. But unless the comedian laid off the bottle, there'd soon be no money to be generous with. The comedian's usefulness was coming to an end. In the past they had brushed shoulders with nobility and gentry at the races at Epsom and Newmarket, gambled with the toffs around the boxing ring at the National Sporting Club, Covent Garden, or at the less prestigious fight arena at 'Wonderland', the former music hall in the heart of Whitechapel. But Granville was no longer popular with the gentry. There had been too many drunken scenes. That was the life he wanted for himself, and as Tanya's husband he would have it.

His step was jaunty and he paused to admire his reflection in a tobacconist's window. His looks were his fortune. They had never failed him. He could charm a peanut from a monkey. Women could not resist him and no male lover had denied him. London was his oyster, the heart of a mighty empire the riches of which were his to plunder.

His dark eyes were brooding with malice. It was very different from his childhood when he'd been taunted by the other kids for being a bastard. He'd only been tolerated by his foster father for the few guineas each quarter which were sent to him by his mother's family – guineas spent down the pub while he was half-starved and beaten on any drunken whim. He'd never had a single cuddle from his foster mother, Annie Shore. She'd been too busy protecting her own five kids and herself from her husband's brutality. Any blow delivered to him was one less her children received.

He was told little of his parents, but his mother was gentry. He hated her. Any woman heartless enough to abandon a child to the cruelty of Bert

Shore had no place in his heart.

A twisted smile revealed Archie's teeth as he savoured the revenge he'd had on his foster father. On his fifteenth birthday he'd gone to the pub where Bert was drinking that night. It was located in one of the dimly lit back streets. He'd waited nearly an hour for Bert to come out. When he did he was alone, his gait uncertain from the quantity of rum he had drunk. Hidden in the shadows, he'd watched Bert weave level with him. Then he'd smashed the iron bar down on his head.

'What the bleedin' 'ell...' Bert groaned.

Those were the last words he spoke. Four blows later he lay dead on the cobbles, his blood soaking into the moss and debris of the runnel in the centre of the road.

'That's for all the beatings you gave me.' Archie spat on the lifeless form. Then he'd rifled through Bert's pockets. It was pay day and Bert had not yet been home. There were only seven shillings left from his wages after the drinking bout. It was enough to get Archie to London.

There he'd met Scribbler Sorrill. In his time Scribbler had been the best forger in London. Drink had given his hand the shakes. He also couldn't leave youths of Archie's age alone. Scribbler owned his own house. That was riches to Archie and he'd absorbed everything the forger could teach him. Forgers were the elite of the underworld. He'd also learnt how to pick pockets during that time. Finding Sorrill in a back alley with his throat slit was Archie's first encounter with the vengeance of the Gilbert brothers. Sorrill had bungled a job for them. Word reached Archie that the Gilbert brothers were looking for him. It could only be to continue Sorrill's work. He didn't fancy that. He wanted riches, not a slit throat. He'd changed his name and taken work on a cargo ship. For a year he'd sailed the globe, but the work was too menial for his taste. When they docked in Southampton he worked around the country trying his luck in Liverpool, Birmingham and other cities. But the riches of London beckoned and he was lured back.

Within a month of returning five years ago, a chance encounter on the street had changed his life. A well-dressed, middle-aged woman had approached him in Cheapside. He had just lifted a wallet from a city gent. She was staring at him as though she had seen a ghost and was visibly shaking.

'Forgive me, sir, did you once live in Tilbury?'

'It is the port which gave me my name,' Archie quipped, his ready tongue seemingly giving her the answer she needed.

'Were you by any chance fostered?' she persisted. If she hadn't been so richly dressed he'd have dismissed her as a madwoman. Even so, he'd hesitated in answering. He didn't want any reminders of that part of his life. But something in the woman's expression prompted him to reply, 'I was, ma'am.'

She had turned deathly pale and swayed. Catching her arm, he led her into a nearby Lyons coffee house. The story she had told him had moulded his future from that day. She was convinced that he was her illegitimate son taken from her as a baby.

'You are so like your father,' she had startled him by announcing in a whisper. 'It isn't uncommon for a fostered-child to be given the name of the town they are raised in.'

Her obvious wealth intrigued him. When she asked him to meet her again, he'd readily obliged. His heartbeat had quickened as she spoke of her plans for his future. They continued to meet once a month. When she started to buy him expensive clothes, he was happy to humour her. She had refused to tell him her family name, saying that he would learn it when he could walk into any drawing room in London and be accepted as a gentleman.

She gave him a taste for a style of life which he realised could have been his. He strove to better himself easing the roughness from his speech, studying the manners of gentlemen at every opportunity. Last year she had finally accepted that he was ready and she had revealed her identity, 'I am Stella Summersfield. I can never give you my name, but I can ensure that your rightful inheritance, our family home in Pilgrim's Crescent, will be yours. My niece is seventeen; by marrying her all the Summersfield property and wealth will be yours when she inherits on the death of her father.'

Only a fool would let such an opportunity pass. His looks had always been his fortune and now he ruthlessly applied charm to natural cunning. How could he fail? Parading as a gentleman, he found it easier to mingle with the rich outside the theatres in the West End or Hyde Park. His agile fingers would dip undetected into pockets which produced more lucrative prizes.

Six months after returning to England he had also caught the eye of Granville Ingram and moved in with him to become his lover. But aping the gentry was no longer enough. His ambition was fired. He would become one of them. He had started practising his old forgery skills and in the last year they had paid off and the rewards had been high.

He was jolted from his reverie as the Tube pulled into Embankment and he alighted. In the warm sunshine he wandered aimlessly along the river, mixing with the crowds outside the Houses of Parliament and Westminster Abbey. His gaze scanned the people but there was no opportunity to lift a wallet from the hurrying gentlemen going about their business. He decided that he would be better employed strolling through St James's Park. He felt confident and in high spirits. Things were progressing well with the Summersfield woman, albeit slower than he would have wished. Life was good and it was going to get better.

It was about time he moved from the rooms paid for by Granville to a better neighbourhood. Granville would not be pleased, but that was his problem. Archie was weary of the comedian's possessiveness. Even when he married Tanya there was no reason why he should not have his own rooms where he could continue to indulge his pleasures.

He had walked through Horse Guards Parade when he saw an elderly, richly dressed gentleman a few yards away. The man was on the edge of the pavement ogling the cleavage of a courtesan riding past with her paramour in an open carriage. Archie brushed past the elderly man. Seconds later a bulky wallet was secreted in the hidden pocket in the lining of his black frock coat. A tram was approaching and as he reached out to step onto the platform, his arm was grabbed. His heart raced. Had a bluebottle nabbed him?

The voice which rasped in his ear chilled his blood more than any policeman's ever could. 'Keep moving. No fuss.'

The pressure of a knife against his ribs prodded him across the busy road and into St James's Park. With a vicious shove he was slammed up against the nearest tree.

'Well now, if that pretty face don't bring back memories,' a rough voice grated on his ears as he was swung round to face two men. 'Did you think we'd forget, Alfred Turner, old Scribbler's 'prentice?'

Archie's heart plummeted to his shoes and fear churned his stomach. These were the two most evil men in London. From the cruel glitter in the Gilbert brothers' eyes, they were after blood. His blood.

''E don't look pleased to see us, does 'e, Slasher?' Fancy Gilbert sniggered.

Archie strove to appear calm and bluff his way out. 'I don't believe I have had the pleasure of an introduction, gentlemen,' he said.

'Don't get bleeding lippy with us.' Slasher pressed the point of the dagger just hard enough so that it pierced Archie's waistcoat and a trickle of warm blood oozed from the cut. 'What name you going by now? Is it still Arnie Potter the friend of Laughing Granville Ingram, or shall we go back further to Alf Cope, sailor or even Freddie Larkin, pickpocket and gambler?'

'Arnie Potter will do fine,' he croaked. He was relieved that they hadn't yet discovered that he was also known in London as Archie Tilbury. His gaze darted from side to side, seeking a means of escape. Although there were several people waiting at a tram stop twenty yards away, the Gilbert brothers were standing directly in front of him and the tree was against his back. He was trapped.

'We've been expecting you to contact us, Arnie boy.' Fancy Gilbert eyed him malevolently. His cheek was disfigured by a jagged scar and two of his front teeth were missing, making a sneer his habitual expression. He was only fractionally shorter than Archie but carried the bulky weight of a wrestler. His stout figure looked comical in the dandified yellow silk, waistcoat and large checked brown and beige suit. But Archie didn't feel inclined to laugh.

'You aren't always easy to find,' Archie replied in a voice cracked with fear.

'Word is that you reckoned we didn't need to be found,' Slasher Gilbert rasped in a voice which set Archie's teeth on edge. There was brutality in every line of his pug-like face. 'You've bin working our manor long enough to know the rules. No one thieves without paying their dues to us.' He thrust his face close to Archie. Raw onions and stale beer were overpowering on his breath. 'Pickpockets are two a penny but a decent forger ain't so easy to find. Which is why we've put ourselves out to be nice to you.'

'What do you want?' Archie could feel his bladder threatening to disgrace him. He controlled it. Slasher was a menacing sight, but if they needed his skill as a forger they'd not kill him. He forced an engaging smile, his attention on Fancy, but there was no softening in the villain's brutal features. Had he misjudged the gangleader? He knew Fancy liked to break in both the whores and young boys in their brothels. Obviously grown men did not appeal to him. Archie didn't know whether to be relieved or aggrieved that for once his looks had failed to work for him.

'We want a 'undred quid as a gesture of good will,' Fancy gritted through his decaying teeth. 'To ensure our protection like, considering what's owing to us.'

'And if I don't pay, I get my knees smashed, right?' Archie hoped to keep them talking until someone noticed that he was being threatened. Not that he reckoned his chances were high of anyone helping him.

'That would be just for starters,' Fancy jibed.

Slasher raised his dagger. ''Andsome man like yourself could also lose 'is looks.' He flashed the blade within half an inch of Archie throat. His action was shielded from the view of any curious passer-by by Fancy's broad shoulders. 'Or I may take it into me 'ead to slit your throat just for the fun of it. Pity though, seeing as you 'ave such special talents.'

Fancy sniggered. 'Me brother is 'andy with the blade, as you must've 'eard.'

Archie swallowed against a throat dried by fear. 'I haven't got a hundred quid.'

'Don't give us that, Arnie boy.' Fancy's glare was malicious. 'What about that wallet you just lifted? But we'll 'ave that anyway. It were a joy to watch you at work. A natural dipper, that's what you are. By your skill today, we reckon that a 'undred quid should pay us what's owing.'

The wallet appeared in Fancy's podgy hands like a rabbit from a magician's hat. His own wallet followed containing the money for the watches sold to Joe Strong. He hadn't felt the fingers inside his jacket.

Fancy chuckled. It sounded like glass grinding into bone. 'In future you fence only through us, Arnie boy. You can forget about going to Joe Strong. He's part of the Jew Goldstein's set-up in the East End. You thieve in our manor, so you pay your dues to us.'

'I'm telling you straight, I ain't got a hundred quid. There's thirty in me wallet and what I nicked. Take that. It's all I got,' Archie declared, fear making him lapse into rough speech. However frightened he was, he didn't see why he should hand over all his hard-won loot to these fiends.

'We were taking this anyways,' Slasher grinned, evilly. 'But I'll be generous. You've got until Friday week to get the other seventy quid. An enterprising man like yourself shouldn't have no trouble. Once this little misunderstanding is settled we'll discuss our other business.'

Before Archie could reply, Slasher's arm shot out and agony pierced his side. He looked down to see his waistcoat ripped and rapidly soaking in blood where the dagger had sliced through his flesh along his ribs.

'That's just so you don't forget us,' Slasher jeered. Then he allowed his stare to flicker knowingly over Archie's slender figure. 'Be a shame to ruin such a pretty face.'

Fancy sniggered and made a cutting motion across his throat. 'Another seventy quid or... And our lads'll be watching you.'

Archie covered his wound with his jacket and, once outside the park, hailed a taxi-cab to take him to his lodgings. Thank God he had enough loose change to pay for it. He didn't reckon his chances of getting home without fainting on the Tube.

Chapter Seven

With Archie banned from visiting the house, Tanya now met him on the corner of Ludgate Hill where he accompanied her to the class. After waiting fifteen minutes, there was no sign of him. Tanya was frantic. She was due in Aldgate in another fifteen minutes. Having escaped from the house without detection – Sam Hawkes had gone out – she was anxious not to let her pupils down. A final study of the road revealed no sign of Archie. She would have to go alone. If she took a hansom to outside the church hall, surely no harm would come to her.

The class was already assembled. 'Thought you'd abandoned us, Miss Summersfield,' Joe Lang said with a cheeky grin. 'And there was me boltin' down me pint of porter in the Britannia to get 'ere on time.'

Dave Fisher, seated beside him, stared pointedly at the door. 'Isn't Mr Tilbury with you?'

'Not tonight.' She was touched by his concern. 'I've ordered a hansom to pick me up outside after the class.'

'Then me and Joe will wait with you, if you've no objection, miss. I wouldn't have you on these streets alone.'

She accepted his offer with relief. Her arrival in the hansom had attracted several hostile glances which had made her uneasy.

As she handed out the slates and chalk, she paused by Polly. The young woman was leaning back on the bench rubbing the side of her rounded stomach. 'Are you all right, Polly? Would you be more comfortable if you sat in my chair tonight? It can't be long before your baby is due.'

'Little blighter should 'ave been 'ere couple weeks ago by my reckoning. Got a spot of indigestion, that's all, miss.'

When the class filed out for soup an hour later, Reverend Carver poked his head round the door. 'I've received glowing reports from your pupils about your class.'

Tanya smiled. 'I hope I can continue them. They're very enthusiastic.'

'Is there a problem with you teaching?'

'Papa does not approve.'

The reverend frowned. 'Is Mr Tilbury not with you?'

She shook her head. 'Joe and Dave will wait with me. I've ordered a hansom to take me home.'

'You're a brave and determined woman.' Reverend Carver smiled his approval. 'Do you wish me to speak to your father?'

'Not at the moment. He's ill.'

'I'm sorry to hear that.' He turned to leave, then checked. 'Your work here is greatly appreciated. We usually have a float in the August carnival. In recent years Mrs Corbett and her sister have decorated it for us and provided costumes for those on the float. Unfortunately Mrs Corbett was paralysed by a seizure last month and her sister has to nurse her.'

'The poor woman. Is there any way I can help?' Tanya said before considering that her father would not approve.

'I was hoping you'd offer. I remembered that you said you painted and liked to design rooms. Could you design the float? Any theme will do. Would you also be able to manage the costumes?'

'I'm no dressmaker, Reverend,' Tanya apologised, wondering already if she had been overhasty.

'I am,' Polly interrupted. 'I couldn't face the soup and overheard you speaking. I'd be happy to assist Miss Summersfield, if she can provide the materials and a sewing machine. I'll make anything she wants. I work in Reuban Solomon's sweatshop machining shirts. Sal will 'elp me, won't you?'

Her young sister nodded. She was a bright enough pupil, but the girl rarely spoke unless she had to read aloud and then her voice was little more than a whisper. It was as though she wanted to make herself as inconspicuous as possible. Close to her, Tanya was dismayed to see that there was a large yellowing bruise over her eye beneath the matted blonde fringe. From Nan Rudge who liked to gossip, she had learned that Polly and Sal were orphans. Polly lived with a man who was the father of her child, but he was a bully and he resented having to give a roof to Sal. He lashed out at her if she displeased him.

Polly looked happier than she had for weeks at the idea of helping with the float. Tanya hadn't the heart to back out now.

'Are you sure you will be able to manage the extra work, once the baby comes along, Polly?' she asked.

'The carnival is quite an occasion round 'ere. Kids look forward to it all year.' Her enthusiasm brought a glow to her pallid cheeks. 'I'd love to be part of it. I reckon Widow Rudge will do 'er bit as well.'

'What bit will I be doing?' Nan Rudge said, leaning heavily on her tree branch as she paused for breath in the doorway.

Reverend Carver explained.

'Ain't no use with a sewing machine but I can put me 'and to a bit of sewing.'

‘That’s wonderful,’ Tanya said excitedly, her mind buzzing with ideas. ‘I’ll draw up some designs for next week.’

Joe and Dave had also come in and were listening. Wilf Baker, from the chemical works, was scratching his bushy beard. Next to him was his brother Bill who had joined the class two weeks ago. He walked with a crutch after an accident at work when a pile of timber had fallen on his leg. He had been dismissed as a cripple. It was why Wilf was so virulent about fighting for workers’ rights.

‘I can help out if you want a bit of carpentry done,’ Bill offered. ‘I’m a carpenter. Wilf will give us a ’and, won’t you, Wilf?’

Wilf grunted agreement.

‘That would be a great help, thank you both.’ Tanya marvelled at the way everybody was responding.

‘You can count me in for any odd job that wants doing,’ Dave Fisher chipped in. ‘Though you ain’t gonna get me sitting on no float done up like some Nancy-boy actor.’

Tanya saw Joe Lang walking to his seat, his shoulders slumped. His mangled hand was jammed in his pocket. He’d been out of work for a year and with each passing week, the sadness and despair in his eyes deepened. His writing with his left hand was clear and legible, proving that he practised for hours each day. And he had learnt nearly all that she could teach him in mathematics. He had a brilliant head for figures.

‘There’s so much to do and get organised. I

wouldn't know where to start to get wood for scenery or paint, or the cost of it. We will need to stick to a very tight budget. Everything must be costed.' Tanya was watching Joe as she spoke and saw his expression brighten.

'I could do that for you, Miss Summersfield.'

'Then it's settled.'

Sal hugged herself with excitement. 'We'll have the best float in the carnival.'

As Tanya went back to her desk, her pleasure faded. She had yet to get her father to agree to let her do this. He'd forbid it if he discovered that she'd been teaching against his orders.

She was handing out exercise paper for them to do set work in their homes, when a cry from Polly alarmed her. Her face was twisted in agony and on the floor by her feet a pool of water was spreading.

'Gawd, 'er waters 'ave broken!' Widow Rudge declared. 'Baby's started. It'll be a while yet as it's 'er first. Best we get Polly 'ome.'

'It ain't 'er first, it's 'er third in as many years,' Sal wailed, looking frightened. 'Other two died after a few days. Last one only took an hour to pop out.'

Polly screamed, clutching at her stomach. 'Oh lawd, I just wanna push. I can't stop it.'

Nan Rudge shuffled over to Polly and placed her hand on her stomach. She glared at the men. 'Help me get 'er in the corner over there. Then get out. This is women's work. Best see Miss Summersfield gets 'er cab, Dave. I'll stay with Polly. Too late to move 'er now.'

Tanya felt helpless but responsible. 'I won't

leave Polly. And she can't give birth on the floor.'

The widow snorted. 'They sleep on a pile of rags. They ain't got no fancy brass bedstead.' At Tanya's horrified expression, Nan said more kindly, 'Best get 'ome, miss. Ain't nothing you can do. It's dark outside and you ain't got Mr Tilbury with you.'

'I'll stay.' Tanya was adamant. 'I'm not abandoning Polly.'

Joe and Dave shuffled their feet. 'We'll wait outside for you, miss,' Joe assured her. 'We ain't letting you on the streets alone.'

Tanya nodded her gratitude and knelt on the floor by the panting woman. She knew nothing about childbirth and witnessing Polly's pain and struggle was harrowing. All she could do was encourage her and hold her hand for comfort.

The pains were incessant, each onslaught bathing the woman in sweat. Nan Rudge sat back in a chair and lit a pipe. 'Time for a smoke, I reckon. Sal, go tell the kitchen we need hot water and scissors to cut the cord.'

'I have some in my bag.' Tanya handed them to her. Half an hour later, Nan Rudge was not so composed, she was on her knees delving between Polly's legs. 'I can feel the 'ead now, Polly girl. Next pain, you push.'

Polly screamed. Her teeth were bared and her lips curled back, her face contorted in agony as she strained.

Tanya's gaze moved from the tortured face of the mother to between her exposed legs. A tiny downy head appeared, then its face. It was as wrinkled as a walnut. Another scream from Polly and the baby slid into the world. It looked so cross at having been thrust from the warmth of the womb that Tanya found herself laughing and crying with emotion.

Widow Rudge cut the cord and held up the baby. 'You've got a girl, Polly. But I ain't got nothing to wrap the poor mite in.'

Tanya pulled off a lace-hemmed petticoat. 'Use this. Then Polly can cut it up and make the baby some robes.'

'Thank you, miss,' Polly beamed as the baby was placed in her arms.

Tanya brushed a tear from her cheek. 'She's a lovely baby. Have you a name for her?'

'Jane, after me ma who died when Sal were a nipper.'

Joe Lang and Dave Fisher were at the top of the basement stairs when Tanya finally appeared.

'Polly had a girl,' she announced tiredly. 'I want her to have this cab when she's ready. I'll get another from the highway.' She handed a silver crown to the driver and ordered him to wait for Polly.

'We'll walk with you, miss. There's bound to be one outside Aldgate Station.'

'Thank you, Dave.' She glanced nervously up and down the dimly lit street. The excitement of the birth had drained her emotionally and now she was aware of the lateness of the hour. There seemed to be menace in every shadow.

There were no cabs at Aldgate Station. In the press of the boisterous milling crowd, Tanya felt ill at ease and vulnerable. Suddenly there was an eruption of shouting from across the road and several figures spilled out of a pub. One man fell into the gutter and was set upon by another.

'Right barney goin' on over there,' Joe observed. 'Perhaps we should walk on a ways.'

Before Tanya could answer, men appeared from side streets and the scuffle across the road broke into a street fight. Tanya was roughly jostled and Dave turned to the man who had pushed her. Immediately two others sprang on him, fists pummelling.

Joe pushed her against the wall and shielded her. 'Looks like the Courtyard and Flower and Dean Street mob are at each other's throats again.'

Tanya shuddered, seeing iron bars and wooden staves with protruding nails being used as weapons. Dave had been swallowed up in the crowd. 'I hope Dave is all right. I can't see him.'

''E knows how to look after 'imself,' Joe said. 'Best get you away from 'ere though, miss.'

Caps flew up into the air, grunts of pain followed the persistent thud of pounded or kicked flesh. A man was crawling away cradling a bloody ear half torn from his head. Women and children gathered on the outskirts, the women cheering their menfolk and deriding the rival gang. A ragamuffin boy picked up a stone and hurled it into the fighting mass, his aim indiscriminate.

A bear of a man rose up wielding a bloody knife, dancing a jig and swiping his arms in a vicious arch to challenge. 'Scum, all of you. Take me on, you yella curs.'

He was felled by an iron bar. Tanya turned

away, sickened by the violence. 'Where are the police? Someone will be killed.'

'They're coming, Miss Summersfield. Look, there's a cab at the corner.'

Joe grabbed her arm and guided her through the crowd, all jostling to see the fight. An outflung elbow banged into her cheek and her hat was knocked askew as she battled her way through the throng. Tanya glanced back and saw a dozen policemen charging into the mass, their batons raised to break up the disturbance. She shouted out her address to the hansom driver and was about to get into the cab when a furious voice grated by her ear.

'What in the devil's name are you doing here?'

She spun round and faced the enraged glitter in Sam Hawkes' eyes.

Joe shouted above the racket, 'You look like a gent. If you know Miss Summersfield, get 'er out of 'ere.'

'Get in the cab.' Sam gave her a none too gentle shove and climbed in beside her.

All Tanya could think of as the horse inched its way through the people overrunning the road was that Sam Hawkes would tell her father. Why did she have to meet him of all people tonight?

'Archie, why aren't you with Tanya?' Stella regarded him with disbelief.

'Isn't she here? I was detained. I couldn't make our meeting.' His side ached intolerably from the knife wound and he was perilously close to losing both his patience and his temper. He had come here to apologise to Tanya. He did not want to risk losing her favour. With the Gilbert brothers now on to him and causing him problems, he needed the financial security of a wealthy marriage more than ever.

'I should never have agreed to you meeting her away from the house,' Stella groaned, distraught. 'Reginald has already taken against you. Why did he have to return home the evening you kept her out late?'

'Your brother is an unreasonable man. I'm sure Tanya is safe,' he soothed, though he was anxious that if anything had happened to her, it would go against him. Damn the Gilbert brothers. 'The class would have ended by now,' he said heavily. 'Otherwise I would go and meet her.'

Stella wrung her hands. 'If anything has happened to her, Reginald will blame me. And with that damned captain in residence now, it's difficult for me to settle matters.'

He took her hands and forced a reassuring and captivating smile. 'Tanya will be fine. But I need your help. I've asked Tanya to marry me. She says she's not ready for marriage.'

'I'll talk to her.' Stella wrenched her hands from his. 'I thought with Reginald so ill, it'd be easier for you and Tanya to meet. But he's stubborn. He doesn't want you to call on her until he's up and about again.'

Anger flushed his cheeks. 'I can also be stubborn when I want something. And I want Tanya as my wife. What's this about a captain staying in the house?'

'He was Reginald's aide in India,' Stella told him. 'He's constantly at his side.'

Archie's lips thinned. He could feel the situation slipping from his grasp. 'Does he intend Tanya to marry this man?'

'You have no fear of that. He was a non-commissioned officer and was born in Stepney. Even thought Reginald has formed a strange friendship with the fellow – and is even considering going into some sort of partnership with him – he will consider him beneath us and unfit to wed his daughter.'

Maude came into the room and looked uneasy at seeing Archie. 'Is Tanya not back yet? Shouldn't she be with you, Mr Tilbury?'

Stella spoke before Archie could. 'Tanya went without Mr Tilbury tonight. He has just returned from searching for her. The girl is too headstrong for her own good.'

'She could have been attacked,' Maude wailed.

'I'm sure that she's safe,' Archie reassured her. 'The traffic is heavy and will have delayed her, that's all. I'll go and look for her again, just to set your minds at rest.'

'You put yourself to a great deal of trouble for my niece,' Maude stated. 'It is time she was wed and settled down.'

'That is my intention,' he replied. From Maude's dreamy expression, he judged her to be a romantic, and added, 'I find Tanya utterly captivating. Clearly she gets her beauty from her aunts.'

Maude's answering smile told him that he had won her over. Now he must ensure that Tanya was not angry that he had missed their meeting.

Bowing graciously to both women, which

caused his wound to stab painfully, he left the house.

'Do you intend to tell my father where I was tonight, Mr Hawkes?' Tanya glared at him in the dim interior of the hansom cab.

'And risk giving him another heart attack?' he ground out. 'I'd rather not have to tell him of his daughter's shameless conduct. I couldn't believe my eyes when I saw you. No decent woman sets foot in that area after dark. What the devil were you up to?'

She resented his attitude. No harm had come to her. 'You may be a guest in our house, sir, but what I do is no concern of yours.'

'Isn't it, by God?' Fury rippled through his voice. 'I've too much respect for the brigadier to see his daughter bring scandal to his name.'

That brought her head up, her eyes glittering with defiance. 'I was doing nothing shameful. What kind of a woman do you think I am?'

He glared at her frostily. 'Obviously you're disobedient. Headstrong. Hot-tempered. And careless of your own safety to the point of stupidity. Was it an assignation?'

'Certainly not.'

'Then explain what you were up to, risking your life and virtue.'

She was about to tell him to go to the devil but thought better of it. 'First, you must promise to keep my secret.'

'So that you can continue to meet a clandestine lover?' His stare was glittering and scathing.

Her hand came up to strike him and was

caught inches from his taut jaw. 'Don't play the innocent with me, miss. And don't try and lie.' Abruptly he released her.

She was breathing heavily as she glared at him. 'How dare you imply that I am capable of that. You have a sordid mind.'

'Put it down to worldly experience. I saw enough bored daughters and wives who were supposedly gentlewomen dallying with soldiers when their husbands or fathers were on patrol.'

Shock widened her eyes. Then her anger resurfaced. 'It's Papa's fault that I'm driven to subterfuge. He forbade me to teach the poor. I was taking a class of adults who want to better their circumstances. Is that so wrong? Or are you as bigoted as my father?'

His elbow rested on the window rim, his knuckles pressed against his cheek as he regarded her. The shop lights cast light and dark shadows over his face. His expression remained tight and closed to her.

'Do you realise the danger you'd have been in if that fight had spread across the road?' He spoke to her as though she was simple and it fuelled her resentment. 'Even in a hansom you wouldn't be safe. The mob, once roused, has been known to attack cabs, hauling out the passengers to beat and rob them. A young woman would be lucky to escape with just that. Are you courting assault? Have you no sense, woman? What possessed you to travel alone?'

'Duty drove me. Perhaps foolishly,' she conceded, hating to admit that he was right. 'Usually Mr Tilbury accompanies me, but he did not meet me this evening. I didn't want to disappoint my class.'

'Tilbury has a lot to answer for,' he shot back with the brutality of a firing squad. 'No decent man would endanger your virtue as he has. I've never heard such a hare-brained scheme. The man is a bounder.'

Tanya rounded on him. She'd heard enough of his preaching. 'I won't have him maligned. He is honourable and a gentleman. More importantly, he doesn't treat a woman as though she is an imbecile. He's broad-minded enough to help me.'

'Yet he failed you tonight.' There was a darker note to his voice which condemned Tilbury more than her.

'There must have been a good reason. How could I let my pupils down? If I don't teach them, who will? Don't you think they deserve a chance to better their lives?'

His tension was palpable, but he was no longer glaring at her with contempt. 'There are other ways. This was too dangerous.'

She tossed back her head, refusing to lower her defences or give ground on so important an issue. 'My family thrives on danger. They've made a career of it in the army. And why are you being so high and mighty in your attitude? Were you not brought up in the same area yourself?'

He stared out of the window. They were emerging from the main thoroughfare of Cheapside and St Paul's majestic dome was silhouetted against the starry night sky. In truth he no longer knew whether he should lecture this foolish woman or commend her.

'Besides, sir,' she challenged, 'how innocent are you? You were in the same area which you condemn as a den of iniquity.'

'*Touché*,' he surprised her by saying, then regarded her gravely for several moments before adding, 'I was born in Stepney, which isn't much more than a stone's throw from Aldgate. I was visiting friends.' His voice remained terse. 'And yes, the idea of teaching adults who are willing to better their lives is commendable. But you've placed yourself at risk.'

'I'm not a coward. No harm came to me. Two of my pupils escorted me to a cab.' Her voice dropped to a tremulous huskiness and her eyes shone with passionate fervour. 'If you tell Papa, he'll stop me teaching.'

In the gaslight her beauty was ethereal, contrasting with the earthy ardour of her entreaty. It was hard to resist. 'I don't like deception.'

Like a citadel he looked impenetrable, rock-solid, his defences unbreached. 'Neither do I,' she said, softly. 'I hate lies. But there's no other way.'

'The brigadier is not well enough to be upset by such information,' he replied heavily.

The hansom had drawn to a halt outside her house. Tanya opened her purse to pay the driver but Sam Hawkes was there before her. She said softly, 'It's still early. I doubt you'd have returned here at this hour but for me. I have inconvenienced you, at least let me pay the fare.'

The look he shot her warned her not to insult him by persisting. He assisted her from the hansom. 'Your actions tonight were misguided and foolish, Miss Tanya. You were lucky to escape harm. Promise me you'll never again go alone to the East End.'

She smiled at him in relief. They stood under the street gas lamp as the cab pulled away. There was something about the presence of this quiet, unassuming man which dispelled her resentment. Sam Hawkes cut a presentable figure in his dark suit, even though he favoured a cap instead of a fashionable homburg. He carried himself like an officer, but he didn't speak like one. He no longer dropped his aitches but there was a nasal twang to his accent which told of his East End upbringing. It wasn't just the threat that he could betray her to her father which caused a swirling of anticipation to crackle through her veins, it was his physical presence.

His thick, dark blond hair, which fell forward over his tanned brow, was unrestrained by hair oil. And the way he eased his neck against the chaff of his shirt collar showed that wearing a tie irked him. He must have hated the stiff collars of his army uniform. Unbidden, the image of him in an open-necked shirt with his sleeves rolled up came to her. There was a masculine magnetism about him that was unlike anything she had encountered before.

'The brigadier may seem strict to you, but he thinks of your welfare,' he added. The tawny paleness of his eyes was guarded, warning her that his strongest loyalty would be to her father.

'Papa must realise that I will not be ordered into mindless submission like one of his troopers.' She broadened her smile to lighten her words. There was still a flush to her cheeks and an overbrightness to her green eyes from their earlier contest of wills. Sam saw it and was struck by the radiance of her beauty. The gas light enhanced the warm amber sheen of her hair, her pale skin was as unblemished as a pearl. He had been shocked to recognise her in Aldgate. Instinctively, he had reacted to save his friend's daughter from the mob. The haughty way she had confronted him in the cab had ignited his anger. Then her explanation had knocked the sting from his ire.

Now as he stared down at her, he swallowed convulsively. She was exceptionally lovely, but there was something more than that about her, which made her an extraordinary woman. That special radiance came from the goodness within. She was spirited, with a sense of justice. Caring. An innocent who at the same time was provocatively feminine. There was a vitality and strength of purpose about her. All traits which he admired. She was undoubtedly strong-willed and determined, yet her innocence made her vulnerable. It roused in him a need to protect her.

Taken aback by the force of his emotion, he dragged his gaze from her face. This was a woman it would be all too easy to fall in love with. And this was a woman who was barred from him by position and wealth.

The army had taught him to value his own worth. It had also taught him that the lines of class could not be crossed. The brigadier might have offered him a rare friendship, but he'd be outraged if he guessed what his former aide was feeling at this moment. And Sam knew his place; he knew the heights he could rise to within it and the taboos that must never be crossed.

Sam was not the only one watching Tanya in the street. When Archie saw a man help Tanya from the carriage, he drew back into the shadows. He'd been waiting to speak to her and was annoyed that she was not alone. He could not hear their conversation but the gas lamp showed him Tanya's radiant expression. Her companion was staring at her entranced.

When the man entered the house, fury ground through Archie. He had not missed the soldierly bearing, or the self-possession of a man used to being in authority. He must be the brigadier's guest that Stella had mentioned. The man appeared enamoured of Tanya. It was not a situation Archie would permit to flourish.

Chapter Eight

Granville was reclining on a chaise longue wearing a floor-length emerald and black brocade dressing gown. He removed the stem of a Turkish opium pipe from his lips as Archie entered the cluttered parlour. The smell from the pipe made him wrinkle his nose in distaste. Granville's pupils were dilated and his jaw was slack.

'I told you I didn't want that filthy stuff in the

house.' He pointed to the pipe. 'Look at the state of you. Weren't you supposed to be working Hackney Empire tonight?'

Granville peered at him with unfocused eyes. 'I played the matinee. You were supposed to join me afterwards.' He pouted. 'I missed you. I came back to see you. When you wasn't here, I got lonely.'

Archie eased off his jacket. Pouring himself a stiff whisky, he flopped down in a fireside chair.

Granville frowned. 'That a new red waistcoat you're wearing?'

Staring in horror at his shirt, Archie saw fresh blood spreading across the linen. He'd been in such a temper he'd walked back from Pilgrim's Crescent. His angry pace must have reopened the wound. Tugging out the tail of his shirt, he began to remove the bloodsoaked bandage.

'It's not a waistcoat. It's blood,' he snapped.

'How d'you get hurt like that?' Granville gave up trying to rise and remained slumped on the chaise longue.

Archie swore roundly as he struggled to re-dress his wound and directed a hostile glare at the comedian. 'I suppose you can't get your aged arse off there and help me?'

Granville grinned inanely.

'You're useless,' Archie spat as he tore up one of Granville's shirts to make a bandage. At least the wound had not become infected. 'Slasher Gilbert did this.'

Granville waved a finger at him. 'I told you it were dangerous to thieve in their manor. Why were you working without me?'

'The state you're in you'd've been no use, would you?' he goaded. The pain roused his loathing for Granville's addiction. In another few months no music hall in England would employ the comedian.

'From what I've heard of the Gilbert brothers, you got off light,' Granville slurred. 'I suppose it's gonna cost us now.'

'Too fucking right.' Archie's temper soared, his fine airs discarded as he remembered what the Gilbert brothers expected.

Granville's head swayed back and forth as he tried to concentrate. 'Evil bastards, the Gilberts. P'haps it's time we moved on. I could do the clubs in the north. We could start afresh.'

Archie glared murderously at him. 'And miss out on the Summersfield money? I can stop thieving once I marry her and become respectable.'

Granville sat up, fear slackening his lips. 'Perhaps it ain't just the money you want. You've changed since you took up with the Summersfield woman. Always I have to do what you want. What would Miss Summersfield say if she knew the truth about you?'

Archie lashed out at him, sending Granville sprawling onto the floor. Picking up the opium pipe, Archie smashed it against the wall. 'If you know what's good for you, you ain't gonna tell her nothing.' He swayed and clutched at his side, the pain agonising.

Granville was holding his head and his face was awash with tears. He was quivering with terror. Archie stared at him, hatred burning his stomach at the indignities he had suffered, first from the Gilbert brothers then from Tanya and the soldier. He stared at Granville who had drawn his legs up to his chin and was sobbing.

'You ain't got no cause to treat me like that. This isn't one of our games, is it? You meant to hurt me.'

'I'm sick of your games. And I'm sick of you.'

Granville came up onto his knees. Holding out his arms, he beseeched, 'Don't be cruel, Arnie luv. I got a tidy nest egg put by.'

Archie scowled. 'You've spent all your money on opium and drink.'

Granville shuffled over to the fireplace, flicked back the rug and lifted a floorboard. His hand dived inside and he lifted out a tin box. 'I ain't lying. I put this by for a rainy day.'

'So I see, Granville.' Archie lowered himself to the floor and ran his hands over the older man's chest.

Granville's smile was slack and his eyes were glazed with drugs and passion as he reached to unbutton Archie's trousers. 'Don't I look after yer? Ain't I good to you?'

Archie laughed and put both his hands round Granville's neck. The comedian's usefulness was at an end. This way he got what was left of his money and made sure Granville never blabbed what he knew of Archie's past.

Two days later every London paper carried the headline:

Music hall star Laughing Granville Ingram found strangled in a back alley in Soho.

When Stella saw Tanya alight from the hansom in the company of Sam Hawkes, anger channelled through her. She checked it, unwilling to create a scene which Hawkes might overhear. No doubt he would report everything back to Reginald. She could do without her brother's spy in the house while he was bedridden.

The next morning her anger was resurrected when she entered her brother's room with the medicine she had prepared for him and found Hawkes already in attendance. He was holding Reginald against his chest as the invalid vomited into a basin. When Reginald lay back, there was tenderness in the way Sam Hawkes pulled up the bedclothes.

'Leave the brigadier to rest, Mr Hawkes,' she commanded.

'Has the doctor called again?' He had the audacity to question her. 'The brigadier has been vomiting since breakfast and he's very weak.'

'You need not concern yourself over my brother's health. Dr Garrett came yesterday evening while you were out. He bled him. Rest is what my brother needs. You should not be disturbing him.' She spoke to him as if she was addressing a servant.

Sam Hawkes returned her frigid glare. 'He shouldn't be left alone. He's so weak he could choke on his vomit.'

'If he is sick, it's because he's not getting his rest,' Stella declared. 'I will inform you when the brigadier is stronger.'

Tanya had entered the room in time to catch her aunt's remarks. 'Aunt Stella, you are being unreasonable,' she remonstrated. 'Mr Hawkes is the only person who can get Papa to eat.' She noted that Sam wore no jacket. A black unbuttoned waistcoat matched his trousers, his white shirt neck was open and his sleeves rolled up revealing strong brown forearms. His casual attire struck her as more masculine and commanding than Archie in his formal frock coats or suits.

Without a word, Sam picked up his jacket from the back of a chair. His jaw was taut with anger as he left the room.

Tanya followed him out to the landing. 'My aunt did not mean to be rude. We're all worried about Papa.' The stiffness in his manner did not relax. 'I was equally rude to you last night,' she went on, wanting to make amends. 'I was in the wrong and you were right. The mob frightened me and I was angry with you for believing the worst of me.' She smiled wryly. 'It was kind of you to accompany me home. As we will be seeing each other daily, it would be less formal if you called me Tanya.'

A light flickered in his eyes though his features did not soften. He hooked his jacket over his shoulder with his finger, the other hand in his trouser pocket. 'I'm glad I was there to be of service, Miss Tanya. But if others can tend the brigadier, I've me work to attend to. I've premises to look at if I'm to run a garage.'

'You're still angry with me?' At his frown she laughed softly. 'Please let it just be Tanya. And may I call you Sam?'

'You may, it if pleases you, Miss Tanya.'

'Thank you for not betraying my secret to my father.'

There was a sardonic lift to his brow. 'So that's what all this Sam and Tanya business is about. You don't have to pretend that you regard me as your equal, Miss Tanya. Providing you don't teach again without a proper escort, I'll not mention it.'

Green sparks brightened her eyes. 'I was not flattering you. I was being polite to my father's guest.'

She walked away. Sam whistled under his breath as he watched the sensuous sway of her hips. The belt of her white morning gown encompassed a small waist and through the thin silk the swell of her breasts tilted provocatively as she breathed deeply to master her annoyance. Unlike other women of her class, she wore her hair in soft curls high on her head which fell in a mane to her shoulder blades. It would be wonderful to bury his head in the scented depths of those tresses. Feeling his body begin to respond, he marched with a more pronounced limp than usual out of the house.

He had agreed to stay on here because the brigadier had seemed to need him. He remained because he was worried about Summersfield's fading health. In the future he would keep a greater distance between himself and the brigadier's enchanting daughter.

It was Sunday and Tanya was resentful that her father had forbidden Archie to call while he was still ill. The summer morning was glorious, the sky azure and cloudless. It made her restless and she took a book outside to read in the rose arbour. The trelliswork filtered the sun, providing welcome shade, but even here the air was close; any breeze was blocked by the tall buildings around them. Aunt Stella was fussing over her precious flowers. The garden, like the house, was Stella's obsession. Here at least she could create the splendour she craved.

Tanya had to admit that the delphiniums, hollyhocks and foxgloves were beautiful. The border of lavender and pinks filled the air with sweet perfume. They also attracted dozens of butterflies into the garden. Buster, the feral tom cat, was asleep on top of the old stables roof. He stretched out and yawned, too hot and lazy to stalk the sparrows enjoying a dust bath in the baked earth under the wisteria.

Full of suppressed energy, Tanya was frustrated at being cooped up. She put down her book and sauntered to the old stables at the foot of the garden and peered in through the cobwebbed and dusty panes. Her bicycle was propped against those of her brothers. Ben's had been a conventional model like her own; but Harry, always an extrovert, rode a penny-farthing. The high brick walls surrounding the garden trapped the heat. It would have been pleasant to cycle over London Bridge to Greenwich Park.

She stretched, lifting her arms to the cobalt, cloudless sky and twirled round on her toes. Even in her cream muslin gown she was uncomfortably hot. She was a virtual prisoner. Her young body ached to walk, cycle or spend a day on the river. If her father had not been ill she'd have taken off to spend a few days with Clare and Simon. With a sensuous sigh she lifted her heavy hair into a coil on the crown of her head and gazed up at a blackbird singing in a laburnum tree. How wonderful to be as free as the birds, to sing from the sheer joy of life without restriction.

A movement at a window caught her eye and she saw Sam watching her from her father's bedroom window. Self-consciously she waved, then assuming a more decorous manner returned to her abandoned book.

Minutes later Ginny called to her. 'The brigadier asks that you join him, Miss Tanya.'

When she entered the sickroom, she was delighted to see her father sitting by the window. Sam was seated opposite him across a games table set out with chess pieces. On her entrance Sam rose. He was in his shirtsleeves and reached to put on his jacket. She put up a hand to stop him. 'Please, don't wear that on my account. It's far too hot. You're our guest. There's no reason for such formality. My brothers would never have bothered to be so polite.'

He smiled appreciatively and leant against the windowsill, his arms folded across his chest.

Her father grunted as he concentrated on the chess pieces, ignoring Tanya's arrival. 'Damn you, man. You've put me in check again.'

Sam laughed. 'Just because you're an invalid, you wouldn't want me to let you win, would you?'

A noncommittal snort answered him. Tanya regarded her father and wondered why she had been summoned. She had not seen Sam to speak to for two days. He either ate with her father or went out to dine. He kept himself deliberately apart from the family.

Her father waved her nearer. 'Hawkes tells me I'm being unreasonable keeping you shut in the house.'

Tanya glanced at her father's companion with surprise, but did not comment. He also seemed taken aback by her father's words.

'Does that mean you are permitting Mr Tilbury to call upon me?' she asked.

'I haven't decided about that fellow yet. I need to meet him and know more about him, but not until I'm stronger. But you should get out more.' His gaze was approving of her slim figure in the cream gown as he added, 'See and be seen, my girl. That's important. A woman of your age should be seen in certain places, it's expected of them. I'm sure Hawkes will arrange something suitable.'

'I beg your pardon, sir?' Sam looked uncomfortable.

The brigadier regarded him sharply. 'You said yourself the girl needs to get out. And she can't go without an escort. You've got an hour or so to spare this afternoon, haven't you?'

'I have business to attend to,' Sam replied tersely. 'There's a man willing to sell an old Daimler that needs renovating. Thought I'd take a look at it.'

'On a Sunday? That won't do at all.'

Exasperated that they were talking as though she was not present, Tanya announced, 'Papa, I will not be told how to spend my time. Why won't you permit Mr Tilbury to call on me?'

'I know nothing about him. Sam knows his place. I trust him. Besides, he's been shut up with me for hours. He needs to exercise his wounded knee or it will stiffen. The arrangement should suit you both.'

'I would prefer to be consulted, not ordered,' Tanya returned, her cheeks stained with embarrassment.

A muscle flickered along Sam's jaw. 'I think it's time I moved back to me old lodgings. You're recovering, Brigadier.'

'You mean I can stagger out of bed as far as this damned chair.' He thumped the chair arm in exasperation. His face was turning crimson and his breathing became laboured as he accused. 'So you'd desert me, Hawkes, because I ask you to give an hour of your time to ensure that my daughter is safe on the London streets?'

'You forget, I'm not your servant,' Sam clipped out. 'And you'll make yourself ill carrying on as you are.'

Puzzled, the brigadier studied the two young people who were both bristling with indignation. 'Now what have I said? I don't regard you as a servant, man. It was your idea, wasn't it, that Tanya looked bored and needed to get out? I thought you'd both be pleased.'

At their silence he added, 'You can't desert me, Sam. I need you here. I thought you'd enjoy a couple of hours outside on a summer's day. What's all the fuss? You could hire a couple of hacks and go riding.'

'I've no riding habit that fits me, Papa.' Tanya fixed on the first excuse that came to mind.

'Don't you want to get out, girl?' Her father eyed her sternly.

'Of course, but...'

'Got no objection to Hawkes escorting you, have you?'

'No. But Mr Hawkes has his own interests to pursue and friends to visit. Can't you see you are putting him in a difficult situation and embarrassing us both?'

'Nonsense. You're not embarrassed, are you, Hawkes?' The brigadier leaned back in his chair. 'It was your suggestion, after all.'

Sam pushed away from the window. He'd been put into a corner. To refuse would only cause offence. 'If Miss Tanya wishes to accompany me, I would be pleased to escort her this afternoon.'

She inclined her head in acceptance, though the stiffness of her shoulders and the brittle light in her eyes were evidence that she resented her father's command as much as he did.

'Can you ride a bicycle?' she asked.

'I haven't done for some years.'

'You could use one of my brothers'. Perhaps we could visit one of the parks. It is such a lovely day.'

'As you wish, Miss Tanya.' He saw a flash of annoyance cross her face at his stiff answer.

'Are you sure that such a ride will not adversely affect your knee? It is quite a recent wound, I believe.'

The concern in her voice and her willingness to accept him as a guest dispelled his antagonism.

Even so, it didn't make him their equal. Why did that rankle more than usual? It hardened his reply. 'It needs exercise.'

Sam was standing to attention, his voice clipped with formality. Tanya inwardly groaned. He was the image of the soldier she had feared would be thrust upon them. It was at odds with his casual dress and the natural confidence in him which she found attractive. Out of misplaced kindness he had suggested that her father give her more freedom. Obviously, he had not expected the brigadier to involve him.

'I must change,' she replied with equal formality. 'I shall be ready in half an hour, if that is convenient to you?'

'Perfectly.'

When she left, Sam turned to the brigadier. 'I don't take orders any more, sir.'

'Did that sound like an order?' Summersfield frowned. 'It wasn't intended as such. Truth is, I fear the girl may be infatuated with Tilbury. There's something about the man I didn't take to. She's been isolated from male company. Both her brothers were dead by the time she was thirteen. Best way to stop her getting romantic notions about Tilbury is to give the man more competition.'

'I'm hardly an acceptable rival, am I?'

The brigadier bayoneted him with a stare. 'You'll do as a companion. Once I'm up and about she can mix with the cream of society and be introduced to the right sort of men. You don't have to give up your own female companions. Just treat Tanya as a cousin or sister. Is that too much to ask?'

It was a great deal to ask if the brigadier but knew it. Since Thursday Sam had been unable to banish thoughts of Tanya from his mind. He controlled his resentment. The brigadier was telling him not to overstep his place, while throwing them together. Was he unaware of Tanya's beauty, her enthusiasm for life which was contagious and exciting? Watching her in the garden he had been captivated by the way the sunlight turned her hair honey-gold. When she had lifted her hair and arms in pagan abandonment to the sun, her body graceful as a wood nymph as she pirouetted, desire more profound than anything he had experienced before overwhelmed him.

He felt as if he was sitting on a powder keg with the fuse already burning.

Chapter Nine

Tanya entered the garden to find the bicycles propped again the garden wall. She flinched with surprise at seeing Sam's head appear above the high wall of the side alley. He looked eight feet tall. When he wobbled precariously she realised he was riding the penny-farthing.

'Are you going on that?' she called. She had changed into a burgundy skirt and square-necked, cream blouse. Her hair was drawn up from her face and fell loosely around her shoulders, her eyes were shaded from the sun by a large straw boater decorated with silk camellias.

'Not likely,' he answered with a grin. 'I just couldn't resist trying it out. Devil of a thing to keep your balance on.'

With that he cried out and disappeared from sight. Tanya ran through the garden gate into the alley, worried lest he had injured himself.

Sam was crouched over the largest of the wheels examining its frame. 'It hasn't come to any harm.'

'What about you?'

He dusted the seat of his cream trousers and the sleeve of his striped blazer, his grin returning. 'Ego's a bit bruised.' He eyed the wicker basket she was carrying.

'Aunt Maude was anxious that we'll miss lunch. She insisted Cook made us up a picnic hamper,' she explained as she tied it behind the saddle of one of the bicycles propped against the wall.

'Watch your skirt on the chain,' he advised. 'I've just oiled it and I also checked the brakes.'

Wheeling the penny-farthing back into the garden, he entered the old stables which had once held half a dozen horses. When he did not reappear, Tanya peered inside. She could not see him.

'Sam!'

'Over here.' He was crouched over an object in the first stall and stood up to beckon her. 'Look what I've found. Could be just the thing for the brigadier.'

'That's Grandma's Bathchair.' She studied the

wicker seat and the long handle which steered it.

'Needs some work done on it,' Sam observed. 'But it would do the brigadier good to get out in the sunshine. He hates being stuck in the sick-room. I could push him in it.'

'If he agrees.' Tanya was doubtful.

Sam chuckled. 'He'll agree.'

She hid her astonishment that he was so certain of her father's moods and handed him a rolled tartan blanket to secure behind the saddle of his bicycle. They would sit on it when they ate.

Sam pulled a tie from his pocket and was about to fasten the top button of his shirt when she said, 'Isn't it too hot for that? Don't wear a tie for me, Sam. Be at ease and enjoy yourself.'

The tie was stuffed back in his pocket and they wheeled the bicycles into the cobbled alley. She had to admit that with his harvest-blond hair falling over his brow and his shirt open at the neck he cut a dashing figure.

'Where would you like to go?' Sam enquired.

Now that she was out in the sunshine with the prospect of a few hours away from the house, Tanya was determined to make the most of it. Just because Sam Hawkes' company had been forced on her, she would not let it spoil her pleasure. Unaccountably, she also wanted him to enjoy the afternoon. 'Surprise me,' she challenged.

'Since we're not expected back for lunch, I hope you've strong legs.'

They cut through the back streets, passing the law courts of the Old Bailey being built on the site of the infamous Newgate Prison demolished two years before in 1904. Avoiding the congested thoroughfares, they headed towards Holborn. Cyclists were everywhere, sometimes in large groups as a local club headed towards one of the London parks or further afield to Wanstead Flats or Hampstead Heath.

From the direction they were taking, Tanya wondered if Sam had decided they were going to Hampstead Heath. Minutes later he veered from the route. They cycled past elegant terraces and round large squares. Hurrying servants emerged from basement steps, chauffeurs or coachmen sweltered outside porticoed entrances waiting for their masters. Tanya's cheeks were flushed. The press of people promenading in their Sunday best clothes and the constant steam of traffic was making the air oppressive in the summer's heat.

Sam grinned. 'Not too tired, are you?'

She shook her head. 'It would be nice to stop for a drink before too long.'

'We're nearly there.'

A short time later Tanya's eyes widened with pleasure as they entered Regent's Park. Sam halted by the boating lake and propped his bicycle under the shade of a tree.

'You chose well, Sam. Of all the London parks, I've never been to this one.' She stared around her and laughed. 'There are so many people enjoying themselves. Look at the children paddling in the water.'

A spaniel bounded up to them and ran round Tanya's skirts. She stooped and ruffled its ears and the dog enthusiastically licked her hand and leapt up to graze its tongue against her cheek. Its master called it to heel and it ran round in an excited circle before scampering off.

'What an adorable dog,' Tanya remarked wistfully. 'Aunt Stella refuses to have any animals in the house. I've always wanted another dog since Harry's old Labrador died.'

'I would have thought you'd find a way to get what you want,' Sam said wryly.

'I've only been back from boarding school one term. It wouldn't have been fair to have a dog while I was away. Perhaps now I shall, though Aunt Stella will make a song and dance about it and I shall be constantly rescuing the poor thing from being shut out in the garden. Stella is an old dragon.'

Sam chuckled. 'Your other aunt is very different.'

'Maude is a dear. Stella is a stickler for propriety and convention. A typical spinster.' The shadow which had crossed her face lifted. 'Are you ready to eat? All that cycling has made me ravenous.'

Sam unrolled the tartan blanket and spread it under the tree as Tanya opened the wicker food hamper. Kneeling on the ground, she unpacked it with a laugh. 'There's enough food here to feed a small army.'

Looking up she saw Sam standing like a sentry on duty, his injured knee bent as though it pained him. 'Aren't you going to sit down?'

He sank down onto the blanket, long legs stretched out, propping himself on his elbow. He took the chicken and ham pie she handed to him and ate it in silence. It had been difficult to converse freely as they wove through the busy traffic and now he seemed ill at ease. Or was it that Sam was still annoyed at being commandeered into escorting her today?

The ride had been invigorating. She had enjoyed it and she wanted the day to be a pleasure for him, not an onerous duty. In the distance she could hear the roar of lions from the zoological gardens.

'Could we possibly go and see the animals? I've never been. Though Ben always promised to take me, we never went there.'

'Of course.' He stared at her in a way which was disconcerting. 'When the brigadier said that your life had been sheltered, I had not realised to what degree.'

'With my parents and brothers abroad, often I remained at the school during the holidays. Twice I was taken to Bognor Regis by my aunts when they visited an elderly cousin. It wasn't much fun. They sat in the garden all day gossiping. I was always in trouble for wandering to the beach. I loved the sea.'

'I never saw the sea until I sailed to India,' Sam said. 'But as kids we used to swim in the canal. The streets were full of kids. I may have been poor but I was never lonely.'

Had he deliberately emphasised the differences in their childhood, when she had been trying to break down the barriers between them? Piqued, she replied, 'I wasn't lonely. I had my drawing. My own company doesn't bother me. I suppose with my brothers so much older than me I got used to playing alone. The last few years I always stayed with my schoolfriend Clare in the country. She married a few months ago and now lives in Tunbridge Wells. Most of my other friends from school went out to India when they were fifteen and married officers. I'm glad I was spared that marriage market by Papa.'

'I can't believe you have no friends in London,' Sam said, surprised.

She shrugged. 'I've plenty of acquaintances, mostly the daughters of the regiment. It's almost like a club. But all they think of is marriage and the latest fashions. It is all trivial and boring. Clare is my best friend. A true friendship is rare and precious.'

Tanya tucked into the picnic with relish. Catching Sam's thoughtful expression on her, she reached into her skirt pocket and said quickly, 'Please don't be offended, but will you take these guineas to pay for the entrance to the zoological gardens and anything else we may purchase this afternoon?'

There was a tightness to his jaw as he replied, 'I won't take your money, Miss Tanya. It's the man who pays when he takes a woman out.'

'But this wasn't your idea. It was Papa's. I feel uncomfortable enough at having taken so much of your time. I'm sure there are other women you would rather be spending your Sunday afternoon with.'

She dropped the two guineas into the top pocket of his blazer. He fished them out and flipped them onto the blanket. 'If I'd had other plans for today, noting the brigadier could say would make me change my mind. And there is no particular woman I would wish to spend Sunday with.'

Why that information should make the day seem even brighter, Tanya did not know. But it did.

'Then this afternoon there will be no more Miss Tanya. It makes me feel like some decrepit spinster, for heaven's sake.'

When he did not reply, she smiled and, eager to dispel the awkwardness between them, asked, 'What was India like?'

He bit into a teacake and ate it before answering. 'It's an impressive country. But a country of extremes. The brigadier can tell you about it better than I can. He's an exceptional man.'

She did not inform him that her father had no time for polite conversation with his daughter. The brigadier was virtually a stranger to her. They had been locked in confrontation since his return. She had been seven last time she saw him. He'd had little time for a child. Obviously, Sam had seen a different side to her father's despotic nature, which he admired.

'In what way is my father exceptional?'

He looked at her with surprise and ran his hand through his hair. A lock flopped attractively over his brow, softening the angular lines of his face. 'He cared about the welfare of his men. That's unusual. Most senior officers regard the rank and file as little more than cannon fodder.'

'Papa thinks highly of you, or he would not have been so insistent that you stayed with us. Do you miss the army?'

'I thought I would. You can't spend nine years

of your life constantly surrounded by scores of men, following orders, every minute of your day accounted for, without expecting to miss it. But I don't.' He leaned back on his elbow, gazing out at the rowers on the lake. 'I didn't mind taking orders when they made sense. Too often they didn't. I like the feeling of freedom since returning to England. Still, the army taught me many things. Through it I encountered the great passion in my life.'

'And that is?'

He grinned, his teeth white against his tanned face. 'Automobiles. Such transport was an infantry soldier's dream. Soon as the first trucks arrived I badgered one of the drivers to teach me how to drive it. After that I couldn't leave them alone. I wanted to learn how they worked and how to repair them. Every spare minute I could, I spent with the vehicles. My path had crossed the brigadier's a few times and when he saw my interest I was assigned to drive his staff car.'

'I thought you were his aide.'

'That came later. The brigadier got me out of a spot of bother with a major I'd fallen foul of.' His expression hardened as though the memory angered him in some way. He sat up, bending one knee and resting his elbow on it. He flicked a piece of bread to a foraging mallard close by. 'But enough of me. Let's go and see the animals.'

He helped Tanya pack up the remains of the picnic and, securing their bicycles, they entered the zoological gardens.

Tanya was entranced. Her excitement and

pleasure bubbled over as they saw the lions, tigers and polar bears. The snakes in the reptile houses gave her the shudders and the antics of the seals at feeding time made her clap her hands with pleasure. But it was the chimpanzees which really captivated her. Tears of laughter streaked her cheeks as she watched them play. Without thinking she clung to Sam's arm as she pointed out two baby chimpanzees, arms locked round each other as they rolled over and over along the ground.

'I can't remember when I last laughed so much,' she said, self-consciously removing her hand from his arm. 'Thank you for bringing me.'

His eyes crinkled with pleasure at witnessing her happiness. The restraint of their earlier conversation had dissipated in the enjoyment of the sights. Sam was an entertaining companion and their laughter had become free and easy as though they had been friends for years.

'The parrot walk is very popular,' he said. 'We should be able to see that before the penguins are fed.'

The path was packed with people exclaiming at the radiant plumage of the birds. The perches were strung on lines between the trees, the leaves dappling the ground with shadows and flowering shrubs perfuming the air.

Tanya laughed. 'The parrots are as proud as any Guards officers in their scarlet uniforms. See how they preen and puff out their feathers. They are as conceited as any colonel.' She gasped and clapped a hand to her mouth. 'I'm sorry, Sam. I didn't mean that to sound as it did. I wasn't implying that you preen yourself in your uniform or…'

He laughed, dispersing her embarrassment. 'Thank you for that. I know exactly what you mean. At least the parrots know when fine plumage is simply that, and underneath they're simply birds. Look at them now. They bob their heads and parade along their perches, then without warning they hang upside down. Would that certain aristocratic officers remember that under the scarlet and gold braid, all men are the same flesh and blood. Your father is such a man.'

'I doubt he thinks any woman is the equal of a man,' Tanya quipped.

His stare was serious as he answered, 'But you're the woman to re-educate him, aren't you?'

His compliment heartened her. 'If I want to lead my own life, I shall have to.'

The parrot walk was above the canal. They paused to watch a steam-driven red and green boat chug past, its cabin decoratively painted with roses and anemone-like flowers. There was a cry from the walkway and Sam gently took Tanya's arm to guide her to the edge of the path. An elephant shambled towards them led by its keeper. High on its back was a wooden carriage-like seat which carried half a dozen excited children.

'What a magnificent beast!' Tanya said, awed by its sedate pace, the trunk swinging out searching for titbits from the crowd. 'Have you ever ridden one, Sam?'

'I accompanied your father on a couple of tiger hunts on them.'

'That must have been exciting.'

His expression was grave. 'Yes, to start with. The thrill of seeing a tiger in the wild for the first time is breathtaking. But to kill them for trophies I found distasteful. It's different if they've turned man-eater, and terrorise villages, but not otherwise.'

She had not expected him to be sentimental. Most soldiers were proud of their animal trophies, her ancestors no exception. Sam was an intriguing man, his qualities more admirable with each meeting.

The shadows were lengthening when they left the zoological gardens, though people still lounged in deck chairs and children ran across the grass bowling their hoops. Shading her eyes against the sun, Tanya watched a young man launch a kite into the air. It soared heavenwards, dipping and swaying, its long tail of ribbons streaming behind it.

'I remember Harry used to have a kite when I was little,' she said wistfully. 'Although he was fourteen years older than me, he never tired of flying it. He could make it dip so low that I could chase the tail ribbons.' Her expression saddened. 'He loved that kite. He would have loved flying it here today, a son watching him in awe.' She sighed. 'It wasn't meant to be. The army is a cruel master. The sacrifice of young men's lives is high. I miss Harry and Ben. Papa never speaks of them to me. I wish he would. Why should the memories of them be buried just because they have died?'

'Their deaths hit him hard,' Sam confided. 'He

was very proud when Ben received the Victoria Cross.'

'I never knew Ben won the VC!' Tanya's voice cracked and she turned away, blinking against the scald of tears. 'Why does Papa shut me out?' she whispered. 'Doesn't he know that I loved them and am proud of them?'

'Don't take it so hard, Tanya.' Sam gently turned her to face him.

'What hurts most is that I never really got to know them.' She shook her head, a single tear overflowing onto her eyelashes. 'Forgive me, I grow morbid.'

'Sometimes it's good to talk about such things.'

His understanding eased her pain. 'You're a good listener. You take me seriously. I appreciate that.'

For a long time they held each other's stares. Tanya saw his eyes darken with sensual promise. It evoked an indefinable longing deep within her. It was a honey-and-vinegar ache, poignant and evocative.

'Would you like to take one of the boats onto the lake?' His voice was like a ray of sunshine entering her veins.

'Could we?' Her eyes sparkled with anticipation. 'That sounds fun.'

The lake was less crowded as the afternoon drew to a close and it was growing cooler. Tanya did not notice. She lay back in the prow of the boat, a hand trailing in the water. With a sigh she closed her eyes and smiled.

'What are you thinking?' Sam enquired as he rowed into the lake's centre where fewer boats jostled for space.

She giggled throatily and blushed. 'Very unmaidenly thoughts. After all that cycling and walking I feel so languid lying here. It is almost magical with the warmth of the sun, tigers roaring and elephants trumpeting in the distance. I daydreamed I was in a faraway land. There's something rather decadent about lying back in a boat on the water. Is this what Cleopatra, the Queen of the Nile, experienced when she was rowed to one of her palaces? Or our own Queen Elizabeth in her royal barge, being wooed by the great men of her time – Raleigh, the Earls of Leicester and Essex.' She smiled, her voice dreamy with contentment. 'You must think me a hopeless romantic, Sam.'

'Quite hopeless. But that's what young women are supposed to be.'

The tenderness and teasing in his eyes made her heart race. She stared silently at him. In the exertion of his rowing, the ends of his hair had curled in the heat. An impulse to reach out and touch one where it wound round the lobe of his ear was powerful. She resisted. Had Sam sensed her need? His throat worked as he swallowed and for a second there was starkness in his eyes which made her breath catch in her throat.

Abruptly he looked away. The spell was shattered.

'Have you seen the swans over there with their cygnets, Miss Tanya?'

Confused by his reserved tone, she followed his gaze. He had deliberately distanced himself. Acknowledgement wrapped barbed wire round her pleasure. He rowed for some minutes with neither of them speaking. Then she asked. 'Do you think my father will recover? I'm worried about him. He seems to get stronger then has some sort of a relapse. He keeps little of his food down.'

He paused in his rowing, his gaze on the swans. 'He's strong and a fighter. Without meaning to speak out of line, he doesn't like your aunt fussing over him. And she obviously resents my presence in the house.' He angled the boat back to the landing stage.

'Stella is over-protective. She doesn't even want me in his room.' She didn't add that her aunt had been horrified that her father had insisted Sam escort her this afternoon. Stella considered him no better than a servant who had inveigled his way into her brother's affection. She was a dreadful snob. Had she attempted to put Sam in his place? Tanya suppressed a smile. It was unlikely that she would have succeeded. There was something very singular about this man.

Once ashore, Sam took Tanya's hand to assist her out of the boat. It rocked and, off balance, she fell against him. His arms went round her and he held her close. Her hand trapped between their bodies felt the hard beat of his heart. It echoed the rapid pounding of her own. Gazing up at him, her eyes smiled into his. 'It's been a wonderful afternoon. I don't think I have ever enjoyed myself more.'

Golden motes speckled his irises. There was a fierceness in their depths which she did not understand. The heat of the day emphasised the masculine scent of him. It was pleasant and dangerously seductive. All around them lovers strolled arm in arm. She envied them. She wanted to feel the power of his arms crushing her against him. Her gaze lowered to his mouth. What would it be like to be kissed by him? A lover's kiss, tender and compelling. The thought made her light-headed. Her eyelids became heavy and her mouth dried. The sun must be getting to her. She ran the tip of her tongue over her lips and widened her eyes to dispel the image of Sam kissing her.

As carefully as though she was made of porcelain, he put her from him and walked to where they had left their bicycles. There was a tension in his body and his limp was more pronounced.

Tanya could still feel the tingling imprint of his hands on her flesh through the silk of her dress. When Sam held the bicycle for her to mount, their hands touched. Her fingers coiled round his, her voice sibilant. 'This afternoon has been wonderful. I shall never forget it.'

Before Sam realised what he was saying, he suggested, 'Perhaps one evening we could visit Earl's Court to enjoy its entertainments.' He gently removed his hand from her clasp.

'That sounds marvellous. Don't they have exhibitions there and a pleasure garden?'

Her excitement was tangible and refreshing. It was infectious. And despite his reservations about becoming too involved with this vivacious woman, he hadn't felt this carefree for years.

'It may have changed since I was last there some years ago, but it's still popular. There used to be a roller coaster and a Chinese dragon railway runs round a lake. Everywhere is lit up with coloured lights.'

'I should like to go very much, Sam. Thank you for inviting me.' The wonderment in her eyes was a joy to behold. She was natural and unaffected, taking pleasure from the simple things of life. He could show her so much. Chase away her loneliness, draw the sparkling laughter from her. Brutally, he checked his thoughts. Green, enticing eyes were making a fool of him, lulling him into forgetting his place.

'Tilbury might object,' he commented. The brigadier wanted to know whether Tanya was more involved with the man than she had so far led him to believe.

'Why should he?' she replied guilelessly. 'We work together for the benefit of the poor. I have only been to the theatre with him once.'

Tanya had no reservations about seeing Sam again. He made her feel alive and more feminine than Archie with all his glowing compliments had ever done. In Sam's company she could be at ease and enjoy herself. After so many years of repression, it was a heady experience.

Chapter Ten

Archie moved lodgings to Holborn to put more distance between himself and the Gilbert brothers. Since he had dumped Granville's body, ransacked the flat for valuables and moved here, he had not gone out during the day. The police were looking for Arnie Potter to question him. He reckoned he could outwit any dumb policeman, but if it hadn't been for the lure of the Summersfield fortune so close to his grasp, he'd have left London until things cooled down.

He studied his reflection in the mirror as he wiped the shaving soap from his cheeks. He'd sacrificed his moustache and the long side whiskers which he had thought so distinguished, but the face that stared back at him looked younger than his thirty-one years and that pleased him. There was only a thread or two of silver in his dark hair and as he looked down at his trim naked figure he felt a customary glow of pleasure. While he kept his looks, he could achieve anything.

His appreciative smile turned to a scowl. It was too hot to be inside but until it was dark he did not want to risk going out. The Gilberts were likely to track him down before the police. He balked at getting involved with the gang. Once in, always in – if you wanted to stay alive.

Getting his hands on the Summersfield money

was proving more difficult than he had expected. The brigadier was the main problem and Hawkes wasn't helping. He was beginning to suspect that Tanya was not as indifferent to the soldier as he would wish.

'Damn the woman, she's too wilful,' Archie cursed. With Hawkes on the scene, he couldn't force her. He had to curb his impatience. Nothing too suspicious could happen to either Hawkes or the brigadier as yet. He couldn't risk the name of Tilbury being connected with that of Potter. Granville's death had complicated matters.

The handsome reflection in the mirror smiled back at him with cocky assurance. 'Play your cards carefully and you can't lose,' he said aloud. 'Patience. Just a little patience. Those who get in the way will be dealt with, as you've dealt with others in the past.'

Alone in his bedchamber after putting the bicycles away, Sam discarded his blazer and rubbed his knee. It ached dully, but the exercise had loosened some of the stiffness. His expression was bleak. Unexpectedly, he had enjoyed the afternoon. It had changed his opinion of Tanya Summersfield. He could understand her resentment of the brigadier's disapproval of her teaching. She had a tender, caring nature. There had been childlike innocence in the pleasure she took from the animals. It had changed to sensuality when she lay back in the rowing boat, a sensuality the more profound because she was as yet unaware of it.

He had been unprepared for the devastating effect she had on him when she smiled. And her laughter was as stimulating as a swim on a hot day. Not for her a polite stretching of the mouth in genteel amusement at the frolics of the monkeys. She had thrown back her head and given a heartfelt laugh. She had no false airs. Her naturalness and sincerity were captivating.

That she wished to teach the poor proved she had a tender heart but he suspected that beneath all her womanly softness there was a core of steel. He admired that. During his years in India he'd had no time for the spoilt and petted daughters of the army officers. They were career wreckers. Too many came out to India to enter the marriage showcase – a ritual Tanya professed to despise. Those women were only interested in ensnaring a wealthy and positioned husband. A non-commissioned officer was beneath their notice. They scorned the men who by courage alone had risen from the ranks.

Not so those already wed. Bored wives left in the garrison while their husbands were on patrol wanted entertainment at any cost. Several such women had made it obvious that they would welcome him in their beds. He had declined the invitations. He was proud of his rise from the ranks. Only a fool would jeopardise his career by such a liaison.

Since he had no inclination to frequent the bordellos close to the garrison, he had taken a mistress. Lori was a beautiful half-caste and he had remained faithful to her. Fifteen months ago she had died giving birth to his stillborn son. Lori had been special and he wished he could have given her more of himself. She had captivated him, given him love and comfort from the horrors he witnessed in battle, but he had not loved her.

There had been no other woman since. Tanya's company had made him aware how long it had been since he had made love to a woman. He frowned. Tanya Summersfield might be desirable, but she was not for him. The daughter of a brigadier was far above him in station. Even as her father's business partner he would never be considered her equal. Women from a family as old as the Summersfields only married their own kind, or found themselves ostracised by society.

He had plans to become rich. To make something of himself. He was only twenty-six. There was a fortune to be made in motor vehicles which was the expanding transport of the future. Once he had his garage, he would deal in secondhand cars and provide a maintenance and repair service. He'd never been much of a drinker and had saved a tidy nest-egg from his army pay to start a car business. Although his leg made him unfit for duty, thanks to a recommendation from Brigadier Summersfield, he would be receiving half pay until the end of the year. Once his business was running he planned to plough every spare penny back into it. Life had shown him that those who had money acquired more money. Without it you were nothing.

Sam reflected on his relationship with the brigadier. It had formed out of mutual respect. In a way Sam regarded the brigadier as the father he had never known. As for the brigadier, the old man mourned his two sons.

Sam was a realist. He had been born in the workhouse and orphaned an hour later. At seven he had run away and begun a life of living off his wits in Stepney. He scavenged for morsels of food. Before dawn he'd be outside one of the markets offering his help to the costers for a penny or something to eat. Not once did he consider stealing. He took pride in his honesty even though his belly rumbled with hunger.

For a year he'd done his share of mudlarking before progressing to running a rag-and-bone round for a wizened old Jew whose meanness would have put Fagin himself to shame. Despite starting work at dawn every day, Sam always attended the ragged school. When the classes finished, he resumed his rag-and-bone round until ten o'clock at night. Intuitively he had known that education could help him make something of his life. That was why he respected Tanya for what she was doing.

At fourteen he was apprenticed to a carriage maker and it was then that his fascination for vehicles took root. But he hated being shut away inside a workshop all day.

His seventeenth birthday in 1897 coincided with Queen Victoria's diamond jubilee celebrations. After a weekend of drinking and revelry, he and his mate Podge Harris, in a fervour of patriotism, had lied about their ages and enlisted in the army. They had boasted of the new lands they would see and the honours they would win in battle. They were sent to the North-West

Frontier. It was a brutal initiation. Within a month of arriving and still raw recruits, they were plunged into subduing a revolt by hill tribes.

They had faced an ignominious retreat when the Khyber Pass fell. By the time the revolt was crushed, winter was approaching. The rebels' villages were destroyed and the crops trampled. Such wholesale destruction had sickened Sam. He and Podge had survived three battles without a scratch. Then Podge had died from dysentery. More troops were lost through disease than ever were slain on the battlefield.

Eighteen months later, having won his corporal's stripes, Sam saw Brigadier Summersfield pitched from his horse as it was shot from under him. The officer hit his head on a rock and lay unconscious. When the enemy surrounded him, Sam ran forwards, despite the close fire. Crouching over the brigadier, he kept the enemy at bay with his musket and then with the brigadier's revolver until that, too, was empty and he had to resort to his bayonet. When the brigadier regained consciousness, Sam helped him to safety. His bravery had earned him his sergeant's stripes and marked the start of his unusual friendship with the brigadier.

He received his captaincy two years later and lost it within a year when he refused to obey an order which would have seen his troop massacred. It had taken another eighteen months before his rank was reinstated.

His knee wound had seen the end of his army career, but Sam had tasted ambition. Never again would he take orders from anyone. He would be his own man and build his own future. That future was with motor cars.

In Maude Summersfield's room along from his he heard Tanya's laughter and was reminded of the pleasure her company had been that afternoon. She was a remarkable woman. Regret furrowed his brow. He should never have invited her out again. What madness had possessed him? Looking into her radiant face, he had found the words tumbling out, caution forgotten. It must be the last time.

'You're a selfish and impossible woman, Maude,' Stella snapped, looking around her sister's sitting room with mounting anger. The new carpets and curtains were bright and cheerful, so different from the rest of the house. 'You live here yet you pay nothing towards the upkeep of your home. We need new curtains for the family parlour and dining room. It's a disgrace.'

'I will not pay for such luxuries,' Maude declared. She had been admiring her latest hat in the mirror. It was a frothy royal blue net and silk creation with a fan of exotic bird feathers at the back. Stella had spoilt her pleasure in it. 'I've already spent this quarter's income. I will not touch the money which came to me on dear Bernard's death. It's for Tanya. You must speak to Reginald.'

Stella rounded on Maude, her expression fierce and menacing. 'He's as miserly as ever. All he thinks of is this new business venture with Hawkes. How much is he putting into that, I wonder? We live in squalor while our brother squanders his capital on a whim. And you're just as mean. You were born in this house. How can you let it go to ruin? You have your rooms all nicely redecorated so your friends can visit you. I'm too ashamed to ask anyone to dine. How do you expect Tanya to meet the right sort of gentleman if we cannot entertain?'

Maude removed her hat and placed it on a cluttered table. Her gaze was drawn to the sepia photograph of Bernard and herself on their wedding day. 'I will not touch that money. And I'm tired of you always trying to bully me.' Her lip trembled. 'You don't want the parlour decorated for Tanya's benefit, but for yours. And I thought you were keen for Tanya to make a match with Mr Tilbury. Is it because he reminds you of your lover?'

Stella gasped and clutched her hands to stop them shaking. She had refused to sit down on entering the room, preferring to use her height to intimidate her petite sister. 'Nonsense, Maude.'

'But you have to agree that he has something of the look of your artist Geoffrey,' Maude persisted.

Her composure regained, Stella regarded her sister coldly. 'He has the same dark hair and dark eyes. So do thousands of other men. You know I don't like to be reminded of that time, Maude. It's cruel of you to mention it.' She folded her hands across her waist, her vast bosom puffing out with indignation. 'Mr Tilbury is a man highly regarded in the city. It is time Tanya was engaged. She's too headstrong. Heaven knows what trouble she will get into if she isn't married soon.

She's seeing too much of that Hawkes fellow. He's quite capable of compromising her. He's ambitious. But Reginald won't see it.'

Maude sat down and picked up her embroidery, needing the comfort of something to do when Stella was so bossy and domineering. But where Tanya was concerned, Maude always found resources of courage. She didn't like the way Stella was trying to manipulate their niece. 'You're too much of a snob to see that Sam would make Tanya a good husband. There's something about Archie Tilbury I don't like. I think you've been taken in by his looks, Stella. And the attention he pays you.'

'Don't be ridiculous,' Stella scoffed.

'I'm not, but I believe that you are,' Maude countered with spirit. 'He's too charming, too solicitous in his manners. Have you noticed that his eyes always remain cold no matter how much he smiled?'

'You've only met him once,' Stella blazed. 'What would you know?'

'I met Frank Gilbourne last week. He was Bernard's close friend. The Gilbournes are bankers with links throughout the city. He had never heard of an Archibald Tilbury. Don't you think that rather odd?'

'Mr Tilbury told me that he had been abroad for some years and has but recently returned to England. Mr Gilbourne cannot be expected to know every one of London's businessmen by name.' Her voice rose bombastically.

'Don't get so touchy, Stella.' Maude shrank from her sister's rising anger. 'I thought I'd just mention it. But I think Reginald should know what I've found out.'

'Reginald is too ill to be troubled,' Stella snapped. 'Do you want him to have another attack?'

'Of course not.' Maude hated dissent and was upset by her sister's attitude. 'I'm concerned for Tanya. How do we know that Mr Tilbury is a fitting escort for her? What if anything happened and her reputation was damaged?'

Stella strode across to her sister and towered menacingly over her. 'What would a stupid, ineffectual woman like you know about men? Bernard was chosen for you by Papa because he was wealthy. He was fifteen years older than you. You fell in love with him because you're an idealistic, romantic fool.'

Maude burst into tears. 'That's a wicked thing to say. Bernard loved me. I loved him. He was good and kind.'

Stella laughed cruelly as she walked to the door. 'He was dull, boring and plain. But then so are you, sister.'

'I know I'm right about Archie Tilbury,' Maude sniffed as she dabbed at her eyes. 'If his intentions were honourable, why did he agree to continue to escort Tanya to her classes knowing it was against her father's wishes?'

'You've changed your tune,' Stella scowled. 'I thought you supported Tanya in her teaching. Reginald is just being unreasonable.'

'It was different before he returned. Now I'm worried about her. I don't trust Mr Tilbury. If she continues to teach against her father's wishes, it will only court disaster.'

Stella laughed. 'The girl has backbone, unlike you.'

Maude sobbed into her hands when Stella left. Her sister was getting worse. Why did she have to say such wicked things to upset her? She was too distraught to leave her room that day.

'Has Stella upset you?' Tanya asked, dropping in to see Maude when she did not come down to dine.

'She said some nasty things about dear Bernard.' Maude's tiny figure was crumpled like a discarded puppet in her chair, her face pale and her eyes red from weeping.

'You shouldn't let her upset you.' Tanya hugged her. 'Why don't we go to Oxford Street tomorrow and you treat yourself to a new hat?'

Maude shook her head. 'I shall visit Mrs Rivers, she's such a comfort. And it will annoy Stella to know that's where I've gone. She's getting more bossy than ever.'

From the stairs they heard Sam laugh as he spoke to Ginny.

'Sam Hawkes is a nice man,' Maude observed.

'He is. He's offered to take me to Earl's Court pleasure garden.'

Maude frowned. Stella had undermined her confidence in her judgement. 'I wouldn't like to see you get hurt. Although Reginald has befriended Sam, he would not condone a match between you.'

Tanya blushed. 'I enjoy Sam's company. I will not have Papa dictating to me who I may see.

He's been difficult enough over Archie.'

'Archie Tilbury shouldn't be encouraging you to teach behind your father's back. How much do you know about him? He seems a bit of a dark horse.'

'Archie always behaves like a gentleman. Though Sam is more fun.'

'You're young and susceptible where handsome men are concerned,' Maude warned. 'I'm not so sure I trust Mr Tilbury. And as for Sam, Reginald trusts him not to cross the boundaries of propriety but don't be careless enough to allow yourself to fall in love with him.'

Tanya laughed. 'I want to see something of life before I marry. As for teaching behind Papa's back, I intend to speak to him about it today. I only put off the confrontation because he was so ill.'

Tanya had just returned from Trafalgar Square where she had been inspired by a six thousand strong meeting addressed by Emmeline Pankhurst. The suffragette's impassioned words still dominated her thoughts: 'We have been patient too long, we will be patient no longer.' It was time that women had more say in their lives. The words had charged her with determination to confront her father and continue to help her pupils.

Her father was sitting on an iron seat by the oval fishpond. Herringbone brickwork formed a pathway round it and a wooden pagoda was draped by the fading blooms of a wisteria. His eyes were closed and he was dozing. The mid-

June sun was warm and his colour looked healthier from the fresh air. At Tanya's approach he opened his eyes.

'How nice of you to join me.'

'We have to talk, Papa. And I fear you will not be pleased with what I have to say. I would have spoken sooner but your ill health prevented me.'

He regarded her without speaking and she plunged on, 'I have been teaching adults two evenings a week in a church hall in Aldgate.'

'The devil you have,' he exploded. 'I told you–'

'Papa, please let me finish. I take no payment for this. The Reverend Carver is delighted with the results. I'm helping men and women better themselves. Reverend Carver has asked if I will design a carnival float and I've agreed.'

Angry colour flooded his face. 'How dare you flout my wishes. I forbade you to teach. And as for this float nonsense–'

'This is important to me,' she interrupted. 'Mr Tilbury escorts me so I am quite safe.'

'You will stop at once. And as for that bounder Tilbury–'

'Don't judge Archie when you haven't even troubled to meet him properly.' Her eyes sparked with combat. 'My pupils need me. I won't abandon them. I've given my word to Reverend Carver that I will design the carnival float. A Summersfield does not go back on their word.'

'I will not tolerate this defiance,' he bellowed. 'You deliberately disobeyed me.'

She stood tall, her head held high. 'I will not break my word.'

'Then you are no daughter of mine. Get out of

my sight. Get out of my house. You've brought shame to this family.'

Tanya trembled as she fought to contain her outrage. She was too furious to consider the consequences of being cast from her home and refused to concede defeat. 'If that is what you wish, I shall leave. Though when it is learned that you threw your daughter out for helping those less fortunate than herself, I do not think that it will be my name that is scorned by society.'

His face dappled with angry colour and he waved his walking cane at her. 'Get out! I will not tolerate this insubordination.'

Her temper got the better of her. 'And I'm not a mindless trooper to be ordered what to do. My motives are worthy. Are you such a despot that you will not even hear me out? Even a soldier has the right to speak at his court martial.' She strode away from him. 'I shall be out of your house in an hour. I'll inform Ginny where to send my things. I'm capable of supporting myself by teaching which is better than suffering this tyranny.'

'Tanya, come back here!'

She halted, stiff-backed and shoulders squared. Slowly she turned, her eyes bright with defiance.

'You will apologise and forget this nonsense,' he commanded.

She held his forthright glare without wavering. 'I can't believe that I've done anything so terrible, Papa. I will not go back on my word. That would be dishonourable.'

She was startled to see that he was looking at her with dawning respect. 'So I raised a daughter with some fire in her blood. Tyrant, am I? Is that how you see me?' He looked aggrieved. 'Come here, girl. Tell me something about these classes.'

Her face was animated as she sat beside him and told him of the successes she had achieved.

'I still do not approve,' he said gruffly. 'As for Tilbury encouraging you in this, he has much to answer for. Was he aware that I would not approve?'

'He intended to speak to you but you were taken ill before he could. It was never my intention to deceive you.'

He digested this but his expression remained dour. 'I suppose if Stella approves of this fellow, he must be all right. But I shall retain my reservations for the moment. Get him to call on me Monday evening. It's time I learned the man's intentions.' His eyes gleamed as he regarded her. 'It couldn't have been easy for you telling me this, knowing I would disapprove. Your ideals were noble, if misguided, so I shall allow you to continue. But once this carnival is over, we will review the situation. The East End of London is no place for a gentlewoman to be traipsing about in the evening. I forbid you to make any further commitment to Reverend Carver. Is that clear?'

'Yes, Papa.'

Delighted at this reprieve, she bent to kiss his cheek. He wasn't such a despot after all. But then she wondered whether her father's change of heart owed anything to Sam's influence.

'Remember, it is only until this carnival.'

Tanya nodded. She would cross that bridge when she came to it.

Chapter Eleven

Archie was getting hot under the collar. For an hour Brigadier Summersfield had been firing questions at him about his background. The old buzzard was astute and twice he'd almost made an error when repeating his fabrication of his past.

They were taking tea in the shade of the rose arbour, and throughout the brigadier had been pompous verging on the bombastic. With increasing unease Archie was aware that he was failing to charm him. That angered him. The man was stubborn and his health far more robust than he had expected.

'Papa, must you drill Archie so with your questions?' Tanya interceded. 'You've already asked him about his business and parents.'

'Every father has the right to know what a man's background is when that man shows an interest in his daughter,' Reginald insisted.

'I assure you that my intentions are honourable, sir.' Archie favoured both Summersfield and Tanya with his most sincere and respectful smile. When the brigadier did not respond he felt his temper begin to slide. And Tanya needed reminding how much he had done for her. 'Your daughter is dedicated to teaching the poor but I would like to think that she regarded me as more than just a patron for her work. Her company is delightful and I would like your permission to take her to the theatre and to dine from time to time if it pleased her.'

Summersfield studied him, his stare seeming to bore into his mind and expose all the devious and treacherous schemes that resided there. Then his gaze turned to Tanya.

'Does it please you?' he asked bluntly.

'I always enjoy Archie's company, Papa.'

The brigadier stood up, his arrogant gaze once more on Archie. 'It disturbs me that none of my acquaintances have heard of your family. You will understand that in the circumstances I wish to make further enquiries. I will inform you of my decision in due course.' He left the garden leaning heavily on his walking cane.

Archie's cheeks had paled at this summary dismissal.

'Pay no heed to my brother,' Stella placated in a trembling voice.

'I think he has made his position perfectly clear,' Archie said tersely. 'Good day, ladies.' By God they would pay for the insults he'd received today.

He did not leave through the house but used a side gate instead. He'd been humiliated and he did not trust his anger. Also he was deeply troubled. The police were asking too many questions about Arnie Potter, and wanted to question him about the death of Granville Ingram. Also the Gilbert brothers were putting pressure on him to work for them. He could not keep fobbing them off with excuses for much longer. His gut twisted with fear. Had he been too hasty in stalking out of the Summersfield house? They were the means of him making a new life for himself after all.

'Tanya, go after Archie,' Stella wailed. 'Your father was rude and insensitive.'

Tanya was aghast at her father's behaviour and it was obvious that Archie was offended. Yet she knew that if Archie began to escort her to functions then gossip would link them together, and she did not want that. But if she did not go after him, he might stop supporting her in her teaching. She was torn. She didn't want to use him. He had been kind and generous to her. Her father should not have been so insulting.

She ran out into the alley. 'Archie, please wait.'

He did not immediately halt and was in Pilgrim's Crescent before she caught up with him.

Sam was whistling as he passed the elderly flowerseller by the corner of the crescent.

'Flowers for your sweet'eart, mister?' the woman called. Sam waved the bouquet of roses aside.

As he entered the crescent he frowned at seeing Tilbury emerge from the alleyway at the side of the Summersfield house. Seconds later Tanya ran after him. Tilbury swung round. From his stiff manner he was clearly furious. Tanya appeared to be trying to placate him but it seemed to be having little effect. There was something about Tilbury's attitude that Sam resented. He was clearly giving Tanya a hard time. His antagonism towards the businessman surfaced. Tilbury thought too much of himself.

Sam scowled, but much as he wanted to strike the self-satisfied smirk from the other man's face as Tanya pleaded with him, Sam knew that Tilbury would feel the sting more if it struck at his ego.

He backtracked to the flowerseller. Several buckets were filled with scarlet carnations. He scooped up the contents of three of them so that they filled his arms and tossed the money to the flowerseller. Striding towards Tanya and Tilbury, he saw that they still had not resolved their differences. When Tilbury saw him approaching, he broke off his speech. There was menace in his glare as he regarded the vast bouquet.

Tanya's eyes widened with surprise at the sight of the flowers.

With a flamboyant bow to her, Sam presented the blooms. 'The sweetest smelling flowers for the prettiest woman in London.' His tawny eyes were bright with mischief as he held her astonished gaze. 'They are a thank you for making me so welcome in your home.'

'Sam, there was no need for that.' She inhaled their scent and her eyes shone with something deeper than pleasure.

'Ah, but beauty and kindness should always be rewarded.'

He realised then that she might misconstrue his gift, believe it was a token of his affection and read more into the gesture than he intended. Tipping back his cap, he nodded to Tilbury. The black eyes regarding him were hostile. Then he was ignored as Tilbury touched his homburg to

Tanya, exuding charm.

'Good day, Tanya. I shall call for you for the class on Tuesday.'

Never trust a man who was too charming, Sam reflected. He had found in the army that they were the first to further their careers at the expense of yours.

By the end of June, Tanya had finished her designs for the float and costumes. She had raided the old clothes trunks in the attic to provide material for the garments. Her grandmother's and aunts' crinoline-style dresses provided ample material and trimmings. She had decided to model the characters on those in Lewis Carroll's *Alice's Adventures in Wonderland.* As her pupils' reading had improved, she had used the novel in class. An unexpected find in the attic had been an old sewing machine, a relic of more affluent days when her grandmother's ladies' maid had also been a skilled seamstress.

Tanya was sorting through the clothes when she heard Sam's voice as he left her father's room. She went onto the landing.

'What were you telling Papa about hot air balloons?'

'The first race of its kind in the United Kingdom took place yesterday. The brigadier has a fancy to go up in one. I told him I'd arrange it once he was better.'

'He needs something to look forward to. Flying higher than the trees and rooftops must be a wonderful experience.'

'For now the brigadier has agreed to go out in

the Bath chair, starting tomorrow,' Sam said, abruptly changing the subject.

Tanya had an uncomfortable feeling that he thought she had been angling for an invitation to join them in the hot air balloon. Despite the carnations he had presented to her and his light-hearted flirting in front of Archie, he had not mentioned taking her to Earl's Court as he had suggested after their bicycle ride. Her disappointment was acute, but she would not let him see it.

'That's good news. It must mean Papa is feeling stronger.'

Sam shrugged. 'He's improving slowly but he still gets bouts of vomiting which weaken him. He's not the best of patients, I'm afraid.'

'It's good of you to spend so much time with him. He doesn't want me in the room unless it's to play chess or backgammon with him.'

'He dislikes the fussing of women.' He hesitated before adding, 'Could you have a word with your aunt? She's always bringing him teas and broths and she harasses him until he's finished them. Often they end up arguing and the brigadier has another of his attacks.'

'Stella is a law unto herself. She won't listen to me, I'm afraid. She's only following the doctor's instructions. But I shall mention it to her. I've been so worried about Papa. I spoke to Dr Garrett asking him why he was not getting better. He told me that set-backs must be expected in tropical ailments.'

'We must take hope that he has periods when he is stronger.' Sam hid his fears for the brigadier's health. He had seen how diseases in India could eat into a man's body and strip it of vitality. He began to walk towards the stairs.

'Sam, I know we keep imposing on you, but do you think you could get something out of the attic for me? It's too heavy for Ginny to move. If you were about to go out, some time later will do.'

'Now is fine.'

'I'll just fetch an oil lamp from my room. It's very dark up there.'

He followed her up the narrow uncarpeted stairs to the top of the house. Here the air was musty with damp. There was a mildewed patch in one corner and the paint on the walls was cracked and peeling. 'When Papa is stronger, he must arrange for the roof to be fixed. The walls up here are running with damp.'

She opened the attic door and lifted the oil lamp high to cast its yellow light further into the gloom. The silhouette of a dark figure leapt out at them from a corner. Sam moved protectively in front of her, calling out, 'Who's there?'

Tanya nearly dropped the lamp, she was laughing so hard. 'There's no one there. It's an old suit of armour.'

Sam relaxed and put his hand over his heart. 'It gave me a turn. I didn't know whether it was a burglar or a ghost.'

'It's given me a fright before now,' Tanya confessed, advancing further into the room. 'But it could have been a ghost. Ben and Harry used to swear they'd seen a man all in white walk through the wall over there. They reckoned it was the spirit of our great-great uncle Lucien Summersfield. He was a friend of Beau Brummell and ran up vast gambling debts which his father refused to pay. Rather than face the disgrace, he shot himself. He was only twenty-two.'

'There is something spooky about this place,' Sam said with an exaggerated shiver. 'They always say the temperature drops just before a ghost appears and it's certainly cold up here.'

Something soft and cold crept over Tanya's cheek and she gave a stifled scream. Sam chuckled, waving a mildewed ostrich feather at her. She slapped his arm with her hand. 'You scared me half to death. You're as bad as my brothers. They used to give me nightmares with their stories when I was little. You're a wicked tease, Sam Hawkes.' The sparkle in her eyes belied the sternness of her words.

'And you rise to the bait,' he taunted.

The warmth in his voice caused a shiver of expectancy to expand low in her stomach. Inadvertently she swayed towards him, her lips parting.

Sam swallowed and threw the feather aside, his manner abruptly distant as he asked, 'What did you want brought down from here?'

The rapid change in his mood dismayed her. Just as they seemed to be getting on so well together, he would become formal. 'It's that sewing machine cabinet.'

He dragged the cabinet to the head of the stairs.

'It's rather bulky, let me help you,' Tanya suggested. She gripped the rim and helped him ease it step by step down the stairs to the first landing.

'Where do you want it?'

'By the front door,' Tanya replied. 'I've hired a van to take it to the home of one of my pupils. Reverend Carver has asked me to design a float for the carnival and Polly is making the costumes. Everyone in the class has offered to help.'

He lifted a dark blond eyebrow and regarded her gravely. 'Is the brigadier aware of all this?'

'He reluctantly consented since I had given my word. And he has also agreed to my continuing the class until the carnival. I'm sure you had something to do with it.'

'He isn't the ogre you would make him,' Sam stated.

'We got off on the wrong foot when I came home so late the evening he arrived. And I made matters worse by losing my temper.' She grimaced then laughed. 'I'm glad I don't have to deceive him any more. This means so much to the class. They are so enthusiastic. We're taking a theme from *Alice's Adventures in Wonderland.* Lewis Carroll's novel. Do you know the story?'

Sam's expression tightened. 'I'm not a great reader. Never had much time, though I've read a bit of Dickens and Stevenson. I liked *Treasure Island.*'

'Since you have a fascination for motor cars, H.G. Wells's fantasy about an ideal society of the future whereby new inventions and technology are used for the benefit of all should interest you.'

'You refer to *A Modern Utopia,*' Sam answered.

'Yes, it was recommended to me, but I've had no chance to read it.'

'Then you may borrow my copy. It's very different from the world which Alice discovers.' It was suddenly important to her to have his approval for the carnival float. Briefly she outlined the plot of Alice and added, 'Would you like to see my designs for the float? They're in my studio.' The room was opposite where they were standing and she walked inside, looking over her shoulder, expecting him to follow. His step was slow and reluctant. On a table was a vase containing some of the carnations Sam had given her. The rest were in her bedroom filling the room with their heady scent and reminding her of the happiness they had shared on their outing. She saw him stare at the flowers and a muscle worked along his jaw as though he was displeased. Did he regret the impulse to buy them? Had he only flirted with her to annoy Archie because her father disapproved of him?

Sam propped one leg over the corner of the table and folded his arms, his expression polite but guarded.

Tanya spread out her drawings of the costumes and the scenery, her face becoming flushed with excitement as she explained her ideas. Finally running out of words, she said, 'What do you think?'

'I think you'll be bringing fairyland to the East End. The children will love it.' The admiration in his gaze faded as he said, 'And I suppose Tilbury is your accomplice in all this. That will not please the brigadier.'

She bristled. 'I won't have Archie criticised by you or my father. He made my work in the East End possible.'

'The brigadier suspects he is an upstart who wants to marry you. What do you know of the man?'

Tanya's cheeks scalded. 'He's generous and I enjoy his company.'

'Do you love him?'

'That's none of your damned business,' she flared.

Sam marched out of the room. 'I'll see if Parkins is here to help me with the sewing machine.'

'He isn't. Besides, it's only two more flights of stairs. I can help you.' She stood by the cabinet, her expression as stubborn as his. He shrugged and they were both breathing heavily when it finally rested by the front door.

Grateful for his help and wanting to ease the tension that had sprung up between them, Tanya said softly, 'I don't wish to quarrel with you, Sam. I don't understand why you are so against Archie.'

He didn't answer and his eyes remained shielded, leaving her unsure whether she should say what was on her mind. An impulse overrode caution and she added softly, 'Because we were going to visit Earl's Court and you have not mentioned it since.'

'Isn't it more fitting that Tilbury takes you?' His stare was cold and again judgemental.

'I expect he would take me if I asked. But he is not my beau. And I would not encourage him to think that he was. I'm sorry I raised the subject.' She turned away to enter the parlour.

'If you are free on Friday evening we could go to Earl's Court then.' His tone was neutral but even so his words thrilled Tanya.

'I would like that very much, Sam. Thank you.'

Every afternoon, weather permitting, Sam would take Reginald Summersfield out in the Bath chair. The fresh air tired him so that he retired early. Today Sam had carried him down the stairs and he had tottered into a waiting hansom cab. They had gone off saying that they would not return until tomorrow. Stella was furious. She was in the scullery pulling the lower leaves from the stems of a large bunch of flowers.

'He'll have a relapse,' she raged, stabbing roses into a crystal vase. 'He's barely out of his sickbed and he goes gallivanting out God knows where. Said it was business. That Hawkes is behind this. He'll be the death of Reginald.'

'Sam has Papa's welfare at heart,' Tanya reasoned. 'He will not let any harm come to him.'

'Hawkes will benefit from this, see if he doesn't.' Stella attacked some lilies, thrusting them into a blue and white jug. 'He wants your father's money for a business venture they're involved in. That's why he hangs around him all the time. He's only after his money!'

'I don't believe that,' Tanya protested. She sniffed as she bent over a saucepan of boiled leaves on the table by the vases. It smelt unpleasant. 'What's in that?'

Stella tutted. 'Didn't they teach you anything at

that Ladies Academy? The liquid obtained from boiling foxglove leaves keeps the cut flowers fresh longer.' She finished arranging the lilies before adding in a more social tone, 'At least Reginald had finally agreed that Mr Tilbury may call and take tea with us on Sunday. Though I must say that the way Reginald has been asking questions of any neighbour who calls on him and also writing letters to his associates in the city, is quite deplorable. He was closeted with Mr Fairchild, the accountant and alderman who lives at number five in the crescent all afternoon yesterday. Mr Fairchild praised Archie highly – as well he should since Archie donated fifty pounds to the church fund where Mr Fairchild is the choirmaster.'

The remaining flowers were jammed into the arrangement as Stella's irritability mounted. 'Reginald takes too much upon himself. As if I would introduce you to anyone who was not of impeccable character and position.'

'But don't you think it strange that Papa's acquaintances in the city have had no dealings with Archie?' Tanya voiced a concern which nagged at her.

'Why is it strange?' Stella rapped out stiffly, her colour high. 'Do you think that I am not capable of knowing a true gentleman when I meet one? Archie does not move in the same circles as Reginald's acquaintance. And where he banks his money is his concern not ours.'

Stella scooped the leaves into an old newspaper and screwed it into a tight bundle, pushing past Tanya to put it in the dustbin outside. Tanya followed her. 'Why won't Archie speak of his business? Is he then of independent means?'

'I would have thought that was obvious,' Stella snapped.

Her aunt could be evasive as Archie himself. She really did not like having her integrity questioned. But was her father just being overprotective? Tanya shrugged. Personally, she could not fault Archie's conduct as a gentleman, yet why did he make such a mystery of his background? It made her uneasy. She was grateful for Archie's escort twice a week but there was something about his manner which had changed. He was still charming and well-mannered, but there was a tension in him. He clearly disliked Sam staying at the house and was always asking questions about him.

'You are fortunate that Archie is so understanding,' Stella scolded. 'No man gives a lady so much of his time unless his intention is to marry her. You shouldn't be seeing so much of him if you are not considering marriage.'

'But you agreed to Archie's escorting me to the classes,' Tanya protested.

'I didn't think they would go on for so long. And how else were you to get to know such an eminently suitable man?' She pinioned Tanya with a condemning stare. 'I trust that you have not been trifling with Mr Tilbury's affections. That would be too bad of you, Tanya.'

'Why must men always seek to manipulate us?' she flared. 'I will not marry Archie just because he has enabled me to teach.'

'You must consider your reputation.'

'Why? I have done nothing wrong.'

Tanya was still fuming when Archie called and they took a hansom to Aldgate.

'It's not like you to be so quiet, Tanya.'

'It's Aunt Stella. She says I'm wrong to allow you to escort me since we are not engaged.'

He smiled. 'The remedy is easy.' He took her hand. 'Marry me, Tanya. You know I adore you.'

Why hadn't she kept quiet? She'd made matters worse by speaking. 'Give me more time, Archie. Please.'

A harsh indrawn breath was her reply. 'I will not be used, Tanya.'

Guilt assailed her. She liked Archie even if he was rather stiff and formal compared to Sam. She closed her mind to that train of thought. Sam invaded her thoughts too often.

Archie was sitting poker-stiff, his eyes glittering with anger. 'Please, Archie. Don't rush me into such a decision.'

The cab halted at their destination. 'I will wait for your answer until after the carnival. No longer.'

The staccato words sounded uncomfortably like a threat to Tanya. Her spine stiffened. 'In that case my answer will be no. I will not be bullied, especially by a man who wishes me to spend the rest of my life at his side.'

She pushed open the door of the hansom cab and leapt nimbly onto the pavement before he could reply. She was halfway along the side street to the church hall when Archie caught up with her after paying their fare.

'I'm sorry, Tanya. I didn't mean it to sound like

an ultimatum.' His voice was soft and cajoling. He should have realised that she could not be forced into a decision. But he was getting desperate. Slasher had been pestering him to copy some company shares which had come into his possession. For anyone but the Gilbert gang he would have been tempted. As it was he'd had the devil's own job to raise the money Slasher had demanded and now they wanted a cut of all his takings. Word was out that the Gilberts were using him as a forger and no one else would risk giving him work. It was also harder to work the streets without Granville as an accomplice. At least there had been no complications arising from Granville's death. The comedian was estranged from his family, having been disowned by his father when fourteen after being caught dressing up in his mother's clothes. The police had not connected Arnie Potter with Archie Tilbury and Arnie Potter had, to all intents and purposes, disappeared without trace. Marriage to Tanya would give him the respectability he craved and the wealth, especially since Stella had told him that Tanya would also inherit Maude's money which was considerable. He would have to be patient.

Archie assumed his most disarming smile. 'You are right, my dear. I shouldn't rush you. We have hardly seen each other outside this classroom. Your father's return stopped me showing you the life we will lead once we are wed. There will be the opera, dancing, the theatre and entertaining friends. You will be the belle of London.'

'All those things sound exciting, Archie, but

there is more to life than living it in a social whirl.'

The smile did not falter. 'Everything you desire will be yours. I would not stop you teaching, if that's what you fear. If I'm impatient for your answer, it's because I care so deeply for you.'

His false sentiments had their effect. Tanya's expression softened as she regarded him. 'You are very understanding.'

Archie raised her hand to his lips. In the coming weeks he would court her as no other woman had been courted before. He would shower her with flowers and gifts, show her sights her sheltered life had never dreamed of. She would be wooed with passionate words to melt even the stoniest of maiden's hearts. There would be moonlight, dining and dancing, though God alone knew where he was going to find the money for it.

When Tanya swept ahead of him down the basement steps to the hall, his eyes were cold and unforgiving. Winning her should have been a formality. For a young, inexperienced woman she was exasperatingly headstrong.

He calmed his resentment with thoughts of the money that would come to him on their marriage. For he would marry her. If charm and flattery failed to win Tanya, there were other ways to ensure that she would be his wife.

As Tanya and Archie entered the classroom, Polly leapt from her chair and held up a pale blue velvet costume. 'This is for Alice. Sal is so pleased she's to play the part.'

Tanya smiled at the shy young girl. 'You'll look

lovely, Sal. And you can keep the dress after the carnival.'

The girl's eyes widened and with a sob she ran to Tanya and flung her thin arms round her waist. 'Miss, you're so good. Ta ever so much. Ain't no one got a dress like that in my street.'

'You shouldn't give it to her,' Polly said. 'My Frank will only 'ave it down the pawnshop for what 'e can get.'

There was a fresh bruise on the side of Polly's face. ''E threatened to take the sewing machine, but I told 'im you'd get the law on 'im as it were only lent me.'

Widow Rudge said, 'Don't know why you stay with that bastard. Pretty thing like yourself could 'ave any man you want.'

'Frank ain't all bad.' Polly's hunched shoulders and jutting lower lip showed her resentment of the criticism.

'Until 'e starts drinkin',' Widow Rudge snorted. 'And 'e's drunk every night. 'E's a bad un, Polly.'

'How is little Jane?' Tanya changed the subject and peered into the basket where Polly's baby slept.

'Little angel.' The sullenness left Polly as she glanced towards her child. 'Don't know I've got 'er most of the time. It's good of you to let me bring 'er 'ere, miss. A neighbour has her during the day when I'm at work, but it wouldn't be fair to put on her of an evening as well. Frank wouldn't give up an evening at the pub either.'

'I didn't want you to miss your schooling, you're doing so well.'

Dave Fisher walked in and removed his cap.

'Scenery for the castle you wanted is out the back. Reverend said we can keep it there. I'll have the trees finished by next week and also the boards for the playing card characters, which they'll be strapping to their chests and backs.'

'Let me see it.' Tanya hurried out. The fairytale castle with tall pointed turrets was exactly as she had drawn it. 'You've done a wonderful job. I'll come over and get it painted one morning.'

Sal's eyes were wide with wonderment. 'Oh, miss, we're gonna 'ave the bestest float ever.'

Chapter Twelve

On Friday evening Sam paid their shilling each at the turnstiles of Earl's Court. Tanya felt she had walked into fairyland. A lake glistened in the moonlight, the water reflecting hundreds of coloured lamps strung through the trees. Further along they reached a grotto and as they crossed a wooden bridge several electric launches fashioned into swans came into view.

'Where do you want to go first?' Sam asked. 'There's a theatre, an exhibition hall, music in the bandstand, a fairground.'

'You decide. It all sounds exciting to me.'

'No one could say you're difficult to please,' he laughed. 'Hold on to your hat. We'll start with the watershoot, then the roller coaster.'

Tanya clung to Sam's arm as the flat-bottomed boat set on rails climbed high up on its framework. She had never had much of a head for heights and as the boat rounded the top curve it felt as if they were suspended precariously. The air was filled with music. An orchestra played a waltz in a dance marquee, the brass band in the bandstand played a military march and from the fairground two organs played different tunes.

'It's a wonderful view across the gardens,' Tanya managed stoically while her head spun with vertigo. Her next sentence was cut short as the boat thundered down the steep slope towards the lake. Her stomach felt it was being pitched into her throat. She screamed and clutched tighter to Sam's arm as the water shot up high around them, a light spray fanning her face.

'That was terrifying and exhilarating,' she laughed.

'Wait until you get on the roller coaster.' There was devilment in Sam's eyes as he escorted her to the huge wooden structure. By the time their car came to a halt after its rattling journey, Tanya's heart was hammering. Her throat was scratched from screaming and her legs felt they could not hold her weight. A rosy hue dusted her cheeks and her eyes were sequin-bright as Sam slipped his arm about her waist to steady her.

'Can we go on it again?' she pleaded.

He chuckled. 'That was meant to put you off fairgrounds for life.'

After their second ride they headed laughing towards the sideshows.

Unseen by them, a scowling figure swiftly moved behind its companion to step into the shadows of an ice-cream seller's cart. Archie was furious at seeing Tanya here, especially in the company of that damned soldier who was living with them. And the wench looked as if she was enjoying herself. Why did he have to run into them when he was with Marcus Bennett? Marcus was the son of a bishop and he had insisted that they come here.

Unfortunately Marcus enjoyed shocking people. His mincing walk and feminine gestures flaunted his sexuality. Short and slim, he dressed flamboyantly. His cream suit was accompanied by an emerald brocade waistcoat and flowing cravat. Usually Archie avoided being seen in public with men like him. He had no intention of getting arrested for his vices. But Marcus was the most exciting decadent man he had ever met. Now he couldn't relax and enjoy himself for fear that the soldier and Tanya might see him.

Archie's second shock of the evening came ten minutes later. He was tapped on the shoulder outside the main exhibition hall and turned to stare into the pockmarked face of Fancy Gilbert.

'Good to see you working,' Fancy jibed. 'Not been getting much stuff off you lately. Ain't been fencing to Strongarm, 'ave you?'

Worried lest Marcus overhear the conversation, Archie glanced in his direction. He was absorbed in watching a strongman outside his booth lift a heavy bar.

'Ooh, the muscles on him,' Marcus crooned.

'I can't talk about it now,' Archie whispered, 'but I've laid off the thieving since Granville was killed.'

'Nasty business that.' Fancy eyed him belligerently. 'But I see you've got a new partner.' There was a keener interest in Fancy's gaze now as he regarded Marcus. 'Bit obvious though, ain't 'e? That sort can be trouble. Not seen 'im around before. New to London, is 'e?'

'He don't thieve. No need to. His father's rolling in it.'

Fancy jabbed a finger in Archie's chest. 'I can't 'ave me men stop working or I'll end up in Carey Street workhouse.'

Archie's throat tightened with fear. 'It's not been easy. Granville and I worked as a team.'

'But you've got other talents. Clever with a pen since you were Scribbler's 'prentice. We don't like to see such talents wasted.'

Marcus was eyeing Fancy uneasily and Archie was fearful that Tanya might see Fancy speaking to him. The gangleader's squat figure shouted that he was a villain. 'I can't discuss it now,' he said.

Fancy rubbed the side of his nose. 'Aye, not the place. But think on my words. I've just taken over the Merry Monk Club just off the Haymarket. I'll expect you there a week on Sunday, in the evening. Bring your friend. There'll be plenty to keep him occupied.'

It wasn't an invitation that a person would live to boast they'd turned down.

Something about the stocky man, with the physique of a gorilla, on the walkway ahead attracted Sam's attention. He slowed his step, only half listened to Tanya's excited chatter as he watched the gorilla sharply poke a finger in a taller man's chest. There was menace in every line of the shorter man's body. A menace which emanated evil. He was shocked to recognise Tilbury as the man he appeared to be threatening. There was definitely a sinister element in the short man's smile which revealed missing teeth.

Guiding Tanya to one side so that she would not see the confrontation, he watched the shorter man appear to deliver some kind of ultimatum. Tilbury was deathly pale when his antagonist walked away. It was the shorter man Sam was now interested in. He'd seen henchmen like him when he lived on the streets as a lad. They were scum. But this one was dressed well enough to be a high mobsman, an underworld leader. With his curled sandy-gold hair, missing teeth and gorilla body, it would not be hard to learn his identity. If Tilbury had dealings with that sort, he was clearly up to no good.

'Sam, did you hear what I said?' Tanya asked.

'Sorry, I was miles away. I thought I saw an army friend in the crowd.'

'Where?'

He glanced in Tilbury's direction and was relieved that he had disappeared. He didn't want Tilbury to know that he had seen his meeting.

'I was mistaken,' he told her, then spotting Tilbury standing by a nearby booth, he took Tanya's hand and swung her round. 'That's a waltz I hear the band playing and I have a notion to dance.'

His arm about her waist, he expertly pirouetted round in time to the music until they were safely out of sight of Archie Tilbury.

Tanya was laughing as she protested, 'Sam, people are watching us as though we are mad.'
'They are envious. Ignore them.'
Sam gazed down into her laughing face and experienced an overwhelming urge to kiss her. He released her abruptly. 'Time to get you home. It's almost ten o'clock. Your father expects you back by ten thirty.'
Again, his swift change of mood disconcerted her. He had made her feel alive and carefree. She didn't want the evening to end.

'I'm not going to listen to any more of this, Stella,' Tanya heard Maude declare from the dining room as she came down the stairs the next morning. Her aunt sounded upset. 'You can be cruel and bullying but I won't change my mind.'
'And you are a selfish old woman,' Stella spat nastily.
Tanya sighed. Why did her aunts argue so much lately? They had never been close but there had never been this ill feeling between them before. Maude had a handkerchief pressed to her eyes as she hurried from the room.
'Don't get upset.' Tanya put her arm round the small woman's plump shoulders. 'I'm sure Aunt Stella didn't mean it.'
'She can be so spiteful. I had forgotten how much.'
'We are all on edge with Papa being ill. None of us is used to having men around the house,' she soothed.
Maude dabbed at her eyes. 'I think I will go and lie down.'

Tanya shook her head. 'It's a lovely morning. Why don't we go shopping together? I don't know why you didn't buy that cornflower blue hat last week. It suited you so much and was exactly right for your new skirt and jacket.'

Childlike, Maude brightened. 'Stella was making me feel guilty about spending my money on myself. But why shouldn't I have a new hat? You always know how to cheer me. And I think I shall treat you to something special.'

'There is no need for that, Aunt Maude.'

'It will give me pleasure.' She dropped her voice to a conspiratorial whisper. 'Besides, it will annoy Stella. First we will attend the morning service at St Paul's. The peace in the cathedral always calms me.'

Tanya preferred the parish church for her devotions but the sound of the cathedral choir, their voices lifting to the galleries in the dome, could not be equalled. There was a stillness and peace to be found within the symmetrical white walls, the clean lines rising up to the great dome, uncluttered by the fan vaulting of earlier great churches.

An hour later, as they walked down the steps, the tarnished silver sky threatened rain and the wind had strengthened. Tanya linked arms with her aunt and searched the street for a hansom to take them to Oxford Street. Aunt Maude refused to travel by any other form of transport.

'I can't abide being crushed in an omnibus or tram. And the thought of going down into the bowels of the earth to ride on the underground trains makes me feel faint. A hansom is the only civilised way to travel, unless one has one's own carriage of course. Such a pity Reginald got rid of the horses and family carriage when Papa died. I did so enjoy riding through Hyde Park on a sunny day.'

'They were an extravagance we can survive without,' Tanya replied.

Maude sighed. 'I'm beginning to sound just like Stella, pining for our past glory.'

A horse-drawn delivery van drew away from the kerb as they turned into Ludgate Hill. The main thoroughfare was always crowded with trams, horse-drawn omnibuses and trade vehicles. The stiffening wind was causing whirlwinds of paper to scuttle along the gutter. Bowler-hatted men on top of the open-roofed buses clutched at their headwear, coachmen and motorists also exposed to the weather huddled into their protective clothing. Tanya saw Sam walking towards them from Fleet Street. She had not seen him for three days and wondered whether he was avoiding her.

At that moment a gust of wind snatched at Maude's hat and she raised her hand from Tanya's arm to secure it. Tanya's gaze remained fastened on Sam's striding figure. His limp was less pronounced than when he had first come to their house. He had seen her and lifted his hand, and shouted something. There was urgency in the movement but his voice was drowned by the clop of hooves and rumble of traffic wheels. When he broke into a run, his eyes wide with horror, she had her first intimation of danger.

She spun round and cried out in alarm. 'No! Aunt Maude! Dear God, no!'

Her cry was carried away on the wind. She was rooted to the pavement, unable to move. Maude's hat had blown onto the road and was cartwheeling along the cobbles. Head down and scurrying after it, her aunt was oblivious of the traffic. A horse-drawn van was bearing down upon her. The horse shied away nervously from the flapping skirts of the figure under its nose and whinnied in fear. Tanya screamed. Too late, Maude looked up and threw up her hands, her face slack with terror. Vicious hooves windmilled in the air above her. They came down, striking her temple. Maude was knocked sideways down onto the cobbles, blood pouring from her head.

The driver's cap was pulled low over his eyes as he sawed at the reins. Tanya's gaze was riveted on the figure in the road. One hand was outflung, the fingers jerking towards the flattened hat.

There was a sickening thud and crunch of bones as the wheels of the van bounced over Maude's back. Maude twitched spasmodically then became still. Tanya pushed her way through the pedestrians who were frozen into gaping statues around the scene. She was about to throw herself onto the ground beside Maude's still figure when Sam dragged her back on the pavement.

'Good God, woman, you'll get yourself killed as well,' he shouted, his voice fractured with fear.

A brewery dray drawn by four shire horses missed her by inches. The drayman was wrestling with the reins to guide the frightened horses into the centre of the road to avoid Maude's body being further mangled. A motorist slammed on his brakes but was too late to avoid colliding with the dray.

Pandemonium broke out around them. The horses were skittish and people were screaming or shouting for assistance. Even in her dazed state, Tanya was shocked that the driver of the delivery van leapt out of his seat and ran off into the crowd and down a nearby alleyway. Was he going for a doctor or just running away?

'Someone get after that driver,' Sam ordered.

Two men rang after him but they were hampered by the press of the curious bystanders.

Sam held Tanya tight, preventing her from going to her aunt. 'There's nothing you can do. She's dead.'

'No. I've got to help her.'

Sam's fingers were manacles on her arms, forcing her round to face him. 'Try not to look. It will upset you.'

Tanya wrenched free and glancing over her shoulder saw the pool of blood seeping from beneath her aunt's figure. Nausea rushed to her throat, and her knees buckled. She fought back the sickness and bowed her head against Sam's chest, her body trembling from shock.

He held her against him and whispered, 'It was quick. There's nothing you can do.'

'Move along there, people,' she heard a policeman command. 'Let's get the road cleared. An ambulance is on its way.'

'The woman is this lady's aunt,' Sam informed him. 'I'll tell the family.'

The stout, ginger-whiskered policeman nodded sympathetically to Sam. 'I'll need a statement later, sir. Best take the young lady home. The ambulance will take the body to the mortuary.'

'The driver responsible ran away,' Tanya said, dazed with shock.

The two men who had run after him shook their heads, intimating that the driver had got away. The sobs she had been struggling to contain broke free. Sam led her gently away. She resisted, turning back in time to see her aunt's broken body covered in a blanket being lifted into the ambulance.

'Why did the driver run away, Sam?'

'He was young. The accident probably shook him up,' he lied. He could see no point in telling her that the driver had deliberately run Maude Summersfield down. It made no sense. Who could possibly want that sweet old lady killed?

Tanya feared that news of his sister's tragic death would make her father suffer a relapse. Instead he seemed to rally and was determined to attend Maude's funeral.

The day was disrespectfully sunny and hot for such a sad occasion. It was a small affair, for Maude had no relatives other than her brother, sister and niece. The brigadier, still too weak to walk, attended in the Bath chair pushed by Sam.

'A sad day,' the brigadier sighed. 'Never thought my little sister would be in her grave before me. Take me back to the carriage, Sam.'

Sam tucked the scarlet plaid blanket round Summersfield's knees before wheeling him back along the narrow path between the family tombs and yew trees.

Mrs Rivers had attended the service and as the door on the family vault was being closed, she approached Tanya. The spiritualist was different from how Tanya had imagined her. She supposed it was superstitious prejudice that had made her conjure an image of a crone-like, half-demented figure who consorted with the dead. Mrs Rivers was in her twenties, fashionably dressed in a large black picture hat and fitted suit, similar to Tanya's own. A worldly serenity emanated from her, together with an air of sympathy and compassion.

'Hurry along, Tanya,' Stella fussed. 'It's so hot and you've no parasol to protect your complexion.'

Mrs Rivers regarded Stella with chill disapproval. 'Your aunt would rather I had not come,' she said to Tanya.

'You were Maude's friend and I know you gave her a great deal of comfort,' replied. Tanya. 'I'm glad you came.'

'She was a lovely woman, a kindly soul. Not like that one.' Her eyes were chips of flint as she watched Stella climb into the carriage. 'Nothing is as it seems. Be warned, Miss Summersfield. I had felt for weeks that Maude was in danger. I can still feel it. You take care, Miss Summersfield.'

The spiritualist's words made Tanya shiver. The fine hairs on her arms rose with premonition. 'Maude said those same words to me not long ago.' She checked her unease. Funerals were always charged with emotion, the mind more susceptible to superstitious fears. 'My aunt's death was an accident,' she declared, refusing to believe there could have been anything sinister behind the tragedy. 'Good day, Mrs Rivers.'

Tanya regarded the reading of Aunt Maude's will as a formality; she was stunned when she learnt that she was to inherit nearly five thousand pounds when she married.

The brigadier's health continued to improve, so much so that a week after Maude's funeral he accompanied Sam on a business trip. They stayed away overnight. Stella had made her disapproval obvious, but to no avail.

Through the scullery window Tanya saw her aunt working in the garden, collecting seeds to be potted next year. Tanya was looking for a vase in the scullery to arrange some flowers a florist had delivered from Archie. Remembering Stella had told her that an infusion of foxgloves helped to preserve them, she called out to her aunt who was tending the garden.

'How do I make the foxglove infusion for these flowers? I can't remember if it's the leaves, seeds or flowers I have to boil. You've so many jars of dried herbs here, you should label them as to their uses.'

Stella stripped off her work gloves and hurried into the scullery looking flustered. 'I don't like anyone touching my jars. Did Archie send the flowers you want arranging?' She made a visible effort to calm herself. 'Such a generous man. Every week he buys you flowers.'

Millie came into the scullery, looking dejected. 'I've finished bundling up Miss Maude's clothes to be given to a charity for the poor.' She wiped a tear from her eye. 'I do miss her.'

Tanya put her arms round the maid. 'We all do. And I'm pleased that you decided to stay with us. Stella and I could not cope without you.' To Tanya's delight, her father had suggested Millie should stay on. He would pay her the samc wages Maude had paid her.

'I don't have nowhere else to go.' Millie wiped at her tears. 'I've lived here for fifteen years. I'd miss Ginny and Cook, and of course yourself Miss Tanya. You're all the family I've got.'

Stella sniffed the contents of a jar of herbs, then announced, 'Now that you have sorted out Maude's things, I shall move into her room.'

Tanya was shocked. Stella had shown little grief over her sister's death, but unless angry her older aunt had always kept her emotions hidden. Tanya was constantly battling against a wayward tear which escaped her lashes. She missed Maude's loving presence and cheery inconsequential chatter. Guilt nibbled at her conscience: if she had hadn't been so excited at seeing Sam ahead of them in the street that day, she might have been able to have stopped her aunt running after her hat.

Ginny came rushing in waving a feather duster and tripped over the corner of the mat in her excitement. 'The master has returned,' she said recovering her balance. 'And in such style. You should see the grand motor car they've rolled up in.'

'Motor car?' Stella peered through the window up through the basement railings into the road. Her face twisted with anger as she choked out,

'Hawkes is at the wheel of an expensive automobile and Reginald is in the back looking like the King of Siam.'

'Sam mentioned that their business was to do with motor cars.' Curious, Tanya joined her aunt at the window. 'I think it's exciting.'

'It will be the ruin of us,' Stella seethed. 'I knew Hawkes was up to no good. This proves it. How dare Reginald squander his money on that contraption? He always was selfish. A car like that costs a fortune. The money could have been better used on this house.'

Tanya was appalled by the hostility and rage mottling her aunt's face.

Stella stamped up the back stairs to the hallway, her black taffeta skirt with its bustle quivering with outrage. Tanya followed her. In this mood Stella was bound to be rude to Sam and Tanya wanted to try and forestall her. She was pleased with the purchase of the motor car. Perhaps now there would be drives out to the country. Stella was obsessed with redecorating the house. She wanted it to be a showpiece. Although the roof was in urgent need of repair to stop the damp, the century-old furniture from the elegant Regency age appealed to Tanya's taste more than the more cumbersome furniture produced in Queen Victoria and King Edward's reigns. The house might be shabbier than their neighbours' but it was comfortable. Even in her fanciful designs for the rooms, she had kept much of its lovely old features, changing only the lighting and wallpaper to lighter colours.

Reginald was holding on to Sam's shoulder as

he walked slowly towards the stairs. Stella was waiting for him, her eyes glacial and her lips pursed with outrage. 'You won't be happy until you bankrupt us, will you?' she shrilled. 'What do you need an automobile like that for?'

'You forget your place, sister.' He dropped his hand from Sam's shoulder and regarded Stella sternly. 'My good will has supported you these last thirty years.'

'Supported me?' Stella's face turned puce. 'I've been an unpaid housekeeper.'

Tanya interceded. 'Aunt, clearly Papa is tired after his travelling. Of course he appreciates all you have done.' She looked at her father. His mouth was turned down and his eyes were narrowed with dislike as he regarded his sister. A noncommittal grunt was his answer.

'He has never appreciated the sacrifices I have been forced to make,' Stella declared.

'I've honoured my duty to an unmarried sister.'

Stella reeled back as though he had struck her. She was trembling. Her voice sounded as though she hated him. 'And who ensured that I did not marry? I will never forgive you for that. Never.'

Chapter Thirteen

'Women!' the brigadier declared, brandishing his walking stick as Stella returned to the garden. 'Never could understand them.'

'And I doubt you've ever tried,' Tanya retorted.

'Stella has devoted her life to keeping this house for you. She spared herself nothing in caring for you when you were ill. And you cannot even be civil to her.'

'Go to your room, Tanya,' he thundered. 'And stay there until you learn to respect your betters.'

Her eyes flashed. 'Respect is something which is earned, Papa. And it works both ways. If you took the trouble to talk to the women in this house instead of demanding mindless submission, you might be surprised at your discoveries.'

'It has always been a man's place to make the decisions and women to obey.'

Hands on hips, she confronted him. 'A decision made by a man, I warrant.'

He waved his stick threateningly until Sam took it from him. Then Sam stood back, clearly unwilling to become involved in a family argument.

'You're insolent and insubordinate. Go to your room, Tanya.'

'A typical soldier's reaction to failed diplomacy. I shall be sketching in the conservatory. I'm prisoner enough in this house without being further confined to my room.'

Sam watched Tanya glide along the hall. Like all the family, she wore black in mourning for her aunt. It made her look more mature, even with her upswept curls flowing in a mane to her shoulders. The freedom of her hair echoed the freedom of her spirit. Not for her the tortuous padding and wiring of the powder-puff style fashionable women favoured.

'Insolent chit,' Summersfield grumbled. 'I don't know where she gets it from. Her mother was a gentle creature.'

Sam laughed, earning himself a wrathful glance from the brigadier. Unabashed, he commented, 'It couldn't be that she takes after you, could it, sir?'

The brigadier looked taken aback. Then he nodded, not displeased. 'Perhaps she does. Pity she wasn't a son. Could have gone far in the army with spirit like that. But it doesn't do in a woman, does it? I've never heard such nonsense. If she's been going to those damned rallies where women are demanding their rights, there'll be trouble.'

'Your daughter spoke from the heart,' Sam countered. 'Perhaps you should listen to her more often. She's no one's fool and an intelligent woman.'

'Sounds like she's made a conquest,' he barked. He leaned on Sam's shoulder as they mounted the stairs. His hand tightened and there was a warning in his eyes. 'Don't misplace my trust in you, Sam. You're good man. But the girl is not for you. And never can be. It's down to breeding in the end. Like must marry like.'

Sam kept his expression impassive. He agreed with every word the brigadier said, but each syllable was like a bayonet thrust straight in his heart.

'I suppose this Tilbury chappie will be all right for her,' Summersfield bludgeoned on. 'Pity he made his money out of the country so his credentials can't be checked. But one thing Stella does have a nose for is status.'

'I'm not so sure about Tilbury,' Sam replied, 'not that it's my place to comment.'

'Do you know something I don't? I grant you the man's too smooth for my taste, but that isn't a crime.'

'I saw him talking to an unsavoury character the other evening – though that on its own means nothing. I think Miss Tanya deserves better, that's all,' he replied guardedly.

'Can't be much wrong with him.' The brigadier flopped into the chair by his bedroom window. 'Stella would never allow Tanya to be courted by a man who wasn't up to the mark. My sister is an inveterate snob.'

Sam kept his opinion to himself that Stella had a spiteful, vindictive streak in her nature. She had never troubled to conceal that she resented his presence in the house. He had seen how she bullied Maude and more subtly tried to manipulate Tanya. It was obvious that the woman was bedazzled by Tilbury. For reasons of her own she was determined that Tanya should marry him. If she was so shrewd, why couldn't she see that Tilbury was not all that he seemed?

He waited while the brigadier set out the chess pieces on the board before speaking. 'Now that you're recovering, I shall be moving out.'

'You can't do that.' Reginald Summersfield was aghast. 'I've come to rely on you to keep me sane in this infernal house full of women. You haven't taken offence over what I said about my daughter?'

Sam shook his head. 'I am aware of the gulf between us.'

The brigadier rubbed his moustache. 'I wish it could be otherwise. You're a fine man, Sam. But the girl must marry someone of wealth and position. Her legacy may seem a lot to you, but it isn't. Once that much would have been my great-grandfather's yearly allowance. This place costs a fortune to run. I've just enough in the bank to stay above water for another year. Unless we make our fortune in this new venture, I'll have to sell the house. I want to see Tanya settled before that happens.'

'I understand that, sir,' Sam replied. 'But there's a couple of rooms over the garage we've just bought the freehold on. I'd rather live on my own. I only stayed here because you were so ill. Now that we've acquired those premises, I should be working every day. I'm not a gentleman of leisure. The garage is just the start. Part of the premises will be adapted into a showroom for the second-hand cars we're selling.'

The brigadier preened the waxed ends of his moustache and regarded his business partner thoughtfully. 'You always were your own man. That's why I like you, Sam. But stay here until you have the room fit to live in.'

Reluctantly Sam agreed. Even if he had to do the work himself, he'd have the place cleaned, painted and ready to live in by next week. Being in the same house as Tanya was becoming a daily torture.

Leaving the brigadier's room, Sam wandered into the games room. Restless, he opened a walnut veneered cupboard, looking for billiard cues and balls. His protective feelings towards Tanya were getting out of hand. The thought of Tilbury being encouraged to court her angered him.

Sam removed his jacket and rolled up his shirt sleeves. Having set up the balls, he began systematically to pot them. His mood made him play aggressively and the balls rattled into the pockets with a loud thud. He had started his second game and some of his frustration had cooled when he looked up to see Tanya standing by the door watching him.

'My, someone has ruffled your feathers. I've never seen the game played with such violence.' Her light tone was like salt in an open wound.

He did not answer but potted the last two balls. Retrieving them from their pockets, he rolled them on the table. She had moved to the games cupboard and laughed as she picked up a broken stringed battledore racket and a warped billiard cue. 'These are all sadly neglected. Even the darts feathers look as if mice have been at them. Yet these look in good shape.' She picked up two ping-pong bats and a box which held half a dozen undamaged balls. 'Come on, Sam. I'll give you a game. I haven't played ping-pong for years. Lift that hard cover over the billiard table and I'll unravel the net.'

She was hitting the ball up and down on the bat and laughing. Sam stood by the billiard table, his cue propped on the floor like a pikeman's staff beside him.

'Don't you wish to play?' she asked, her laughter fading.

'Another time perhaps,' he answered stiffly.

Tanya had recovered her good mood after her father's outburst. The scenery for the float was all painted and she was delighted with the results.

Polly had brought in the costumes for the Mad Hatter and White Rabbit, Widow Rudge was finishing off the trimmings on the Queen's gown and the King's cloak, then everything would be finished.

The costumes surpassed her expectations. Polly was an accomplished seamstress. The success was exhilarating and even her father's argument with Stella could not spoil it. Stella was becoming more unreasonable since Maude's death.

Sam was standing so stiffly he could be on regimental parade. His manner was so unlike the fun-loving man who had taken her to Regent's Park and Earl's Court. She longed for a return to that camaraderie.

'I thought a game of ping-pong would be fun. Better still, would you teach me how to play billiards?'

'Women do not play billiards,' he remarked.

She snatched up a cue and advanced towards the table. 'Poppycock. I've never heard such nonsense. This is one woman who will play.'

Knowing that you had to aim the white ball at one of the red ones to get it into the side pockets, she bent over and squinted along the cue. It curved to one side and when she struck the white ball it bounced off the raised edge of the table and was caught in mid-air by Sam, a good two feet from where she had been aiming it.

'At least use a straight cue before you break a window,' he remonstrated, handing her his. 'And spread your fingers like this on the table, letting the cue move easily between the thumb and forefinger.'

She copied his pose, the tip of her tongue protruding between her teeth. This time she was successful in getting the white ball to hit a red one but it went nowhere near the pocket she was aiming for.

'What am I doing wrong?'

Sam moved to her side. 'It's the way you're standing and you're holding the cue too tightly. It should be like this.'

She followed his instructions without success. With an impatient tut he stood behind her as she bent over the table to line up the next shot. His body folded over hers as he repositioned her back and drew her arm lightly back and forwards to align the cue. The touch of his breath was warm against her cheek; the heat of his body, so close but not actually touching, permeated her clothing. It made her flesh tingle with awareness of his masculinity. He didn't use cologne or Macassar oil on his hair; he smelt of cedarwood soap, fresh air, and a faint muskiness which was uniquely his own scent. It was as exciting as he was exciting. When they potted the red ball, she looked over her shoulder at him, her face alight with pleasure. What she saw in his eyes made the breath catch in her throat. There was a longing so profound it arrowed into her heart.

Immediately he stepped back, a shutter coming down over his eyes. 'You wanted a game of ping-pong.'

'I was enjoying being taught this.' She could not keep the disappointment from her voice.

His stare was fierce. 'There are some games which are too dangerous for us to play.'

'I would have thought you man enough for anything.' She was being provocative, taunting him for the pain he caused her by distancing himself from her.

'You don't know the implications of what you're saying.' He stood with his back to the window so that she could not see his expression.

Tanya bowed her head. How could she tell him that she enjoyed his company without sounding too forward? Her heart ruled more strongly than her head. 'Why are you erecting barriers between us?'

'Your father would not approve of us seeing too much of each other.'

She laughed softly. 'You live here. Papa cannot stop us meeting.' The challenge brightened in her eyes. 'I thought you vowed on leaving the army to take orders from no one.'

'That has nothing to do with it.' His manner had changed, no longer fun-loving and teasing, but cold and uncompromising.

What had she done wrong? She would never understand this man. Or the power he had to wound her. With a defiant flick of her head, she forced a smile. Her pain was hidden under a polite mask. 'Clearly you are too busy, so I'll take up no more of your time.'

When again he did not answer, her temper got the better of her. 'Damn you, Sam Hawkes, I thought you were my friend.'

His brittle laugh was mocking. 'There is no such thing as friendship between a man and a woman.'

'Poppycock!'

'There speaks the young and innocent.'

They faced each other, both tense, their eyes glittering and their breathing sharpened.

'Don't patronise me,' Tanya flared.

'Like so many of your kind, you don't like hearing the truth if it crosses your will.'

Her head tilted, her eyes sparking with a dangerous fire. 'Why do men always behave as if they are so superior? Confound you, Sam Hawkes. I was trying to make you feel comfortable in this house, to show you how much we appreciate what you have done for Papa.' The rigid way he held himself and the coldness in his stare snipped at her composure. She was a fool to allow herself to be hurt this way. Injured pride gravelled her voice. 'I apologise for mistaking your kindness as something more, for believing that we could be friends when the idea is obviously loathsome to you.'

He was struggling to master his own temper. 'It is not loathsome. It simply is not possible.'

She would not yield. 'Because I'm a woman.'

'A beautiful and desirable woman. Now are you satisfied?' he fired back.

'Am I desirable?'

Suspecting that she was flirting and demanding attention, he was about to walk out. This argument was pointless. Instead he saw her puzzlement, her vulnerability. The light outside was fading to a crimson sunset, turning her complexion to pale rose. The tremulous jut of her lower lip was almost his undoing. She was temptingly lovely and unaware of the power she could wield over men, or to what danger that power could lead.

The house was quiet. They were alone. Temptation threatened to overwhelm him. An iron will controlled it.

Tanya held out a hand, entreating. 'We had such fun at the zoo and Earl's Court, now you sound as if you hate me. What have I said or done?'

A groan was torn from him. Instead of leaving the room, he found his hands reaching for her shoulders, then his lips were hard and punishing upon hers. The sweetness he found there was as unexpected as it was harrowing and profound. He had wanted to repel her, show her the violence and carnality of men. But when the fresh scent of her hair and skin assailed him, his kiss became tender. His arms encircled her, drawing the softness of her against his hard body. The tip of his tongue parted her lips, compelling and coercing. It wasn't until her mouth moved in response – at first virginal and hesitant, then her tongue was teasing and tempting – did he realise he had understimated his own desire. The pressure of her figure moulded to his fired his passion. He was on the brink of an abyss, teetering, and imperilled. Her soft moan of pleasure and the touch of her fingers entwining in his hair was shredding his control. Cold reason doused him. This was the brigadier's daughter!

To draw back took all his willpower. He forced contempt into his voice as the only means now to shock her. 'Some men would misinterpret the friendship you so freely offer, Miss Summersfield. When news spreads of the money you have inherited, there will be a stream of suitors calling at your door. A fortune-hunter will use your innocence to compromise your reputation. Let that be a lesson for you to be on guard against them.'

Tanya put her hand to her lips as the door closed behind him. Her body trembled with shame. Her senses careened from Sam's kiss. At the touch of his tongue, invading her mouth, a delicate heat had unfurled in the pit of her stomach until she had swayed against him. Her body had burned to be crushed in his arms, feel the firm muscles of his chest and thigh contoured against her own. Then he had spoken those hateful words which brutally rejected her. How dare he treat her so callously? He wasn't kind. He was hateful.

Sam swore roundly under his breath. Now he felt guilty for wounding her feelings. Yet he had taken the only course possible by ignoring her challenge. With each meeting he was becoming dangerously attracted to Tanya and he was aware that it was reciprocated. It would only lead to heartache. The brigadier was recovering and no longer needed him. Even if the rooms over the garage workshop were not finished, he would leave tomorrow.

Archie was drinking in the Merry Monk. He was alone. He hadn't wanted Marcus Bennett along to complicate matters. Nor did he want his lover to learn of his involvement with the Gilberts. He wouldn't understand or approve. He was here because he was too scared to ignore Fancy's order.

He eyed the other customers over the rim of his

glass. Several showed their interest in him. His handsome looks ensured that he was popular. Tonight he hadn't the enthusiasm to smile back. They were the usual crowd. Transvestites parading in gaudy dresses. One in a showgirl's spangled tights and tight-fitting costume was singing a bawdy song on the stage. Young painted catamites touted for custom. A few of the men were masked. These were politicians or men of business. They paid highly for their anonymity though Archie doubted that their identity was unknown to the Gilbert brothers. Blackmail was too lucrative.

Archie sipped at his whisky. He needed it for courage but dared not let it blur his judgement. When he saw Slasher Gilbert heading towards him, his flesh broke out into a cold sweat. His confidence in his ability to charm his way out of anything ebbed. He needed sharp wits to survive tonight.

'You've not been keeping your side of our bargain,' Slashed grimaced. 'Missing Granville, are you? Terrible, 'is death. But 'e must've been worth a few bob, though according to the newspapers nothing was found in 'is flat. They reported 'e died skint. You and me know different. He didn't believe in banks.'

Archie shrugged. He had a nasty feeling where this was leading. Did Slasher suspect that he'd murdered Granville Ingram? Archie swallowed against a lump of fear rising in his throat. 'Granville was a drunk and an opium addict,' he said. 'He didn't work much in the last months of his life. His money went on his vices.'

Slasher grinned. 'And you were one of those vices, weren't you, lover boy? Scribbler Sorrell taught you more than forging, the randy sod. Was Ingram getting troublesome?'

Archie pulled at his shirt cuff in a practised show of nonchalance and gave Slasher a lopsided smile. Inside he was quaking. 'What are you getting at?'

'Don't like murders close to our manor unless it's us who's done 'em.'

Archie downed his drink. There was no point in lying. 'I dealt with it. Though a seaman who owed me a favour helped me deposit the body. He's since sailed to South America.'

Slasher leant back against the bar, his stare acid. 'Ingram's body being found near the Chink's opium den took some heat off us. The bluebottles were sniffing round that club for days and five arrests were made. For that I'm prepared to overlook your involvement.' The gangleader winked at him. 'Maybe you've 'eard that Bull brown 'ad a similar accident a week ago. Brown were me right-'and man after Fancy got above 'imself. Tried to sell us out to a rival gang.'

Archie resisted the need to loosen his collar. His neck was slick with sweat and his shirt was sticking uncomfortably to his shoulders. He stared at his elegantly manicured nails and ran a finger and thumb along his forefinger. His lovers always praised his tapering fingers and when he saw Slasher moisten his lips, he knew that he was not unaffected. Slasher, like his brother, took his sport from both men and women. It boosted Archie's confidence.

'What's that got to do with me?' he asked, his voice heavy with injured innocence. 'I had nothing to do with Bull Brown.'

'It's time you and I talked. Private like. Come into my office.'

Archie's guts clenched. Had he gone too far? He'd meant to charm Slasher not seduce him. He wasn't into the sadistic perversions Slasher enjoyed, not when they were directed at himself at any rate. He had a horror of experiencing pain and Slasher enjoyed inflicting it. He looked around the room. He could run for it. But his reprieve, even if he gained it, would be shortlived.

He straightened his tie and smoothed the oiled sides of his hair, checking his image in the bar mirror. Satisfied with what he saw, he followed Slasher. If you looked the part, you became the part was his motto.

Inside the office, panic again knotted his guts. The walls were decorated with instruments of torture and in one corner stood an iron maiden, its door open to reveal the spikes which would pierce a man's eyes, heart and gut. A thick bull-whip hung above a lead-tipped cat-o'-nine-tails and on one wall were a dozen vicious-looking daggers. All were gruesome reminders of how Slasher Gilbert had acquired his name.

Fancy was standing by a leather daybed pulling on his jacket. A silver-turbaned Negro youth lay shivering and naked, his buttocks covered in welts from a whip. 'That'll teach you to do as your told,' Fancy growled. 'Now get back outside and if you refuse another customer, it won't be a beating you'll get, it'll be a knife cutting off your balls. Now get outta me sight.' He flung some purple satin trousers at the youth.

Slasher stared after the boy. 'Waste of time beating 'im. Get 'im on the opium. The boy will work 'ard enough then, to pay for 'is dope.'

Archie kept his face expressionless, but his chest was tight with fear. He had mixed with some unsavoury characters but the Gilbert brothers were pure evil. He must have been mad to work their district and think he could get away with it.

Slasher swaggered to a door which opened onto steps leading down to the cellar. He gestured for Archie to follow him. Archie's legs trembled and almost betrayed him. He'd heard rumours of what went on in these cellars where the screams of Slasher's victims could not be heard above ground.

Three oil lamps spread their yellow light over the macabre tableau in the room. Two poor wretches were manacled, arms spread, against a rough brick wall. Each had been stripped to their waists and cuts criss-crossed their bloodied torsos and arms. From the grotesque way their fingers were distorted and swollen over the iron chains, it was obvious every bone in their hands had been smashed. Their heads were bent, their bodies sagging and unconscious. Slasher nodded to a gargoyle-like creature squatting in the corner. The spindle-legged dwarf shuffled forward and grinned toothlessly at the gangleader.

The villain ruffled the dwarf's long, lank, mousy hair as though he was a puppy and the pug-nosed creature responded with an animal purr. 'You've done well, Titch. Ain't dead, are they?'

'Nah, ain't dead,' the gargoyle wheezed. 'You don't like it if they dies before you sees 'em.'

''Ow long they been 'ere now, Titch?' Slasher askcd for Archie's benefit.

'Three days, Mr Gilbert.'

'Throw water over 'em,' Slasher ordered.

The dwarf obeyed. Only one of the men responded. Guttural sounds emitted from his throat. When he lifted his face to the light, Archie saw that the man's eyes had been gouged out and his tongue docked.

Sickened, he looked away.

Slasher's grin was diabolical. 'Bull Brown got off easy. 'E died when me men tried to take 'im. These buggers were gonna inform on us. Pity, 'cos Rick were me best forger. The other is James Fenton. Refused to sign over his property to me when 'e lost everything in a poker game. And I mean everything. Owned four clothes factories and a row of 'ouses in Mile End.'

'But isn't he the brother of Harold Fenton, one of the top inspectors at Bow police station?' Archie battled against his rising nausea.

Slasher grinned. 'Yeah. Thought that would keep 'im safe. But no one gets one over on me. That's where you come in. I want Fenton's signature forged on the papers. They better look real legal like, or you'll find yourself awaiting the pleasure of Titch's artistry. Get me meaning?'

Archie nodded. His stomach churned and he saw himself walking down a dark tunnel which led to torture or the gallows. Once he got his hands on Tanya Sumersfield's money, he'd be on the first boat to America, far away from Slasher Gilbert's malignant clutches.

He was sweating with fear and blamed Stella for getting him into this. She had promised so much and come up with so little. She'd sworn her niece would be engaged to him before the brigadier returned. The woman was blinded by her obsession for retribution against her brother.

And Tanya was proving difficult. She was also to blame for his dilemma. If she'd agreed to marry him when he'd first asked her, he would never have got embroiled with the Gilbert brothers. And even now the wench prevaricated. Despite her denials, he suspected that she was becoming interested in Hawkes.

Hatred spattered him. He channelled his fear into thoughts of his own revenge. It was time Hawkes was dealt with. Once he was out of the way, the conquest of Tanya Summersfield would be just a matter of time.

Chapter Fourteen

Throughout August England sweltered in a heatwave. The day of the carnival was the hottest yet. Tanya had put the finishing touches to the float on Friday evening. The castle rose up behind a raised platform holding two thrones for the King and Queen of Hearts. At the far end a woodland scene was the setting for the Mad Hatter's tea party. The playing cards were to walk beside the float, collecting the money thrown for the charities supported by the carnival.

Even Joe Lang and Dave Fisher were excited about the float. Joe had shown a talent for figures in costing the enterprise and it had prompted Tanya to teach him how to keep basic accounts. It had been one of the subjects taught at the Ladies Academy. Miss Stockwell believed that every wife must be manager of her own household accounts.

Reviewing the costumes, Tanya enthused, 'You all look wonderful. Thank you for your hard work.'

'Didn't seem like work,' Polly said smiling. 'It were fun making something different from shirts.'

'Will you be staying for the judging of the floats before the carnival starts, Miss Tanya?' Joe asked. He jammed his cardboard crown on his head and adjusted his long fur-trimmed cloak to hide his crippled hand. He made an impressive King of Hearts.

'No. I said I'd watch with Reverend Carver by the church.'

'But what if we win the prize for best float?' Sal fidgeted excitedly. Her long blonde hair was neatly combed and a blue satin bow, which matched her dress, was fastened to it. She was bursting with pride at playing Alice.

'Have you seen how grand some of the floats are?' Tanya laughed. 'It's not the winning that's important, it's the taking part.'

'But wouldn't it be great to win?' Sal persisted

and Tanya marvelled at how she had changed in the weeks she had been coming to the class. She was no longer timid and her animation gave a hint of the beautiful woman she would soon become.

'Keep your fingers crossed for us, Sal,' Tanya smiled.

Her smile broadened as she looked at Dave Fisher in his white fur suit and crimson waistcoat; a mask over the top part of his face gave him the features of a rabbit. Nan Rudge was parading grandly as the Queen of Hearts, her face heavily rouged and her purple and scarlet costume as outrageous as any pantomime dame's. It had surprised Tanya that Wilfred Baker, the hardened socialist, had offered to dress as the Mad Hatter. He was already in place on the float. Dave and Wilf had both been reluctant to wear a costume at first but they were now as keen as the others.

'All set, Wilf? Don't forget, the tea party is under your control,' Tanya prompted. 'But it's supposed to be fun. Don't go organising it like one of your Labour Party meetings. Dave says you're a devil with the gavel.'

'Passions run high at our meetings, miss. I just keep the men in line. I'll not have hecklers stopping us recruiting new members. It's not a year since James Keir Hardie founded the party.'

She held up her hands to stop a political lecture. 'No politics today, Wilf. Everyone must enjoy themselves.'

The students working together on the float had formed a strong bond and Tanya was saddened that the work was over.

Joe Lang held out a bouquet of flowers to her. 'For you. You've done so much for us.'

She blinked aside her tears of happiness. 'Thank you. You have given me as much as I have given you.'

She would miss these people. She would speak to her father and try to convince him that her work was worthwhile. It reminded her that she also had to deal with Archie. He was another problem. He continued to press her to agree to their marriage. Her teaching forged a link with him which she was finding increasingly disquieting.

Refusing to ruin this festive day by dwelling upon problems, she bade them good luck and left to join Reverend Carver.

The street was lined with spectators; children jumped up and down with growing excitement and buskers entertained the crowed. One in a battered top hat and a long, russet coat had a big drum strapped to his back with a string attached to his right heel to enable him to beat it. Bells, cymbals, a tambourine and a motor horn were strapped to his knees and elbows and he played a banjo. Following him was an organ-grinder with his dancing monkey and two accordian players. Flag-sellers paraded with Union Jacks stuck in their hats. Ice-cream and drink vendors cycled slowly past with their goods in a barrow over the front wheel. Muffin-sellers and piemen strode along with their trays of food balanced on their heads.

The sound of the Salvation Army band announced the arrival of the carnival and small children were lifted onto shoulders to view the spectacle. Altogether there were four bands, followed by a circus parade led by an elephant advertising the circus performing in Victoria Park. The children cheered the Italian acrobats and men whistled at the female bareback rider in a brightly sequinned costume which displayed her shapely legs. There were gasps of astonishment when the Indian fire-eater performed, his breath a dragon's tongue of flame.

Then came the floats. The crowd roared approval at the depiction of various nursery rhymes and Bible stories, while amateur musical and dramatic societies sang along to pianos or performed a scene from a play. Between the floats clowns capered, animals frolicked, a harlequin danced and stately historical figures paraded. There were also jugglers, stilt walkers, and Morris dancers.

When Tanya's float appeared the crowd laughed at the antics of the Mad Hatter and White Rabbit and shook their fists when Nan Rudge pointed at Alice and roared, 'Off with her head!'

'The float looks splendid, Miss Summersfield,' Reverend Carver congratulated Tanya. 'The costumes are superb, as is the scenery. You have hidden talents. Oh, look! There's a banner proclaiming it won first prize.'

'That's incredible,' Tanya gasped. 'I never expected that. But I'm pleased for the pupils. They put so much hard work into it. It's a tribute to their talents, not mine.'

'You are too modest.' The reverend turned to a bewhiskered, middle-aged man in top hat and morning suit who stood at his side. 'The costumes for *Alice's Adventures in Wonderland* are outstanding, are they not, Mr Vernon?'

'Indeed they are.' Mr Vernon studied Tanya. 'And you say, Reverend, that this young lady is responsible?'

'Miss Summersfield devised everything herself.'

Tanya blushed at the praise. 'It was nothing. I enjoyed it.'

Mr Vernon continued to regard her with interest. 'You have a special talent. Have you done this type of thing before?'

'Only when a play was put on at school. I taught art for a time and designed the costumes and scenery.'

His interest intensified. 'You should take it up professionally, Miss Summersfield.'

'My father would never consent to me working in a theatre, sir.'

'Indeed not.' He sounded shocked. 'That was not what I meant. Would I be presuming on this chance acquaintanceship if I asked you to design a fairy grotto for my shops for the children at Christmas? I own Vernon Emporiums. We have a branch in Regent Street and several others throughout the London boroughs.'

'I would be happy to, Mr Vernon,' Tanya said enthusiastically. Then her expression sobered. 'Of course, I must consult my father. He would never consent to my being an actual employee. It would have to be a private business arrangement.

He's rather old-fashioned about such matters.'

Mr Vernon nodded. 'You have a talent which should not be wasted, Miss Summerfield. I would gladly call upon him and discuss the matter.'

'There is no need for that.' She hesitated at becoming too heavily involved. 'I fear Papa is unwell at the moment. I will talk to him and inform you of his decision.' Then caution was cast aside as her excitement refused to be dampened. 'I'm sure he will agree.'

'Have no fears, Mr Vernon,' Reverend Carver said with a laugh. 'Miss Summersfield can be most persuasive. Her father was originally against her teaching adults at the church hall in the evening. Her work here has been very successful.'

Mr Vernon handed Tanya his business card. 'I am free at ten o'clock Tuesday morning. If you will attend my office in Regent Street, Miss Summersfield, we can discuss the details then.'

The last of the floats had passed and the crowd was beginning to thin. Some people remained dancing in the street as a piano was wheeled onto the pavement from a pub. Mr Vernon tipped his top hat to her and moved through the press of people to where a chauffeur awaited him in a gleaming open-topped Lanchester motor car.

Tanya stared at the business card in disbelief. 'Was he serious, Reverend?'

'Certainly.' The clergyman smiled at her. 'His emporiums are prestigious establishments. His grandfather built up their business empire from a small shop in Whitechapel. His father married money and continued the expansion. Mr Vernon's grandfather is in his eighties, but he will not allow his family to forget their roots. They donate generously to the poor of this parish. There is nothing about their reputation or status that your father could object to.'

Tanya was not so certain, but she had enjoyed working on the carnival float. It wasn't as though Mr Vernon was suggesting a permanent position, just a few months of preparation on the grotto and possibly a week setting it up in the stores by the end of November. It was an exciting prospect, a way to bring some magic into children's lives. And it was suddenly very important to her. She was determined that her father should not stop her.

She was walking towards the omnibus stop when she recognised Sam's voice calling out to her.

'I caught the end of the carnival,' he said, his eyes sparkling like golden wine. 'The float was spectacular. Everyone was commenting upon it. congratulations for winning the best float award. What was the prize?'

'I don't know. But that wasn't the most wonderful thing that happened.' She was bubbling with excitement. 'Mr Vernon who owns the Vernon Emporiums has asked me to design a fairy grotto for his shops this Christmas. Isn't that astounding?'

They reached the stop just as the omnibus pulled up. Sam said, 'Vernon knows talent when he sees it. I'm about to visit your father. Do you mind if I travel with you?'

'Of course not. I'd enjoy your company.'

They broke off speaking as they filed onto the omnibus and it set off with a clanging of its bell towards the centre of the city. Once they were settled, Sam smiled to her. 'If men like Vernon are interested in your talent, you could have quite a career starting for you. But will your father permit you to take paid employment?'

'I've been thinking about that. My pupils did so well with the float, they could help me. It would give Polly extra money and also Joe, who could help me cost everything. He still hasn't been able to find work with his crippled hand. I'd arrange it so that I was working for myself. It is only for a few months. Christmas is only once a year, after all.'

'I hope the brigadier agrees to your idea.' Sam grinned. 'Wait until I come back from my business trip next week, you may find he is in a better frame of mind.'

'You sound very mysterious. What will you be doing on this trip?'

'Wait and see,' he teased.

Tanya was aware of the heat of Sam's body as he sat on the wooden seat beside her. 'Why won't you tell me?'

'Because the deal may not come off. And it don't do to count your chickens before they're hatched. You'd do well to remember that before you get too excited about this scheme. I can't see the brigadier giving in to it easily.'

Her eyes widened artfully. 'You could put in a good word for me. He listens to you, Sam.'

He shook his head. 'The brigadier has strong

views about what he considers right for his daughter. Personally, I think it's a great idea. I can't see any harm in it. You've a talent for this work and it will give a great many people pleasure.'

Tanya sighed. 'If only I didn't have to wait until I married to receive Aunt Maude's money. I could live independently and do what I liked.'

Sam raised an eyebrow. 'Happen that's why your aunt made the stipulation. For all your headstrong ways, you're only seventeen. No respectable woman leaves the protection of her family before she marries if she wishes to keep her reputation untarnished.'

'Then I hope your business deal goes well and you put Papa into a good mood. I hate being cosseted. I want to be independent and do something worthwhile with my life. Marriage is not the be all and end all of every woman's aspirations.'

'Just don't let the brigadier hear that,' Sam cautioned, 'or any man you intend to wed. It will be a crushing blow to their ego.'

She regarded him seriously. His expression was taut and guarded, revealing nothing of his emotions. Had he truly not felt anything when he kissed her? He had moved into the rooms above his garage the next day and had taken to visiting her father on the evenings when she was teaching.

'How is business?' she asked, changing the subject.

'Business is good. People are prepared to buy second-hands cars. The industry is improving car models so quickly that the wealthy are keen to sell their older vehicles for the latest ones.'

'I'm pleased for you, Sam. And also that Papa is your partner. The army meant so much to him. It has given him a new interest and I'm sure has contributed to his recovery.'

He shrugged aside her praise. 'And how are you, Tanya? You look very well. Are you still seeing Tilbury?'

'Occasionally we dine or go to the theatre.'

'Is your relationship serious?' His tawny stare was fierce and his voice gruff.

After the way he had rejected her friendship, she resented his enquiry. 'Why must people put labels on relationships? I enjoy his company.'

'A man does not call regularly upon a woman unless his intentions are serious.'

'You sound just like Stella. Am I supposed to become a recluse for fear of gossip?'

'I would not see you hurt.'

'Why should I be hurt?'

He did not answer but there was tension in the tilt of his jaw as they disembarked and walked towards Pilgrim's Crescent.

'Answer me, Sam.'

Still he hesitated until they were on the steps of her home. 'It's just a feeling I have about the man.'

She rounded on him, her eyes blazing as they entered the house. Sam had made it clear that he was not interested in her as a friend. Why then was he so against Archie? Men were such peculiar creatures. Why did they always think they knew best? 'If I didn't know you better, Sam

Hawkes, I'd think that you were jealous.'

The angry rustle of the silk of her black dress accompanied her rapid progress up the stairs to her room.

Sam whistled through his teeth. She hadn't liked him passing judgement on Tilbury. Was she in love with him? Pain stabbed him. A pain he had no right to feel.

He frowned. Was he jealous? To dwell on that thought was to walk on quicksand. Tanya's involvement with Tilbury certainly troubled him. The incident at Earl's Court continued to plague him. By asking around he'd learned that the man Tilbury was talking to was the gangleader Slasher Gilbert. No respectable man kept such company. He was determined to find out more about Tilbury. Tanya's safety could depend upon it.

Tanya had reached the landing. Sam took the stairs two at a time to overtake her. His hand caught her wrist to halt her. The touch of her skin scorched his palm. There was an uncomfortable knot in the pit of his stomach. He wanted to protect her, to shield her from pain. Yet how could he? She was so proud and beautiful. Too proud and beautiful for his peace of mind. Her will was indomitable, but all women were vulnerable to man's greater strength.

'Why don't you visit your friend in Tunbridge Wells? It would do you good to get away for a while.'

'Papa will not allow me to travel unescorted and Stella says she cannot spare Millie from her duties.'

He did not release her and she made no

attempt to pull away. 'I could drive you down in the car and collect you when you wish.'

His generosity banished her resentment at his questions. 'That's very kind of you, Sam. I'll write to Clare. They are in the south of France until the end of September.'

Impulsively she stood on tiptoe and kissed his cheek, her eyes shining with excitement. 'Thank you.'

Inexorably his head bent towards hers. He couldn't take his eyes from her lips which were parting in silent invitation.

'Sam! Is that you I hear?'

The brigadier's strident voice from the study broke the spell and they pulled apart. Without a word, Sam hurried down the stairs, feeling as if all the temptations of Hades were ready to swamp him.

That evening Tanya wrote to Clare. It wasn't just the thought of a visit to her friend which made her sing as she wrote. It was the long drive in Sam's company.

When she had finished her letter, she sought her father's permission for Mr Vernon's proposal. On entering his study she was delighted to see how much better he was looking. His complexion was a healthy pink and his eyes were bright though he had lost a lot of weight with his illness. He was still unable to shake the bouts of sickness.

'Tanya, you're looking pleased with yourself. Sam said you plan to spend some time with Clare Grosvenor. That's a splendid idea.'

'Has Sam left?' She had hoped that Sam was

still with her father.

'He's gone to get me some tobacco as I forgot to ask Ginny to buy it earlier.'

'You don't mind me visiting Clare?'

He looked at her and sighed. 'Am I such an ogre? Sam says I should trust you and that I should listen to your views. But convention is there to protect you.'

In recent weeks they had spent more time together and she had encouraged him to tell her of his time in Africa and India. At last they seemed to be building bridges of understanding. She kissed his cheek and sat in the leather chair opposite him.

'Sam said that you'd won the best float award in the carnival. Well done! I'm proud of you,' he pleased her by saying. 'The Summersfields have risen high because they give an example to others. But I trust that will be the end of this episode. Have you informed Reverend Carver that you will no longer be teaching?'

'I did not want to spoil the pleasure my pupils had in their achievement today by telling them that I could not teach.' She mastered her resentment. He was at least talking to her as an adult and not bellowing orders to be mindlessly obeyed. 'I will do so on Monday.'

'Good. I understand your wish to help these people but such work is unsuitable for a woman of your position. I'm glad you've come to your senses.'

She kept her voice neutral. 'I'm obeying your wishes, Papa. It does not mean that I agree with them. I'll go mad if I have to mope around the house all day with nothing but menial duties to perform. My design for the float has led to a proposition.' At his frown she ploughed on. 'Mr Vernon who owns Vernon Emporiums has asked that I design the Christmas grottos in his stores.'

He eyed her stonily. 'It's out of the question. I'm surprised you even considered it. It's preposterous. My daughter a paid employee? Never.'

'It will not be like that. Please hear me out, Papa.'

A nod indicated that she should proceed, but he was twirling the waxed ends of his moustache, his flushed cheeks warning her he was controlling his disapproval.

'I find the prospect exciting. It would also give much needed work to my pupils. If I take the work on, it will be for a set fee. I will design the grottos and employ people to make the costumes and build the scenery. I shall be the artistic consultant.'

'Tanya, the Summersfields do not engage in trade.'

'Do we not, Papa? Then pray what is this partnership you have with Sam if it is not trade?'

His colour deepened alarmingly. 'That is different. I hope to persuade Sam to race the Panhard at Brooklands. It is a gentleman's sport. I have nothing to do with the business side of our arrangement, other than as an investor.'

'You are splitting hairs, Papa. Why shouldn't I use my talent as an artist to give people pleasure?' She struggled to stop her voice rising. If she lost her temper she would lose the argument. Instead, she sought to reason. 'It would pay to have the roof repaired. This house is going to ruin because there's no money to maintain it. What's the point of outmoded ideals when we no longer have the money to preserve our status?'

'So you think I've failed in my obligations.' Spittle flecked his moustache at the force of his anger. 'I suppose you are disappointed that I have not launched you into polite society or taken you to more regimental balls?'

'No, Papa. I have no intention of being put on display to attract a wealthy husband. I would rather save the finances of our family by working for my living than by degrading myself in that fashion.'

'And what is your role in life, if not to marry well?' he bellowed.

Tanya gripped her hands together to control her temper. 'I have a brain and I want to use it. I'm your only surviving child. You would not have condemned Harry or Ben if they had applied their ingenuity to improve the family finances. So why condemn me? I will not be doing any manual work myself, if that's what you fear. I shall be employing people for that.'

'The idea is preposterous. A woman setting herself up in business … the very idea…'

Instinct told her to appeal to the qualities he admired and had instilled in his sons. 'It takes courage for a woman to enter a man's world. But it's not unknown for a woman to have inherited a business and succeeded. If I were intimidated by a male-dominated world I would not be confronting you now. I thought you admired courage, Papa. Please, give me this chance.'

'The idea is outrageous. I do not want this subject mentioned again.'

His words crushed her. She had begun to hope that she had won him round. 'What are you afraid of, Papa? That I might succeed?'

'That's enough, Tanya. You forget your place. You are a Summersfield.'

'You don't have to remind me of that. I've been brought up on the stories of my ancestors' courage and bravery. I had not realised that the men were also bigoted and despotic. I will call on Mr Vernon and inform him that my father is too entrenched in male supremacy to allow his daughter to face the challenge of succeeding in a man's world.'

'A woman's place is in the home,' he shouted.

'What as? A prisoner? For that is how you would treat me. And if you had your way I'd exchange this gaol for another when I marry.'

'And you had better get used to the idea. No decent man allows his wife to work. Not only is it his job to provide for his family, but any work done by a woman is taking the job a man could be doing.'

Until now she had been too concerned with gaining some independence to consider she could be taking employment from a man. Even so, she still rebelled. If her talent as an artist was the greater, then didn't she have the right to use it? And wasn't she intending to employ men to build the scenery? Stealing a man's job indeed! If she had her way she'd be providing employment for them.

She stormed out of the study and collided with

Sam who had been waiting to enter. Her cheeks burned with humiliation that he must have heard her father treating her like a halfwit.

'Tanya,' he said consolingly.

Her green eyes glittered with mutiny. 'I suppose you agree with him. You don't know how lucky you were to be born a man. I wish I had been, but without your inbred narrow-mindedness. Why must you all treat us as inferior and only fit to pander to your needs? What are you afraid of? That women might be better at some things than men?'

Sam bit his lip to stop a smile. She was glorious in her anger. And probably right.

'I suppose you must have heard some of that, Sam.' The brigadier shook his head wearily when Sam entered the room. 'I don't know what gets into the girl.'

'What would you expect from a Summersfield, sir? She's a fighter. And is what she's asking for so terrible?'

'You think I am wrong to stop her?' The brigadier rubbed his moustache, his manner stiff with affront.

'If she was my daughter I'd be proud of her for having both the talent and the determination to succeed.'

'Wait until you're a father,' the brigadier scoffed. 'You'll feel differently then.'

'I sincerely hope not, sir.'

'You're impertinent.'

Sam picked up his cap and gloves where he had tossed them onto a chair. 'Goodnight, sir. I'm pleased that you are obviously stronger. Unlike your daughter, I don't have to tolerate your rudeness.'

He had reached the door before he was called back.

'So you think I was too hard on the girl?'

'I think that you should listen to Tanya. As I have said before, she's an intelligent and talented woman.'

The brigadier pulled the bellrope. When Ginny appeared, he barked out, 'Inform my daughter that I will discuss the matter of her visit to Mr Vernon with her in the morning.'

When they were again alone, he shook his head and sighed. 'She should have been a boy, Sam.'

'Her sentiments exactly. But I think Tanya will give any man a run for his money. She is your daughter, after all.'

Summersfield threw back his head and laughed. Pride roughened his voice. 'Ay, she's a fighter.'

Chapter Fifteen

It was four days before Tanya saw Sam to thank him for his intervention. He had called on her father in the evening and when she heard him leave, she waylaid him in the hall. He shrugged aside her gratitude as she led him into the conservatory where two oil lamps cast a warming glow over the fading tapestry on the chairs.

'Papa was not going to listen to me,' she insisted. 'I am in your debt. But I did have to agree to give up teaching. Reverend Carver was very understanding. Archie was annoyed. He regarded it as a slight after all the trouble he had taken.'

'Will you still be seeing him?'

'Occasionally, and there is no reason why I should not. He is a charming companion.' Her tone had inadvertently sharpened. 'He has asked me to dine and afterwards see a play next week.'

Sam stood ramrod straight, a muscle pumping along his jaw. For a moment her heart seemed to stop. Would he tell her not to see Tilbury and invite her out instead.

'How did your meeting with Mr Vernon go?'

Concealing her disappointment, she managed a weak smile. 'I saw him today. Sit down while I tell you, Sam. You don't have to rush off do you?'

Sam was reluctant to stay. Tanya was in his thoughts too often and he avoided being alone with her. But it would be unfair to leave when she was so excited about her new adventure. She sat opposite him on the chaise longue. The light behind her gave her hair a halo of golden amber as it curled over her shoulders. As she spoke she glowed with an inner radiance. Each time he saw her she was more lovely.

'I had drawn several sketches for him to approve. He liked them all. He wants a different idea in every store. He hopes it will encourage his customers to visit more than one of his emporiums over the Christmas period. It's a lot of work and organisation. And at first he was against me employing my own staff for the work. I insisted on it and eventually he agreed.'

'Have you spoken to Polly, Joe and the others yet?'

'I'll call on Polly tomorrow.'

'Where does she live?'

When Tanya told him, he frowned. 'That's in the Courtyard, one of the worst rookeries in the East End. You can't go alone.'

'I'm not seeing Archie until Saturday. I must visit Polly now. She lost her job at the shirt factory last week for hitting her employer when he caught her alone in the storeroom and tried to molest her. Besides, it will be daylight.'

'If you leave it until lunchtime I'll come with you. I don't like you going there by yourself.'

'You've your own business to run, Sam.'

'Can't I help out a friend?'

She smiled and teased, 'I thought you believed that a man and a woman couldn't be friends, Sam.'

He glowered at her and stood up. 'I'll call at midday.'

Tanya wore a black tailored suit. Even dressed so plainly, she regretted that the cut of her suit and the rich material would make her stand out among the poverty of the East End. When she voiced her misgivings to Sam, he laughed.

'It isn't what you wear which places you apart from them. It's the way you carry yourself. You've a noble grace and bearing which would draw eyes to you even if you walked along Pall Mall in rags.'

Tanya blushed and looked away. She had missed Sam since he moved to the rooms above his garage. The thought of spending an afternoon with him set her blood sizzling through her veins. Today he looked exceptionally handsome. He rarely wore a cap now and dressed as a gentleman in a dark grey suit and homburg.

'I didn't bring the car,' Sam said. 'I thought it best we took the tuppenny Tube.'

'I've never been on it. Aunt Maude always refused to travel underground like a mole.'

'It can get crowded at times, but at this time of day it shouldn't be too bad.'

Tanya shivered as they walked through the white tiled tunnel and descended the steps to the platform. After the heat of the afternoon sun, it was cool underground and she was surprised by how many people were waiting for a train, ranging from men in top hats to women with young children.

'The Tube is often quicker than travelling by road now that the traffic is so heavily congested in the city,' Sam explained.

There was a fierce gust of air which made her reach up to secure her hat. A loud whoosh was followed by a rattling which sounded as though the Devil was trying to burst out of restraining chains. Then the train hurtled out of the far tunnel. Tanya was nervous as they sat side by side in the swaying carriage. Though it was lit, she felt the black walls of the tunnel closing in on her as they sped towards the next station. Sam took her hand and squeezed it and her fear dissipated at the feel of his warm fingers wrapped round her own.

'Quite a feat of engineering, this,' Sam said wryly, 'but I admit it gave me the collywobbles the first time I used it.'

At last they emerged from the gloom of the underground station into the dazzling daylight at Tower Green. They walked past the sinister walls and turrets of the Tower of London to enter a maze of back streets. Immediately Tanya was struck by the change of atmosphere. In the city everyone was rushing between offices or to the chophouses for their lunch. Their expressions were grave and harassed. Here the people were shabbier and more vociferous; there was a large immigrant population and foreign phrases were to be heard as much as native English. The different nationalities and cultures tended to keep to themselves so that certain streets were predominantly inhabited by the Irish or European Jews or by Chinamen or Negroes, and every street carried its own cooking smells – onions, cabbage, tripe, fish or exotic spices. Yet despite the poverty there was often laughter from the women sitting outside their front doors. They gossiped with their neighbours as they shelled peas, patched a pair of trousers or darned socks.

Tanya stepped carefully over the debris accumulated in the central runnels between the terraced houses. It wasn't yet one o'clock in the afternoon yet Sam guided her round a drunk snoring in the gutter. Several young boys wearing clothes cut down from their father's cast-offs poked at the drunk with sticks.

'Clear off, you little beggars,' Sam shouted at them.

'Who's gonna make us?'

'I could bang your heads together or,' Sam tossed some coppers into the air, 'you could go and get yourself some sweets down the corner shop.'

Bare feet were trampled under oversize boots as the boys scampered for the coins. Then yelling and pushing each other, they ran off to the sweet shop.

'Kids don't change, do they?' Sam chuckled.

Tanya was filled with pity for the children who looked half starved and she did not answer. They were nothing like the plump satin and velvet clad children of her childhood. These were the type of streets where Sam had grown up. Several of the houses had smashed windows.

'What's that awful smell?' Tanya would have liked to raise her scented handkerchief to her nose, but too many curious glances from the women prevented her.

'It's the communal middens out the back,' Sam whispered. 'The wind is blowing in this direction.'

They approached a corner shop where a lad stood on duty outside, protecting the household goods on display on the pavement from being stolen.

'I've got to get some cigarettes,' Sam said, walking inside.

Tanya stared around the tiny shop, amazed at the assortment of wares it stocked. Tin baths battled for space with vegetables, sweets, saucepans and hammers. Wooden tubs of sugar and tea stood in front of the crowded counter, the brass scoops used to weigh out each customers' order sitting on top. A man wearing a muffler despite the heat was rummaging through a box of tools and while the shopkeeper served Sam, Tanya saw the customer pocket a brass door hinge and handle, then walk to the door.

''Ere, mate. You buying them?' the shopkeeper yelled.

'Not bleedin' likely, mate. Too bloody dear.' He scarpered before the shopkeeper could get from behind the counter.

Seeing Tanya's shocked expression, Sam winked. 'Thieving is a way of life here. It's a wonder some shopkeepers make any profit.'

They arrived at Polly's house. It's front door was hanging off its hinges, one panel of the wood splintered as though it had been kicked open.

A woman scrubbing the doorstep of the next house eyed them belligerently. 'Who are you?' she demanded. Her voice was antagonistic and she lisped through several missing teeth. 'Bloody toffs stickin' their noses in where they ain't wanted. There ain't no charity created to 'elp the likes of those two poor sods. Go back to your bloody soup kitchen.'

'I've come to offer Polly work,' Tanya returned.

'You that Summersfield woman?' The woman stood up. She was less than five feet and almost as round, her huge breasts resting on the waistband of her apron. Her straight hair was pulled into a tight bun at the nape of her neck. Two snotty-nosed toddlers peered from behind her, their arms speckled with bedbug and flea bites.

'I am.'

The antagonism vanished. 'Then 'appen you're welcome. Poll's spoken of you. Thinks the world of you, she does. If you can get 'er away from that bastard Frank, then you're an angel, Miss Summersfield. 'E's turned vicious lately. A real nasty piece of work, 'e is. All 'ell broke loose in there last night.'

'Stay here, Tanya. I'll go and look.' Sam moved inside, but Tanya followed. The place was tidy but bare. The only furniture in the downstairs room was two wooden chairs and scarred oak table. The fire was out in the kitchen.

'Are you upstairs, Polly?' Tanya called.

There was an indistinct noise which sounded like a sob. Staying close behind Sam, Tanya climbed the creaking stairs to the single room above. The window was covered and she had difficulty discerning anything in the gloom. There was a groan from one of the mattresses laid on the bare floorboards.

'It's Tanya Summersfield, Polly. Are you ill?'

'You shouldn't 'ave come, miss,' Polly croaked. 'It's Sal. She's real bad.'

Tanya flicked back the sacking which acted as a window curtain. What she saw made her gag. Both women's faces were bruised and beaten. Polly was kneeling and cradling Sal in her arms. The girl was staring wide-eyed and unblinking at a mildew patch on the wall. The blue dress she had worn as Alice was in tatters on her thin body which was gripped by violent shudders.

'That bastard Frank came 'ome drunk last night. While I were tending to the kid, who were screaming with colic, 'e came up 'ere and raped

Sal. By the time the kid were settled and I heard Sal's cries, it were too late. I 'ad to bash 'im over the head with the kettle to get 'im off 'er. Then the bastard 'ad a go at me. As we were fighting 'e tripped over the bedding and I 'eard 'is arm break. Frank made more noise than a cockerel getting its neck wrung and staggered out vowing to kill us when 'e got back.'

Polly rocked Sal back and forth like a baby, tears flowing down her cheeks. 'I can't rouse, Sal. I've been trying to get 'er away from 'ere before Frank returns. The sod lost 'is job because of the drink and now 'e reckons the two of us can whore for 'im.'

'We're here to help you, Polly,' Tanya said.

'The bastard went back on 'is word and never wed me like 'e promised,' Polly continued as though Tanya hadn't spoken. 'Frank were al right till the drinkin' started. I were afeared for Sal. That's why I made 'er come to your class. I 'oped it would save 'er from this.'

'Clearly you cannot stay here,' Tanya said. 'Wrap Sal up in that blanket and get yourself tidied and collect the baby's things. You're coming with us.'

Polly did as instructed and Tanya knelt on the mattress and held Sal against her breast, speaking to her softly. 'We're taking you away from here, Sal. He won't touch you again. You'll be safe. It's all right, dear. Everything will be all right now.' She looked up into Sam's angry face. 'Do you know of any rooms away from here? I'll pay the rent until Polly starts work.'

'There's a place going near the garage,' he answered. 'In fact I was going to suggest you might want to rent it for a workroom. It's got rooms above. They could stay at my place until I sort it out with the landlord.'

'That's good of you, Sam. I'll stay with them. Polly has enough to do looking after the baby.'

'I'll get a couple of hansom cabs to take us there.'

Sam returned quickly and Tanya held the sleeping baby while Polly wrapped the blanket gently round her sister's thin shoulders. Sal remained in her petrified trance. It wasn't until Sam stooped and put his arms round her to carry her out of the house that she flinched back.

'No. No. No! Get off me! No!' She struck him wildly with her fists.

Realising that the touch of a man resurrected the terror she had lived through last night, Polly took her hand. 'This is Sam, Miss Summersfield's friend. Sam ain't gonna hurt you. We're leaving 'ere, Sal. We gotta get away from Frank. I ain't gonna let this 'appen to you again.'

When Sal continued to hit Sam, Polly slapped her face. The girl fell silent, but the terror remained in her eyes.

Polly said gently, 'Sam needs to carry you down the stairs, Sal. We're takin' you somewhere you'll be safe, love.' She kept repeating the words until they reached the pavement.

Polly had thrown the possessions they owned into the thin blanket covering the other mattress and tied the corners in a knot. Outside in the street, several children had gathered around two horse-drawn cabs.

'You off then, Poll?' the neighbour who had spoken earlier asked.

'Yeah, and I ain't comin' back, Meg.'

'Then good luck.' She stared hard at Sal and her eyes misted. 'You never did see what a bastard that Frank were. Too soft 'earted, you are. My Sid will get the blokes on to Frank. That bastard will wish 'e'd never been born for touching Sal. She ain't more than fourteen, is she? There's a lot that's hard to stomach round 'ere, but Sid and 'is mates ain't about to let Frank get away with that. Blimey, 'e could be at their own girls next.'

As they were speaking, a driver of a small cart drawn by a shaggy pony drew up. 'What furniture you want shifted?' he demanded.

'Sam, you're a wonder,' Tanya declared. 'I was so worried about Polly and Sal, I didn't give their furniture a thought. And my sewing machine is still here. We'll need that to start our business.'

Polly looked worried. 'I'll need me stuff from the kitchen. What furniture there is I bought meself.'

Meg stepped forward. 'Get on your way, Polly. Me and the other women will get your stuff packed up. Ain't no one gonna nick nothing. You've always been there for any of us when we needed you.'

Sam told the man with the cart where to deliver the furniture.

Polly hugged the older woman. 'Thanks, Meg.'

Without a backward glance she climbed into the hansom beside the shuddering Sal. Since

Sam had placed her in the cab, Sal had not made a sound and continued her unseeing wide-eyed stare.

Tanya sat beside Sam as the two carriages pulled away. 'I can't understand men like that.'

'He'll get his comeuppance,' Sam ground out. 'I'm afraid that against man's superior strength women will always be at risk of becoming victims of violence and rape.'

'At least we can help Sal. I'll get a doctor to see her.'

Sam shook his head. 'It will only frighten her – any man will frighten her in her present state. It's a stable and safe environment that she needs. And you're giving them that.'

A church clock struck three as they passed the Monument, the column that marked the start of the fire that destroyed London in 1666. In a side street close to London Bridge the cab halted outside a warehouse. There was a faint smell of fish in the air from Billingsgate market further along the river.

An hour later Polly and Sal were settled in Sam's lodgings. There was a kitchen, two bedrooms and a bay-windowed sunny parlour.

Sam returned from an apothecary's with some laudanum for Sal. 'Mind you keep to the dosage,' he warned Polly. 'You don't want her getting reliant on the stuff.'

The laudanum sent Sal into a deep sleep. Seeing the dark circles under Polly's eyes, Tanya made her a cup of tea. 'It's going to be all right, Polly. Sal is safe here. She's a strong child and will recover in time.' She went on to talk about her plans for the future and offered Polly the job of seamstress.

'It's a kind offer, Miss Tanya. But it's temporary, ain't it? What will 'appen after Christmas?'

'You're a fine seamstress,' Tanya declared. 'Your work on the costumes proved that. There will always be work for you. I promise you that.'

Polly hesitated. Then looking into Tanya's determined face, she nodded. 'I'll not let you down, Miss Tanya.'

Tanya relaxed. 'Now all I need is to send word to Joe. I'd like him to cost the work for me. As part of his wages he'll be instructed by a retired accountant on how to keep detailed books.'

Sam caught Tanya's attention. 'I'll go and arrange with the landlord for the rooms and workshop along the road. The rooms are identical to the ones here.'

'All right, Sam,' she answered.

By the time he returned with the keys, Polly's furniture had arrived. It didn't take long to arrange it in the upper rooms.

'Already the place is looking like a home,' Tanya encouraged.

To her dismay, Polly burst into tears. 'I don't know how to thank you, Miss Tanya.'

'It was nothing. I needed a workshop and it would be a shame for these rooms to go to waste.'

Sam touched Tanya's shoulder. 'It's getting late. It wouldn't do for your father to get worried that you've been out so long.'

Tanya looked at her watch and was astonished to see it was almost five o'clock. She turned to Polly. 'I'll call tomorrow to see how Sal is.'

'Bless you, Miss Tanya.'

Sam laid two half-crowns on the table. 'Get yourself some pie and mash from the shop down by the wharf for tonight. The rest will get you some food for a couple of days.'

Polly blushed as she stared into his handsome face. 'You're a good man, sir.'

Sam waved aside her gratitude.

Tanya followed him into the street, saying, 'I'm so grateful to you for all you've done, Sam. I've kept you too long from your work.' She turned to look at the double doors of the garage beneath the rooms, with their fresh coat of green paint and white lettering, EVERYMAN MOTORS. 'So this is where you work,' she said. 'How many motor cars have you sold?'

'Two. But I've bought three more this week which had been mouldering in private garages after the coachwork was damaged. I advertised in *The Times* and have several more to see. I have to be careful not to overstretch my capital. I'm hoping an old friend of mine, from the carriage builders where I worked before the army, will help out. It should be very profitable, although to collect some of the vehicles I'll have to travel to Berkshire and Sussex. That means I'll not be able to visit the brigadier so often.'

'I'm glad you're doing so well, Sam. The garage looks impressive.'

He whistled to a hansom driver waiting on the corner. 'I'll come back with you and call on the brigadier. I'm away for the next two days.'

The hansom cut through the traffic past Billingsgate fish market, the smell of fish pungent in the air. As they approached Pilgrim's Crescent, Tanya saw Archie walking away from their house. His face was pale with anger.

'I wasn't aware that Archie was calling today,' she said, puzzled. 'Stella must have invited him to take tea with us. Now she'll be irritable that I'm late.'

'Does he call often?' Sam's voice was strained.

'You don't like him, do you? Why?' She held her breath waiting for his answer. Today more than ever she had been aware of him in a way that she never was of Archie.

'I don't trust him.'

'That's not good enough, Sam.' Her voice was husky.

Sam shut his mind to its invitation, concentrating instead on Tilbury. He hated to admit that Tanya was right. He had no proof that Tilbury was up to no good. Since the brigadier had first asked him to make enquiries about Tilbury and he'd refused, his need to protect Tanya had made him change his mind. So far he had learned nothing incriminating. But he was convinced that Tilbury was not what he seemed. He couldn't shake off the feeling that the man was hiding something and he was determined to find out what.

Archie was finding it difficult to control his anger with Tanya. All Granville's money was gone and still she hadn't agreed to marry him. He wanted to cut his losses and run, but to leave for America without any money behind him was not in his plans. He was going to live there in style not squalor.

At least his work with the Gilbert brothers had turned out better than he'd anticipated. Slasher and Fancy ruled by brawn and terror. Neither of them were particularly bright. Within a week he'd come up with a plan to improve their organisation and a forgery scam to make their fortune. But it would take a couple of months to complete and Slasher had demanded three-quarters of the profits. Archie was in no position to argue. He had to keep the Gilbert brothers sweet until he could flee to America, and now, as he regarded the two villains over lunch in the back room of one of the clubs, he felt the pressure on him building.

The papers he had forged so that Slasher could steal James Fenton's property had caused a devil of a rumpus. Harold Fenton, the police inspector, had been stirring up trouble for the Gilberts. They had brazened it out. They'd paid enough in bribes to the police to feel secure. Although Inspector Fenton suspected that the papers were forgeries, they had been declared legal by an eminent London barrister and a banker.

Archie had lived in terror while the papers were being investigated. If Slasher was implicated in forgery, they would be after the man who had forged the papers. He could spend the rest of his life in prison if he went down for a crime like that.

There had also been the rumpus caused by James Fenton's disappearance.

'That were clever of you, Archie, suggesting the

body become part of the foundations of that new picture palace,' Fancy had sniggered. 'Without a body there ain't no murder case.'

Archie had suggested the plan to preserve his own hide. He was still uneasy. 'Inspector Fenton won't let it rest,' he warned.

'Nothing 'e can do.' Slasher sharpened one of his daggers on a grindstone. 'Didn't I get witnesses to swear that James Fenton 'ad left a card game declaring 'e couldn't face the shame of it. I told the police I reckoned 'e'd scarpered. 'Appens, don't it? Couldn't face the shame or bear to see 'is family thrown out on the street.'

Fancy chuckled. 'Ain't got nothing on us. Wasn't there that suicide last month when a banker threw 'imself off the roof of 'is bank because 'e'd lost 'is fortune on the Stock Exchange?'

'You're forgetting that with a suicide the body is usually found,' Archie cautioned. 'It doesn't do to assume Inspector Fenton is a fool. We're talking about his brother, for Chrissakes!'

Slasher brushed down the lapels of his jacket, his expression grim. He wasn't about to brag how Inspector Fenton had gone for him in an alley when he had caught him without one of his body guards. Slasher had been shaken. Fenton had sneaked up behind him before he could draw his knife and thrown him up against a wall.

'I'll nail you, Gilbert,' Inspector Fenton had raged.

Slasher had forced a laugh. 'You ain't got nothing on me.'

'Not yet, Gilbert. But I'm a patient man. You're

a villain and I'm the man who's going to put you away for a very long time.'

Slasher didn't get frightened, he got angry. Inspector Fenton must die. But to kill him too soon after his brother's disappearance would throw the guilt in his direction. He had to be patient even though it went against his nature. Even the police he'd bribed would turn against him if he had one of their own killed.

Slasher smiled evilly at Archie. 'Fenton will end up like 'is brother before 'e can even get close to nailing us.'

Archie didn't have Slasher's confidence. They were bullies and Inspector Fenton was smart. His involvement with the Gilbert brothers' schemes made his flesh crawl with fear. He couldn't shake the notion that he was living on borrowed time.

'You've done well for us lately,' Slasher said now, sitting with one chunky leg propped over the arm of a chair. 'We need brains like yours. I want you to be in on all the meetings in future. I could do with a right 'and man who knows the ropes like you do.'

Greater involvement with the Gilberts was the last thing Archie was seeking. To hide his alarm he checked his appearance in the cracked mirror on the wall and sleeked back a lock of hair which had fallen forward on his brow. He lifted his mouth into a winning, confident smile.

'Always willing to be of service, Slasher.'

'Just keep it that way. I hear you've got plans fer a grand marriage, but you're one of us now. Think of our partnership like a marriage – till death do we part.'

Archie's lunch curdled in his stomach as he left the club. Carved in his mind were the tortured figures of Slasher's men who had betrayed the gangleader.

A figure detached itself from the shadows of the alley opposite and Archie's guts nearly betrayed him, bile rising to his throat as he held Inspector Fenton's hostile glare.

The inspector haunted the back streets of London searching for clues to condemn his brother's murderers. It was the first time Archie had come face to face with the man. Fenton was tall, wiry, with a piercing, intelligent stare that missed nothing. His pinstripe suit fitted his broad shoulders and narrow hips to perfection. An educated man from a wealthy family. Slasher was a fool if he thought he could outwit this policeman.

It was as well that he was dressed in cap and waistcoat, Archie thought as he hurried past. The disguise should stop him being recognised as Tilbury. But it could link him to Arnie Potter who was still wanted for questioning about the murder of Granville. Panic gripped him. He suspected that the inspector would recognise him again. That was dangerous. He didn't want his links with the Gilbert brothers becoming known to the Summersfields. He ran his finger along the damp collar of his shirt. He couldn't afford to delay marrying Tanya. She wasn't responding to the impressive places he had taken her and remained cool towards him if he spoke of their future. He'd have to take more drastic action over her. How long would his luck hold before someone rumbled him? It wasn't just Fenton who was interested in his movements. Hawkes had started to ask questions about him according to one of Slasher's henchmen.

Now he was in thick with the Gilberts it did have compensations. He'd set a couple of thugs to follow Hawkes. He had to get the soldier out of the way soon. The business had been delayed too long as it was.

Chapter Sixteen

Tanya was in her nightgown, seated on a stool in her bedroom while Millie brushed the tangles from her long hair. The middle-aged maid was used to gossiping with Maude, which Tanya often found wearying.

At least Millie's endless chatter took her mind from the heartache she was feeling. She could no longer deny her attraction to Sam. But he continued to treat her as a sister. While he was closeted with her father she had played the piano for an hour hoping that he would come to her. Instead he had taken the brigadier out in the car.

Male voices carried to them and her father broke into a song.

Millie giggled. 'That's your father back and he sounds rather merry. Mr Hawkes is helping him to his room. Such a nice man, Mr Hawkes. And so good to the brigadier.'

Tanya did not answer, hoping Millie would

change the subject. The maid continued to babble on. 'He has a way about him. He makes people feel special. You must have noticed it. If I were twenty years younger, I'd be hopelessly in love with him. And Miss Maude, God rest her loving soul, liked him. Even Ginny has her eye on him – little good it will do her. He's going far, that young man. A captain, even a non-commissioned one, won't be courting no parlour maid.'

Was he as charming to the parlour maid as he was to her? Tanya wondered wretchedly. Jealousy burned in her breast. She was his commanding officer's daughter. He could hardly be rude or ignore her. She put up a hand to stop Millie brushing her hair.

'Like must marry like,' Millie continued. 'Though I wouldn't be surprised if Mr Hawkes doesn't better himself by marriage. Got his own business now. That makes him middle-class and with those handsome looks, he could marry an heiress.'

'That will be all, Millie,' Tanya interrupted. 'I'll not need you further tonight.'

Millie picked up the discarded clothes and proceeded to hang them in the wardrobe. 'I expect you'll be next to hear wedding bells now Mr Tilbury is a regular caller. Miss Stella implied as much while I was helping her dress this morning.'

'I have no intention of marrying Mr Tilbury.' Tanya's voice showed her irritation. 'My aunt, for some reason, seems set on the match.'

Millie lowered her voice to a conspiratorial

whisper. 'Miss Maude reckoned it was because the brigadier was against him. Miss Stella never liked to be crossed. If you were to wed Mr Tilbury she would see it as a triumph over her brother. She'd rather you wed someone she introduced to you than any suitor first approved by the brigadier.'

Tanya lost patience with the subject. 'I'll not be part of petty family squabbles. I shall marry the man I love or I will not marry at all.'

She drew a sapphire satin robe over her night-gown and lifted amber-gold curls free to fall to her waist.

Millie smiled. 'I know you will choose wisely. Miss Maude had a secret fancy that you would wed Mr Hawkes. She thought that he was the right man for you.'

'Dear Aunt Maude was a romantic dreamer.'

The grandfather clock in the hall struck ten o'clock. Outside on the landing a man's tread approached her door. Tanya's heart missed a beat at the curt rap on the wood.

'Miss Tanya,' Sam clipped out.

Tanya was at the door before Millie could reach it. The oil lamp on a nearby table threw Sam's face into shadow. He looked haggard and worried. 'You'd best go to your father. It looks like his heart again. It came on sudden after he took his medicine. I'm going to fetch the doctor.'

As Tanya crossed to her father's room, Stella opened her bedroom door.

'Did I hear that Reginald is ill?'

'Sam is going for the doctor,' Tanya explained.

Stella's eyes blazed with hatred as she glared at

Sam. 'This is all your fault. Reginald needed rest and you took him out. And he's been drinking. If he dies, you are to blame.'

Sam paled as he hurried to the top of the stairs.

Tanya ran after him. 'Pay no need to Aunt Stella. She didn't mean that.'

'She meant it.'

'But it's nonsense. You've done so much to help Papa. You must not blame yourself.'

'If anyone is to blame in this house, it's not me.'

With those disturbing words he bounded down the stairs, holding on to the banister to favour his injured knee.

Tanya was appalled at how ill her father looked. He seemed to be barely breathing as he lay unconscious on the bed. When Dr Garrett arrived, he shook his head. 'It doesn't look good. It's his heart. There's nothing anyone can do. I shall call back in the morning.'

'I don't understand it,' Tanya cried. 'He was so much better. Perhaps an army doctor should examine him, one who is familiar with foreign diseases.'

'Another doctor can do no more than myself, I assure you, Miss Summersfield. But you are entitled to a second opinion.'

'I have complete faith in Dr Garrett,' Stella announced, planting herself in the chair by the bedside. 'I shall watch over him, Doctor. I shall give him my most devoted attention.'

Tanya hovered. Sam was escorting the doctor to his motor car.

'Go to bed, Tanya,' her aunt instructed. 'There's nothing you can do. I got him through the last crisis. I shall do so again this time.'

'I shall telephone the regiment in the morning and ask for a doctor to attend him,' Tanya insisted. She had to do something.

Stella sucked in her cheeks. 'As you will, if it puts your mind at rest.'

The next afternoon an army doctor arrived to examine the brigadier; by then even to Tanya's inexperienced eye her father was looking much stronger.

'I agree with Dr Garrett's diagnosis. It is his heart. Plenty of rest is what he needs, a light diet and no alcohol or cigars. If he is so much stronger today, your aunt must be taking good care of him.'

Tanya's spirits were heavy when he left; clearly her father was not recovering as she had hoped from his earlier attack. It looked like he would be an invalid for some time. Returning to his room, she said, 'I will sit with Papa for a while. You also need your rest, Aunt. Do you think that we should engage a nurse for Papa?'

'Certainly not. I won't have it said that I failed in my duty to look after my own brother when he has need of me.'

'Then show me what I must do and I will assist you.'

'You have enough to deal with working on the grottos for Mr Vernon.' Seeing the stubborn look in Tanya's eyes, Stella added, 'You can sit with Reginald while I prepare a strengthening tisane for him. Perhaps I will rest for an hour or two.'

She stayed with her father while he dozed

through the afternoon. Thankfully there was no sign of the vomiting which had previously accompanied his attacks. She had insisted that he eat some chicken broth; his colour was more healthy by the time Sam arrived in the early evening and she left the two men together.

Too restless to return to her room, Tanya roamed the house, drawn to the glass conservatory with its potted palms and cool tiled floor. The conservatory was bathed in moonlight, the palm fronds dark and casting long shadows. She sat on the cushioned window seat and leaning her head against a window pillar drew up her legs beneath her. The evening was warm without even a breeze to cool it. Unbuttoning three buttons on her bodice, she fanned herself with a piece of sketch paper. Staring up at the full moon, she prayed that her father would recover from this latest attack.

A footstep from the adjoining room startled her and she turned to discover Sam watching her. His gaze was drawn to the open neck of her gown and with a start she realised that she had revealed the upper curves of her breasts.

Hastily she pulled the edges of the bodice together. 'I thought you'd gone, Sam. But I'm glad you're here. How did Papa come to have a relapse? Had he drunk too much yesterday? Overexerted himself?'

'He'd only had a couple of brandies and some wine with his meal. He seemed fine. He complained at having to take his medicine when your aunt brought it in. She stood over him while he drank it and lectured him on overdoing things and of course drinking too much. Then she gave me a tongue lashing for encouraging him. Though stopping your father from taking a brandy is nigh on impossible when his mind is set on it. I'm glad you insisted that another doctor examine him.'

Sam was holding a brandy decanter and glass and looked questioningly at her.

'Please help yourself to a drink, Sam,' she said. 'Not that the doctor was any help. He did insist that Papa have no alcohol or cigars and that will not improve his temper. Aunt Stella means well, I suppose. But she can be overbearing at times. That can't help Papa. I often hear them quarrelling.' She watched Sam toss back his drink, then added, 'I hope that Papa is going to be all right. After Aunt Maude…' Tears overwhelmed her.

'He's already improving,' Sam reassured her. His arm slid round her shoulders and he held her close without speaking. His arms were a haven. She clung to him as her grief washed over her, unstoppable. Gradually her sobs quietened and she was aware of the smell of brandy on his breath and of the heat of his body through the thinness of her gown. Embarrassed, she pulled back and swept her hair back from her eyes. He held a clean handkerchief to her cheeks and tenderly dried her tears.

'Here, have some of this. It will help to calm you.'

He raised the brandy glass to her lips and unthinking she drank deeply. The fiery liquid made her gasp, but as its heat spread through her veins, she felt a languor settle over her.

'I'm sorry, Sam. I'm not usually the weeping type.'

His hand remained on her shoulder and she could feel his fingers burning through to her flesh. Her heavy-lidded eyes lifted to meet his gaze. The longing she saw there made her heart sing through her misery. He swallowed hard, the hollows beneath his high cheekbones were pronounced as he stared at her.

'Oh, Sam. Sam!' she breathed. She touched her fingers to his lips.

Sam knew he should leave. It was madness to stay.

He stared down at her, enslaved by her beauty. Her hair was silvered by the moonlight, tendrils curling along her neck and tumbling over the full curves of her breasts. Mesmerised, he wound a thick curl round his fingers.

Tanya leaned towards him and his free hand traced the line of her jaw, the warmth of her breath fanning his skin. Of their own volition his fingers trailed along her throat and he felt the rapid beat of her heart. At her soft sigh, reason disintegrated. Passion resurged. His lips claimed hers, parting them to taste the sweetness of her breath. As his kiss deepened, her hands clung to his shoulders, moulding the firmness of her breasts against his chest. His need for her built to an intolerable ache. Her body moved sensually against him, her mouth opening with answering longing.

He was lost. Drowning in the sensuality of her. Barriers dissolved. Time, place and differences were irrelevant. Bodies demanded. Souls responded.

Tanya succumbed to the clamouring of her senses. Insidious as water lapping the shores of a lake, desire bathed her body. She loved him … wanted him…

She surrendered, moving restlessly so that his hand touched her breasts. To deny him would have been to deny breath itself. When the buttons of her bodice were unfastened, her blood quickened in anticipation. She felt no shame. Guilt was for those who gave without love. How could this be wrong? Sam loved her. The passion in his eyes spoke more profoundly than words.

Her hands were in his hair as she arched her back. His mouth caressed her breasts and her head rolled back, her hair a dark gold moonbeam cascading to the floor.

'Tanya, my darling.' The murmur was indistinct against her flesh but she had not imagined it. His tongue stroked delicately over her receptive nipple and pleasure welled up inside her, drowning modesty. Sam wanted her, cared for her. She lay full length on the window seat, a willing sacrificial virgin on a moonlit altar. An initiate to the Goddess of Love.

Sam was above her, the evidence of his arousal against her stomach. Sensuously, shockingly, her body craved to be caressed by him, possessed by him. A storm of emotions was evoked as his hands and lips played over her flesh. His kiss was endless, infinitely tender, his tongue teasing, demanding, leaving her trembling with desire.

When his hand moved to her thigh, stroking the silken softness, a myriad of thrills pulsated through her. She was damp with yearning, her love transcending morality. When his fingers moved along her thigh to enter her they were tender, experienced, deliciously enthralling, evoking an all-consuming passion. She had no will to stop him, no wish to. This was right. They were meant for each other. She moaned her pleasure, sinuously moving beneath him. There was a stab of pain as his finger encountered her hymen and she gasped. Inadvertently her body tensed with surprise.

Instantly he withdrew. 'Hell, Tanya. This is wrong. The brigadier trusts me.'

She was about to protest when the creak of a stair warned her that someone was approaching. There was a flickering light from an oil lamp in the hall.

Tanya sat up and fastened her bodice and straightened her gown. Sam stepped back into the darkest shadows and Tanya held her breath.

It was Aunt Stella. She had come down to prepare the brigadier's medicine. The light from the oil lamp faded and indistinct noises came from the kitchen.

Sam was at the door. 'I must go.'

Tanya stared at him confused. There was no tenderness in his voice. The moonlight showed his expression was shuttered and he was holding himself as though he was angry.

'Do you despise me now, Sam?' She could not believe that he was acting so heartlessly. Didn't he know that she loved him? That she would never have permitted him to touch her if she did not?

'No.' He whirled round. 'It's not you. It's me. I should never…' His voice was gruff and abrupt. 'We are worlds apart, Tanya. This was madness.'

Her shocked expression pitted his heart like shrapnel.

'So I mean nothing to you?' she said hollowly.

He swallowed against his pain. He could never tell her the truth that he loved her. If they had met in another five years when his business was established and he was financially secure, it would have been different.

'I love you, Sam.'

He steeled himself against her words. 'Don't say that. You've little experience of men. I took advantage of you. You're not free to love me. Nor I you. I'm an orphan who has risen from the gutters of Stepney. I know my place, Tanya, even if you do not realise yours.'

They heard Aunt Stella returning from the kitchen. Tanya pulled Sam back into the shadows beside her until her aunt had climbed the stairs out of sight.

Her hand was on his arm, her eyes large and beseeching. 'You're Papa's friend. We do not have to marry yet. I'll wait until your business is established.'

'Forget what happened tonight,' he grated out, putting her from him. 'Friendship or not, your father will never accept me as your husband. With my background I cannot marry into an army family that has served the sovereign as officers since the Stuart kings.'

Tanya shook her head, refusing to accept his words. 'My family dwells too much upon its past glory. We aren't rich any more. I don't care about tradition. A man's worth is more important than his background. You're more than worthy to be my husband. You're a fighter, Sam. Aren't I worth fighting for?'

Sam flinched from hurting her, but he had to make her see reason or she would ruin her life. The scandal would destroy her and it would quite likely kill the brigadier.

He raised a mocking brow. 'You've just inherited a fortune from your aunt. Your concept of wealth is different from mine.' His expression hardened. 'Besides, you're overlooking one thing. I haven't asked you to marry me. I do not love you.' The lie clawed at his throat, threatening to choke him. But it had to be said. How else could he stop her destroying her life?

Tanya stood up. Her body was trembling and her eyes bright with disillusion. 'Get out of my sight.'

He had never felt more wretched in his life. As he left Pigrim's Crescent, St Paul's clock struck midnight. There was little traffic and he had walked some distance before he became conscious of a steady tread following him.

It wasn't the first time he had sensed that someone was trailing him. He stopped. The footsteps stopped. He walked faster. They increased their pace. Abruptly, he spun round. A couple of pedestrians continued to walk on, one casting him a curious glance. No one appeared to be following him. An empty hansom clattered past.

It was a rare extravagance for Sam to use one, but he could not rid himself of the unease he felt. Was it the pain he had caused Tanya as well as worrying over the health of the brigadier which was making him edgy?

He whistled to the hansom driver and got in. As it pulled away from the curb, he leaned out of the window. A shadow expanded in a doorway, convincing him that he had not imagined being followed.

By the next evening Sam had forgotten the incident. He had called to see the brigadier in the afternoon, but there was no change. He had left before Tanya returned from a shopping errand for her aunt. Stella Summersfield had made it clear that she blamed him for the brigadier's condition.

'That woman is a trial,' Sam said to himself as he made his way to Stepney later that evening. His thoughts were gloomy.

'I'm sure all that stuff she keeps insisting is medicine is not helping the brigadier.'

He pushed away the depression which threatened to settle over him. He would visit his old haunts and drinking cronies of Stepney. It had been raining all day, the coolness a welcome respite from a month-long heatwave. He had been back to Stepney several times since his return to England to look up old friends but had been disappointed to discover how little they now had in common. Two were doing stretches in Wormwood Scrubs for robbery. Another childhood friend had died from typhus. Only Smiley

Richards remained. He still worked at the carriage works in Bow where Sam had served an apprenticeship. In his youth, he, Smiley and Podge had been inseparable. Sam had been stunned to learn that Smiley was married and was struggling to raise seven children.

It was Smiley he wanted to see tonight. He had been visiting him on the evening he met Tanya when the fight broke out at Aldgate. Smiley had been far from the jovial companion he remembered. His friend was only five feet to Sam's five feet eleven. Beneath his frayed cap his dark hair was already thinning and feathered with grey at the temples. The thick moustache he had so proudly grown at sixteen still hedged his upper lip. At recognising Sam his mouth had split into a familiar wide, toothy grin. But it was no longer a permanent feature. His youngest child, no more than a baby, had just died and his one-year-old was weak with the same fever. Smiley was distraught that he had no money to pay for the medicine the child needed to survive.

Sam had happily loaned him some, but Smiley had refused any further offer of help. It was obvious that his family could not live on his wages. The two rooms they rented in a damp and draughty tenement were cramped and reeked of stale cabbage water and overflowing privies in the back yard. There was no running water and his wife, Rosie, had to lug buckets back to the house from the pump at the end of the road. Was it any wonder the ready smile, which had earned Smiley his nickname, had gone, replaced by lines of worry?

Sam hoped to change that for Smiley. He needed someone to work on the bodywork of the cars while he did the mechanics, and he wanted Smiley for the job.

Sam absorbed himself in thoughts of Smiley to forget what had happened with Tanya yesterday. But it was impossible. He was deep in thought and unaware of the three men who had been trailing him since he got off the Tube train at Stepney Green.

He was within sight of Smiley's local pub when his soldier's sixth sense for danger finally alerted him to the stealthy sound of footsteps behind him. The narrow side road was deserted and bordered on two sides by factories. The earlier moonlight had vanished behind heavy cloud. There was the sound of smashing glass and the single gas lamp was extinguished.

With the street plunged into darkness, fear chilled Sam's blood. Stepney was dangerous at night. Any shadow could conceal a villain, and in these parts a thief would have no conscience about killing for a few shillings. The street was blacker than a tar barrel. Sam swivelled but could see no one. He could smell them though, hear the rasp of their breathing. The scrape of a boot on cobbles made him veer to the left. The blow of a cudgel bounced off his shoulder. The pain numbed his fingers. He had no weapon but his fists. They had served him well in the past.

When instinct and senses warned of a figure to the left of him, he lashed out. Heat flared through his knuckles as they connected with a bristled jaw. The assailant went down. Another loomed up to replace him. Several of Sam's punches connected, flesh crunching against bone, but Sam knew he was outnumbered.

A punch to his head followed by two to his kidneys and liver sent him reeling against a wall. Before he could retaliate, his arms were caught by two men and wrenched behind him. He lashed out with his good leg, hearing a shriek of pain as his shoe rammed into a man's groin. Then a blow to the stomach doubled him over. Another to the groin sent an explosion of crippling agony through him.

His body felt as though he had been tossed into a cauldron of fire, its vicious tongues touched everywhere. A kick to the side of the head sent him sprawling onto the cobbles. Half unconscious, he spat the filth from the gutter from his mouth and raised a hand to protect his head from the barrage of blows.

The previous attack had been but a prelude. Knocked to the ground he was defenceless against boots hammering into him. Long before they stopped kicking him he was unconscious.

Archie Tilbury watched the men from the Gilbert gang pound into Sam's body. He'd waited four nights for this chance. Until tonight every time Sam left Pilgrim's Crescent he'd gone straight home and too many people were still about. He didn't want Sam done over in his lodgings. Better in the street where no guilt could fall upon him.

Tonight they had almost lost him when he went down into the underground station. They had seen him enter a train and jumped on it seconds before it left the station. By good fortune Hawkes had travelled to Stepney. When he entered this side road, Archie had gestured for the men to attack.

He was elated as he watched the man he regarded as an enemy being beaten. He hadn't expected him to put up such a fight. But no man could win against the Gilbert brothers' thugs. Using them would mean he was more deeply indebted to Slasher, but it was worth it. With Hawkes dead, the road would be clear for him to win Tanya.

A pub door close by was opened and several men spilled out. Two urinated against the nearest wall. A third, less drunk than his companions, yelled out, ''Ere, someone's getting done over. At 'em, lads.'

They all looked like dockers. Archie had no intention of being caught and beaten by them. He cursed at being unable to dispose of Hawkes' body in the river as he had originally planned and ran off. His bullies followed.

One of the dockers struck a match and stared down at Sam's bloodied face and still figure. 'Poor bleeder looks like 'e's 'ad it. Anyone know 'im?'

'No.'

'Aint from round 'ere.'

''Arf a mo, Ted.' A man bent and gently rolled Sam over. 'Weren't 'e in the pub with Smiley Richards couple of weeks back? Bought me and me mate a drink, 'e did. Ain't tight with 'is dough. Used to live round 'ere, as I remember.'

Ted backed away. 'I'll fetch Smiley. 'E came in

for a pint a short while back. Should still be at the bar.'

When Smiley saw Sam he almost brought up the pint of porter he'd just downed. His friend was barely recognisable.

'Sorry, mate,' Ted said. 'Reckon 'e's a gonner. Best notify 'is family.'

Smiley was on his knees. His hand on the battered chest detected the faintest of beats.

''E's alive. Praise God, 'e's alive. We've gotta get 'im to the infirmary.'

Chapter Seventeen

To try and forget the way she had responded to Sam's passion, Tanya immersed herself in designing the grottos. She had received a reply to her letter to Clare and her friend was excited about her visit. But it was impossible to forget the wanton passion with which she had succumbed to Sam's lovemaking and his reaction.

She was not surprised that Sam stayed away from the house, but by the evening of the second day her father was complaining of his absence. Tanya became uneasy. It was unlike Sam not to send her father a note with some excuse for not visiting. Sam would never neglect the brigadier while he was ill.

Dr Garrett was with her father now. When Tanya later escorted him to the door, he said, 'Your father must have the constitution of an ox.

But you must be aware that these attacks are steadily weakening him. He must rest more and stop fretting about his friend not calling.'

'Papa should not expect so much from Sam,' Tanya responded. 'He has called every day and he does have a business to run.'

Stella had followed the doctor from her brother's room. 'Now that fellow has tricked my brother out of his money, I don't suppose we shall see much of him.'

Despite her anger at the way Sam had treated her, Tanya wouldn't allow him to be maligned unjustly. 'Sam wouldn't do anything to harm Father. He's been delayed today.'

'Time will reveal to us that Hawkes is a scoundrel.' Contempt deepened the lines of bitterness about Stella's mouth.

'I shall call back tomorrow,' Dr Garrett informed them.

They had reached the foot of the stairs and Tanya heard Ginny addressing someone angrily.

'You ain't got no right to come to this door. Servants and tradesmen go to the basement door.'

Tanya heard the deep rumble of a man's reply and Ginny fell back against he wall, her hand to her mouth, her eyes wide with shock. 'Oh dear God, no. Not Mr Hawkes.' The maid burst into tears.

Alarm spurred Tanya forward. 'What is it, Ginny?'

Ginny was too upset to answer. Tanya saw a short man standing on the doorstep, cap in hand, shifting uncomfortably from one foot to the other. She addressed him. 'Has something happened to Mr Hawkes?'

The man nodded sorrowfully. ''E were set upon last night in Stepney. 'E's been taken to the infirmary. Sam told me last time I saw 'im that 'e were staying 'ere. I came as soon as I finished work.'

'Are you a friend of Sam's?'

He nodded. 'I'm Henry Richards, but everyone calls me Smiley.'

'Come in, Mr Richards.' She waved aside her aunt's protests and led Smiley into her father's study, leaving Stella to show the doctor out.

'How is Sam?'

'Bad, miss. Real bad. They'd put the boot in good. I called in to see 'im after work and 'e were still unconscious. They won't let no one but family near 'im. But 'e ain't got no family. Ain't right 'im being so poorly. Someone should be with 'im. 'E's got three broken ribs and the wound in his knee is inflamed. Doctor says 'e could lose 'is leg if it don't respond to treatment.'

Tanya's knees buckled and she sank down into the swivel chair behind the desk. 'Why would someone do that to him?'

Smiley shook his head. 'There'd be some from that area who'd resent that Sam 'ad come up in the world. Could just've been a robbery. His money were taken. And if Sam put up a fight, they'd 'ave laid into 'im.'

'I'll go and visit him,' she said shakily. 'Thank you for informing me, Mr Richards.'

'There ain't much point, miss. 'E won't be conscious. And as I said, it's just family.'

'I shall call and enquire anyway.'

Smiley looked at her with greater interest. 'It's just 'it me. You must be the woman who used to take the school of an evening. Sam mentioned you were a rare one.'

Seeing her perplexed look, he flashed his toothy smile. 'That's a compliment coming from Sam. Mind you, 'e kept it to 'imself that you were such a looker.'

Tanya blushed as Smiley went on, 'Joe Lang who lives in the same tenement block as me never stops praising you. It does me 'eart good to see the way that man's changed. 'E used to be right down in the dumps. Never reckoned 'e'd work again. Joe's quite chirpy now since doing that figure work with an accountant. 'E blesses the day 'e met yer, miss. Joe thinks you're a regular angel.'

'Then he flatters me.' Tanya was overcome with embarrassment at so much praise. She liked Smiley's irrepressible manner which was natural and unaffected. Her pain at Sam's treatment of her paled beside her fear for his safety. No matter what he said, it hadn't stopped her loving him. She had to help him.

'You must be a good friend of Sam's. Have you known him long?'

'Since we were raggedy-arse kids.' He looked appalled at his blunder. 'Sorry miss, forgot meself. Didn't mean to use such language. Me and Sam go way back. There ain't nothing I wouldn't do for 'im. Reckon me little Annie would be with her baby brother in 'is grave if it weren't for Sam buying 'er medicine. She's running about full of mischief again.' He laughed. 'There I go rabbiting on and you a busy lady an' all.'

Tanya held out her hand. Smiley stared at it for a second then he wiped his palm on his greasy trousers and took it.

'I wish we could have met in happier circumstances, Mr Richards.'

'Just Smiley if you please, miss,' he answered with a grin.

'Will you wait here a moment, Smiley?' Tanya went into the parlour and picked up a large box of chocolates which Archie had given her last week. They had not been opened. She returned to the study and held them out to Smiley. 'Would you give these to your little Annie?'

'Oh my, miss, she nor the other kids ain't never 'ad nothing so grand. I couldn't take it from you.'

'Nonsense,' Tanya laughed. 'I'll be offended if you refuse them.'

'Sam were right.' Smiley beamed at her. 'You're a rare one.'

When Smiley left, Tanya looked at her watch. It was six o'clock. If she was to visit the infirmary tonight, she must leave now.

'If I'm late back, will you give my apologies to Archie?' she asked Stella. 'We were going to the theatre tonight. I must find out how Sam is.'

'You can't go gadding about London on your own. And visiting a man in hospital is most improper,' Stella remonstrated.

'I'm not going to quarrel with you, Aunt. Papa will be worried about Sam. I want to put his mind at rest.'

'I don't know what Mr Tilbury will say.'

Tanya lost patience. 'While I appreciate everything Archie has done for me, I'm not accountable to him.'

'How can you risk losing the respect of Mr Tilbury because of Hawkes? He's an upstart and a scoundrel. And don't forget, he was your father's servant.'

'He was a captain in the army and Papa's aide,' Tanya returned tartly. 'I don't know why you've taken such exception to him.'

Her aunt's eyes slanted with malice. 'He's only after our money. If you're too taken by his handsome looks to see that, then you're a fool. You cannot slight Mr Tilbury by dashing to the bedside of another man.'

Tanya smiled thinly. If her aunt but knew it, Sam wasn't interested in her at all. 'Since you are so eager for me to keep in Archie's good grace, you'll ensure that he does not take offence at my absence. But if he does, then he is not a man I'd wish to spend the rest of my life with.'

Stella cursed the day Sam Hawkes had entered this house. She recognised that almost animal male magnetism he had, which any young girl as spirited as Tanya would be attracted to. But Stella was determined that Tanya should wed Archie Tilbury. She had done so much towards that goal. And she was not a woman who backed down from a decision or allowed her will to be thwarted. As Reginald would soon learn.

The infirmary ward Tanya was directed to smelt

of carbolic, stale urine and vomit. It permeated the tiled corridors. The small windows of the ward let in little light, adding to the atmosphere of illness and depression.

On entering the ward, a frigid-faced sister, her starched cap concealing all her hair, glared at Tanya. The woman's pale gaze flickered over the expensive material of Tanya's black suit and her eyes were hostile.

'Visiting time is over,' she rapped out.

'I have only just learned of Mr Hawkes' condition. Could I not see him just for a minute.'

'If I make an exception for you, everyone will expect it.' There was no sympathy or compassion in her stare and Tanya pitied the patients enduring her tyranny. 'Rules are rules. I can't have the ward filled day and night with visitors who come when it suits them.' The woman might not speak with the rough dialect of the area, but Tanya could feel her antagonism towards someone with apparent wealth.

She scanned the ward but did not recognise Sam in any of the beds. One bed closest to the ward sister's desk was surrounded by screens. 'Is that Mr Hawkes' bed over there?'

'You can't see him until visiting time tomorrow.'

'Could you at least tell me how he is? I understand that he was severely beaten and could die. I'd also like to speak to a doctor.'

A large dewdrop had formed on the end of the woman's thin nose but she made no attempt to wipe it away. 'You can't come in here with your hoity-toity demands. The infirmary has rules.

They are for the good of the patients. And the doctor is busy.'

'I appreciate that.' Tanya swallowed a heated reply. 'Please, I am worried about Mr Hawkes.'

'Only family are allowed to visit or are given information,' the ward sistcr fired at her triumphantly. 'From our files, Mr Hawkes comes from Stepney and has no family.' Her gaze raked Tanya's immaculate figure. 'This is a hospital for the poor.'

'Is there a problem, Sister Marsh? A man whose eyes were red with fatigue approached. The dome of his pointed head was almost bald and the remainder of his lank blond hair stuck out, making him look like a startled hedgehog. He ran his fingers through it now, his expression harassed. From the stethoscope round his neck Tanya assumed that he was a doctor.

'I wished to see Mr Hawkes,' Tanya persisted. 'Sister Marsh says that only family are permitted.'

'Yes, especially in cases as severe as his. We can make no exceptions.' The doctor regarded her kindly.

'Even to his fiancée?' Tanya blurted out, the lie her only means of seeing Sam. Her eyes, wide with pleading, strayed to the screens round Sam's bed. Her head was throbbing from worry over Sam and she put a shaky hand to her temple. 'I've only just learned that he was attacked.'

The doctor's harassed expression softened. 'If you are his fiancée you may see him for a moment. He's unconscious. Until he comes round it's difficult to assess the extent of his injuries.'

'He will live, won't he?' Her voice broke.

The doctor shrugged. 'He was viciously beaten. His looks will shock you. I must insist that you do not become hysterical. If you think his appearance may upset you, I advise you to return in a couple of days when the swelling and bruising have gone down.'

The gravity of this information alarmed her. 'I won't become hysterical.'

Her movements were wooden as the doctor led her behind the screens. The extent of Sam's injuries appalled her. His head and torso were covered with bandages. Both his eyes were cut, swollen and blackened, as was most of his face. One arm was in plaster and the leg which had been wounded in India was bandaged and supported on some kind of pulley.

'Oh, Sam. Who could have done this to you? And why?' She wiped away the tears blurring her vision. Her heart ached to see him looking so close to death. She longed to hold him close, to let her own vitality flow into his body and by will alone aid his recovery.

'What other injuries are there? I was told he had some broken ribs.'

'Three ribs are broken. Fortunately they did not pierce his lungs. From the extensive bruising on his body we assume that his kidneys and liver are bruised but not fatally damaged. We had to operate on his stomach to stop him haemorrhaging. He was lucky he was found so quickly. It is also likely he will need an operation on his leg.

The tissue from an old wound is badly damaged.'

'Will he lose his leg?'

When the doctor did not look at her, her fears were confirmed. 'Please, do all you can to save it. He is such an active man.'

'We haven't the facilities here to do much. We rely on charitable donations to keep going. There is also the possibility of brain damage in such cases, which we cannot treat here.'

'Then he should be moved to a hospital with such facilities. Whatever it costs, I shall pay.'

'He really needs a specialist hospital,' the doctor advised. 'I will arrange it, Miss...'

'Summersfield.' Her eyes again filled with tears as she regarded Sam's battered face and body. A brown hand, its knuckles dark with dried blood, was spread on the coverlet. Clearly he'd put up a fight. Overcome by fear that he might die, she took his hand and raised it tenderly to her lips. 'You must get well, Sam. You have so much to live for,' she said softly. She blocked from her mind the possibility of brain damage and its consequences. It was too frightening to consider. 'Fight on, Sam. Don't let those blighters win.'

The doctor took her arm and led her gently away. At the foot of the bed she stopped and looked back. There was nothing recognisable about his battered face. She pictured him as he had been on the day they went to Regent's Park. She saw vividly the strong body, his handsome face, the sheer power of his presence and his energy and vigour. *Fight, Sam. Fight!*

Her mind, body and spirit willed him to recover. Her heartache was so intense she knew irrefutably that she loved him. At this moment it didn't matter that he did not return her love. She would do everything in her power to ensure he had the best treatment.

'Thank you for letting me see him, Doctor. The care he has received here saved his life. Without infirmaries like this many people would die. Our family will show our gratitude by donating funds to the infirmary. May it help save other lives.'

The money came from the advance payment from Mr Vernon for the work she was doing for him. She would spend every penny she had if it meant that Sam could keep his leg.

'Damnation!' Archie swore, his face tense as he regarded Stella. 'I can't believe Hawkes survived that beating. Why didn't you stop Tanya running off to see him?'

'Tanya is like a steam train out of control when she gets a notion in her head,' Stella replied. 'You should know that by now. You should have made sure that Hawkes was finished off before you left the scene.'

'And the old man upstairs.' Archie jerked his head towards the ceiling. 'He's still alive and causing problems. You swore I'd be wed to the girl by the end of summer.'

'It's Hawkes that is the problem,' Stella said fiercely. 'Now Tanya is bound to see him as some kind of victim and it will rouse her compassion. If you want her, you must sweep her off her feet while Hawkes is in hospital.'

Archie was staring into the mirror, his eyes dark and forbidding. 'Do you think I haven't tried in the last weeks? She refuses to allow me to talk of the future, or marriage. If I press her too hard, she will refuse to see me altogether. But I tell you this, I'm not hanging round forever for that young madam to make up her mind.'

'No, Archie,' Stella said, her voice impassioned. 'Why are you so impatient to marry her? Give her time.'

He rounded on her. 'I can't afford to wait. I've mounting debts and obligations to meet.'

'Then let me help you.' She pulled off a garnet necklace and earrings and pressed them into his hands. 'Sell those. They are Georgian and should fetch a good price. Just be patient, Archie.'

He looked at the jewellery, assessing how much it was worth, and nodded reluctantly. He didn't see that he had much choice. Damn these Summersfields. They would all pay dearly for the extra risks he was being made to take.

During the next two days, working on the designs and costumes for Vernon's Emporiums helped Tanya to cope with the worry over Sam and her father's survival. Reginald had started vomiting after hearing that Sam was in hospital. He was growing rapidly weaker. Sam had been transferred to a specialist hospital and she visited him daily. He was still unconscious. Dr Musgrove, who was in charge of his case, had been sympathetic and reassuring.

'I've seen men in comas for weeks and suddenly they wake up and are perfectly well. There is no sign of paralysis and we are optimistic that his head wound has caused no disability.'

She clung to those words but they did not stop her worrying. The visits to her workroom were not much happier. Sal was withdrawn and did not speak but seemed content to stitch the trimming on the green and red elves' costumes Polly was making, or sit playing with the baby if she was awake. Joe Lang reported the costing he had made for the scenery materials. Tanya nodded absently and was only vaguely aware of him expressing his gratitude that he was now attending the accountancy lessons.

For an hour twice a week after work she used the warehouse as a classroom, Joe having contacted her old students and also some new ones. Her father had not been pleased with the arrangement, but he had eventually given in.

'At least it's not in the East End or so far from home,' he finally conceded. 'I must be getting soft in my old age at the way you get round me.'

She kissed his cheek. 'It's because you know that it helps others.'

Whenever she walked past Sam's garage, her heart ached. His business had been doing so well but without someone to run it, it would suffer. She wanted to help, but without Sam's approval she could not interfere. At least the premises were all secured and no harm could come to the cars garaged there.

Returning to the house, she tapped lightly on her father's door. There was no answer but she could hear Stella's voice rising angrily from within. Why must her aunt keep upsetting her father? It was not helping his recovery. She entered his bedroom to find Stella forcing medicine into her father's mouth. He was resisting, moving his head weakly from side to side and making tight-lipped grunts of protest. Her aunt was so engrossed in making him drink that she did not notice Tanya behind her.

Her father wrenched his head away from the cup and gasped, 'No, I won't take it. I'm always sick after it.'

'Nonsense, it's making you better,' Stella insisted, jamming the cup against his lip.

The brigadier's hand flailed weakly against his sister's strength.

'Drink it, damn you!' Stella shouted. Holding the cup against his mouth, she pinched his nose so that he couldn't breathe. 'Drink it!'

Her father's eyes bulged as he struggled for air. There was a look of such grim satisfaction on Stella's face that Tanya flew at her and knocked the cup away. The unappetising brown liquid tipped onto the coverlet. It smelt disgusting.

'Stop that at once. That's no way to treat a sick man,' she raged.

Stella was breathing heavily. 'He has to take his medicine.'

Tanya picked up the cup and sniffed the dregs. 'This isn't what Dr Garrett prescribed.'

'How would you know?' Stella snapped. 'You're hardly ever here. You're too busy with your precious business or visiting that scoundrel Hawkes to care about your father.'

'That's not true. You made it clear you resent my presence in here.' Tanya gazed at her father. He was panting but there was a look of gratitude in his eyes. Obviously this was not the first time that Stella had forced the medicine down his throat.

'I will speak to Dr Garrett when he next calls. And if this is how you look after a patient then I shall tend Papa's needs myself from now on.'

'I won't be told what to do by a chit of a girl who knows nothing. This is my house–'

'There you are wrong, Aunt. It is Papa's house. And as his daughter and heir, I am its mistress. I will not have him bullied this way. I shall nurse him in future.'

Stella was shaking with anger, her jowls wobbling as she spat, 'I saved him before. You know nothing of nursing. You won't stop me.'

Tanya had heard enough. She turned to her father. 'Do you wish me to tend you, or Aunt Stella?'

'You.' He reached out and took her hand, gripping it tightly. 'You are mistress here. I don't want Stella in my room.'

'So that's the gratitude I get for nursing you. For putting up with your insults and your bad temper.' Stella's voice rose hysterically. 'I've dedicated my life to running this house while you reduced it to a ruin. I am mistress here. Not Tanya.'

'The house will be Tanya's when I am gone,' her father gasped. 'It is for her to run it now.'

Stella's eyes were venomous. 'So I am to be cast aside like an unwanted shoe. Curse you both. I shall never forgive this.' She left, slamming the door.

Tanya sighed. Later she would have to calm her aunt. But Papa was right. It was she who should now be running the house, not Stella.

'How are you feeling, Papa?'

'Better for not being forced to take her witch's brew,' he answered weakly.

Tanya sat on the bed. 'That's rather hard on her. We're all worried about you.'

'Stella has no love for me. She enjoys the power she has over me as each day I become weaker.'

Tanya pulled off the coverlet which was stained by the medicine and replaced it with a fresh one. 'Try and sleep now. I'll ask Millie to answer your bell if you ring for anything. I'm going to see Sam later.'

'Do all you can for him. I feel so helpless. I don't understand this illness. I never had anything like it until I returned to England.'

'Sleep, Papa, and regain your strength.'

'Stay with me.' He smiled wanly. 'Stella won't forgive you for this. She'll make your life difficult if she can. I'm proud of the way you took her on.'

'The Summersfields are headstrong – which is why Stella can be so volatile.'

'You have your mother's generous heart. Stella unfortunately takes after our grandmother. There was no charity in that woman. The only love she gave was to her horses. And one of those she whipped so badly it had to be shot when it threw her during a hunt.' His eyes closed from the effort of talking. Tanya stayed with him until she was certain that he was asleep. Before leaving the house she sought out Millie and was horrified to find her cleaning the silver.

'That isn't your work, Millie.'

The maid was looking unhappy. 'Miss Stella

told me to do it since there was nothing else for me to do. She said since the brigadier was paying my wages I had to fill my hours with work.'

'I am taking over the running of the house. You are a ladies' maid, not a menial. But I'd appreciate it if you would sit with my father. Stella has upset him and he doesn't want her in his room. Ensure that she obeys him and that she doesn't prepare any tisanes for him to take. I alone will give him the medicine prescribed by the doctor.'

The maid smiled. 'Miss Stella has got worse lately. I'm happy to do anything for you, Miss Tanya. Since I've only one more piece of silver to clean, I might as well finish the job.'

Tanya discovered that Stella had locked herself in Maude's old rooms. There was no answer to her knock on the door. Unwilling to add to the bad feeling, she said, 'I'm sorry it has come to this, Aunt Stella. You ran this house superbly. But I'm old enough to be its mistress now. I've instructed the servants accordingly.'

'Do as you like. I am free of the burden of any responsibility.' Her voice was hoarse from weeping.

'I am truly sorry, Aunt Stella.'

'Go away. I don't want to speak to you. I shall never forgive you or Reginald.'

Chapter Eighteen

Tanya was playing chess with her father in his bedroom when Millie announced that Archie Tilbury had called. Tanya had forgotten that they were to dine out this evening.

'Better not keep your young man waiting,' her father said. His colour was better and he had managed to keep down the beef broth Cook had prepared for his supper.

'He's not my young man, Papa. He's a friend. And I don't feel like going out tonight.'

He studied her sombrely. 'I doubt Tilbury regards your relationship as friendship. Not that I think he's the right man for you. Can't say I take to the fellow, myself. Neither did Sam. It's a pity you cancelled your visit to the Grosvenors for this weekend. You need to meet more people your own age.'

'I can't leave London while you and Sam are ill.'

He patted her hand. 'I don't feel queasy since you've been nursing me. But I didn't mean you to be tied to an invalid – though I do miss Sam coming in.'

'It's probably the new medicine Dr Garrett prescribed which is helping. And I can visit Clare later in the year.'

He looked at her affectionately. 'You're a good woman. I appreciate all you're doing for me and

Sam, but,' he paused, his voice heavy, 'Sam hasn't got anything to do with you not taking Tilbury seriously?'

Her emotions about Sam were in turmoil. She loved him. But it was obvious from her father's manner that he would never approve. She had wondered if it was loyalty to the brigadier that had made Sam reject her so brutally. Loyalty was important to Sam. For him to fall in love with her would be a betrayal of the brigadier's trust. He had implied as much as he backed away from her. The resilience she admired in him and which he would draw upon to recover from his wounds was the same resilience he would use to maintain the barriers he had erected between them.

She could only wait and hope that when Sam recovered – for she would not consider the possibility that he would die – he would accept that the difference in their births was unimportant to her. If it took a lifetime, she would wait.

'Papa, I'm not ready for marriage,' she evaded.

'You should be thinking about it. I hate to think that I'm the reason you rely on Tilbury for company when you could be enjoying yourself in Tunbridge Wells. You're looking tired.'

'I'm fine, Papa. I had better see Archie. Are you going to sleep, or do you want Millie to read to you?'

'I've had enough of women fussing round me. I enjoy your company, but I can do without the others.'

She kissed his cheek. They were growing closer and that pleased Tanya. He did look better this evening. She prayed that the latest attack had been a false alarm. It would be too cruel of fate to rob her of her father just as they were getting to know and understand each other.

Archie lifted a dark brow when she entered the withdrawing room. She was still wearing an afternoon tea gown. 'I'm sorry, Archie. I don't feel like going out this evening.'

He looked displeased. 'You are exhausting yourself by your visits to the hospital, and people will talk because you are also paying Hawkes' expenses.'

Her temper was triggered by his mood. She was not going to compromise her ideals by pandering to Archie's ill humour. Archie was always so derogatory about anything to do with Sam. Did he guess that she cared for him?

'Let people talk. Sam's life is more important than gossip. And Papa relies on me to tell him of Sam's progress.'

'I worry about you, that's all.' He smiled engagingly.

It failed to move her. 'I'm horrified at the way that Sam was attacked. He could die. How could anyone be so evil as to beat him so viciously?'

'The streets are dangerous at night,' he replied gruffly. 'Thank God you are no longer teaching in the East End. I should never have encouraged you.' He moved closer and reached for her hand but she sidestepped to sit by the window. He tensed, his tone accusing. 'Do you hold some special regard for Hawkes?'

'My father does.' She felt like a Judas denying her love. 'Sam has no family. I could not abandon a family friend in need.'

'Of course not.' Archie's voice was clipped. He paced the carpet before her, his glance sliding to the mirror to check his appearance as he passed. She could sense his resentment but his manner remained smooth and charming, his smile coercing when he continued, 'I'm jealous that your time at the hospital takes you away from me.'

Tanya knew his pride was hurt. And she had caught him glancing at his image in a mirror too often not to be aware of his vanity. She had considered it a small failing, especially as he was so handsome. He had been kind to her and she wanted to let him down gently. 'My life would be dull without your friendship, Archie. I don't want it placed under any false illusions.'

His expression cleared. 'I adore you so. It is not always easy to contain my ardour but I have never gone beyond the bounds of propriety, have I, Tanya? I respect you too much for that.'

Tanya could not dispute that. Sometimes she wondered why Archie was so circumspect. He had never tried to kiss her. Was it out of respect? He was twelve years older than she was and rather aware of his own importance. She hadn't thought him a prude. Was it just high moral principles which prevented him kissing her when they were not engaged? She wasn't sure she wanted him to kiss her. Perhaps he sensed her ambivalence and feared being rejected.

The following afternoon Tanya arrived at Sam's bedside and was dismayed to find him still unconscious.

'Is there any improvement, Sister O'Rourke? It's been four days now.'

'Nothing, miss.'

The swellings on his face had gone down but his skin was still purple and blue from the bruising. Drawing a chair close to the bed, she took his hand as she did every visit and willed him to regain consciousness.

'Fight, Sam. Come back to us. You've got to fight.' Anger at what his attackers had done to him burst through her distress at his condition. 'Fight! Don't let the buggers win.'

There was a slight movement of the fingers between her own. 'Come back to me, Sam,' she urged. 'Please. Fight on.'

The eyelids lifted and tawny eyes slowly focused. Tears of joy spilled down her cheeks. 'Oh, Sam. You gave us all such a scare.'

'Couldn't … let the … buggers … win,' he croaked.

Tanya laughed softly not realising until now how unladylike her language had become in her need for him to recover. It seemed to have struck a chord in Sam which had made him respond.

'Sister O'Rourke, Sam is conscious,' Tanya called.

The ward sister hurried to the bed. 'That's more like it, Mr Hawkes.'

'Hurt … like the … devil. Was I … in a … battle? Don't remember.'

'You look like you've been trampled by a tribe of whirling dervishes,' Sister O'Rourke observed in a booming voice which would have done justice on the parade ground. She was a big, rosy-cheeked woman in her mid-thirties and had been on duty every day Tanya had visited. 'But it wasn't a battle. You're in London and were beaten up and left in the street, Mr Hawkes.'

'Don't remember,' he croaked.

'You will in time,' Sister O'Rourke smiled at him. 'Now rest and no speaking. Your fiancée can come back later once the doctor's seen you.'

Sam turned to Tanya, his expression blank. 'Fiancée?'

Tanya blushed.

'Best leave him to rest, miss. It isn't unusual for them to be confused when they come round.'

Sam's hold on Tanya's hand tightened but he had closed his eyes, his face contorted with pain.

'The doctor will give him something for the pain,' Sister O'Rourke said. 'Once Dr Musgrove has seen him, we'll know better how he is.'

'I have to go, Sam.' Tanya gently disengaged her hand. He opened his eyes and so great was her relief that he had recovered consciousness that she stooped to kiss his cheek. 'Just get well, Sam.'

Pain clouded his tawny eyes and when he tried to smile he winced. 'Thought I was still dreaming, seeing you here.'

'I'll come again tomorrow.'

Already his eyes were closing again. Had he really been dreaming about her? She felt she was drifting on a raft of happiness as she left the ward.

Stella was agitated as she joined Archie in the family parlour. 'Tanya's not here again. She's at that damned hospital.'

'Is there something between her and the soldier?' Archie demanded.

Stella shrugged. 'If there is, she's keeping close about it. I'm sure it's you she cares for.'

'I'm no longer certain.' Archie smoothed back the oiled sides of his hair.

'Tanya can be stubborn.' Stella stifled her anger at her niece's behaviour. Things were not going as she had planned. Why did the girl have to be so difficult? She couldn't understand why she had not fallen in love with Archie. He was so handsome and charming.

'The brigadier's illness is going against me.' He glared at her. 'I thought the matter would be done with by now.'

'These things can't be rushed. Be patient, Archie.' She didn't like him criticising her. With an effort she forced a smile. 'Did I not promise you that all you wish for will be yours? Tanya has been seen often in your company, people will expect an announcement. Otherwise her reputation will suffer. To a Summersfield, reputation is everything.'

'And the brigadier?' The question needed no elaboration between them.

'Leave him to me.' She held his dark gaze. 'I will not fail you.'

A week later when Tanya visited the hospital Sam was propped up on pillows, his leg in a pulley. The bruises on his face were fading and his colour was much better. The stitches had been taken out of the cuts on his cheeks, jaw and brow. The weight he had lost hollowed the contours of his face, making his features more angular.

'You're looking so much better today, Sam.'

His greeting was cool as she pressed a copy of *A Modern Utopia* by H.G. Wells into his hand.

'I remember you saying that you hadn't got round to reading this.'

'Thank you. You don't have to feel duty bound to visit every day.'

'Would you rather that I didn't?' She was instantly defensive.

He regarded her for a long moment before saying tersely, 'What made you tell Sister O'Rourke and Dr Musgrove that you were my fiancée?'

So that was why he was so angry. She was careful to mask her emotions before she held his condemning stare. 'It was the only way they would allow me to see you since I am not a relative.'

'You could have said that you were a cousin.'

'Because you were close to death, only immediate family would have been allowed in,' she dissembled. 'I will inform them now that I'm not your fiancée, if you've not already done so.'

'I would not wish to embarrass you. You have done so much.'

Her gaze dropped from his probing glare. 'I never liked the deception. I shall inform them that you are a family friend.'

'They told me how you paid to have me moved from the infirmary and that you are paying for specialist treatment to save my leg.' Anger rasped his voice. 'I don't want your money, Tanya.'

He sounded as though he hated her. Pride

masked her hurt and when her gaze lifted to hold his, it sparked green fire. 'Papa insisted that we pay for any treatment to save your life and leg. Is that acceptable?'

'You are splitting hairs. I don't want charity.'

His obstinacy goaded her into retaliating. 'Can you afford to pay for your treatment? I thought all your savings had gone into your business. Or would you prefer to go back to the infirmary and gamble that you still have two legs when you leave?'

His mouth clamped shut as he glowered at her. Finally he said, 'I'll take my chances.'

'For God's sake, man, don't be so stubborn! If you must, then regard the money as a loan. You can repay it when your business is established.'

'The business will go under while I'm stuck in here. Unless I sell some cars, I won't pay the rest on the garage, and I'll also lose the cars I've already negotiated to purchase. Once the owners realise there is a market for them, they will sell them elsewhere.'

'Weren't you going to ask Smiley to come into the business with you? Tell him what needs to be done.'

'Smiley is a hard worker but he can't read or write.'

'Then I'll write to your contacts and explain what's happened. Joe Lang could help out. I haven't enough work to pay him full time. He needs extra money. Give him a list of the prices you negotiated and how much the cars in the garage should be sold for. He'll do the deals for you.'

'It won't work.'

'Yes, it will. Joe's good with figures. He's costed my materials and labour expenses and ensured I make a good profit. He can do the same for you.'

Sam remained obdurate. His broken arm was folded over his chest and his jaw was clenched with anger. 'It's my business. I should be running it. Not some stranger.'

Tanya sighed in exasperation. 'You will be running it. Joe will follow your advice. He need only complete a few transactions to tide you over while you're in hospital.'

When he continued to object, she said impatiently, 'Don't forget that my father's money is also tied up in this.'

'That gives you the right to give me orders, does it?' he rapped out.

She was mortified. 'Is that what you think? I wouldn't dream of ordering you to do anything. I'd hate to see you lose the business, that's all. You're being pig-headed by not allowing anyone to help. You've done so much for Papa. Won't you let me repay that kindness?'

'When I left the army I vowed I'd be my own man,' he persisted.

She stood up. 'As you wish, Sam. There's no reasoning with you in this mood. My suggestions were meant to put your mind at rest, not antagonise you. I'll not come again as you seem to resent my company.'

As she turned to go, her hand was gripped by iron fingers. 'Don't go, Tanya.'

She didn't look at him. She didn't dare. Her eyes had filled with tears and she felt foolish. Her love for him was overwhelming her and she didn't want him to discover her feelings. It would only drive him further away. 'It's better if I leave. I shall tell Sister O'Rourke that I'm not your fiancée, merely the daughter of your business partner who is too ill to visit you himself?'

'I've upset you. I'm sorry.' His voice was mellow with regret. He pulled her closer to the bed and she could feel his stare compelling her to look at him. Unable to resist, she glanced at him through tear-misted lashes.

He groaned. 'I'm sorry. I've made you cry. I don't deserve your help. You're right. I'm pig-headed and stubborn.' His eyes crinkled with self-mockery. 'Can you forgive me? Your visits make being trapped here bearable. But your father wouldn't approve if he thought either of us was allowing a deeper emotion than friendship to form between us.'

Tanya swallowed against a resurging pain. He was trying to be kind, but his words were like darts piercing her heart. Somehow she sketched a smile on her lips. 'Whatever you say, Sam. All that matters at the moment is for you to get well.'

Dr Musgrove joined them. He was a short, stout man, his thick, waving grey hair brushed back from a wide forehead. The gravity of his expression alarmed Tanya.

'We must operate if we are to save your leg, Mr Hawkes. We will do it tomorrow. An operation will mean several weeks of convalescence. But, given time, you should make a full recovery.'

When the doctor left them, Sam stared bleakly at the wall. Guessing that he would prefer to be alone, Tanya picked up her gloves and handbag from the bedside table. 'Is there anything you need that I can bring you?'

His eyes were haunted as they held her stare. 'Aye, you'd better ask Lang if he'll undertake the work. Looks like I'm going to need him now.'

She smiled encouragement. 'You'll be up and about in no time, Sam. The operation is just a temporary setback.'

Nurse O'Rourke came and took Sam's temperature. 'Sure you will, Mr Hawkes. In three months you'll be waltzing your fiancée at a New Year's Eve dance. When Miss Summersfield leaves, your cousin is waiting to see you. One visitor at a time is all you're allowed.'

Tanya glanced at Sam when Nurse O'Rourke left them. 'I didn't know you had a cousin.'

'I don't. But then I didn't know I had a fiancée.'

Colour flamed Tanya's cheeks. 'You should have told Nurse O'Rourke that I was not.'

Sam grinned but it ended in a painful grimace. 'And lose the envy of every man and doctor on this ward? I'd not embarrass you like that. And my "cousin" is Polly. They were still only allowing close family to visit when she came a couple of days ago to see how I was. She wanted to know if I needed anything. She's grateful to me for the part I played in finding her somewhere to live.'

Tanya recalled Polly's eager questions about Sam's progress each time she went to the workshop. Was Polly attracted to Sam? She stifled a pang of jealousy.

'It's good of Polly to call. Time must drag for you in here. So what do you need Joe to do for you?' She drew a pencil and a small notepad from her handbag and wrote down his instructions.

'The keys to my workshop are in the top drawer of this cabinet,' he finished by saying.

Tanya took them. 'I'll come again the day after tomorrow when you've recovered from your operation. Don't worry about your business, Sam. Joe can be relied on.'

'Haven't you forgotten something?' There was a devilish glimmer in his eyes. At her puzzled frown, he grinned. 'Aren't fiancées supposed to kiss their loved ones goodbye?'

Sam took her hand and drew her to him. Was this his way of punishing her in front of the other patients? She kissed him demurely on the cheek and hissed, 'Satisfied?'

'Bit chaste, wasn't it?' he taunted.

Her eyes blazed. She'd give him chaste. Goaded, she took his face in her hands and kissed him full on the mouth, her lips parting in a lingering and sensual kiss.

'That's it, Sam. Give her one for me,' a patient shouted and wolf-whistled.

Tanya drew back, her cheeks crimson, but there was mischief in her gaze. 'Was that more to your liking, sir?'

Then her courage deserted her and, unable to look at him, she hurried from the ward before he could deride her.

It wasn't derision Sam was feeling as he watched Tanya leave. It was dangerous to tease her. He hadn't realised how much he had wanted her to kiss him. Or how sweet it would be.

Frustration ground through him. He was helpless in this bed and while Tanya continued to see Tilbury he was jealous and plagued by fears for her. All he could do was lie here thinking. And his thoughts were unsettling. There was something sinister about the brigadier's illness and he was still convinced that Maude Summersfield's death was no accident. He was also uneasy about Tilbury. He should be out there watching over Tanya. A niggling thought was fast becoming a certainty. He had no enemies he knew of. The beating he'd received was meant to kill him. He would have died if he hadn't been found so quickly.

No one was beaten like he had been just to rob them. Someone wanted him dead. A man who had dealings with the vicious Gilbert gang perhaps. A man who feared that he was a rival. A man such as Archie Tilbury.

Dr Garrett finished examining the brigadier and put his stethoscope in his bag. 'It's remarkable,' he said. 'Even your heart sounds stronger. It must be some foreign disease which ailed you.'

It was six weeks since her father's last attack. In the last two weeks he had been able to get downstairs and his strength was building with every day. In all that time Stella had not spoken to Tanya. She remained shut in her room, even eating her meals there.

Wind and rain were battering the windowpane. 'Looks like we're in for a gale, Doctor,' Tanya said. 'Thank you for coming out in such bad weather.'

'I shall restrict my visits to once a week to keep a check on your father. This illness has me baffled. And I don't like mysteries.'

There was a loud clatter on the garden path.

'Sounds like you've lost some roof slates,' the doctor commented.

Tanya stared at a yellowing patch on the bedroom ceiling. Water had begun to drip from it. After the doctor left, she fetched a bucket to catch the leaks and then helped her father downstairs into the library. 'The roof is getting worse, Papa. It has to be repaired.'

'Miss Tanya,' wailed Millie, entering the room with her hair and dress splattered with brown spots. 'Oh, Miss Tanya. My bedroom's flooded.'

'Move your things into Stella's old room for now,' Tanya suggested. She turned to her father. 'The money I shall earn from Vernon's grottos will cover Sam's hospital fees and stretch to repair the roof. Let me call the tilers or we'll have the rafters crashing down around our ears while we sleep.'

'It's not for you to spend your money on such things,' he began, then sighed in defeat. 'Very well. Lang and Richards have been carrying out Sam's instructions and the garage is doing better than I expected.'

'To continue to do so, you must plough the profits back into the business for at least another six months, Papa.'

He frowned. 'I suppose so. But I shall pay you back then. I don't want you using this as an excuse to continue working when your obligation to Vernon is finished.'

Tanya did not argue. At least the roof would be repaired.

'In that case, Papa, I will pay for gas or electric lighting to be installed. Oil lamps are so smelly and dangerous.'

'What is it about women that once they get the itch to spend money they don't know when to stop?' he groaned. 'Make the arrangement. The place will need decorating in the next few years so we might as well have proper lighting installed. Let it be electric. Never did trust gas. A person could get poisoned by it if the flame blew out.'

Leaning on his stick, he chose a book from the shelves. When he swayed, Tanya caught his arm and was shocked by its thinness. He had lost a great deal of weight since his illness.

'Would you play the piano for me? I can hear it from here. I'll sit and read awhile. Play some Mozart. It's my favourite.' He picked up a letter from the table. 'Get Ginny to post this, would you? It's to my solicitors. I've asked Mr Dodds to call on Wednesday. It's time I put my affairs in order. And it's time your future was settled.'

'Ginny will post the letter when the storm dies down. As for my future, it will take care of itself.'

'Nonsense. I've been too indulgent allowing you to work for Vernon. It's time you married, Tanya. Should anything happen to me, I worry about you being on your own.'

'Nothing is going to happen to you, Papa. Each day you're stronger.'

He waved her comments aside. 'In the event of my death before you marry, I intend to appoint Sam your guardian. But I'd be happier if you were wed. Stella assures me that Tilbury is of good character, though Sam had his reservations about the man. Mr Fairchild, however, spoke highly of him.' He studied her narrowly and pulled his moustache. 'Sam was becoming rather too protective towards you before his accident. I had to speak to him about it. His operation was a success, and although I know it will be weeks before he can walk unaided, there's no need for you to visit him every day. You're seeing too much of him. I don't want you getting too involved.'

Since Sam had taunted her into kissing him goodbye, he had again become guarded towards her. When she greeted or left him, she kissed him on the cheek. Her father's words nevertheless ruffled her calm. 'Would it be so terrible if I did come to care for Sam?' She kept her voice light.

He glowered at her. 'Don't even joke about it. All Sam can ever be to you is a friend or adviser. Never a husband. Do you understand?'

He was breathing heavily and, knowing that it was dangerous for his health to get excited, she did not pursue the matter. It did not change her feelings or intentions towards Sam. If she did not marry him she would remain a spinster.

'You had better decide about Tilbury,' her father added sharply. 'How long have you known him? Six months? People will expect an announcement. Or it will be your reputation that suffers.'

'I will not marry him because convention demands it.'

Her father banged his stick on the floor, his

figure tense. 'Then stop seeing him. I won't have your name linked to a scandal.'

'That seems rather unfair after all Mr Tilbury has done. I may not love him, but I enjoy his company.'

His expression was forbidding. 'If I thought that you cared for Sam, I'd have to end our partnership. You two were thrown together in this house. It's just as well I warned him off. He has more sense of what is acceptable than you have.'

Even in the interests of her father's health this was too important a matter for her to back down now. 'You'd ruin Sam if you withdrew your investment while he's convalescing,' Tanya said, aghast.

'So you don't deny that you're attracted to him? It's infatuation, not love. I own Sam is a rare type of man, but he's not for you.'

'Why not?' she challenged. 'In five years or so he will be a wealthy man if the business continues as it is.'

The brigadier pulled his pipe from his pocket and packed it with tobacco before answering. 'Sam is the best man I know. But it's a matter of background. It's time you met more people. If the weather were not so atrocious, I'd insist you visited your friend in Tunbridge Wells though I've never met the Grosvenors and I'm not sure they are suitable chaperons. Stella considered the husband a country bumpkin.'

'She has never approved of any of my friends, except Archie who she introduced me to.'

A blue haze of smoke formed over his head as he puffed on his pipe. 'Then I shall write to the colonel's wife. They live in Mayfair. She can take you under her wing, get you to meet the right people.'

'No, Papa. At least not until after Christmas. I have my work for Mr Vernon to occupy me. With you ill and so soon after Maude's death, I have no wish to socialise. Neither have I the appropriate clothes.'

'Very well, but once you have the necessary clothes I want you to mix more. Your mother adored balls.'

Stella entered the library looking so outraged that she must have been listening to their conversation outside the door.

'If we had a decent room to entertain in, we could have more dinner parties and musical soirées for Tanya to meet people. Although Archie–'

'I don't want to hear another word about Archie,' Tanya exploded. 'I shall marry the man I love or not at all.'

She left the room and the brigadier exhaled sharply. 'Have the damned work done on the parlour. I've a mind to entertain this New Year. Only wait until I get some more money from Hawkes. You women will bankrupt me yet. But let it end there, Stella. I'm not made of money. Enough has been spent on the house.'

He rubbed his moustache, unable to shake Tanya's departing words from his mind. Was she falling in love with Sam? And would it be such a disaster if she did?

Chapter Nineteen

Sam was discharged from hospital at the end of November. On Tanya's last visit he walked out to the garden and sat on a bench in the watery sunshine, his crutches propped beside him. Tanya had cut her visits to twice a week when her father insisted he was strong enough to travel to the hospital himself by cab.

'I wish you'd come back to Pilgrim's Crescent until you're walking without crutches,' she told Sam.

'I'd prefer to go back to my rooms,' he said flatly. 'I'm having a bed brought down to the back of the garage until I get rid of the crutches. Polly has offered to cook for me.'

'That's very kind of Polly,' Tanya said. She knew it wasn't kindness at all. Polly never stopped talking about Sam and was clearly attracted to him.

Sam glanced at her. 'I told Polly that I prefer to eat out. I made several contacts that way before I was set on.'

'Do you like her, Sam?' Tanya found the words tumbling out and hated herself for asking.

'It would be difficult not to like Polly. She's always laughing. Nothing gets her down. Though Sal is still acting strange and refuses to leave the workshops. Poor kid. I'd like to get my hands on the man Polly lived with and give him a taste of his own medicine. Still, he got a right pasting, by all accounts, and left the district to move in with a woman in Balham. Polly's well shot of him.'

Seeing the shadows in Tanya's eyes, Sam reached for her hand. 'I shall never forget what you've done for me. I wouldn't have a business but for you. I know you've done all the correspondence even though you say it's been Joe.' He turned the subject before it risked becoming too intimate. 'And are the grottos progressing? Are they finished in all the stores yet?'

'There's one left to complete in Stratford. The rest open to the public on Saturday.'

'That's good. Are you pleased with them?'

Tanya shrugged. 'Yes, but it's not what I feel that is important. It's the children and customers' reactions which will prove their success or failure.'

'I'm sure they're fantastic, if the carnival float is anything to go by. What other news have you? The brigadier was talking about giving a New Year's Eve dinner at your house if the dining room is redecorated in time. He's not overdoing things, is he? Though I must say he looked very well when he called in yesterday.'

'The doctor is amazed at the way he's recovered. He's even putting on weight. He spends much of his time at his club to get away from Stella's nagging. Once the work on the house began, she emerged from her self-imposed banishment to her rooms but her resentment continues to fester and she's still not satisfied. She wants the music room and family sitting room redecorated now. I told Papa that any money I received from Mr Vernon would be used for the renovation work. But I'm not sure it will stretch to such extravagance.'

'And you and the brigadier? How are things between you?'

Tanya was aware that Sam had carefully seated himself a good two feet away from her and was keeping his conversation noncommittal. But he could not always stop a degree of tenderness creeping into his eyes. When she glanced at him quickly she would see it before he lowered his lashes, blocking his emotions. To have seen it was enough to sustain her hope that one day he would acknowledge that he loved her.

She laughed softly. 'Papa grumbles about me going to the workshop every day. He insists my place is at home so I tease him that he can't wait to get away from it himself. I think he understands how important it is to me. I've persuaded him to come to the Regent Street emporium on Friday to see the grotto before it opens and gets too crowded. I've enjoyed the challenge of the work.'

'You do too much.' Sam regarded her with concern. 'You look pale. Are you still giving evening lessons in the workshop?'

'Only twice a week.'

Concern crinkled Sam's eyes. 'You should try to get away to your friend in the country.'

'I would have, but Clare has been ill. She miscarried and Simon took her to southern France for a month to regain her strength in a warmer climate. They will be in London for the New Year so I will see her then.'

'Are you still seeing Tilbury?' He did not look at her but stared fixedly at two sparrows splashing in the bird bath by the shrubs.

'Occasionally we go to the theatre or a concert. And he calls to take tea with Stella. But Papa rarely joins us. He has little time for Archie and I don't understand why.'

'The brigadier isn't taken in by his charm.' Sam's tawny lion's stare was accusing. 'Why do you think he visits your aunt? I thought it was you he was interested in.'

'I suppose he sees her as an ally. He's asked me to marry him and at the time I felt I was being pressurised into giving him an answer. He agreed to give me more time.' She saw Sam's throat jerk convulsively as though the news pained him. His profile was forbidding as he turned away from her.

'You mustn't marry him, Tanya,' he declared. 'There's something not right about Tilbury, but stuck in hospital I've been unable to prove anything.' Sam pivoted on the bench and his leg rubbed against hers, but he was too troubled to move back. 'What do you know about him other than what he or your aunt has told you?'

Tanya frowned. Neither of them had told her anything of substance. Archie had always skilfully fielded her questions about his family and she had given up trying to get him to open up about his background for fear of seeming to pry. He never mentioned his family himself and spoke about his business interests only in the vaguest terms. She had been too wrapped up in her own work and concern for Sam and her father to give

Archie much thought in recent weeks.

'I'm sure you're wrong, Sam,' she said, trying to blot the awareness of his thigh pressed against hers.

Unexpectedly Sam took her hand. 'Just be on your guard, Tanya. That's all I ask until I can find out more.'

Tanya saw little of Archie in the next few weeks, though regular bouquets of flowers from him were delivered by the florist. She suspected that he was staying away because he expected her to miss his company. It was his way of punishing her for refusing his proposal.

With the grottos finished, Tanya was worried that she had no immediate work to employ Polly and Joe.

A thick yellow fog hung over the city, obscuring landmarks. Traffic was crawling along Cheapside as she walked to her workshop. Her hands were thrust into a fox fur muff and a matching hat combated the December cold. A cashmere scarf was draped across the lower half of her face to mask the choking fog. Other pedestrians' faces were huddled in mufflers, their noses reddened and eyes watering. She stopped first at Sam's garage and found him leaning on a walking stick, his head over the bonnet of an open-topped black Daimler. He wore an oily overall and there was a smear of grease on his chin as he conferred with Smiley who was lying under the car on a blanket. There were five cars in the showroom and another four were in the garage being renovated.

Sam looked up as she approached and momentarily his gaze softened with tenderness as he regarded her. Then the emotion was erased and his stare was no more than friendly. She wanted to shake him, to shout at him to stop fighting his feelings. But she knew it was useless.

There was a rustle of skirts from a chair behind the car and Polly stood up. 'I'll be going, Sam.'

He nodded absently at her. 'Thanks for the sandwiches, Polly. I'd starve without you making sure I eat properly.'

Tanya saw Polly in a new light. That of a rival. The young woman had changed since they had first met. Some of it was due to her own influence. Polly had modulated her voice so that her speech was no longer harsh and rough and she enunciated her words without dropping her aitches. She copied Tanya's graceful walk, no longer rushing everywhere with her tattered shawl clasped tightly to her. Today her dark hair was neatly coiled at the nape of her neck and her maroon dress was one she had recently made. Its long tight sleeves and high neck were demure, the bodice with its row of tiny buttons was shaped to enhance her breasts without flaunting them. She looked neat and respectable. Able now to afford proper food, her face had filled out and her pale skin was unblemished and pearly. She was an attractive woman.

Polly's gaze was adoring as it rested on Sam, but he did not see it. He was looking enquiringly at Tanya.

'I need Joe for a couple of hours,' she said, relieved that her voice showed none of her jealousy. Sam and Polly were together so much and she saw less of him than ever. 'I need him to go through the invoices for Mr Vernon before I send them out.'

'Fine,' Sam agreed. There were dark smudges under his eyes and he looked tired. He was working too hard. 'Are the grottos popular with the customers? The brigadier was impressed. He's proud of your work though I doubt he said as much to you. He still doesn't approve, does he? Was Vernon pleased with them?'

Tanya's heart warmed to the praise from her father even if it came indirectly. 'Mr Vernon is delighted. The shops are crowded and he says his sales are a third up on other years. He has ideas for a big Easter display and a small one for Valentine's Day. But I'm not so sure. The grottos were fun but...' She shrugged. 'It's better than nothing, I suppose. I'd hate to have to lay off Joe and Polly as they worked so hard to make it a success.'

'How's Sal? Polly says she's less nervous but she refused to attend school or leave the workshop. Polly is so grateful to you for taking the time to get her books and teach her all you can. She's a bright girl.'

'Sal wants to become a teacher herself, but she's still so wary of men. I suppose it's understandable. It's difficult to imagine the trauma she went through that night. I've spoken about it to Dr Garrett because she won't speak to him or allow him near her. He says that giving her a secure home and being understanding is the best cure. It's a matter of time. She's young enough that hopefully it will not blight her future or chance of a happy marriage.'

Sam nodded. 'Time is always the best healer. And how's your father? I've been too busy the last few days to get to see him.'

Tanya knew that part of the reason for Sam's absence from the house was herself. Since he had left hospital he had made sure they were never alone. She had begun to wonder if there was a woman in his life. Was it Polly? She did so much for him. To earn extra money she cleaned his office and garage showroom. Polly and Sam were perfect for each other in many ways. The thought devastated her and she left the garage quickly before she betrayed her emotions to Sam.

Joe Lang produced the invoices for Tanya and agreed to accompany her to the three nearest Vernon Emporiums. She was eager to discover whether they were giving the children the pleasure she had hoped for. Each of the scenes had four people dressed in costumes to play the parts. With a system of weights and pulleys, several of the toy characters moved mechanically. Tanya wasn't disappointed.

'It's just like fairyland,' she heard one young mother enthuse to another waiting in the long line to enter the grotto. 'Young Mary hasn't stopped talking about it since she first saw it last week. And they say every one of Vernon's shops has a different theme which is just as spectacular.'

Her companion nodded. 'Aye, me sister said they've got an elves' cave in the Stratford Broadway branch and at the big store in Regent Street an enchanted forest. I like this idea of pixies and fairies making the toys come alive at night.'

Satisfied that her work was giving so many people pleasure, Tanya dismissed Joe and with the invoices in her bag called on Mr Vernon in Regent Street. To her surprise a woman was standing by the office window tapping the sill with long manicured fingernails. Her pale blonde hair was swept up into a padded and elaborate style beneath a feathered picture hat. She had removed her coat and wore a pink velvet gown, which from its narrow cut and style looked French in origin.

'Good morning, Miss Summersfield.' Mr Vernon rose from behind his desk and held out his hand for her to take. 'May I present my wife. She is very impressed with your work.'

'I had not expected you to be so young,' Sarah Vernon frowned. 'But the grottos are remarkable. I particularly like the subtle blend of colours. Usually they are garish and rather tasteless.'

Tanya inclined her head in acknowledgement. 'Thank you. I visited three of the stores and the children seemed to be enjoying themselves.'

Mr Vernon beamed. 'From the accounts I've heard, they are begging their mothers to take them to see other displays. I'm delighted with your work.'

'And you designed them all yourself?' Mrs Vernon spoke in a soft cultured voice, her haughty tone surprising Tanya until she remembered that although Mr Vernon's family originally hailed from the East End, the last two generations had married rich wives.

'Yes, although I employ a carpenter and handyman for the scenery, and two seamstresses for the costumes and any drapery in the background. An artist worked on the murals from sketches I supplied.'

'Have you done much of this work before?' Mrs Vernon's manner was less stiff now that she understood that Tanya did none of the menial work herself.

'No. As a hobby I enjoy redesigning rooms and my ideas have been used at home. Papa does not approve of me working. Since this work was for the enjoyment of children, I was able to persuade him.'

Mrs Vernon's mouth formed a moue of disappointment. 'So you do not take commissions for such work?'

'I had not considered it.'

'Would you undertake to redesign the rooms in a house we have just purchased which overlooks Hyde Park? It may look very grand on the outside but inside it is a positive fright. In every room the wallpaper is brown with age. I had a mind to have it decorated in the style of Lady Peterswood's house in Eaton Square. Do you know Lady Peterswood?'

'I do not. My family is an army one. Our only acquaintance in Eaton Square is Lord Bradstow. He and my father were in the Sudan together.'

'But Bradstow is an earl. What was he doing in the Sudan?' Mrs Vernon queried.

Tanya hid a smile at the woman's ignorance. She was clearly a social climber. One of the *nouveau riche* Aunt Stella despised so much. 'He was fighting for Queen and country, but he was only the Honourable James D'Arton then. He became Viscount Greysford when his elder brother died tragically in a hunting accident and inherited the title on his father's death five years ago.'

Mrs Vernon looked impressed. 'So you are friends of Lord Bradstow.'

'No, I did not say that. My father was an officer in the same regiment. I do not believe he has seen Lord Bradstow for fifteen years. Papa has only recently returned from duty in India.'

Hugh Vernon coughed in embarrassment. 'Sarah, is this relevant?'

'I was hoping that I could persuade Miss Summersfield to design the modernisation for the house.' Mrs Vernon turned to Tanya. 'You have an original flair and a way with colours which I admire.'

Tanya hesitated. She wasn't sure her father would approve.'

'Price is no object. Your fee is immaterial,' Mrs Vernon declared.

'How many rooms are there?'

'Fourteen in all.'

Tanya wavered, it was a project she had always dreamed of doing. How could her father refuse if she priced it high enough so that the profits paid for the renovations needed to their own home.

'I shall need details of your requirements. And I only use my own workmen.'

Mrs Vernon gave her a card. 'If you meet me at the new house tomorrow, we could inspect it together and discuss what is needed.'

'Agreed,' Mr Vernon said. 'My daughter is to be

presented next season and the house must be ready for the ball we shall be holding.'

Tanya left the office in a daze. They even wanted furniture selected for the dining and reception rooms. Two bathrooms were to be installed and the kitchen modernised with the latest equipment. The work was to be completed by the end of May.

'Joe, what have I let myself in for?' She was working late at her desk in her workshop. Her brow creased as she looked at Joe's calculations. The profit from the Vernons' house looked immense. 'I can't possibly charge them so much.'

'Don't undersell yourself, Miss Summersfield. You'll need to take on more workmen to get the work completed by June. They are willing to pay for the originality of your designs. Mrs Vernon wants to impress her friends. They can afford it. You're an artist and now employ a dozen people.' He held up his crippled hand in its leather glove. 'You've given me back my respect, Miss Summersfield. You aren't afraid to give work to others with a disability and save their families from the workhouse. Most employers shun cripples as useless.'

'I get good value from those men and women. They're grateful for the chance to work and reward me with loyalty and diligence. But what about you, Joe? Are you going to be able to manage the extra work involved now that you're also working with Sam.'

Joe grinned. 'I'm delighted to be of service. And I can find good men to work for you. You'll need skilled plasterers in addition to electricians, carpenters and decorators.'

'It looks like we're in business, Joe. If I can persuade my father. It won't be easy.'

Tanya was right. It took three days of heated discussion before Reginald finally agreed, and then it was only when she insisted that her money should be spent on Pilgrim's Crescent as the builders had found rising damp and woodworm which needed immediate treatment.

'I suppose we must have this work done and there's the brickwork at the back of the house and on the chimney stacks to be repointed. One of the chimneys is in danger of toppling down. The builder also reckons that the porch roof is cracked and its supporting columns need to be rebuilt. Damned house eats money. But I suppose if your children aren't going to inherit a ruin, we have no choice.'

'Don't you want the house restored to its former glory, Papa?' Tanya asked. 'It's been in our family for two hundred and fifty years.'

'And for it to stay in our family, you must marry, girl,' he barked at her. 'You are the last of the Summersfield line. You're eighteen in February.'

'Which hardly makes me an old maid, Papa.'

He snorted disparagingly. 'Why couldn't you be more like your mother? Not once during our marriage did she dispute my wishes.'

She laughed. 'The trouble with children is that they can take after either parent.'

'God knows where you get your stubborn streak,' he retaliated.

'Sam says it's from you.'

He glowered at her. 'Sam says too much. Go on, away with you. I've had enough of your insolence for one day.' There was affection behind the gruffness in his voice.

'It's settled then that I can accept Mr Vernon's commission?'

He sighed. 'Very well. Since it will pay for the work here.'

Tanya was elated. Her father was not the ogre she had believed him. And if the Vernons were willing to pay so highly for her expertise, why not others? She could be independent.

Archie was having to spend time with Fancy and Slasher Gilbert. They were like great spiders weaving a web of intrigue and villainy round him until he felt he would never escape their evil machinations. The Gilbert brothers were bullies without the brains to plan complicated robberies. A short spell in prison years ago had brought Archie in contact with the best in the business and he'd listened to their bragging about the jobs they'd pulled. Once Slasher realised this, he insisted that Archie plan their robberies on a grander scale than they had previously attempted. Archie's cut had been generous by Slasher's standards.

The trouble was, Slasher saw Archie as his property and kept him busy working in the more prestigious of their sporting clubs when he wasn't forging documents for them. He had little time to spare for Marcus Bennett and his lover had become difficult. Archie could put up with his jealous tantrums, but not when he suspected that Marcus was seeing someone else. He'd ended the liaison and a week later sent a sneak-thief round to break into Marcus's rooms to steal everything of value.

He'd decided to keep his relationships casual in future until he reached America. He indulged his appetites during the weekly bacchanal Fancy insisted that he participate in. Every vice was pandered to at a price. And all too often the price never stopped being paid. Fancy's most profitable sideline was blackmail.

After the frustration of dancing to Tanya Summersfield's tune, Archie needed the outlet Fancy's orgies provided. Hawkes also needed to be dealt with. The man still had too much influence with the Summersfields. The only thing that now stopped Archie having him killed was that Inspector Fenton was taking too much interest in Slasher's affairs. Twice Archie had only narrowly avoided being arrested and questioned. Now he made it his practice to move lodgings every month. He had too much to hide to want the police nosing into his background.

Archie grinned evilly. He threw back his head and laughed. What would the pompous brigadier think if he ever found out the truth about himself?

Chapter Twenty

On New Year's Eve Reginald Summersfield entertained in a style the house had not seen in twenty-five years. Waiting for the guests to arrive, Tanya surveyed the dining room with its pale yellow silk wallpaper. Dark gold curtains with draped pelmets made the windows look larger and set off the cream Indian carpet with gold and green flowers. Eight full-size portraits of Summersfield ancestors, all in their military scarlet, decorated the walls and added colour to the room. The long table was set with sixteen places and crystal glasses sparkled in the light from ten electric wall lights and a chandelier centrepiece. The meal was to be served on the hand-painted gold-leaf dinner service presented to her great-grandfather by Queen Victoria for services to the Crown. So far the electric lighting had only been installed downstairs but Stella was overjoyed. All her acquaintances still lit their rooms with gas.

The withdrawing room where the guests would relax after their meal had also been transformed according to Tanya's designs. The walls were pale green with a plain olive carpet and matching curtains. Oil landscape paintings by Landseer, Turner and Constable brightened the walls. In the two alcoves each side of the fireplace two large gilt mirrors had been placed to reflect the light from the adjoining glass conservatory which ran along the entire back of the house. To create more light, Tanya had removed the large-leaved aspidistras and potted palms from the window and put these in the conservatory. To give added colour and cosiness to the room, the vases on the ebony pedestals in each corner were filled with hothouse blooms and orchids. The atmosphere created was tranquil and restful.

Tanya was delighted with the results and she felt confident about her designs for the Vernon house. Joe had engaged a dozen workmen and by Christmas work in the master bedroom, hall, dining room and withdrawing room were well under way. Already Tanya had received three more commissions from acquaintances of the Vernons. She had enough work to keep her busy until late summer and she had taken on another dozen workmen, many with disabilities, whom other employers refused to engage.

Aunt Stella swept into the room on her way from checking that everything was in readiness in the kitchen, and that the extra staff employed to serve the meal knew their duties. She eyed Tanya with approval.

'I'm glad you've discarded your mourning black for this evening. That pale green silk is most becoming.' Her rare compliment acknowledged Tanya's influence in having the house redecorated. In other ways Stella was just as belligerent. She had insisted that Archie be invited tonight. Her benevolent expression became a frown of disapproval as she regarded Tanya more closely. 'That neckline is rather low. Couldn't you pin some flowers across it? And you'll need a lace stole as it hasn't sleeves. It is December, not June.'

Tanya glanced in the gilt-edged mirror above the fireplace. The bodice of her watered-silk gown was close-fitting and although it revealed the upper curve of her breasts it was modest compared to many of the styles she had seen at the theatre and opera. The skirt fell straight and narrow at the front, an overskirt drawn back over a small bustle at the back to fall into a tiered train behind her. She had drawn her hair back from her face with pearl combs to fall in amber curls to her shoulders. A five row pearl choker necklace was at her neck, long pearl ear drops swinging against her neck as she moved.

There was a slow tread in the hall and the brigadier in his scarlet and gold-braided dress uniform appeared. Since Tanya had forbidden Stella to force her potions on him, he had gained weight. For weeks now there had been no vomiting or problems with his heart. She hoped that providing he did not drink to excess or overexert himself that he could lead an active life. Sam was several paces behind him. He was also in uniform and cut a magnificent figure.

Tanya swallowed, erasing her love for him from her eyes as she greeted him.

'You look very dashing, Sam.'

He grinned. 'Since the brigadier insisted I attend I'm more comfortable in uniform than top hat and tails.'

'You should be proud of your rank, Sam,' the brigadier said sternly. 'You're entitled to wear your uniform at an informal gathering like this, I would be insulted if you did not. But you'll have to get used to formal dress now that the business is doing so well. You're on your way to becoming a gentleman, Sam. No more cloth caps for you.'

Sam tensed. 'I'm not ashamed of what I was. Nor shall I dandify myself just to please others.'

'Wear what you're comfortable in,' Tanya agreed. 'Men always look so starchy in their top hats and penguin suits. But then we women are just as bad.' She breathed in sharply to emphasise the constriction her rib cage was suffering. 'We endure torture to appear fashionable. And fashion so often has a way of making fools of us all.'

'There is nothing foolish in the way you look.' Sam smiled in a way that made her heart turn over. 'You look very elegant and beautiful.'

To hide her blushes she poured the men a whisky each. She heard Trent, the butler they had recently employed, announce the arrival of Mr Tilbury. Archie entered the room with Aunt Stella smiling up at him. He was dressed impeccably in evening dress, his high, winged shirt collar forcing him to hold his head stiffly. Archie bowed to the brigadier and raised a dark eyebrow at Sam's uniform. Then with a broad smile he took Tanya's hand and lifted it to his lips.

'You look enchanting, Tanya.' He swept his hand theatrically around the room. 'And all this was your creation. It is magnificent, so refined and elegant. Like you.'

He stayed fastened to her side like a safety pin as the other guests arrived and were introduced. They were mostly retired officers and their wives, who were accompanied by their unmarried sons. To make up the numbers of women, four of Aunt Stella's friends from her committees had been invited and a couple of neighbours and their daughters.

The last couple to arrive were Clare and Simon Grosvenor. Clare swooped on Tanya, drawing her away from Archie. Her dark hair glittered with diamond stars and her aquamarine silk gown inset with diamanté and lace panels must have come from Paris.

'You look ravishing,' Clare said fondly as she held Tanya at arm's length. Her eyes sparkled. 'I insist you come back to Oaklands with us for at least a month. It's been so long since we were together.'

Tanya noted the sad shadows in her friend's eyes and the powder and rouge on her cheeks. Clare never usually used make-up. She must be hiding an unhealthy pallor and her figure had a willowy fragility. Losing the baby had deeply affected her; the invitation was a plea from her heart.

'I've missed you, Clare, but I can't come to Oaklands for longer than a week. And then not for another month. I've gone into business. I'll tell you about it later.'

'You always were one for radical ideas. I see Mr Tilbury is still on the scene. Any announcements yet?'

'Don't you start,' Tanya shuddered. 'I get enough of that from Papa and Aunt Stella.'

'How is the old battleaxe?'

'Razor-edged and twice as lethal when crossed.

But she's been better since Papa agreed to have the house decorated.'

Clare sighed as she scanned the room. 'What an improvement. I remember at school you used to sketch rooms. Is this your work?'

Tanya nodded.

'You have hidden talents. Has this anything to do with your business? The women guests are drooling with envy and trying not to show it. I bet it's put their fusty old rooms to shame.'

'I'm working on several houses, which is why I can't come to Tunbridge just yet. I'll have to plan ahead so that the men have everything they need before I leave London. But enough of me. How are you? I was so sorry to hear about the baby.'

Tears filled Clare's eyes and she blinked them away. 'Simon has been wonderful.' She gazed lovingly at her husband who was laughing at something Sam had said. 'I love him so much.' Her eyes widened as she took in Sam. 'I can see why you haven't accepted Tilbury. Sam Hawkes is so much more...' she laughed, 'well, more manly. And in that uniform I could fall for him myself.'

'Sam is a friend.'

Clare looked at her mockingly. 'And I'm your Dutch aunt. He can't take his eyes off you. And you're blushing, which confirms it.'

Tanya was saved from replying by Stella who commandeered Clare to introduce her to her friends. Stella was gloating with pride, informing everyone that Clare was the daughter of the millionaire Tobias Havistock. Her snobbery was unlimited. She was never happy unless she was impressing people. The pettiness of it irritated Tanya.

Sam was still conversing with Simon, and seeing Archie threading his way towards her, Tanya slipped out of the room. Her father had wandered into the dining room looking furtively over his shoulder to ensure that Stella had not seen him. Intrigued, Tanya followed. He was changing the dinner settings which had been arranged by his sister.

'Stella spent hours sorting out who was to sit with whom. She'll be furious,' Tanya chided.

'I see she put Tilbury next to you. If she's so fond of the man, she can entertain him herself while we dine.'

A gong was sounded in the hall and Trent announced dinner. Tanya returned to their guests. Stella was about to foist a dragon of a matron on Sam, so she darted forward and rescued him. As her arm slipped through his, she encountered Archie's furious glare. Wickedly, she was delighted that Archie had no choice but to escort the dragon himself. Stella looked as if she wanted to throttle her.

'Thanks for rescuing me,' Sam whispered against her hair.

'I am growing tired of Stella trying to manipulate me. Are you enjoying yourself?'

'I rarely socialised in the officers' mess. But Simon Grosvenor is interesting. He's often down at Brooklands for the racing and has seen the big races in France. He's organising some kind of local rally on a circuit round his estate for next spring. He's invited me to take part.'

'Then you must,' she encouraged. 'It would be good for business and you'll enjoy it. I like Simon. He adores Clare. She was always terrified that someone would marry her for her money rather than herself.'

'I gathered they were pretty loaded from the way your aunt was badgering her to support one of her charities.'

Tanya groaned. 'That woman is incorrigible. Clare donates vast sums to charities every year. Stella knows that. I told her not to approach Clare for money.'

When they entered the dining room, her father was making a show of escorting the ladies to their seats, which stopped Aunt Stella from interfering. Her aunt looked displeased at discovering that Archie had been placed in the middle of the table between herself and the wife of a retired general. When she noticed that a young major and a lieutenant were seated on either side of Tanya, her glare could have soured cream.

Archie was glowering darkly until a guest opposite asked him a question. He answered and smiled so engagingly that Tanya was taken aback. For the first time she saw the insincerity and falseness behind his practised smile. Was Sam right and Archie not all that he seemed? It wasn't just politeness which made him charm those in his vicinity. She saw it now as something sinister, a power exerted to cloak his other motives.

She was disappointed that Sam was seated at the far end of the table next to her father. It was obvious that the brigadier was trying to matchmake for her tonight. Yet the only man she was aware of was Sam. It took all her willpower not to keep glancing in his direction. When she did, bittersweet ache pitted her heart. Seated on Sam's right was Felicity Fanshawe, a vivacious, beautiful, blonde widow who had just moved into Pilgrim's Crescent with her young child. Her father was a senior member of the Civil Service. She was reputedly wealthy. Had the brigadier heard of her wealth and hoped Sam would be taken with the woman? He would be delighted if Sam married into a good family, as long as it wasn't theirs.

From the way Felicity was staring starry-eyed at Sam, she was certainly attracted to him. And Sam seemed to be enjoying every second of her rapt attention.

Tanya's hands tightened over her fork as she forced her attention on what Lieutenant Redwood, on her right, was saying. A smile was etched on her lips as she strove to combat her boredom. Both soldiers were arrogant and filled with their own importance. She had been brought up on feats of glory and usually enjoyed having battles related to her, but Redwood was a braggart, his boasting giving the impression that his colonel never made a decision without consulting him, which was preposterous. Major Jordan, on her left, was little better. He had already drunk several glasses of wine and was becoming morose. He was a cynic and proceeded to tell her everything that was wrong with the army. He eyed her blearily.

'Time I settled down,' he drawled, his gaze lascivious as it rested on her breasts. 'Get myself a pretty wife to look after me. And give me a brace of strapping sons to carry on the family name. A woman who knows her place. Not like these damned suffragettes. They should be horse-whipped. It's shameful the way they degrade themselves.'

Tanya regarded him stonily. 'They are brave and courageous women. It's time women had a voice. Why should men presume to know what is best? Did not nature bestow upon woman the bearing and rearing of the next generation?'

'And where would women be without men to provide for them?' Major Jordan declared pompously.

'They would provide for themselves, always supposing that their fathers allowed them an education that matched their sons'.'

He gulped and was stopped from commenting by the lieutenant's guffaw. 'Miss Summersfield is a woman with spirit. My sister has been to prison five times under this infamous "Cat and Mouse" Act. She refuses to eat in Holloway. When she is too weak from hunger they discharge her to recover. Once her strength returns, she is put back in prison. Father keeps threatening to disown her each time it happens, and Mother takes to her bed for a week in mortification. I rather admire her spirit.'

Major Jordan grunted. 'Your sister needs a decent man to keep her in line.' He inspected Tanya. 'That's all any woman needs. Someone with good child-bearing hips like yourself would suit me nicely.'

Tanya bit her lip. She despised men who

regarded women as nothing more than brood mares. The major's attitude was medieval. Before the second course was finished she was dredging her control to remain civil to both the soldiers. Throughout the eight courses of the meal the major drank copiously. His eyes were glazed by the time Tanya rose and invited the ladies to leave the men to their brandy and cigars.

The women sighed over the beauty of the withdrawing room and two of them asked Tanya if she would consider redesigning rooms for them.

'Father is against me working,' she prevaricated.

'This isn't like work,' one matriarch expounded. 'It's a valuable service you're offering. You have a gift for elegance and originality. You should use it.'

'It's not as though you actually do the menial work,' another said patronisingly. 'You would meet your clients as an equal. And I insist on being the first to have my withdrawing room redecorated to your designs. Horace has agreed that the house is looking positively tawdry. The last work done on it was in the old Queen's reign and she, God rest her soul, has been gone for six years. This style is so different. It will be all the rage.'

'The Christmas tree looks lovely,' Felicity Fanshawe said, posing decoratively by the candlelit spruce. 'How unusual to decorate it only with red plaited ribbons and bells. And the holly and ivy garlands on the walls are almost pagan, yet very dramatic.'

Clare, who was standing next to her, laughed. 'Tanya is interested in folklore. I remember one Allhallows Eve at school when she–'

'Miss Fanshawe doesn't want to hear that story, Clare,' Tanya hastily intervened. 'It was a schoolgirl prank.'

'I love disreputable secrets,' Felicity confided. 'Do tell me.'

Clare needed no encouragement. 'Tanya persuaded a group of us to dress all in white and cover our hair and faces with flour. About half a mile across the fields from our school there was a pile of stones from an old convent which was supposed to be haunted. We were to sneak into the stables and ride across the parkland and pretend to be the avenging spirits of the murdered nuns who were killed by Henry VIII's soldiers during the dissolution of the monasteries.'

Tanya saw Felicity stifle a yawn; she was clearly not interested in the tale.

'The others lost their nerve before they got to the stables and Tanya and I were the only ones to do it,' Clare went on, her face animated. 'It was in the local paper that ghosts had been sighted. All the girls in our dorm were sworn to secrecy and Tanya was the heroine of the year for that exploit.'

'I thought you were going to tell me of a romantic escapade,' Felicity replied languidly, 'about meeting secret lovers.' She leaned towards Tanya and lowered her voice. 'What would fascinate me is everything you know about that divine captain I sat next to at dinner.' The musky perfume she wore was too powerful for Tanya's taste and the woman kept glancing at the door, obviously impatient for the men to rejoin them. 'I understand he's a friend of your father's and that he stayed here for some weeks. Lucky you. Not that I suppose you noticed, having that delicious Mr Tilbury so often in attendance. Tell me about Captain Hawkes. There's no woman in his life, is there?'

'I do not believe so.' Tanya's throat was so tight she almost gagged on her words. 'Please excuse me, I see the maids have forgotten to set out some delicacies for the ladies.' She looked apologetically at Clare who smiled understandingly. Tanya couldn't bear to stay in the room a moment longer. She had no intention of being cornered by Felicity Fanshawe again.

When the men joined them, the women flocked round Reginald, demanding that Tanya be allowed to redesign rooms for them. Felicity was at Sam's side the moment he walked through the door. He was smiling at her, clearly enjoying her company. So that she would not have to watch them, Tanya wandered into the conservatory. There was no escape. Here memories of Sam kissing her were overwhelming. Her cheeks flushed with colour as she remembered how wantonly she had responded.

A footfall made her whirl round. Archie was watching her. It was an effort for her to smile a welcome. Sensing her reticence, he frowned.

'Your father has made it obvious that he would have a soldier as a son-in-law,' he said curtly.

'This is a regimental family, officers are always shown deference,' she said, sounding unconvincing to her own ears.

'Hawkes seems taken with the Widow Fanshawe – a woman with a reputation, according to Stella. Didn't she marry an older man who died within six months of her marriage? And there was talk that the child born within a month of his death was not his.'

'Papa would not have a woman with a tainted reputation in our home. Gossip is often malicious where a beautiful woman is concerned.'

'She cannot compare with you for beauty.' He groaned softly. 'Tanya, I adore you.' To her embarrassment he went down on one knee. 'Say you will be mine. Make me the happiest of men by agreeing to become my wife. It's New Year's Eve, what better opportunity to announce our engagement?'

She was horrified lest someone come upon them. 'Please stand up before someone sees you.'

'You cannot refuse me.' He stood up and moved closer, his voice strained. The smile was pasted on but there was no accompanying tenderness in his eyes. 'Think of your reputation.'

This sounded uncomfortably like a threat rather than a proposal of marriage.

'Archie, I do not love you. I'll not be blackmailed by convention into marrying you. If people are being led to expect an announcement between us, it would be better if we did not see each other again.'

Her arms were gripped in bruising fingers. There was a feral glitter in Archie's eyes which sent shivers of alarm through Tanya. He looked as if he hated her.

'I've given you the time you asked for. I will not be made a fool of in this way.'

'Archie, you're hurting me.' She struggled to release her arms. The grip tightened and she gave a low cry. Then outrage filled her. 'Let go of me at once,' she commanded, her voicc icy, 'or I shall be forced to call out. That would be an unnecessary embarrassment to us both.'

Her arms were released as though their touch had burned him. 'I can only surmise that you are distraught and do not know what you are saying. Once you have considered the damage to your reputation by refusing me, I shall call upon your father.'

'Don't threaten me,' she said, backing away, her fear mounting.

'Tanya, are you all right?' Sam demanded from the doorway.

Archie stepped back and fury darkened his face.

'Archie was just leaving,' she answered coldly.

'Goodnight, Mr Tilbury,' Sam said and held out his arm to escort Tanya back to the guests.

Archie brushed past them so violently that a button on his frock coat grazed Tanya's arm. He marched through the guests, throwing Stella an enraged glare before the front door slammed behind him.

'What was that all about?' Sam asked.

'I told him I would not marry him.'

'You're well rid of the bounder,' Sam said, feeling easier. He had learned some disturbing facts about Archie Tilbury. And it seemed that he was not the only one making enquiries. This afternoon his source had told him than an Inspector Fenton was asking after a man called Arnie Potter who bore a strong resemblance to Tilbury. And what he had learned about Arnie Potter had alarmed him. But he still lacked the proof he needed to convince Tanya. It was as well that she had finished with Tilbury.

Even so, he remained uneasy. There was something about Tilbury that he distrusted deeply. Tomorrow he would call on Inspector Fenton and hear what the policeman had to say.

Stella dragged Tanya away from Sam and snarled in her ear, 'What did you say to upset Mr Tilbury?'

Tanya eyed her coldly. 'He again asked me to marry him and I refused. Then he started to threaten me.'

Stella paled. 'What nonsense. Both you and your father have insulted him in front of our guests.'

'What's the long face for, Stella?' Reginald demanded as he joined them.

'Your daughter has turned down Mr Tilbury's proposal of marriage,' Stella fumed. 'She's led him on for months. Her conduct is disgraceful.'

'This is not the place to discuss it,' Tanya said softly, aware that their guests were listening.

Her father chortled. 'You can do better than him, my girl. Never did take to the fellow. Something shifty about him. What about Lieutenant Redwood? Good family. He'll rise high in the army.'

'Papa, I am not looking for a husband.' Her gaze had caught Felicity Fanshawe sidling up to

Sam and possessively taking his arm. She had suffered enough. 'Excuse me, Papa.'

Lieutenant Redwood shouted, 'It's almost midnight. Anyone coming down to St Paul's to see the New Year in?'

Felicity Fanshawe grabbed Sam's arm. 'Yes, let's join the celebrations there. Will you be my escort, Captain Hawkes?'

Sam effortlessly disengaged her arm. 'I've already promised Miss Summersfield that I would escort her.' He beckoned to Redwood. 'I'm sure that Lieutenant Redwood will be delighted to escort you, Mrs Fanshawe.'

Only the younger guests were going to St Paul's. While they waited for their cloaks to be brought to them, Tanya smiled at Sam. 'I thought you were rather taken with Mrs Fanshawe.'

His eyes were dark and fathomless as they stepped out onto the pavement. 'I'd rather see the New Year in with you. You still look shaken from your confrontation with Tilbury.'

Outside Pilgrim's Crescent they merged with other revellers converging on the steps of St Paul's to await the cathedral clock striking midnight. They became separated from the rest of the party as the crowd thickened. A discordant wail of bagpipes came from a group of kilted Scotsmen. A barrel organ played and couples swung each other round in a boisterous dance. Others linked arms and sang and swayed from side to side. Sam and Tanya were frequently jostled. When she was almost whisked from Sam's side by a top-hatted reveller reeking of brandy, his arm went round her waist to hold her tight.

The first chime from the cathedral silenced the gathering. Then the clock began to boom out midnight. At the last stroke, everybody yelled and cheered, the men grabbing women and kissing them.

'Happy New Year, Tanya,' Sam said, drawing her round to face him.

'Happy New Year, Sam.'

In a surging mass of people they could have been on an island alone as they gazed into each other's faces. Sam stooped to kiss her. It wasn't the passionate kiss she craved, but its lingering restraint told her of the curb he was putting on his desire.

Her arms wound round his neck and her lips moved over his, refusing to allow the kiss to end. His kiss deepened with hunger and longing until she was breathless and elated.

When they broke apart she expected to see Sam's answering love blazing in his eyes. Instead they were guarded, his tone hoarse as he murmured, 'We must return to the house.'

'Are you angry with me, Sam?' she asked, feeling that she had again made a fool of herself.

'Tanya, I don't want you to be hurt,' he returned gruffly. 'There can be nothing more than friendship between us.'

'Your kiss told me there could be more,' she pursued. 'Or is that how you'd kiss any woman to celebrate the New Year?'

'Only the beautiful ones, given the chance,' he said flippantly.

'Then go and find Felicity Fanshawe for more sport.' Twisting away from him Tanya pushed her way through the crowd and ran without stopping to Pilgrim's Crescent.

Outside her home she held her side to recover her breath before entering. From a darkened doorway she heard a giggle and saw Lieutenant Redwood and Felicity Fanshawe in a passionate embrace.

Clare called out her name and Tanya waited for her and Simon to join her. Sam was behind them, watching her, his expression shuttered.

'Don't I get a kiss, Tanya?' Simon said, planting a loud one on her lips. 'Happy New Year. Have you made your resolutions tonight?'

Tanya forced a smile. Sam had obviously resolved to put loyalty to her father before his feelings for her.

Clare laughed. 'Only young women make resolutions and that's to be married before the year's end. Isn't that right, Tanya?'

Tanya looked pointedly at Sam, but did not answer. When she entered the house, Stella waylaid her. Her aunt drew her into the empty study and before Tanya realised her intent, Stella slapped her cheek.

'I know what you've been up to, you little slut. You'll never have Hawkes. And you'll regret making a fool of me.'

Chapter Twenty-one

Within days of the dinner party the brigadier suffered another seizure. It was worse than any of the others. Just after waking, a scream from Ginny took Tanya to her father's bedroom. Inside the door the breakfast tray was on the carpet, tea stains spreading from the broken teapot.

Tanya cried out at seeing her father. His upper body had rolled out of the bed and his head lay on the floor. He was unconscious, his breathing rasping like broken bellows. His face was pale as tallow and a blue tinge coloured his lips. With Ginny's help, Tanya lifted him back into bed and sent for the doctor.

Dressing hurriedly, she returned to his side, fearful at leaving him alone and feeling wretched and helpless.

Dr Garrett examined him, his expression bleak. When he turned to Tanya, he shook his head sorrowfully. 'It's his heart. He's dying. There's nothing I can do.'

'No! That can't be,' Tanya cried. 'He's recovered before. He's only middle-aged and strong. He's a fighter.'

The doctor sighed. 'I'm sorry, but even the most valiant warriors run out of strength.'

'Is there nothing we can do?' Aunt Stella asked. 'My infusions of herb teas have helped him before.'

‘Get him to take as much liquid as you can,’ Dr Garrett advised. ‘But I doubt he will last the day.’

The sound of horses’ hooves striking the cobbles at the front of the house made Tanya frown. She ordered straw to be laid in the road outside to deaden the sound of passing vehicles to aid her father’s rest. Word was also sent to Sam.

Desolate, Tanya sank into the chair by the bed and took her father’s hand in hers. His breathing was an intermittent wheeze. Her throat was tight and the sound of the black marble clock ticking on the mantelpiece echoed through the room. Ginny crept in and banked the fire high with coals, sobbing quietly as she performed the task.

Stella sat by the window, a dry-eyed sentinel of duty. ‘I told him he was doing too much,’ she said, self-righteously. ‘He’s been out in this cold weather with Hawkes. Sheer madness when he’s been ill. But would he listen? No, he would not. It’s that fellow Hawkes’ fault for encouraging him. All he’s interested in is Reginald’s money.’

‘Sam cares for Papa,’ Tanya retaliated. ‘And keep your voice down, Aunt. How do we know that Papa cannot hear you?’

Stella sniffed disdainfully. ‘Are you telling me how to behave in a sickroom? Wasn’t I the one who tended him day and night during his first seizures? I don’t know why I put myself to so much trouble. He never appreciated it, I was just an unpaid servant as far as he was concerned.’

‘That isn’t true. And this is not the time to speak of such things. Why must you always blame Sam? He was as good as a tonic for Papa. Few men would have given so much of their time.'

'You've a soft spot for that scoundrel,' Stella sneered. 'Is that why you refused Archie? Hawkes is a common man. A–'

'Stop it!' Tanya said quietly but firmly. 'Sam is a most uncommon man, if you must know. His loyalty to Papa is unquestioned. I refused Archie because I do not love him.'

Stella glared at her. She had been ill-tempered towards Tanya since the dinner party and had not forgiven her for refusing to marry Archie.

Why did her aunt always want to organise other people's lives? Tanya wondered miserably. It wasn't as though Archie was anyone special to Stella. He was only one among many businessmen who contributed to her charity work.

Tanya picked up a guitar and began to play a classical piece her father had always liked. She needed to do something to help her father and perhaps, even while he was unconscious, the music would help him.

She lost herself in her playing. She had always loved the guitar although the piano was the instrument every gentlewoman was expected to be proficient upon. When the music teacher at school had encouraged her pupils to try other instruments, Tanya had chosen the guitar. It had been her companion during many lonely summer holidays when only a few of the girls remained boarders at the school. She was unaware of the tears streaming down her cheeks as the haunting harmony reflected her grief. Her father was no longer the tyrant she resented. He had listened to her and allowed her to continue her design work for clients. She had glimpsed the other side of his nature, the leader of men, the diplomat and the intellectual, a man she could admire and respect as Sam did. It was cruel that just as they had become close, death was robbing them of something precious.

By the time Sam arrived, the brigadier looked even greyer and more hollow-cheeked. The once strong and vibrant man was withering before their eyes.

From Sam's haggard expression, it was clear to Tanya that he was grieving as much as she was. Stella remained like a black shadow sitting by the window, her accusing glare on Sam throughout their vigil.

At midday Reginald's breathing changed. It soughed from his lungs in painful bursts. He opened his eyes and when Sam leaned forward into his line of vision, he seemed to recognise him. His blue lips moved but no sound rose from his throat. Sam swallowed and blinked against his unashamed tears.

'Don't try and speak, my friend. Rest easy.'

Tanya squeezed her father's hand and with her head close to Sam's gazed down at her father. The brigadier licked his lips, his Adam's apple working as he tried to speak.

Then the light in his eyes faded and vanished.

'He's gone,' Sam croaked and closed the staring eyes.

Stella stumped forward from her chair and rudely pushed Sam aside. She studied the still figure of her brother for a long moment. 'I'll send Ginny to fetch the undertaker and inform

Dr Garrett,' she said and left the room.

It was snowing the day Brigadier Reginald Victor Alexander Summersfield joined his ancestors in the family vault in Bunhill Fields Cemetery. Tanya had planned a small funeral service in the parish church close by but a visit from General Waymark had informed her that the regiment would make all the arrangements and the service would be in the early morning at St Paul's Cathedral. The cortège would have a mounted escort.

The coffin was laid on a gun carriage for the procession to St Paul's. Resplendent in his scarlet officer's uniform, Sam led a black stallion with riding boots reversed in the stirrups to signify an officer's death. Tanya could have done without all the pomp and ceremony of a regimental funeral but Stella revelled in it, declaring that it was no more than Reginald's due. Over sixty officers from various regiments attended.

Tanya was aware of little of the church service or the procession. Her gaze remained upon the coffin draped in the Union Jack. When the coffin was placed in the vault, a salute of musket fire resounded in the air. The gunfire brought her abruptly back to an awareness of her duties. The snow had numbed her fingers and toes and the mourners were restless to return to the warmth of the house.

It was only then that she realised that Archie Tilbury was among the gathering. Stella must have invited him. Her aunt was talking earnestly to him as the mourners paid Tanya their condolences before leaving the churchyard. Then leaning heavily on his arm, Stella walked back to the waiting horse-drawn carriages which would return them to Pilgrim's Crescent for the funeral tea. When Archie also entered the carriage, Tanya felt uneasy. She didn't want to have to face him back at the house. She resented the way he had tried to manipulate her at the dinner party into accepting his proposal. His behaviour had revealed a side of his character that she did not like or trust.

She turned towards a different carriage. At least she could avoid travelling with them. Sam was at her elbow, helping her inside.

'Join me, Sam. I don't want to be alone. Or face the condolences of the others. I don't know most of these people. And Stella has invited Archie back to the house. Do you think we could stop somewhere by the river for a short time? Everyone is so well-meaning with their condolences but...'

'Of course,' Sam agreed. 'But first you must have a hot drink. The snow is beginning to settle and your hair is wet.'

They stopped at a refreshment booth by Tower Bridge and Sam ordered the cabbie to wait. Holding the cup of steaming tea in both hands, Tanya stared up at the twin turrets of the impressive bridge. The central section was raised to allow three tall-masted ships through. The jetties and warehouses on both sides of the river were bustling as vessels loaded and unloaded cargo. From a two-masted brig, seamen were disembarking, their canvas kit bags on their shoulders.

‘I wonder where their voyage took them?’ Tanya remarked. ‘What exotic countries did they visit, what strange customs did they witness? Papa saw so much of the world. Africa, Europe, Asia. He experienced so much and I know so little about that life. I wish we’d had more time together.’

She finished her tea and shivered. The snow was falling thickly now, covering the roofs of the warehouses and blurring the massive battlements and turrets of the Tower of London. Stepping back into the carriage she stopped Sam ordering the driver to move on. ‘Tell me about Papa. About the real man, not the soldier.’

Sam stuck his head out of the carriage window and flipped a silver coin to the carriage driver. ‘Get yourself a whisky to keep out the cold. We’ll be staying here a while yet.’

He had removed his steel-domed helmet with its horsehair plume and several flakes of snow clung to his wheatgold hair, the dampness making it fall forward over his brow. The impulse to touch it was so overpowering Tanya gripped her hands together beneath her black fur muff.

‘I’d never met an officer quite like him. He cared for the welfare of his men and never regarded them as cannon fodder, as do so many others. He always had time to listen to their problems. But he could be strict if discipline was necessary.’ Sam spoke hesitantly at first, his expression tight with grief. As he expanded his reminiscences, his face relaxed and his tawny eyes glowed with affection.

They sat in the stillness of the carriage. The falling snow formed a lacy curtain round them, sheltering them from the outside world. Tanya listened with rapt attention, the huskiness of Sam's voice warming her as he conjured images of her father which she had never seen in life.

At last, he said, heavily, 'He was a great man. I shall miss him.' He leaned forward and gently wiped a tear which clung to her cheeks.

'Oh, Sam.' She raised her hand to keep his palm against her skin. 'Now that Papa has gone, will I still see you?'

For a long moment he stared into her eyes, his gaze so profound and magnetic that she swayed towards him. For a second she thought he intended to kiss her, and her lips parted in anticipation. Then abruptly he sat back and dropped his hand back to his knee.

'Of course we shall see each other. Your workshop and my garage are only a few doors apart. And you'll inherit your father's share of the business.'

The carriage dipped as the driver climbed onto his seat and Sam rapped on the roof with the hilt of his sword for them to move off. He looked far from pleased at the prospect that they would now be business partners. Sensitive to his moods, Tanya was wounded by his withdrawal. She had almost made a fool of herself again. Polly had excitedly told her of the three occasions when Sam had taken her and Sal for a drive in the country at the weekend. Sam had said it was to get Sal out of the house, but Tanya was beginning to suspect that there was more to it than that. In the last few weeks Polly had been doing her work in a dreamlike trance. It was how Clare had looked and acted when Simon first courted her.

'The lawyer has insisted that you should be present when Papa's will is read,' she informed him, forcing neutrality into her voice. A glance at her wristwatch showed her that they would have been expected back at Pilgrim's Crescent an hour ago.

'Have you had any further trouble from Tilbury since he stormed out on New Year's Eve?'

'This is the first time I've seen him. It was good of him to come to the funeral, though I would rather not have to face him today.'

'There is nothing good about Archie Tilbury.' Sam studied her before continuing. 'I'd not blacken a man's character without cause, but I don't trust him. An Inspector Fenton has been asking questions about a man of his description who goes by the name Arnold Potter. I suspect Tilbury is also Potter. Why does he use two names? He's hiding something.'

His measured speech suggested that he had weighed his words carefully. 'You're not telling me everything, Sam,' Tanya said.

Sam already felt he had said too much without proof. He didn't want to frighten Tanya but she had to be warned. There was no point in telling her that he believed it was Tilbury who had paid thugs to beat him up. Or that Inspector Fenton was making enquiries about the death of Granville Ingram, the music hall comedian who had been murdered and was once a friend of Arnold Potter.

'I've been making enquiries and I should have more answers in a few days. You've enough to worry about. Just take care, that's all.'

'I want nothing more to do with Archie,' she said, truthfully.

When they entered the house, only a few of the mourners remained. Four officers, her father's closest friends, were talking in a corner. Clare and Simon were chatting to a neighbour and Archie was seated beside Stella, his smile at its most disarming. It failed to beguile Tanya.

Immediately she entered the room, Stella stood up, her glare hostile as she announced. 'You have kept the lawyer waiting. We will hear your father's will now.' She turned to their guests. 'Please, help yourself to more refreshments, brandy or sherry. Our business with the lawyer will not take long.'

Sam was talking to Simon Grosvenor and Tanya saw Mr Dobbs approaching her. He was a thin, stoop-shouldered man, with thick white side whiskers, who had been the family solicitor for thirty years.

'I'm sorry to have kept you waiting, Mr Dobbs.' Tanya shook her head. 'But I couldn't face so many people.'

He nodded with understanding. 'This is a sad day. Your father will be greatly missed. When you are ready, I shall be in the study.'

When Tanya caught Archie's brooding stare on her, it unaccountably made her shiver. To avoid him she joined Clare.

'Thank you for coming, especially in this atrocious weather.'

'How are you, Tanya?' Clare asked. 'Your father's death must have been a shock. He looked so well last week.'

'I feel dazed. It hasn't sunk in yet. Thank goodness I've got my work to throw myself into. They say it's the best cure.'

Clare hugged her. 'I wish we didn't have to return to Oaklands today but Simon is worried that the road could be cut off if this snow keeps up. Promise you'll visit soon. I intend to throw a birthday party for you in February, so no excuses to avoid that.'

Simon and Sam joined them. Clare took her husband's arm, her love for him shining in her eyes. 'I've invited Clare down to Oaklands for her birthday.' She turned her attention to Sam. 'You won't mind driving her down, will you, Sam?'

'Yes, you must,' Simon insisted. 'We can go over the rally circuit at the same time. I really would value your advice.'

'How can I refuse such an offer?' Sam laughed, but Tanya saw from the stiff way he held himself that he had reservations about the visit.

Stella was bearing down on them. From her angry expression she had overheard Simon's invitation and did not approve. She gave Sam a malignant glare. 'I suppose you were responsible for the way Tanya has neglected our guests.'

'No,' Tanya interceded. 'I asked Sam to take me to the river. I couldn't face all these strangers – Clare and Simon excepted of course.'

'Mr Tilbury is not a stranger and you've ignored him,' Stella returned tartly. 'I made the excuse that you needed to collect some papers from the garage in connection with your father's partnership with Hawkes. But I dread to think what your father's friends thought of such conduct, especially with a non-commissioned officer. You have no protector now that your father is dead. You must safeguard your reputation.'

Sam's jaw tightened at the insult. Simon tactfully intervened. 'Thc brigadicr told me how you got your commission, Sam. For exceptional courage, wasn't it? You led a vital attack after your commanding officer was injured. Your men regarded you as a hero.'

'Hardly that,' Sam parried modestly, and excused himself to join the solicitor in the study.

'I would trust Sam with my life as well as my reputation,' Tanya defended Sam.

'Any hint of a scandal and no decent man will wed you,' Stella snarled. 'You have to be especially careful now. Doesn't she, Clare?'

'Tanya would never dishonour her family,' Clare returned.

Stella poked a finger at Tanya. 'I won't have you gadding about the country with that man. I heard them invite Hawkes.'

'You can't stop me, Aunt. Millie can accompany me.'

'And how am I supposed to manage without a maid? Pride cometh before a fall, my girl. Carry on acting as you are and no respectable woman will want you designing her rooms. That's important to you, isn't it? Though why you want to degrade yourself by working when a husband could keep you in style and comfort is beyond me. There's no glamour in being a spinster. You are at best pitied, at worst indulged. You are barren in heart, body and soul. And often lonely.

Is that what you want?'

'I'm sorry if that is how spinsterhood has been for you. My work will ensure that I am fulfilled.'

Stella glowered at her. 'You know nothing of society and how it can shun its own. No matron will allow an attractive and unwed woman into her home to become a temptation to her husband. A woman in business will be considered fast and loose.'

Tanya refused to rise to her aunt's baiting and excused herself. She went to the study and took a seat next to Sam. Stella moved her chair closer to the fire and seated herself in frigid silence.

The will was short but full of surprises. Sam inherited Reginald's share of the motor business. Although Tanya was pleased that this would help further Sam's career, she was disheartened that it removed an excuse for them to meet in future.

Stella was bequeathed a small annuity and several pieces of valuable porcelain and silver. It meant that she remained dependent on Tanya for support. What shocked Tanya most was discovering how heavily the house was mortgaged and that there were death duties to pay as well.

Mr Dobbs looked at her over the top of his horn-rimmed spectacles. 'Miss Summersfield, I would advise you to sell this property and the more valuable paintings and contents. You could then live comfortably in a smaller house on the outskirts of London.'

'We couldn't possibly sell the house,' Stella declared. 'It's been in our family since it was rebuilt after the great fire of sixteen sixty-six.'

'As its new owner, that is for Miss Tanya to

decide.' Mr Dobbs dismissed the older woman's outburst. 'My company will of course be happy to advise on any sale. Until Miss Tanya either marries or reaches the age of twenty-five, I am to be trustee of her inheritance. Mr Hawkes is co-trustee.'

'That's outrageous!' Stella spat.

'It is what the brigadier wished for his daughter. Mr Hawkes has already agreed to uphold the conditions of the will.'

'Not all the conditions,' Sam interrupted. 'I never expected to be given the brigadier's share of our partnership. His financial backing got me started. So far we have been fortunate and it brings in a handsome profit. I want Miss Summersfield to keep the brigadier's share of that income.'

'But the will states–'

Sam put up a hand to halt Mr Dobbs. 'It's not that I don't appreciate the brigadier's intentions. He was a man I greatly respected and I'll not see his family go without. Draw up what papers are needed for Miss Summersfield to receive half the profits from the partnership.'

'No, Sam. I will not take the money. Papa wished to be yours.'

'Take it and don't be such a fool, Tanya,' Stella urged.

'My mind is made up.' Tanya was adamant. 'I shall renovate every room in the house and then sell it. That way it will be worth a great deal more than it is now.'

Sam looked distraught. 'Then at least accept your father's share of the profits until you marry.

It will give you more independence.'

Hearing Sam talk so dispassionately of her marriage to another man bruised Tanya's heart.

'Don't be so stubborn, Tanya,' he persisted. 'You agreed to let me repay my hospital fees once the garage was established. There can be no argument about that. More importantly, if you had not helped run the place when I was in hospital, there would be no business. I'd be bankrupt now.' Ignoring Stella and the solicitor, he took her hands. He rubbed his thumbs across their backs in a way which sent her senses spinning. 'Today we share a common grief,' he added softly, coercing. 'You proved a true friend when I needed you. Would you deny me the chance to do the same for you?'

How could she withstand his reasoning, especially as his touch was playing havoc with her emotions? It would mean that they would continue to see each other. That meant more to her than the money. 'Your offer is very generous, Sam. Thank you.'

He smiled, increasing the pressure of his fingers over hers before releasing her. Turning to Mr Dobbs, he held out his hand to the solicitor. 'Good day, sir. I shall sign any necessary papers as soon as they are ready.' He picked up his steel helmet from the corner of the desk. 'Tanya, there are a few things I loaned your father. Would it be all right if I collected them now?'

'Of course, Sam. And I'd like you to have father's ivory chess set as a memento of him.'

'I'll treasure it.' He held her gaze and the tenderness in his eyes set the blood pounding through her veins. His smile was intimate and she almost believed poignant with a hidden yearning. Then his expression became guarded in the way she hated. Holding his helmet against his side he left the room, only a slight limp perceptible after the operation on his knee.

'Such a generous gentleman,' Mr Dobbs observed.

'Ha!' Aunt Stella was rigid with anger and disapproval. 'It was the least he could do. He conned my brother out of his life savings to start that business. Why do you think the house is so heavily mortgaged?'

'That's not true, Aunt,' Tanya defended.

'You are wrong, Miss Stella,' Mr Dobbs intervened. 'The house has been mortgaged since your father's time. He inherited vast debts from his father. The brigadier never failed in the payments and neither did he increase the loan.'

'That aside,' Stella continued vindictively, 'I don't trust Hawkes. He's an opportunist. That's proved by the way he rose in the army. He's nothing but an East End guttersnipe at heart. And they'd steal your last farthing given the chance.'

Tanya looked appalled at Stella's outburst. 'Sam is not like that!' she cried.

'Umph! We'll see about that,' Stella fumed, heaving herself out of the chair and waddling to the door. 'What do you know of the world to judge such a man? Blood will always out in the end. Mark my words. No good will come of this.'

Tanya escorted Mr Dobbs to the door and as she made her way back to the guests she saw Sam descending the stairs. She waited for him. He grinned as he held up a carpetbag belonging to her father. 'Hope you don't mind me borrowing this. I'd left more upstairs than I realised, and I've borrowed some books he suggested I read. I shall miss visiting him.'

'There's always Polly. You see a lot of her, don't you?' She couldn't believe she had said those words.

Sam stared at her blankly then a teasing light appeared in his eyes. Before he could answer, she blurted out, 'I'm sorry, Sam. I shouldn't have said that. Your seeing Polly doesn't affect our friendship, does it?'

'Nothing could affect that.'

Their gazes locked, neither moved or spoke.

'You'll always be special,' he said softly and sighed.

It echoed the longing in her heart. She waited breathless, expectant. Was he going to tell her Polly was not important to him and that only she mattered?

One of the officers laughed and another declared that he was leaving. It shattered the intimacy of the moment.

'I wanted a word with Major Travers,' Sam said, his stare again impersonal.

'And I have neglected the guests.'

Sam hesitated, apparently loath to leave her side. Again her heartbeat suspended in anticipation. 'Will you be at your workshop next week? Work is a good therapy against losing someone you love. It doesn't fill the void, but…'

Damn him for being so practical. 'Oh, Sam.'

Her lower lip quivered and tears glistened on her lashes.

'Hey, where's the brave, strong woman I so admire?'

His hand which had meant to squeeze her shoulder in compassion was suddenly round her waist, drawing her against him. Unconsciously, she was offering her lips to him. The warmth of her breath against his face was as tantalising as a summer breeze. He stooped to kiss her goodbye, intending a salutary kiss of friendship. The touch of her lips parting warm and sweet beneath his made a mockery of friendship. He wanted her. He had tried so hard to forget the madness her kisses could provoke. Restraint shattered. The bag fell from his fingers. He gathered her to him, his tongue tasting the sweetness of her mouth.

A soft sigh was torn from deep in her throat; a siren's call, beckoning, enchanting. Her kiss was both seductive and innocent, reverent yet passionate. The fullness of her breasts was crushed against his chest. His blood quickened and desire throbbed achingly in his groin. Her hip was against his tumescence, her fingers in his hair to lock them closer.

A gruff laugh came from one of the retired officers in the parlour brought him to his senses. 'Sweet mercy,' he groaned, pulling back from her. 'Your father would turn in his grave if he could see us.'

'I love you, Sam.'

'No.' He jammed his steel helmet on his head, the chin strap a barrier across his mouth. 'You don't know what you're saying. It's impossible. Now I must say goodbye to Major Travers.'

He marched into the parlour and she heard him being greeted with hearty affection. Her gaze fell on the carpetbag in the hall. Her heart ached with unrequited love. His friendship with her father had been so special. Why did she confuse his sympathy and friendship with love? This was the third time he had rejected her. She wouldn't make such a fool of herself again.

'Tanya!' Aunt Stella called. 'What are you doing? Our guests are leaving.'

She dabbed at her eyes. At least the guests would not see her tears as other than those of grief for her father.

When she entered the parlour, Clare was still there. She had been speaking to Archie. Coming to Tanya she said, 'That one's a charmer all right and terribly handsome. Knows it, of course. And he can't keep his eyes off you.' Clare's smile broadened as she nodded towards Sam. He was talking to a colonel with an eye-patch. 'But then you have two handsome men to choose from. That one watches over you like the hawk of his name. He's a bit of a rough diamond from what Simon tells me, but I like him. Eyebrows would certainly be raised if you chose him.'

'He's just a friend,' Tanya said more sharply than she intended.

Clare widened her eyes. 'So it is Sam you love. You can't hide anything from me. I know you too well. But is your love wise? We must marry our own kind. Any other marriage would be disastrous. Remember Priscilla Harper from school?

She ran off with her father's groom and was disowned by her family. No one in society will acknowledge her. They say she lives in a dilapidated cottage and her husband is drunk most of the time. That's what happens when you marry beneath you.'

Tanya was scornful. 'Occasionally that may happen. You listen to too much gossip, Clare.'

Clare became unusually serious and her expression was concerned. 'I only want you to be happy as I am happy.'

Tanya nodded. From the corner of her eye she saw Archie trying to catch her attention. When she ignored him, he strode from the room. 'My happiness will come when I marry the man I love. In the meantime I have my business which takes up a great deal of my time.'

Simon came to his wife's side. 'We have to leave, Tanya,' he stated. 'We'll see you soon, I hope. Any time you need to get away, you know you are always welcome at Oaklands.'

As Clare and Simon left, Tanya saw that Sam was also about to leave. Dutifully, he stopped to express his condolences to Aunt Stella. Tanya was surprised that for once she seemed to be making an effort to be pleasant to him. She was so talkative she delayed his departure by more than five minutes. Then with a curt nod in Tanya's direction he moved to the door. At that moment Archie strolled back into the room. The two men eyed each other frigidly. She couldn't see Sam's expression, but his body was stiff with tension. Archie's black stare was filled with hatred when it settled on Sam. There was something in Archie's manner as he joined Stella which caused prickles of unease along Tanya's spine.

Except for Archie, the remaining guests left with Sam. Archie was seated next to Stella in close conversation. Needing to be alone, Tanya wandered into the conservatory and watched the snow falling on the flowerbeds and trellis fences.

'I want to apologise for my conduct at the dinner party. Can you forgive me?' Archie's suave voice directly behind her made her start. She had not heard him approach. When she turned to face him his smile was disarming. Once it would have charmed her, now it left her cold.

'There is nothing to forgive.'

He stepped forward, smiling with bold assurance and arms outstretched as though he intended to hold her. 'I knew you would come to your senses, my dear.'

She sidestepped, uneasy that they were alone. 'I have not changed my mind. I will not marry you. You must accept that.'

He swung away from her and his fist thudded down on a pedestal holding a potted palm. 'You need a man's protection now that your father is dead.'

Outrage welled in her. 'I find this conversation in bad taste after Papa's funeral. Please excuse me.'

Archie scowled as Tanya swept from the room. How dare the wench treat him like a nonentity? He'd spent nine months fawning on her. He'd wined, dined and wooed her with finesse. Lavished his attention on her. Spent a fortune on flowers. The wench should be grateful, not throw his consideration in his face. He'd treated her with gentlemanly respect and this was how she repaid him. No woman would so humiliate him and get away with it.

His face darkened to a demonic mask. Tanya would pay for her insults. He'd see that haughty bitch humbled. And Sam Hawkes too. The day still held some unpleasant surprises for Tanya Summersfield. Stella had seen to that. There was a woman who never allowed sentiment to get in the way of her plans. Especially when she was set upon revenge. She had already triumphed over her brother whom she hated. How many women were capable of such devious murder? Ever since the brigadier had returned to England, she had been dosing him with digitalis, distilled from the foxgloves she tended so lovingly in her garden. Not enough to kill him outright, just enough to establish that he had a heart condition. When she finally increased the dose to kill him, no one suspected her.

And now Stella wanted the house. As Tanya's husband he had agreed to sign it over to her. It was no sacrifice. He just wanted the Summersfield fortune – the inheritance Stella believed her illegitimate son was entitled to.

Chapter Twenty-two

Tanya was helping Ginny tidy the front parlour after the funeral guests had left when Stella staggered into the room and wailed, 'We've been robbed. Robbed! Ginny, fetch a policeman. Be quick, girl.' She leaned against the wall, sobs shaking her large figure.

'Calm down, Aunt,' Tanya soothed. 'No guest would steal from us. You must be mistaken.'

'No,' Stella gasped. 'Ginny, don't stand there gawping. Fetch the police. Now!'

Ginny bolted out of the house, not even stopping for her coat even though it was still snowing.

Tanya put a comforting arm round her aunt and led her to a chair. 'What is missing that you think we've been robbed?'

'The small gold and enamelled clock on the landing cabinet has gone. I then checked the landing for anything else missing. A silver horse and dog on the table outside Reginald's room are no longer there. My jewellery was not touched but I don't know about yours. The house must be checked in case anything else has been taken,' Stella insisted. 'Don't let any of the temporary servants leave until they have been searched.' Her sobs grew louder. 'It's one thing after another. First Maude being run down, then Reginald's sudden death and now a robbery. And on the day of his funeral.'

Tanya rang the handbell to summon Millie who was helping in the kitchen. 'We've been robbed,' she informed her. 'None of the servants engaged for the day are to leave until the police have arrived and questioned them.'

Stella closed her eyes and laid her head back on the chair.

'She's fainted!' Millie cried and drew smelling salts from her pocket to thrust under Stella's nose. She groaned and pushed them away.

'Stupid woman, I haven't swooned. It's the shock.'

From the Crescent the shrill piping of a policeman's whistle calling for assistance sounded. Moments later a breathless Ginny announced, 'Constable Lane is here, Miss Tanya.'

'Show him in,' Stella snapped.

The tall, thin policeman removed his helmet. His short dark hair was parted in the centre and greased flat to his head. 'Your maid has reported a burglary. Is that right?'

'I'm not so sure that someone actually broke into the house,' Stella answered, 'but several articles are missing.'

Tanya moved to the door. 'I was about to check whether anything else was taken.'

Two other policemen appeared at the door and Constable Lane addressed them. 'They've been robbed. Notify the inspector.'

One of the policemen ran off; the other, who was heavyset and freckle-faced with narrow russet side whiskers, remained. Constable Lane took charge. 'This is Constable Bates. I'd appreciate an exact list of the stolen property, miss.

Have you any idea who could have stolen it?'

'The house has been full of guests. We buried my father this morning. And of course extra staff were engaged. None has been permitted to leave.'

He turned to Constable Bates. 'Question the staff and search them.'

Tanya said, 'I'll check the rest of the house.'

She surveyed each room. Nothing appeared to have been taken from downstairs although there were several small silver ornaments which could easily have been carried away by a thief. On the landing a six-inch gold and ivory carriage was not in its place. Nothing was missing from any of the first-floor rooms. Apart from the chess set which she had given Sam, she could see nothing missing from her father's room. Even his gold hunter watch was on his dressing table, together with his gold cufflink and ring box. Opening the box, she studied its contents. A set of matching ruby cufflinks and tiepin was not there, neither was the large oval sapphire ring that her father wore on his little finger. Obviously the thief hoped that by stealing only a few items the loss would not be noticed for some time.

From her own jewellery box nothing had been taken. It looked as if the thief had kept to the landing and her father's room. Constable Lane was writing down her aunt's statement when Tanya returned to the withdrawing room.

She told him what else was missing and he jotted it down.

'Do you know the value of these items?'

Tanya shook her head.

'They chose well,' Stella wailed. 'Small objects of value. They probably thought we would not notice for weeks.'

Constable Bates returned from the kitchen. 'There's nothing in any of the servants' bags and they don't remember seeing anything suspicious, though one said they'd seen an army officer coming down the stairs just before the last of the guests left. He was carrying a carpet bag.'

'That was Captain Hawkes. A friend of my father,' Tanya explained. 'I gave him my father's chess set and he had left some of his own things in my father's room and had gone to collect them.'

'So he was in the room where cufflinks and rings were stolen?' The policeman wrote this down.

Stella's face twisted with anger. 'It must have been him. No one else was upstairs. I want Sam Hawkes arrested.'

'Sam wouldn't steal from us,' Tanya said, appalled.

'What do we know of him?' Stella raged. 'Once a guttersnipe, always a guttersnipe. I never did trust him, He ingratiated himself with my brother so that he invested a fortune in his car business.'

'If Sam was going to steal from us, why did he insist that I keep father's share of the profits from that company?'

'Because he thought we'd be too grieved to notice the theft today of all days,' Stella declared. 'Suspicion was then bound to fall on the temporary staff. Thank God I noticed the clock was missing. He won't get away with this.' Her stare was malicious. 'Constable, Hawkes left here only half an hour ago. Get someone round to search his lodgings and workshop. It's just off Queen Street. The place is called Everyman Motors.'

Constable Lane stood up. 'We shall do that, ma'am. In the meantime, perhaps you could give us a list of your guests' names and addresses so that we can check with them.'

'We haven't got all the addresses,' Tanya answered. 'Many of the officers saw the obituary in *The Times,* as did several acquaintances from his club.' Refusing to believe that Sam was a thief, she defended him forcibly. 'Mr Hawkes would not steal from us. Isn't it more likely that someone broke in while we were at the funeral?'

'There's no sign of a forced entry,' Constable Bates said.

Tanya persisted. 'There have been deliveries from tradesmen and of course the funeral wreaths all morning. With everyone so busy, someone could have slipped in.'

'Accept it, Tanya,' Stella scoffed. 'Hawkes is the thief. A burglar would have taken all our jewellery. Hawkes was in Reginald's regiment. He had the perfect opportunity. No one else went upstairs.'

'That's not true, the bathroom and water closet is on the first floor. Several of our guests used that,' Tanya corrected. 'And what about Mr Tilbury? He left the room for some time.'

Stella glared at her. 'He went out to buy a newspaper.' She turned to the policeman. 'Constable, Hawkes is the culprit and he will have disposed of the evidence if you do not hurry.'

'I am sure my aunt is mistaken,' Tanya insisted.

'That remains to be seen.' Constable Lane replaced his helmet. 'We will inform you of our findings in due course. An inspector may also call to take further statements.'

When he left, Tanya rounded on her aunt. 'How could you implicate Sam that way? He is innocent.'

'I never trusted him.'

Anger stormed through Tanya's blood. 'I'm going to him to explain it is all a mistake and to tell him I never believed him capable of stealing from us.'

Stella grabbed her arm, her thin lips sucked in with censure. 'Have you no shame? You're throwing yourself at that man like a hussy.'

Tanya shook off her hold. She was sick with disgust that Sam was about to be treated like a criminal because of her aunt's spite. And while Sam was being hounded by the police, the real thief was getting away with the crime. Her voice was icy as she said, 'I don't remember Archie having a newspaper in his hand when he returned to the room. Perhaps the inspector should search his lodgings.'

The coat she hastily donned was still damp and more snow was falling. It lay an inch deep on the roofs and fenceposts. She pushed her hands into her muff to combat the biting cold. Traffic was almost at a standstill and she decided to walk the short distance to Queen Street. It wouldn't take longer than ten minutes.

She had underestimated the ice forming under the snow on the pavement; each step was treacherously slippery. It took her half an hour to get to Sam's lodgings. Just as she rounded the corner into Queen Street, she saw two policemen pushing Sam into a Black Maria.

'Stop!' she shouted. 'Mr Hawkes is innocent.'

Constable Lane recognised her. 'I'm sorry, miss. The stolen property was found in his possession. We're taking him to the station to charge him.'

Sam broke away from his captors to throw himself against the barred window at the back of the Black Maria. 'I didn't do it, Tanya. I swear. Someone put those things in that bag while it was in the hall,' he shouted before he was dragged further back inside.

'I believe you, Sam.'

She was sobbing as the Black Maria drew away. If Sam had the stolen items in his possession, someone wanted him arrested. But who?

She remembered Archie leaving the room and returning as Sam left. She lifted a gloved fist to her mouth. Why wasn't Archie carrying the newspaper Stella said he'd purchased? Archie had never hidden his dislike for Sam. Was he capable of incriminating Sam in this way? Once the thought formed, intuition told her that it was possible.

Her breath caught in her throat. Why had Stella been so emphatic that Sam was guilty? She had never concealed her resentment of Sam's friendship with her and her father. Had she planned this with Archie?

It was too absurd. Or was it? Tanya inhaled sharply, the cold air snapping into her lungs. She could not accept that her aunt was part of this but she could not so easily dismiss Archie's possible involvement.

Anger flared. The injustice of it flushed her body with fury and she no longer noticed the penetrating cold from the falling snow.

As she retraced her footsteps along Cheapside towards St Paul's, the streets were almost deserted and the few vehicles that were braving the weather were slithering dangerously. The snow was ankle deep, each step threatening her balance. The treacherous progress added to her frustration. Her first instinct was to confront Archie. He would deny it of course. And what good would it do? Somehow she had to prove that Sam was innocent. But how?

She was still grappling with the problem when she dragged her shivering body up the front steps of the house. The building was gloomy in the twilight. Usually Stella liked every room blazing with their new electric lights. The semi-darkness suited Tanya's mood. She sank down onto a chair in the hall and stared helplessly at her gloves. Her hands were too numb to remove them.

'Millie!' she called.

There was no response. She picked up a brass handbell and rang it. Again, no servant appeared. Cold and tired, she pulled ineffectually at her gloves. Struggling through the snow had drained her strength. Using her teeth, she managed to ease the stiff leather away from her frozen fingers. Massaging her hands, the returning circulation brought them back to painful throbbing life. As she unbuttoned her coat, tears pricked the back of her eyelids. The thought of Sam in gaol for something he had not done crucified her. The malice of the action was beyond her comprehension.

Shivering, she entered the withdrawing room and threw another log on the fire. The eerie quiet of the house struck her. There were no distant sounds of crockery being put away or voices from the kitchen. The servants must have left. But where was Millie? Wretchedness swamped her. Loneliness was a hollow ache in her breast. Maude and her father were dead. Clare was well on her way to Kent by now. Sam, her confidant, was in prison. She shuddered and murmured crossly, 'Sitting here feeling sorry for yourself won't help Sam. Oh, Sam. What must you be feeling?'

She dashed the tears from her cheeks and leaned against the mantelshelf to stare into the flames of the fire, 'Oh, Sam, my darling. My love. I know you are innocent.'

'Tender words for a thief.' She spun round.

'The truth at last,' Archie continued. 'You rejected my suit because you prefer that crass lout Hawkes.'

'What are you doing here?' she challenged. 'Sam stole nothing. But you were out of the room for a long time. Time enough to put those valuables in Sam's bag before he left.'

'And why should I trouble myself to do that?' His face was sardonic in the fading light.

'To get a rival for my affections out of the way?'

Disgust filled her at seeing him for the vain, self-important, cowardly man that he was.

Archie laughed cruelly. 'Hawkes has caused me a great deal of inconvenience. Now he's out of the way, nothing can stop our marriage.'

Tanya's eyes widened with shock. 'I'll never marry you. Sam's done nothing to harm you. You've got to tell the police it was a mistake.'

He walked purposefully towards her. Malice was a fever in his eyes. Frightened, Tanya pulled the bellrope to summon a servant. Archie laughed. 'There's no one to come to your rescue. The servants have gone home and the old maid has been dealt with. She'll be sleeping so soundly nothing could disturb her.'

'My aunt–'

'Has gone out. Even the snow could not keep her from her duty when an emergency committee was called to raise funds to provide wood and coal for the elderly.'

'Then please leave,' she ordered.

His wide smile was sinister and menacing. Her throat constricted with fear. She made a dash for the door, but her long skirts hampered her. Archie blocked her flight and grabbed her arm, ripping the sleeve of her gown as he did so. His nails scratched her flesh, drawing several droplets of blood. The sight of them roused his excitement and tightened his hold on her arms.

'You can't escape me, Tanya. We have unfinished business.'

'Get out!' She slapped his face. 'You disgust me.'

He caught her hand and wrenched her arm up

behind her back. Sharp pain seared through her shoulder blade, making her cry out.

'Why do you deny me? Everyone expects us to marry. I will not be insulted this way.'

'I don't love you, Archie,' she tried to reason. He was a gentleman, surely he did not intend to force her. But encountering the incensed gleam in his eyes, her fear intensified.

'I don't need your love,' he snarled. 'Just your subservience.'

'Never. Get out of this house.' Terrified, she kicked him. Her boot scraped his shin and he grunted with agony. Then pain exploded in her jaw as he slammed his fist into her chin.

'Bitch! No one refuses me.'

A second blow knocked her sideways. She staggered. The room spiralled, red flashes of light exploded in her skull. Another blow felled her to the carpet. Winded and stunned, her blurred vision showed her Archie straddling her, unfastening the buttons of his trousers.

'No! Damn you! No!' she screamed. 'Get away from me.'

Archie fell on her, striking her again as she struggled to regain her breath. Her fear excited him as her femininity never could. He pulled a length of cord from his pocket and bound her wrists behind her. Then, without passion, he opened the front of her dress and pulled it down over her arms. Her corset was tightly laced, pushing her breasts high, and they were covered only by her silk chemise. He exposed them to increase her humiliation. Emitting a harsh laugh, he flipped up her petticoats to her waist and dragged her silk and lace underwear to her knees. Her frantic efforts as she twisted and writhed to stop his violation stimulated him. His hand closed over his penis, working to harden himself sufficiently to penetrate her, her cries of denial a potent aphrodisiac. The haughty bitch was finally in his power.

At the sound of the front door opening, he clamped his mouth over hers to stop her cries and rammed into her. Never having taken a virgin, he was surprised to encounter the membrane. Gritting his teeth, he thrust harder and without mercy until the resistance parted. Her muffled cries sounded like the last throes of her passion, her struggling body gave the impression of a woman abandoned in her lovemaking.

Stella's screams accompanied his ejaculation. A man's shocked voice proclaimed, 'My God, the brigadier's daughter behaving like a hoyden and the poor man barely in his grave.'

'The shame of it,' Stella wailed. 'The shame of it.'

'There'll be no shame,' the man remarked. 'The bounder must marry her.'

'They are about to announce their engagement, Mr Fairchild,' Stella sobbed. 'Just that with my brother dying so suddenly...'

'It is most distressing for you, Miss Summersfield.' Mr Fairchild sounded embarrassed. 'They must marry without delay.'

Archie grinned as he stood up and adjusted his clothing. He knew Fairchild, a sanctimonious church choirmaster and alderman of the city. He frequently visited the Gilbert brothers' brothels in Soho and Piccadilly. The threat of blackmail earlier had ensured that Fairchild spoke well of Archie to Reginald. Stella had chosen their witness well. Tanya lay sobbing, drawing her knees up to hide her body from him. He untied her hands.

'I'd rather die than wed you,' Tanya croaked. 'Get out of my sight.'

Archie walked to the mirror and sleeked back a lock of hair and straightened his tie. A triumphant smile showed the white of his teeth before he adopted a sombre expression. He gestured for Stella to tend to her niece. As she helped Tanya from the room, he whispered, 'She's still being stubborn.'

'Laudanum will settle that,' Stella murmured.

Archie looked suitably abashed as he met Fairchild's gaze. He was a large-boned, ruddy-faced man with grey whiskers and artificially curled hair. 'My fiancée is too distraught to join us. Regrettable incident. But you know how it is. We so rarely have time alone. I have a special licence. We are to marry quietly tomorrow. I hope I can rely on your discretion, Mr Fairchild.'

'As long as the wedding takes place. I would be failing in my duty if I did not protect the good name of this family.'

'You have my word on it, sir.' Archie's practised smile was contrite. 'Perhaps you would care to attend as a witness.'

He nodded. 'I shall look for the announcement in *The Times*. I believe my wife has asked Miss Summersfield to call to discuss the redecoration of our dining room. You may tell her that her services will no longer be required. Good day, Tilbury.'

Jubilant, Archie rubbed his hands and poured himself a whisky. Tanya had no choice but to wed him now. He would be a rich man. The Gilbert brothers could go hang – which they very likely would one day for their crimes.

Stella did not look pleased when she returned. 'Did you have to be so rough with her? She is my niece, after all.'

'She was stubborn and fought me. And isn't it rather late for you to let your conscience trouble you? Where is Tanya now?'

'Sleeping. I gave her laudanum.'

'Then keep her that way until the wedding. I don't want her going to the police. She guessed it was me who planted the stuff on Hawkes.'

'I never thought she'd be so difficult. She's too like Reginald. But I told you it would all be yours. The house. The money. Everything. It's your inheritance.'

'It isn't mine yet. We've been lucky so far.'

'But it will be.' She came to him, her arms outstretched. He turned away to pour a whisky to avoid her embrace. 'Why are you so cold towards me?' she accused. 'I thought you understood why I had to give you up as a baby. Haven't I made it up to you now? Everything I've done was for you.'

He raised his glass in salute. 'We are two of a kind.'

She chuckled, her eyes glowing with adoration. 'Yes. Mother and son. Bonded by blood and suffering. You may have arranged for that truck to run Maude down but I dealt with Reginald. Slowly killing him with my potions. And no one suspected. I did it so that you could take your rightful place in this house. I vowed that Reginald would pay for the suffering he caused me. When I saw you that day on the street, you were so like Geoffrey. But you had my strength, while he was weak.'

Archie shrugged. He'd heard it all before and was weary of the story. But he had to continue to play along with the deluded woman until he was safely married to her niece.

Chapter Twenty-three

The pain in her jaw roused Tanya from her stupor. Pincer fingers were gripping it, forcing her teeth apart. Her bruised flesh felt tortured and something hard was being pressed relentlessly against her teeth until a bitter liquid trickled into her mouth. Her eyes opened to find her aunt standing over her. A flickering candle on the bedside table threw her face into macabre half-shadow. Glittering demon's eyes stared back at her. It was a gargoyle's face, sinister and unforgiving.

'Drink this, it will help you.' Impatience harshened Stella's voice. Merciless fingers continued to prise at her aching jaw.

Tanya tried to wrench her head away. Movement was impossible. Her body was leaden, her mind clogged. Any thought waded through a cauldron of cloying mud.

Fear insinuated itself through her lethargy. An image of her aunt bent over her father's struggling figure punched energy into her limbs. Concentrating all her strength into her arm, Tanya lashed out and spat the foul brew from her mouth. In reality her arm flapped uselessly, the mixture dribbling from her lips.

'Silly girl,' Stella pronounced. 'How will you get better if you don't take your medicine?'

Through the drug-induced haze, Tanya rebelled. She'd been given laudanum for toothache as a child and knew its acrid taste. She managed to latch her fingers over her aunt's wrist. Her lower body ached, the pain dredging up the memory of Archie's violation of her body.

'I was raped,' she slurred.

'Nonsense. Archie loves you. Don't blame him. I saw the wanton way you gave yourself to him. So did Mr Fairchild. Thank God a scandal will be spared. Archie will marry you. Many a decent man would have abandoned you for a trollop.'

'I was raped,' she repeated. 'He tied my wrists.'

'You're a whore who got caught fornicating with her lover,' Stella snarled. 'You will marry him. Or do you prefer to see your reputation and the good name of this family dragged into the gutter?'

The cup with its debilitating brew was again thrust to her lips. Tanya resisted but knew she was too weak and that the battle would be lost. Better to appear to concede, let them think her spirit broken.

Her hand flopped towards her mouth to bar the contents of the cup reaching her lips.

'I don't want a scandal,' she croaked.

The cup receded. 'Then you'll marry Archie?'

She nodded.

'I knew you'd be reasonable.' Stella drew back.

Tanya turned her face away. She wanted to rage, scratch and scream at the injustice of her plight. It would not help her. Instead she must scheme. Archie was not going to get away with this. Once she had shaken off the effects of the laudanum, she would fight them.

Stella left and the key clicked in the lock. Her aunt was taking no chances. As Tanya rolled on her side pain tore at her insides. She was violated. Defiled. Unworthy to be any man's wife.

The room spun into a vortex, dragging her deeper into its whirling. At its centre was stillness, the edges fuzzed with revolting images. She concentrated on the stillness. The eye of the storm.

Shudders of revulsion shook her body. She was still wearing the dress she had put on for the funeral. The unfastened bodice exposing her breasts reminded her of her degradation. Drawing up her knees, she hugged them with her arms. No fire had been lit in her room. The windowpanes were glazed with frost patterns. Yet the cold was as nothing compared to the ice which chilled her blood. The horror of the rape threatened to swamp her. But apathy would lead to her destruction and their triumph. She must rouse herself or all would be lost.

Her determination that Archie would pay for

his crime gave her the strength to roll off the bed and remove her torn dress and underclothes. With every garment she discarded she was forced to pause and steady herself against waves of giddiness. She had to battle against the heaviness and unreality created by the drug. A need overwhelmed her, dominating her reason. She had to wash, to cleanse herself of the filth of violation.

Blood and semen were smeared on her legs and petticoats. She kicked the petticoats under the bed but nothing could hide the shame which ate into her defiled flesh.

Naked and shivering, she stared at her pale image in the cheval mirror. Her hair was tangled and wild looking, her face bruised and cut where Archie's ring had torn her flesh. Her eyes were blackened and swollen and so was her jaw. Studying her slender figure filled her with abhorrence. She turned away disgusted by the image and the abomination she had been subjected to.

The water in her jug was freezing. She plunged the sponge into it, repeatedly scrubbing her breasts, stomach and thighs until they were raw. She could still feel the horror of male flesh and hips hammering against her body. Male scent and sweat choked her senses. Her stomach heaved and her body juddered as she vomited into the chamber pot. Weak and shaken, she crouched on the floor and sobbed until her throat and lungs ached.

Conjuring deeper reserves of strength, Tanya stifled her sobs. Her tears had released her emotion. They could help to heal but they could never cleanse her. To indulge further would weaken her. And weakness was a luxury she could not afford. Not only was her own freedom at stake, she had to convince the police that Sam was innocent.

A moan escaped her as she thought of Sam. How he was truly beyond her reach. The difference in their births had never troubled her, but she could not go to him tainted by another man's violation. How could Sam respect her now that she was not a virgin? Purity was a husband's prized possession. The thought of any man's touch filled her with revulsion now anyway.

Rising, she plunged her face into the icy water, holding it there until her lungs were busting from lack of breath. She repeated it three times. When she lifted her face, her senses were clearer. Cold would chase away the soporific effects of the drug.

Her teeth were chattering as she dressed in her plainest black wool gown. She pulled her hair back into a tight knot at the nape of her neck. Stout boots and a thick coat completed her attire. This time when she gazed into the mirror, her reflection portrayed a woman with eyes darkly circled and staring with shock. Her skin was like bleached linen with livid bruises on her jaw and cheek. Sullied she may be, but she was not defeated.

Tanya moved to the window and surveyed the snow-covered garden. Her bedroom was again her prison. The first glimmer of dawn was silhouetting the tall chimneys of the surrounding houses.

Her expression was bleak but determined. So

they thought they could drug her and lock her in to gain their ends. Archie would not get away with what he had done. He had compromised her to make her marry him. He did not love her. There had been no tender caresses. No kiss to rouse her pleasure. His lips had been the means to silence her. His attack was a sadistic humiliation to break her will. Yet her will was not broken. It was inflamed and outrage fired her resolve. She wanted justice. Not only for herself. To perpetrate this evil they had sacrificed Sam's reputation and honour. His name must be cleared.

She gripped the sill to steady herself, visions of Sam almost destroying her calm. Her love was no longer worthy of him, but she could save him from disgrace.

Lifting the window sash, she stared at the gnarled trunk of the wisteria. At school she had always been in trouble for climbing trees and the wisteria had been scaled many times as a child. But she had been lighter then and more agile. The branch was as thick as her arm but would it hold her weight? Next to it was a new cast-iron downpipe from the guttering. The brackets fastening it to the wall looked substantial enough to provide footholds.

Ducking through the window, she tested the branch with her foot. It creaked alarmingly but held. With one hand on the windowframe she braced herself to reach across to the downpipe. There was a twenty-foot drop to the ground if she fell. Her heart scudded as more weight was taken by the wisteria, then she flung her hands round the iron pipe and began to search for footholds to reach the ground.

At last the frozen earth scrunched beneath her boots. She scanned the brick exterior of the back of the house. No lights were visible. With luck she would not be missed for some hours. Stella never breakfasted until ten and it was unlikely that she would permit Ginny or Millie to attend her.

She kept to the flowerbeds, treading only where greenery had broken through the whiteness so that the snow would not betray her footsteps. The side gate refused to open more than six inches because snow had piled against it. She squeezed through the gap, her breath steaming around her in a misty cloud. The alley was dark and the gaslight at the far end was reassuring. The streets of London had never been so silent. There wasn't a hansom cab in sight on the main road. It was too early for the trams and omnibuses to run. She would have to walk to the police station.

The last of the effects of the laudanum helped calm her rather than incapacitate her. It took away the fear of being set upon by thieves who reputedly never slept. She focused on her goal. The few pedestrians tramping to work were scarcely noticed. Her eyes were riveted on the path as she trudged to the police station.

The bewhiskered police sergeant at the desk looked up as she entered. Taking in her rich attire, he frowned.

'I want to speak to an inspector. I have come to report a crime and also a grave miscarriage of justice.'

'Ain't no inspector 'ere at this time of the

morning,' the sergeant advised. 'Best come back later. In a couple of hours or so.'

'I'll wait. If I leave I may not be able to return.'

She sat on a wooden bench out of the glare of the gaslight to hide her battered face. Dimly she registered the drunken ravings of a woman from somewhere at the back of the building.

'Can't I help you, miss?' the police sergeant offered.

Keeping her head lowered, she asked, 'Do you know of an Inspector Fenton? I have information which may be of help in his enquiries.'

'Ain't no Fenton here, miss. You'll 'ave to speak to Inspector Naylor, I reckon.'

'I must speak to Inspector Fenton. While I wait, could you please find out where he is stationed?'

The sergeant scowled. 'If you've come to press charges there's regulations to uphold. I ain't a skivvy. There's enough to deal with 'ere without me wasting me time finding out about any Inspector Fenton.'

Tanya gripped her hands together. She had not expected it to be easy. And these were just the preliminaries. She had yet to face the ordeal of speaking of her shame to a male stranger. If she didn't speak to Fenton first she would have to repeat everything a second time and that would be doubly humiliating.

'Please, Sergeant. I can't speak about this to anyone but Inspector Fenton. It's partly to do with a robbery in Pilgrim's Crescent yesterday. Sam Hawkes was arrested. I've discovered that the stolen property was planted on him by a man who I believe Inspector Fenton has been investigating. I cannot say more.'

Another policeman, in a cape and helmet, had entered the station and stopped to listen.

'Fenton,' he said. 'Ain't that the inspector whose brother were murdered up West? He came down 'ere after the Hawkes bloke were arrested and brought 'ere for questioning. Hawkes said 'e 'ad information for Fenton. That were before I went off duty yesterday. Fenton is stationed at Bow Street as I remember.'

The sergeant shuffled his papers. 'Is it about that murder enquiry, miss?'

'Please, I must speak to Inspector Fenton,' Tanya repeated.

'You can't wait here,' the sergeant blustered. 'Give me your address and I'll ask him to call.'

'No. I will wait,' she insisted. She was trembling violently from the events of the last hours which were beginning to overtake her.

The second policeman was young and more curious. 'I'll ring Bow Street and leave a message for Fenton,' he said kindly. 'Then let me call a hansom to take you home. A police station ain't no place for a gentlewoman like yourself, miss. Do you live in Pilgrim's Crescent?'

'You can't go there. Not yet. They mustn't know I escaped.' Fear haunted her. They mustn't discover she was missing until she had given her statement. She could feel the hysteria rising and breathed deeply to combat it. 'Sam Hawkes is innocent and the real thief goes free. He … he attacked me.' She lifted her head to show him her battered face and held out her bruised wrists where the cords had bound her. At his shocked expression, her senses began to betray her. The room was dipping and swaying in and out of focus. 'I must speak to Inspector Fenton.'

'Lord, she's keeling over,' the sergeant shouted, but his voice was rapidly becoming distant in Tanya's ears. 'Grab her, man! Did you see those bruises? There's more to this than she's letting on.'

When Tanya's senses recovered she found herself in a small room. Someone was holding her head down between her knees. Upon straightening, a glass of water was thrust into her hand by the young constable.

'Drink this, miss. What happened to you?'

'I will speak only to Inspector Fenton. I couldn't go through it twice. Please.' Her eyes beseeched him. 'It's important or I would not be here.'

'I'll see what I can do,' the sergeant answered more sympathetically.

It was mid-morning when Inspector Fenton arrived. He was middle-aged and of medium height and build, the sort of man who blended in with a crowd, except when you looked into his eyes. They were razor sharp, missing nothing. He listened without interruption while she told him the truth about the stolen property. Her sense of justice enabled her to speak passionately about the wrong done to Sam, but whenever she mentioned Archie's name, revulsion gripped her and she was forced to pause.

'So you see, Inspector, Sam Hawkes is innocent. Archie Tilbury put those pieces in Sam's bag.'

His stare was piercing and forceful. 'I spoke to Mr Hawkes. He gave me information about this Mr Tilbury which was disturbing. He could be involved with criminals. A gang led by the Gilbert brothers. They are evil and ruthless. But there is something more, is there not, Miss Summersfield? Did Tilbury give you the bruises on your face?'

She nodded, finding it difficult to continue and could no longer hold his gaze. 'And more. He ... he assaulted me.' Her voice broke.

'In your own time I'd like you to tell me exactly what happened.'

Shame flooded her and she had to summon all her willpower to force herself to continue. 'The house appeared to be empty. I assumed my aunt and our maid Millie had gone out. He was waiting for me. He compromised me to make me marry him. He doesn't love me. I felt he hated me – hated all women. We thought he was a gentleman of wealth and position. Clearly he wants my inheritance.'

She was trembling so violently she had to stop and drink some water. Resurrecting the memory of her violation meant reliving the horror. She broke down several times but Inspector Fenton was always patient and never condemning. She finished by saying harshly, 'I want Archie Tilbury to pay for what he did. I want him locked away so that he can't terrorise another woman the way he did me.'

'And you had no idea of this man's true character?' Inspector Fenton said more sharply. 'You say you have known him for some months, that he frequently escorted you to the theatre or your classes. Most men would take that to mean you had an understanding with them. He must have told you of his feelings, or tried to kiss you.'

'He asked me to marry him but I refused. He didn't seem able to accept it. He was so charming, insisting that we remain friends. He was always the perfect gentleman.'

'There was no hint that he was capable of such an act before yesterday?'

She shook her head. 'He has great charm which he cultivates to win the adoration of people around him. He is a vain man and likes to be the centre of attention. His good looks drew people to him at any gathering.' The images and revulsion rushed back, leaving her shuddering and nauseous. She put a hand to her eyes to shield her tears and mumbled, 'Forgive me. It's so hard to speak of it.'

Inspector Fenton stroked his chin. 'I'm sorry, Miss Summersfield, but I needed the facts.' He pressed a clean handkerchief into her hands.

Tanya controlled her tears. 'My aunt refused to listen to me. She wants me married to avoid a scandal. But I shall never marry him. I'd rather face the shame than marry a monster capable of such brutality.'

'Regrettably it's not a crime which is easily brought to justice,' Inspector Fenton said heavily. 'It will be your word against his. His will claim that you were willing and that only Fairchild's arrival prompted you to defend your virtue.'

Outrage gouged her. 'Are you saying that you won't charge him? Do you think I inflicted the bruises on my face and arms myself?' Angry colour bloomed in her cheeks and her eyes flashed dangerously. She was no longer embarrassed; she was incensed and intent upon justice. 'Not so long ago a youth could be hanged for stealing a loaf to survive. Men were transported for seven or fourteen years to Australia for poaching. Harsh sentences for petty crimes. But where has there ever been justice for crimes against women – unless they were murdered? Their property can be stolen from them by their husbands or guardians. They can be locked away as mentally insane if they are unmarried and become pregnant. And they are too ashamed to run the gauntlet of a prejudiced society who deem that any woman who his raped probably deserved it anyway.'

'If Tilbury was charged you'd have to appear in court and relate every unpleasant detail of the incident.' Inspector Fenton paced the room. 'Tilbury's lawyer will then proceed to prove his client's innocence by tearing your evidence and reputation to shreds. He will declare that you led Tilbury on. That you were willing. He will dismiss the bruising on your face and wrists. A scandal will be inevitable. The papers will take up the story. You will become notorious, Miss Summersfield. A stain on your reputation such as that would be something you would carry to your grave.' He stood in front of her and his voice was weary. 'Is that what you want? Haven't you suffered enough?'

'I cannot let this rest. If he goes free–'

'He will not go free, I promise. I've followed up

the information on Tilbury which Hawkes gave me. My men have been ordered to bring him in for questioning. I believe I can put him away for a long time without you having to press charges. As for Hawkes, he'll be released this morning now that I have your statement about the robbery.'

Tanya stood up shakily and regarded him grimly. 'If Archie is imprisoned for other crimes, then I will not press charges. But I'm not the first woman to be raped and see the violator escape justice.'

The inspector had the grace to look discountenanced. 'Consider carefully before you act,' he cautioned.

'I come from a family of army officers,' she blazed. 'It is our custom to fight for what we believe right.'

The admiration in the inspector's eyes helped restore her self-esteem. 'You've a brave woman, Miss Summersfield. But I'd rather handle this case my way. You have been dishonoured and that is a grave crime. But I believe Tilbury can lead me to the murderers of my brother. No one doubts your integrity and courage. Don't allow stubbornness and pride to ruin your business and your life. You have my word that Tilbury will not escape punishment.'

Chapter Twenty-four

The hansom halted in Pilgrim's Crescent by Tanya. Even the driver's shout did not prevent her stupor. The door to the cab was pulled open, the driver snapping, 'This is where you wanted, weren't it?'

Tanya turned glazed eyes upon him. 'I'm sorry,' she said slowly. 'Please wait here. I came out without my purse.'

He muttered and grumbled as she climbed down into the street. There had been no more snow and most of it had already melted, leaving compact islands around the edges of chimneys, gateposts and windowsills.

'What time is it?' she asked when no one answered her ring at the door. She had also forgotten her key.

'Eleven fifteen, miss,' the driver growled. 'Got to charge extra for being kept waiting.'

She rang the doorbell again and was surprised when it was opened by her aunt. She was still in her nightrobe and her grey hair hung over one shoulder in a dishevelled plait.

'Where have you been?' she raged. 'I've been at my wit's end. And how did you get out of your room?'

'The driver needs paying,' Tanya said walking past her to the china pot in the hall which always contained coppers and silver to tip any messengers. She emptied the contents into her hand. It amounted to several shillings which she thrust towards the driver.

'Blimey, miss. The fare weren't more'n 'alf a crown.' He ran down the steps whistling.

'So where have you been?' Stella shouted, her eyes wary and the nervous wringing of her hands showing her unease. 'Archie has arranged for the marriage to take place this afternoon.'

The words jolted Tanya out of her lethargy. The rape followed by the ordeal of speaking of her shame to the police had taken its toll on her during the ride home. Now anger revived her.

'There will be no marriage.'

'But your reputation,' Stella wheedled. 'You'll lose your precious business when gossip starts to spread about you.'

'I can always sell the house and move somewhere I'm not known.'

'You can't sell the house!' Stella screeched. 'It's your heritage.'

'It's bricks and mortar. How little you know me if you thought I would marry a man who raped and humiliated just to save my reputation. I have more pride than that.'

Archie stepped from the family parlour, his handsome face sardonic. 'What foolishness is this, my dear? A woman is nothing without her reputation. The world will brand you a whore and you will be fair game for any man. No one will employ you to work on their houses. And think of the people who work for you. They'll be jobless and destitute.'

The sight of him made her skin clammy with

revulsion. She stepped back, the smell of him filling her mind with remembered horror. Terror bleached her face of colour except for the livid bruises. She gripped the newelpost at the bottom of the stairs. 'I won't marry a man who disgusts me. As for my staff, they have all learned new skills and continued their lessons after work. They will find jobs. Now get out of my house, before I call the police.'

His handsome face twisted with anger. When he stepped forward reaching for her, she screamed, 'I've been to the police and reported that you raped me.'

'What lies have you been spreading?' Archie shouted. He halted and she could see that her mention of the police had unsettled him.

Stella looked puzzled at the change in him and blurted out, 'Tanya, be reasonable. You have no choice but to marry Archie.'

'I have many choices. I could prefer death. But that is the coward's way. I did nothing wrong. I was beaten and abused but not cowed. I can still hold my head up. Should I become the subject of scandal then I shall leave London. To safeguard my name I shall visit Mr Fairchild and tell him the truth and ask him to respect my wishes.' She held out her purpled wrists. 'I think these will prove that I was raped.'

Archie's grin was malevolent. He was only four steps away from her. His nearness set her insides quaking, the smell of his cologne and the Macassar oil in his hair brought bile to her throat. She swallowed and breathed deeply to control her trembling.

'They will prove nothing,' he said with a laugh. 'I will say that you liked to be tied up. It eased your conscience by making what happened seem out of your control. Many people enjoy bondage. Mr Fairchild insists on being tied himself when he visits the West End brothels. He won't believe you. Be sensible, Tanya. We shall marry at three o'clock.' He projected his most disarming smile. The falseness of it sickened her. 'You have blown our little fun together out of all proportion because Fairchild walked in on us. That happening on top of your father's death has unbalanced you.'

'I'm not the unbalanced one.' Tanya held her ground, though every muscle and nerve was screeching at her to put as much distance between herself and this demon as she could. 'Inspector Fenton was very interested in the movements of an Arnie Potter to whom you bear an uncanny resemblance.'

The flushed triumph in his face changed to the pallor of a corpse. His dark eyes started in terror. 'Bitch!' he yelled. 'I'm done for. Does he know I'm here?'

Stella was staring at him as though he was insane. 'You've nothing to fear, Archie. I'll tell them the truth. Tell them you are my son.'

Tanya was stunned by this revelation. Yet now she understood Stella's obsession with the man. His birth was the shame her aunt had brought to the family through her disastrous love affair.

He rounded on Stella, his face ugly with hatred. 'It's your fault this has happened. Why didn't you keep her too drugged to escape? You stupid bitch.'

Weeping hysterically, Stella threw herself at him. 'Don't blame me. I did my best. I did everything for you, Archie. You've as much right to the Summersfield money as she has.'

Archie shoved Stella away so brutally that she banged her head against the wall. 'Stupid bitch! By letting her escape you've ruined everything. I should have known not to trust a woman. They always betray you in the end.' He stumbled towards the door.

'Archie, you can't go,' Stella sobbed, holding out her arms to him. 'Haven't I done everything to make up for the years you were fostered?'

'Guilt money,' he spat. 'The money of a whore who gave away a son to save her reputation. Gave him to the misery of being daily beaten by drunken foster parents. Gave him to be ridiculed in his childhood for his bastardy. You saved your reputation at the expense of his. That's why I agreed to your plan. When I raped Tanya, I was making her pay for all the humiliation and degradation I suffered because of my mother's betrayal.'

'But I explained what happened,' Stella cried. 'I had no choice. You are my son. I love you.'

He threw back his head and laughed cruelly. 'I'm not your son, you stupid bitch. I just looked enough like your lover for you to mistake me for him. I was down on my luck. When you swooned in the street and revived to blurt out your story, I went along with it. I told you my name was Tilbury because that's what you wanted to hear. When you began to lavish me with expensive gifts and clothes I played along with your fantasy for what I could get.'

'That's not true. I'm your mother.'

Archie snorted. 'My mother was a rector's daughter who was seduced by an actor. They ran away together. He ditched her when she became pregnant. Her father took her back, provided that I was fostered. She married the squire's son a year later.'

'You are my son,' Stella wailed.

'You used me to get your own revenge upon the brother you despised. I'm not staying around to get arrested.' His eyes were wild as he ran out of the house.

Stella covered her face with her hands. 'It's lies. He is my son.'

Nauseated, Tanya climbed the stairs to her room. She needed a hot bath to wash the taint of her violation from her flesh. These further revelations came too soon after the trauma of yesterday to be fully digested. Archie would not trouble them any more. And she had further evidence to place before Inspector Fenton if it was needed.

The bath water was almost scalding, turning her flesh red as she sank down into it. The discomfort was nothing. It was cleansing her skin but nothing could wash away the defilement which tortured her mind. She lay back and closed her eyes, tears soaking into the water.

The water was cool when she dragged herself from the bath. She was calmer, convinced that Inspector Fenton would bring Archie to justice. And thank God Sam was being released today. She wrapped a towel round her, hugging it close.

Agony lacerated her heart. Sam was now for ever beyond her reach. She loved him too much to fight to win his love as she had vowed. Her shame made her unworthy to be his wife. He deserved better than the sullied phantom of herself Archie's violation had forced her to become.

When Archie ran out of the house and her life, Stella staggered into the withdrawing room. The rich furnishings which always gave her so much pleasure could have been rags now for all she cared. She slumped into an armchair by the fireplace. The fire was unlit. Millie had again been drugged with laudanum and was sleeping soundly. That was how she had kept the maid out of the way yesterday. Stella rubbed her brow. She'd given the servants the day off, fearful lest Tanya proved difficult.

Difficult was an understatement. The girl had destroyed her. She reached for the crystal sherry decanter and filled a glass. She tossed it back and poured herself another.

How could she have been so wrong about Archie? For years she had been buying his clothes and persuading him to better himself. He had been so kind and appreciative.

Another sherry was downed and her unhappiness and bitterness expanded. She'd worked for months ensuring that their plan went smoothly and Tanya married Archie, whereby he would acquire the house and sign it over to her. She would truly be mistress here then and her son would take his rightful place as head of the family.

She had not expected Tanya to be so stubborn. She had thought to dominate her niece as she had dominated Maude. Her eyes slitted with hatred for Tanya. She had ruined everything.

She lay back in the chair remembering, tears running down her cheeks. Thoughts of revenge had soured her years ago. She hated her brothers for their part in ruining her life. That they had been young and goaded into it by their father she discounted. Branded in her mind was the brutality of her lover being beaten by her brothers and their friends and the horror she had endured when her son was born.

Stella dragged her thoughts back to the present and poured another sherry. Her darling baby had been lost to her. Never a day had gone by when she hadn't thought of him. By the time he would be attending school, she found excuses to leave the house for a day and took the train to Tilbury, searching the school playgrounds at lunchtime for a sight of him. Without success. As the years dragged on, she had begun to scan crowds, searching for any likeness to her lover in youths. She had never given up hope of finding her son. When she saw Archie walking down Leadenhall Street, she had nearly fainted from the shock.

Had she really been so wrong? Had Archie played her for a fool and deceived her?

It appeared so. She cackled with malicious laughter, slopping the sherry over her nightdress. At least she had gained her revenge on her brothers and father. She had played the devoted daughter, sister and mistress of the house. She had won the respect of the matriarchs of society by her charity work. It had been part of the role she created to protect herself.

Her father never forgave her the shame she had brought to the family. He had paid with bouts of stomach pain when she put powdered glass in his drinks. The doctor had diagnosed stomach ulcers and his death had been slow and agonising.

Her eldest brother, James, had escaped her retribution by being killed in action. Reginald had married and Stella had resented his wife becoming mistress here. Fortunately Reginald's duties had kept him abroad and she had ruled supreme, revenge tucked away but never forgotten. Yet each year the house became shabbier and more derelict. Each year there was less money to manage the household accounts. Yet she had struggled on to maintain the prestige of the family. She had also studied plants and learned that an infusion made from foxgloves could induce heart failure.

Stella stared into the rich brown liquid in her glass without remorse. The atrocities she had committed were justice for her lover's death. Maude, too, had had to die. Her legacy to Tanya would pay to refurbish the house and keep Archie in the style she had promised.

Her face crumpled and a fresh flow of tears spilled onto her cheeks. She hadn't expected to miss Maude as much as she did. Her sister had always irritated her, but they had been companions, supporting each other over the years.

Another glass of sherry sustained her. She had done it for Archie. Her lost baby. He had lied, her befuddled mind reasoned. He had said those cruel things to punish her. Archie had cared for her. Hadn't he cautioned her to be careful after the manner of Reginald's death? He had insisted on the delay following Maude's death. Too many tragic deaths in a family can rouse suspicion. He had been concerned that the doctor would become suspicious of Reginald's attacks. That was why she had decided on small doses, administered whenever Reginald became difficult.

They need not have worried about that fool of a doctor. He had made it all so easy when he declared that some tropical fever had weakened Reginald's heart. She nodded in satisfaction. She had delighted in seeing her brother suffer, as she had suffered so cruelly in the months before her confinement.

The refilled glass chinked against her teeth and her stare was malignant and crazed. Her thoughts meandered with increasing belligerence. Sam Hawkes had also been to blame. Archie had bungled it by not killing him when he was set on in the street. But her plan to have him arrested for stealing the silver had worked. Caught red-handed with the stolen goods it would be many years before Sam Hawkes again smelt the clean air outside a prison.

The sherry decanter was empty and her eyes were hard with hatred as she gazed through the door to the stairs where her niece had disappeared. Curse her! Tanya had ruined everything by her obstinacy. Tanya had been the cause of Archie saying those cruel words. It was Tanya's fault that Archie had run away. Now she must pay.

The crystal decanter fell to the floor unnoticed as Stella pushed herself out of the chair. The room weaved precariously as she moved to the stairs. Her hip banged against a table, sending a porcelain figure crashing to the floor. Snow clouds had darkened the afternoon sky. Stella clicked on an electric lightswitch in the hall. Its glow did not reach the upper landing.

'We must get electricity installed on the upper floors,' she mumbled as she clung to the banisters to steady her swaying figure as she climbed the stairs.

There was an oil lamp on a landing table and she lit it with difficulty. The glass shade rattled against the inner glass cylinder when she tried to reposition it. Holding it aloft, she proceeded towards Tanya's room. The girl was now at her mercy.

Chapter Twenty-five

Archie withdrew all his money from his bank before returning to his lodgings. He'd pack a few essentials, collect the passport he'd already forged under the name of Arthur Penrose, and be in Southampton in time to catch the steamer to New York which sailed on the late tide.

At discovering the door to his rooms ajar, his heart lurched with alarm.

'Shit!' he swore under his breath and retreated a step. The stair creaked under his weight, making him quiver with fear. Slasher's voice boomed out, menace in every syllable. 'That you, Arnie boy? Ain't thinking of taking flight, are you?'

Archie began to sweat. Slasher's presence here was ominous. He usually sent his minions to summon him. He pasted on his most disarming smile. It never did to show your fear to the Gilbert brothers. They used it to their own evil ends and sadistic satisfaction. His step casual, he sauntered into the room and blustered, 'Good of you to call, Slasher. This is an unexpected pleasure.'

Seeing Fancy preening his hair in the mirror over the fireplace caused his stomach to knot. The brothers rarely went abroad together unless they had some vendetta to settle.

Slasher was waiting in an armchair, his chin resting on his clasped hands in an attitude of prayer. There was nothing holy about the glitter in his eyes.

'We 'eard the police are getting interested in you,' Slasher announced. 'Fenton ain't giving up. Proving a real pain, 'e is. 'Eard tell that some rich bird from St Paul's way 'as been talking to 'im. You're getting careless, Arnie. She the bint you were gonna get 'itched to for 'er dough?'

'Women have their uses, especially if they're rich.' Archie laughed nervously.

Slasher wasn't amused. 'Planting that stuff on 'Awkes were clumsy. Did you reckon 'e were a rival? We don't like personal greed affecting our business.'

Archie froze with fear. For the Gilberts to have

learned so much meant they had someone in the police in their pay. He should have realised that before. How else could they have kept ahead of Inspector Fenton for so long?

'Ain't like you to be careless, Arnie boy.' Fancy pushed his hands into his trouser pockets, revealing a bright yellow and black striped waistcoat stretched over his barrel stomach. Archie could see the outline of the whalebone corset he wore beneath his shirt. He'd always found the ugly man's vanity hilarious. But he didn't feel like laughing now.

Slasher leaned forward. 'We don't like the police getting too close to our business. It ain't 'ealthy. But you've done us proud, Arnie boy. Some of the schemes you thought up made us a lot of dough. You're one of the best forgers in London.'

'Always happy to oblige,' answered Archie, forcing a smile. While Slasher was talking, Fancy had crossed the room to stand behind him. The feel of his breath on the back of his neck increased his alarm.

'So why 'as the bint been welching on you to Fenton?' Fancy rapped out from behind him.

Slasher had left the chair, a dagger in his hand and pressed to Archie's throat before he could answer. The stiff collar of his shirt grew tight as he swallowed hard.

'I don't know,' he managed hoarsely. His starched shirt collar was becoming limp as he perspired and the linen stuck damply to his shoulders. He could taste and smell his own fear. 'She doesn't know anything about my life as

Arnold Potter. She was upset about Hawkes and wanted to help him. She didn't believe he'd rob her family. She was distraught. And refused to marry me.'

Fancy sniggered. 'Ain't so perfect then, are you, Arnie boy?'

Slasher pressed the point of the dagger harder against his windpipe. It pierced the skin and a thin line of blood ran down Archie's neck. 'We don't want Fenton sniffing round our business. And because of you 'e now is. So how you gonna get 'im off our backs?'

'Whatever I can do, I will. You know that, Slasher,' Archie whined. He'd say anything to appease them. All he needed was to get out of here and he'd be on the first boat leaving the docks. He didn't care where it went. He had to get away from England.

'That's mighty obliging, Arnie boy,' Slasher observed. ''Appen there's a bit of paper you could sign.'

Archie felt the bony hand of death reaching for his shoulder as he asked, 'Sign what?'

Fancy stood beside his brother and drew a document from his pocket. 'It's a sort of insurance document. Ensuring your loyalty, so to speak. Wouldn't want you running out on us when you know so much.'

'I'd never do that.' Archie tasted a salty droplet of sweat which ran into his mouth. His bladder was beginning to ache intolerably. He needed to relive himself urgently.

Slasher grinned. 'Course you wouldn't. But just to set the records straight, we'd like it in writing that you killed Ingram.'

'But that would be a confession,' Archie objected. 'If the police got hold of it I'd be arrested and hanged.'

Fancy lit a fat cigar and blew the smoke in Archie's face. 'The police ain't gonna get 'old of it if you behave yourself, are they?'

'Permanent silence would also keep yer quiet.' Slasher lightly drew the dagger across his throat.

Archie's eyes bulged with terror. 'I'll sign,' he croaked.

The document was laid on the table and folded so that he only saw the bottom half of it. Fancy pushed a pen into his hands.

'What does the rest say?' Archie hedged.

'What it 'as to, that's all. You don't reckon we'd trick you, do yer, Arnie boy? Not one of our best forgers. It's just a question of loyalty and trust. You trust us, don't you?'

Archie saw the writing was a good imitation of his own handwriting. They didn't need him for the signature. They'd found another forger as competent as himself. This was one of their sadistic games. If he signed he'd be hanged. If he refused they'd slit his throat anyway. His usefulness to them had come to an end.

Perhaps by signing he'd gain enough time to get away. He was younger and more agile than either of the heavyset Gilbert brothers. The door was still open behind him. He'd make a bolt for it. Then Arnie Potter and Archie Tilbury would disappear like so many of the other personas he'd assumed in the past.

His palms were so slippery he could scarcely

hold the pen as he signed. He waited, holding his breath until Slasher withdrew the dagger. Then he whirled and shot through the door. The solid figure of Punchdrunk O'Hannagan, the meanest of all the Gilberts' bullies, blocked the top of the stairs.

Punchdrunk lunged at him, crushing him in a bear hug as he marched him back into the room.

'Running out on us, Arnie boy?' Slasher accused, his fetid breath whistling through the gaps of lost teeth. 'Can't 'ave that now, can we?'

'I signed what you wanted,' Archie whined. 'I did everything you asked of me.'

'Yeah, but you got above yourself.' Slasher's mouth parted in an evil parody of Archie's white-toothed disarming smile. 'And you got greedy and careless. You always were a cocky bastard, thinking yerself cleverer than us. We ain't survived this long without 'aving some brains, Arnie boy. Fenton is proving a problem. You'll 'ave to oblige us by putting 'im off our scent. You signed not only a confession to murdering Ingram but also Fenton's brother and where the body was disposed of. It says you knew you'd get caught and couldn't face prison. That's why you topped yerself.'

Archie's mind raced. The dagger was brandished in front of his nose. He faced it unflinching. Slasher hadn't gone to all this trouble to rip his throat from ear to ear. He'd want the death to look like suicide. Hope surged. He still had a chance to escape. He could outwit these louts.

Before he could act, his hands were grabbed by

Punchdrunk and Fancy and wrenched out in front of him.

'I'd never betray you, Slasher.' Desperation made him bluster. 'I've this plan to make us all rich. Could be worth a couple of hundred a week when I've finalised the details.'

'Wouldn't be worth much to us if we were banged up inside, now would it, Arnie boy?' Slasher struck swiftly. The dagger glinted. Ruby tramlines channelled across both Archie's wrists.

'No, Slasher. I'll make our fortune,' he cried at seeing his blood spurt onto the floor.

A grimy rag tied across his mouth by Fancy stopped his pleas. Terror made him struggle harder, pumping his blood more fiercely through the severed arteries. Within seconds his shirt cuffs were soaked and there was a growing pool of scarlet spreading on the rag rug at his feet.

Slasher laughed. 'The more you fight, the quicker it's over with.'

'Why did you do it, Tanya?' Aunt Stella screeched. 'Why did you denounce Archie to the police? You're an evil woman. He adored you. He lied about not being my son. He lied because you had wounded his pride.'

Tanya turned from where she was packing a suitcase. The snow had stopped and if the trains were running she intended to visit Clare at Oaklands. She had drawn up enough plans for the house she was working on for her staff to carry on without her for a week or two. She could even send Polly and Joe further details through the post if she did not wish to return too soon.

She had to get away from this house which was tainted with her defilement and recent death.

Stella stood wild-eyed. Her frizzed fringe was matted and her plait was unravelling. She was still in her nightdress. When she leaned against the doorframe, her body rocked back and forth. Stella was drunk. Shadows from the oil lamp in her hand made her face a ghoulish mask.

Even now her aunt put her in the wrong. Tanya couldn't believe it. She had expected some understanding. Why were the pious always so condemning and a reformed sinner the greatest hypocrite? She did not want to argue with Stella. She did not condemn her for having borne an illegitimate child, but she could not understand her continued blindness towards an impostor who had manipulated them all.

'Archie was not what he seemed,' she said wearily. 'You saw how he reacted when I accused him of being Arnold Potter. Inspector Fenton suspects he is connected with at least one murder and that he's involved with a gang of criminals.'

'Not my Archie.' Stella reeled forward, her face contorted with fury. 'He's a gentle, loving son. You changed him. You used him and then discarded him. You made him abandon me. I hate you.' Her eyes blazed with drunken insanity. She lifted her arm to fling the burning oil lamp at her and cried, 'Burn in hell.'

Tanya screamed. 'My God, no!'

Her petrified stare was pinned to the oil lamp in her aunt's hands. Time was distorted and slowed to reveal everything in shocking detail. As Stella's arm went back, the lamp flickered alarmingly. Droplets of oil leaked from the brass neck of its base to spill on her loosely plaited hair and the sleeve of her nightrobe. The movement caused her to totter. She threw out her arms to save her balance and failed. The leaking oil splashed over her clothing. As she toppled sideways, the oil lamp fell from her hand and smashed on the corner of a table. Oil spread on the carpet. Stella's hair was already alight. The oil on the floor ignited and expanded like a nest of escaping snakes. They writhed along the carpet and as Stella fell to the floor they coiled round her in a lethal embrace.

Shrill, agonised screams reverberated through the house as the fire fed on her clothing. Within seconds her scalp was charred as her hair burnt like dry bracken in a heath fire. Stella was kicking her legs and squirming in terror and pain, which spread the flames.

Tanya darted across the room and snatched a coverlet from her bed to smother the fire. In the seconds it took her to toss the coverlet over her aunt and begin to beat out the flames, her body became engulfed by the fire.

'Come away, Miss Tanya,' Millie shouted from the door, obviously roused by Stella's screams. 'You can't save her.'

Tanya couldn't watch her aunt die and do nothing. When she would have thrown herself down over Stella's body to beat out the smouldering coverlet, Millie dragged her away. The coverlet was ablaze, the flames now licking at the hem of Tanya's dress. A dousing of icy water from the washing jug soaked her skirts and Millie attacked her petticoats with an old tennis racket Tanya still kept in her room.

'We have to get out and call the fire brigade. The fire's out of control,' Millie warned.

'But Aunt Stella–'

'It's too late for her. Wc must save ourselves.'

Tanya saw that her aunt's figure no longer moved within the flames. The fire had spread alarmingly from the floor to the bed and curtains. Already a horsehair chair had been incinerated.

Tanya shut her bedroom door, hoping it would halt the fire's progress. When she turned back to look as they reached the top of the stairs, she saw black smoke curling up from beneath the door and the edges of the hall carpet had already begun to smoulder. There was the sound of shattering glass from the bedroom window.

'Fire! Fire!' Millie yelled, running out into the street.

The smoke was rapidly filling the stairway and hall. Her mind too numbed to be rational, Tanya began to gather possessions to save. She dashed into the sitting room and picked up a silver-framed photograph of her two brothers in uniform and another of her parents on their wedding day. A man's voice called her name, but she continued searching for a photo of Aunt Maude.

'You in there, Miss Summersfield? Come out quickly. It's too dangerous.' The voice broke into a coughing fit. 'Where are you?'

By now, smoke was filtering down through the upstairs floorboards and rolling along the ceiling in billowing waves and sprays of sparks. Suddenly the curtains in the family parlour burst into flames. The air was thick with smoke and Tanya was becoming light-headed. She was horrified to see the stairs and hall were ablaze, flames barring her escape by the front door.

The smoke was rapidly overcoming her, clawing at her throat. Her lungs were scalded, her eyes were stinging and coughs wracked her body. Every movement was leaden as she staggered down the stairs to the kitchen door. The precious photographs were clutched like a talisman to her breast. The door in the basement wouldn't open. It was locked and bolted. Her fumbling fingers managed to drag back the bolts but there was no sign of the key.

Panic filled her. She was trapped. The fire was rapidly advancing. Already the kitchen was filling with smoke. Its heat seared her. Dizzy and panting with fear, she careened backwards. Coughing violently, she lifted the hem of her scorched skirt to cover her lower face and staggered to the window. Through it she could see legs and feet running along the pavement and the skirts of women who were staring at the spectacle of the burning house. Frantically, she banged on the pane to alert them that she was in the basement. No one noticed.

The image of her aunt's burning body added to her horror. She didn't want to die like that. She had to escape. Yesterday she had vowed she would rather die than marry Archie. Now life was precious to her.

The heat was growing intense. The smoke thickened ominously. She'd read somewhere that in a fire the smoke filled a room from the ceiling downwards and that pockets of air remained above the floor. Realising that consciousness was deserting her, Tanya sank to the floor, knocking against the table as she did so. A copper pan clattered onto the tiles at her side. With the last of her strength she threw it at the window, shattering a pane of glass. Then darkness claimed her.

Inspector Fenton arrived at Pilgrim's Crescent in time to see the roof of the Summersfield house collapse and flames shoot skywards. Arms of flames writhed from the upper windows. He'd come to report the death of Tilbury so that Tanya need no longer fear for her safety. He did not believe he had committed suicide, Tilbury was not the type. He would have fled the country first. The Gilberts were behind that false suicide note and he'd nail them if it killed him.

The extent of the fire shocked him. The poor woman had already lost so much, now her home was also gone.

There was a crowd outside on the pavement and firemen were directing their hoses onto the building. Fenton's companion shoved past him with an anguished cry. 'Dammit, no. No! Tanya!' He grabbed a fireman, shouting, 'Tanya, where is she? For the love of God, is Miss Summersfield safe?'

'She's still in there, Mr Hawkes.' Millie pushed forward. 'Nothing can save her now.' The maid burst into hysterical weeping. 'First Miss Stella now Miss Tanya. It's too tragic.'

Inspector Fenton made to grab at Sam to stop

him rushing into the house. 'It's no good, Hawkes. You'll kill yourself if you go in there.'

'I've got to try. I can't leave her to die.'

Without hesitation the inspector bunched his fist and crashed it into Sam's jaw, yelling, 'Accept that she's dead. No one could survive that.'

Sam staggered back against the railings and at that moment there was a splintering of glass and a copper saucepan crashed through the window, missing his head by inches.

'She's in the basement.' He bounded down the stone steps with Fenton a pace behind him. When the door wouldn't open, Sam threw himself against it. 'It's locked. Help me! Someone must have an axe to break it down.'

The fire chief joined them, his axe splintering the wood. 'Stay back, man,' he warned. Pulling a wet kerchief round his lower face he disappeared into the kitchen.

There was a pool of water on the basement steps from the fire hoses and Sam immersed his own handkerchief in it, tied it round his face and followed the fireman. It was impossible to see through the smoke. Sam heard the fire chief stumble into a chair on the far side of the room. He dropped to his knees where the smoke was less dense and crawled to the other side.

'Tanya! Where are you?' he called.

His only answer was the roar of the inferno and rafters crashing down onto the floorboards above them.

'Get out, man,' the fire chief ordered as he crawled back to the door. 'This ceiling will go next.'

As the fireman spoke, Sam's hand which had been scything blindly along the ground in front of him encountered a foot, and then another.

'Over here. I've found her.' His shout was cut off by a coughing fit.

He closed both his hands round Tanya's ankles and dragged her to the door. He could feel his senses dulling, the roar of the fire in his ears becoming a distant rumble. Another figure was at his side supporting him and pulling. Then there was a rush of fresh air and two more firemen filled the narrow space between the railings and kitchen door. They heaved Sam and Tanya over their shoulders to carry them to safety.

Sam sat on the kerb staring at the fire chief who was bending over Tanya's prone figure. The man looked up, the whites of his eyes stark in his smoke-blackened face.

'Looks like she'll live. Another minute and the smoke would've killed her even if the flames hadn't reached her. But she's in a bad way. Both of you will have to go to hospital. You'll need to be kept under observation in case the smoke has damaged your lungs.'

Sam put his head in his hands and wept with relief. Then heaving himself to Tanya's side, he took her hand, gently chaffing it and willing her to return to consciousness.

An ambulance clanged into the Crescent and before Tanya could be lifted onto the stretchers, her eyes opened. Overcome with joy, Sam clasped her in his arms. 'My darling, you're safe.'

He felt her stiffen and drew back. Her eyes were round with terror. 'No, don't touch me.' Her voice was gruff, weak and filled with revulsion. 'Don't touch me!'

'Tanya, it's Sam. You're safe with me.'

She began to hit out at him. 'Don't touch me. No. No. Don't touch me!'

Inspector Fenton took Sam's arm. 'Let the ambulance men see to her.'

Sam was shocked by her reaction. She acted as though she loathed him. His touch obviously repulsed her. 'It was as thought she hated me.' He spoke his thoughts aloud. 'Yet she knew I was innocent of the theft. What have I done?'

Inspector Fenton replied softly, 'It's not you she hates. She's in shock. The poor woman has gone through a great deal in the last twenty-four hours and not just burying her father and this fire.'

'What's happened to her?' Sam demanded, his fists bunched ready to fight the world if need be to protect Tanya.

'I had to swear not to tell you.'

Sam glared at him. 'Tell me what happened.' When the inspector remained silent, he growled, 'It was Tilbury, wasn't it?'

The silence confirmed his fears. 'That bastard would have done anything to compromise her so that she'd marry him, wouldn't he? Did he rape her?'

Fenton would not look at him. Sam grabbed the inspector's lapels but kept his voice low so that the gathering crowd of spectators watching the fire would not hear. 'He raped her, didn't he? The bastard raped that fine innocent woman, didn't he?'

'It's not for me to say.'

'So she was raped, since you have not denied it.' Sam wiped his face with his hand. There was murder in his eyes and a pain so acute in his heart that it almost destroyed his reason.

The inspector had been studying him shrewdly and with a heavy sigh said, 'If you care for her, she needs time. I've seen many cases of rape and none are without trauma for a woman. Some are mentally scarred for life. A man's touch can pitch them into hysteria. What is worse, she, the victim, will feel guilty.' He paused and rubbed his temple. 'I'm explaining this because it is obvious that you care for Miss Summersfield. She is strong-willed and I'm sure she'll come through this better than most. Even so, it won't be easy for her. It is a shameful secret she would normally carry to the grave.'

'It's as well that Tilbury is dead, or I'd have done for him,' Sam raged. He stared bleakly at the ambulance. 'I failed her. All I wanted was to spare her pain and protect her.'

'Be there when she needs you. Don't condemn her.'

'I don't, but when I think what that bastard did to her...' Sam shuddered.

'Best get yourself to the hospital, Mr Hawkes. I've got more enquiries to make on the Gilbert brothers. Now I know that Potter, or Tilbury as you knew him, was involved with them, I'll get them for the murder of my brother.'

'I hope you do,' Sam said, shaking the inspector's hand. 'Nasty pieces of work by all accounts, the Gilbert brothers. Go carefully, Inspector.'

Before getting into the ambulance, Sam stared at the burning house. Spirals of smoke trailed skywards like dragon's breath. Nothing had been saved except the three photographs Tanya had been clutching. A coffin was taken in to remove Stella's body.

He groaned. The brigadier's illness had never seemed natural to him and now this. What horrors had Tanya faced here in the last few hours?

Sam turned away, his thoughts in turmoil. The vision of Tilbury violating Tanya was crucifying him. Jealousy and rage stormed through him. Tilbury had taken what he most coveted and like a fool had rejected. Anger perverted reason. He had his own demons to wrestle with.

Chapter Twenty-six

Sam was dismissed from hospital the next day. Tanya was kept under observation for a week. Her burned hands had been bandaged. Their dull throbbing scarcely registered against the wretchedness enclosing her heart. She refused to see Sam when he visited every evening. Her emotions were too raw, too exposed and vulnerable. The shock from the traumatic events leading up to the fire had finally caught up with her. Inspector Fenton had visited to tell her of Archie's death and the confession in his suicide note.

'How could I have been taken in by so evil a man?' she asked wretchedly.

'He used people without mercy. When charm failed he resorted to brutality.' Inspector Fenton's expression was haggard. 'He also confessed to murdering my brother, saying the body was sealed in the foundations of a recently built picture palace. That makes me suspect that Tilbury did not commit suicide but was murdered by the Gilbert brothers. I mean to put Fancy and Slasher Gilbert behind bars where they belong.' He stepped back. 'I just wanted to tell you that you were safe from Tilbury. And there is something else.' He paused. 'You have a visitor waiting to see you. Hawkes says you won't see him. Yet he was the one who dragged you from your home and saved your life.'

Her throat cramped and she battled to overcome a wave of tears. Blinking them aside, she said softly, 'I can't face him. He'll want to know what happened. I could never tell him that.'

'Don't you owe it to him? Besides, he guessed the truth. If he judged you harshly, he'd not be here.'

'I never wanted anyone to know my shame. Especially Sam.' Her voice cracked, her concentration centred upon the white purity of the sheet.

'I've seen the effects of many cases of rape. Don't blame yourself for what happened. And don't let one man's brutality destroy all that is fine in you. Especially as that man was so unworthy.'

Feeling his gaze boring into her, she inhaled

deeply to calm the turmoil of her heart and mind. He was right, but that didn't make it easier to bear.

'Time is the greatest healer, not only of the body but of the mind,' he counselled. 'Shall I ask Mr Hawkes to come in now?'

She knew she must face Sam or it would be even harder in the future. Sam's friendship was valuable to her. At least she could keep that. 'Yes, I would like to see Sam. And I hope you find the men who killed your brother, Inspector Fenton.'

When Sam walked in, her heart constricted. His hair was dishevelled and fell forward over his brow as though he had constantly pushed his hand through it.

Sam hadn't come to terms with Tanya's rape but he couldn't stay away from the hospital for worrying about her. 'How are you?' he asked. He dared not touch her after the way she had responded after the fire. His need to protect her was so overwhelming that to curb it made his manner stiff and awkward.

'I'm feeling better. They're letting me leave to attend Stella's funeral tomorrow.'

'I contacted Clare. She should be here this afternoon. She couldn't come earlier as the lanes around Oaklands were cut off by snow. It's raining now and the snow thawed overnight.' He winced inwardly. Why the hell was he rattling on about the weather like an idiot? 'Clare wants you to return to Oaklands with her and stay as long as you need.'

'Yes, I shall, but I also have a business to run.' A worry which had been troubling her all morning returned. 'Sam, do you know what has happened to Millie? She has no family and she was more than a servant, she was Maude's friend. I hate to think of her being destitute.'

'A Mrs Rivers invited her to stay with her after the fire and she has since found a post as maid to an acquaintance of Mrs Rivers who lives in Ealing.'

'I always liked Mrs Rivers. She's a spiritualist. Stella was set against her but she helped Maude so much. I'll write to them both. I wouldn't like to lose touch with either of them.' She turned to a more painful subject. 'How badly was the house burned?'

He sighed, his rugged face ravaged with anguish. 'It was gutted. I'm sorry, Tanya, nothing was saved. How did the fire start?'

Her eyes widened and she began to tremble.

'You don't have to tell me,' Sam said hastily.

'Stella was drunk,' she answered in a flat monotone. 'She hated me for refusing to marry Archie. She was going to throw the oil lamp at me, screaming at me to burn in hell. It was leaking and set light to her clothing.'

Tears ran down her cheeks. Without thinking Sam gathered her into his arms and holding her close whispered against her hair, 'It's all right, Tanya. No one can hurt you now.'

She leant her head on his chest briefly. Then a violent trembling beset her and she pushed back from him, her eyes wild as she drew her knees up to her chin, her fingers scrunching the sheet as she held it to her mouth. 'Don't ... don't touch me.'

'I didn't mean to … I was trying to comfort you. I'd never harm you, Tanya.' Sam was appalled at her reaction.

She gulped and the terror left her eyes. 'I'm sorry, Sam. It's not you. It's…'

He quickly changed the subject, wishing he could take her hand in the usual way to comfort and reassure her. 'The house was insured, wasn't it?'

His heart ached at the brave way she fought to regain her composure. She was a fighter. Most women would be hysterical at what she had endured.

'The buildings were insured as a stipulation of the mortgage,' she replied. 'I doubt the contents were. It would have meant selling another painting to pay the premium. Stella refused to sell anything unless it was vital. Fortunately, I have my business to support me.' Her voice cracked and she stared at the wall, unable to hold Sam's gaze. 'That's if my reputation is not so tarnished that no one will employ me.'

'Tilbury's death was in all the papers and with the drama of the fire, your names were inevitably linked. There was bound to be some gossip, but only one order was cancelled. Polly says there have been several enquiries.'

The bruising on Tanya's face had almost faded but her eyes were hollow and her cheeks sunken. There was tension in her figure; her green eyes, once so expressive and full of life, were bleak with wounds as yet too harrowing to speak of. Sam ached to hold her in his arms. 'Tanya,' he said gently, 'I'll always be here when you need me.

You know that.'

She nodded, but he could see a tear forming beneath her lashes. His restraint broke and he blurted out, 'Marry me, Tanya. I don't care what's happened. I can provide for you. Your father would understand in the circumstances. I know how important your work is to you and as my wife any gossip will be silenced.'

He could have kicked himself at how badly the words had come out.

Without looking at him, she said hollowly, 'Is there nothing you wouldn't do for the brigadier, Sam? Even marry his dishonoured daughter?'

'Tanya, I… Forgive me, I didn't mean it to sound that way.'

To his relief he heard Clare Grosvenor's voice as she entered the ward. 'Clare's here. I'll go now. She can be more help to you than I can. I never meant to upset you.'

Clare swept over to the bed and kissed Tanya's cheek, heedless of the charged atmosphere between the couple. 'Tanya, my poor darling. Thank God you survived the fire.'

'I'll leave you to Clare.' Sam edged back from the bed. 'Let me know if there's anything I can do. I've had a telephone installed at the garage, Clare has the number. Ring if you need to talk to Polly or Joe about your business. There's enough work to keep the men busy. There's nothing for you to worry about.'

Tanya nodded, her voice hoarse as she said, 'You saved my life, Sam. I shall never forget that. Your friendship means a lot to me, but…'

'Let there be no buts for now, Tanya,' he said

with a slow smile. 'First you must recover and the best place for that is at Oaklands.'

'She will be our guest for as long as she wishes,' Clare stated.

Tanya watched Sam walk away and a single tear ran down her cheeks. 'He asked me to marry him, Clare,' she said brokenly. 'Once I longed to hear those words. But he asked me out of pity and the loyalty he had for my father.'

Clare looked at her with tears in her eyes. 'You have been through so much. You must stay with us until you are fully recovered,' she said firmly. 'And are you sure you're up to attending your aunt's funeral?'

'Yes. She was as much Archie's victim as I was. I have to come to terms with what she did and forgive her, or I cannot forgive myself. A few weeks out of London with you is the best cure I can think of.'

It was not just London she needed to escape from, it was also Sam. She had to come to terms with her loss and the ordeal of recent events. Later, work would be her lifeline.

Tanya spent a month at Oaklands and returned to London briefly to inspect the work done by her men and ensure that they had followed her instructions. She did so on a day when she knew Sam was out of the city inspecting some second-hand cars he wished to purchase. He had phoned Oaklands several times, but convinced that he had asked her to marry him out of pity, or loyalty to her father, Tanya's conversation was stilted.

Putting aside her guilt at avoiding Sam, she

made the most of her day in London. Joe Lang was with her when she exclaimed in astonishment at the work they had accomplished at the Vernons' house.

'The men have been working longer hours and refusing to take any extra money,' he explained. 'It's their way of repaying you for giving them jobs when other employers refused. We shall finish here a month earlier than expected and another two houses will be completed within the next three weeks. You've had several enquiries for more work.'

'I had better visit those prospective customers.' Tanya felt a stab of unease. It had been difficult enough facing her staff for she was not sure how much they knew or guessed about the fire or Archie Tilbury's death. To meet strangers who might have heard gossip was daunting. But it had to be done. She had decided before leaving the hospital that to triumph over Archie's attack she must face the world unflinching. She had been guilty of nothing and she did not intend to become a victim.

Of the four customers she visited, only one declined her ideas. All expressed their commiserations over the fire, but she turned the conversation to avoid the subject. They had been curious about the incident, but their friendly manner showed her that they did not suspect anything more sinister. There had been no comments about her relationship with Archie for which she was relieved. On reflection she doubted whether Mr Fairchild would speak of what he had seen, since his own morality did not bear close scrutiny.

Her three new customers wanted her sketches as soon as possible. It was proof of how popular her work was becoming. Her step was lighter, her mind already planning one of the rooms as she hailed a cab to take her to Lincoln's Inn for an appointment with Mr Dobbs.

The genial solicitor regarded her sombrely. 'I fear the insurance money from the house only covers the mortgage and interest. The property was leasehold. That means you do not own the land. The brigadier had a few hundred pounds in his bank and that is all that will come to you.'

'At least there are no debts,' Tanya said, 'My business gives me the means to support myself.'

Next she went to the workshop. Sal had just returned from school and Tanya was surprised at the change in the shy girl. She had filled out and upon seeing her ran and flung her arms round her neck.

'Oh, Miss Tanya. I thought we'd never see you again. I cried every night after the fire.'

'Sal, that's no way to greet Miss Tanya. She's your employer,' Polly remonstrated.

Tanya held Sal close. 'That's all right, Polly. I'm glad to see Sal looking so well. And you. How is little Jane?'

'I'm fine, miss. So is the baby.' She nodded towards the cradle by the sewing machine where the baby slept soundly. 'When are you coming back?'

'Soon, Polly. This weekend Clare is throwing a birthday dinner and dance for me. I have to return to Oaklands for that. I shall work on the sketches for the customers I saw today while I'm there.'

She looked around the workroom and saw the swatches of material for curtains and the partially sewn, intricately draped velvet pelmet for Mrs Vernon's bedroom hanging over a rail. 'You've coped wonderfully, Polly. I feel guilty leaving you with so much responsibility.'

'I enjoy it, Miss Tanya. And Sam's been a brick. He's always popping in to check if we need anything.' Her eyes glowed as she spoke of Sam and Tanya flinched.

To counter her discomfort, she became practical. 'Mrs Jenner in Sussex Gardens wants a bathroom fitted. I need a larger catalogue of baths and fittings. Could you get Joe to chase up our stockists for that? The customers I saw today will need their rooms measured by Friday. The requirements are listed on this paper.' She tore a page from the notebook she always carried with her. 'Does anything else need my attention?'

'One or two things,' Polly replied.

For the next hour Tanya checked the costing on wallpaper and curtain material, writing out a schedule of work to be completed the following week and discussing any likely problems with Joe.

'That's the second time that supplier has sent us inferior material. Don't use him again, Joe. I shall write to him and tell him why. Our patrons expect the best and that is what they will get. If a supplier thinks that because I'm a woman I can be duped, then they will learn otherwise to their cost. The sooner words get round that I will not be overcharged or accept inferior goods the better.'

There was half an hour before Simon would pick her up. Looking out of the window at the cobbled road, she heard a car engine revving and saw Sam drive into the garage towing a battered and neglected Daimler with Smiley at the wheel. Even that brief glimpse of him pierced her with agony. Why must her heart betray her with longing when her body now shrank from the touch of a man?

She drew away from the window and opened her workbook. A dried red carnation fell out. It was from the immense bouquet Sam had bought her. She picked it up and stared at it. Her eyes closed as she remembered all the tender moments between them. Carefully she put the carnation between two leaves of paper. When she looked up she saw Sam watching her by the doorway. Her heart twisted and she hastily shut the book, feeling foolish that he might have recognised the flower, or its significance to her.

'How are you doing, Tanya?' he said with a grin. He leaned against the doorpost with his hands in the pockets of his black trousers. His tie was loosened and his jacket undone and a lock of his wheatgold hair flopped over his brow. 'It's good to see you back behind your desk.'

'I'm well enough, even my hands are no longer painful.' She stared at the scars which would take some years to disappear and self-consciously hid them in her skirts. A tension began to build between them which had never been present before Archie's attack. Needing to prove her independence, she rushed on, 'I received three commissions today. I've enough work now to keep everyone employed through to the autumn.'

'And more will come in. You can't fail, Tanya.'

'My next priority is to look for rooms. Not too expensive or too far from here. But I can stay in a hotel for a few weeks until that is arranged. I've no luggage and only a couple of black gowns Clare kindly gave me as I lost everything in the fire.'

'Perhaps this will cheer you,' Sam said, his grin broadening. He stepped into the room and Polly put her head round the door as he ordered, 'Close your eyes, Tanya. Polly and I have a surprise for you.'

Tanya did as she was told, but the warmth in his voice as his gaze rested upon Polly disturbed her. Working and living so close to each other was throwing them together. And they were so alike, both conscientious and hardworking, and they made an attractive couple.

There was a rustle of Polly's petticoats and Sam commanded, 'You can open your eyes now.'

She stared at the two velvet dresses spread on her desk. One was black with a high collar and tight sleeves. The other was a sleeveless evening gown of midnight blue with a low scooped neckline decorated with seed pearls.

'Sam brought your ruined gown from the hospital and asked me to make these from the measurements,' Polly explained. 'You'll be wanting something special for your birthday dance which Mrs Grosvenor is giving you. And I thought something smart for when you return to work wouldn't go amiss. I hope you like them.'

Tanya's eyes misted with tears. 'They are beautiful.' She stood up and held the evening gown against her. Its full skirt flowed in elegant lines to the floor without the aid of a bustle. Laying it reverently back on the desk, she smiled at Polly and embraced her. 'Thank you. They must have taken all your spare time to make and you have worked so hard running the business while I've been away.'

'It were my pleasure. You've done so much for me, Miss Tanya.'

She turned to Sam, feeling awkward at the restraint between them. She kissed his cheek. 'That was so thoughtful of you, Sam. Thank you.'

'I couldn't have my partner wearing borrowed clothes for her birthday, could I?' He reached for her hand and squeezed it briefly and from behind his back produced a bottle of champagne and two glasses.

'I can hear the baby crying,' Polly said, her smile enigmatic. As she passed Sam, she touched his arm in what seemed to Tanya an intimate gesture. 'I'll catch you later, Sam. I know you'll be working late on the Daimler with Smiley, so I'll bring you both over some rabbit pie.'

Sam grinned. 'You're a treasure. You spoil me. I could get a meal at the pub.'

'Except that you won't.' Polly laughed and looked back at Tanya. 'Talk to him, Miss Tanya. He'd work through the night on those old cars without eating or sleeping if I didn't keep an eye on him.'

'He's lucky to have you, Polly.' Tanya hoped her

voice sounded natural. It proved that Sam had only asked her to marry him because of his loyalty to her father. He would be better off with Polly. She just wished it didn't hurt so much admitting it.'

Sam was concentrating on freeing the champagne cork and did not respond to Polly's taunting. The cork popped and he poured the champagne. Pressing a glass into Tanya's hand, he lifted his in a toast. 'To the success of Summersfield Interior Designs.' Their gazes met over the rim of the glasses and Sam added more gently, 'And to its beautiful owner. May all her dreams come true.' The tenderness in his gaze threw her into confusion. She felt the wine splashing onto her hands as her body began to tremble.

Sam took the glass from her and placed it on the desk. Her gaze was stapled to the floor.

'You've overtired yourself,' he said. 'Don't rush things, Tanya. Take all the time you need.'

She didn't answer. She couldn't. Everyone had been so kind, especially Sam. Even without his interest in Polly, the spectre of Archie Tilbury would always be between them. It tensed every nerve and triggered the nausea of disgust.

A toot from a car horn sounding outside was a welcome relief. 'That will be Simon,' she said.

As Tanya picked up her gloves an ashen-faced Simon burst into the office and threw a newspaper onto the desk. 'Have you seen this?'

Tanya stared at the headlines in horror: 'Police Inspector killed in Leicester Square'. The article described a tragic road accident when several barrels rolled from a brewer's dray onto the pavement as Inspector Fenton was waiting to cross the road. He was crushed beneath their weight and died instantly.

'It wasn't an accident. He was murdered,' Tanya groaned. 'He was getting too close to the men who killed his brother.'

'Then the police will get them,' Simon said.

Sam shook his head. 'If those gangleaders escaped Fenton, they'll escape any copper. Even an army of blue bottles couldn't flush them out of their midden. They know every secret place there is in their district. If anyone takes the Gilbert brothers out, it will be one of their own kind. And it will probably be a bloodbath.'

His words came true the following year when Slasher's decapitated body was found bound to the railings of one of his clubs. The newspapers reported that he'd fallen foul of opium dealers. Fancy Gilbert had gone into hiding. Sam heard that Fancy's name was later linked to another underworld killing, that of Zach Morton, a nightclub owner. The day after Morton's funeral, Fancy's brutally battered body was found hanging from a lamppost.

Chapter Twenty-seven

Tanya stood on the terrace of Oaklands gazing up at the moon. She had escaped the press of well-wishers, the heat of the dancing had made her head ache. Gazing up at the moon she tipped her glass to it and leaned back against the wall. This was the second birthday dance Clare had thrown for her. Tonight there were sixty guests in comparison to the small occasion of two years ago. Even so Tanya had again chosen to wear the midnight blue velvet dress Sam had asked Polly to make for her then.

Her gaze idly spanned the garden with its Italian statues and Chinese lanterns strung out among the trees to create a festive atmosphere. The last two years had been busy as she had thrown herself into her work to put the trauma of the fire and rape behind her. It was only rarely now that she awoke with nightmares, reliving her ordeal. Summersfield Interior Designs had become one of the most sought-after companies by anyone in society wishing to redecorate a room. She had outgrown her workshop and moved to larger premises across London Bridge in Southwark. She rented rooms in Chelsea but Sam still lived over the garage and ploughed all his capital back into his motor business.

It had paid off. He had prospered and had opened a showroom in Shaftesbury Avenue to sell the more expensive cars he renovated. In the last year, with them both working hard, they rarely saw each other more than twice a month. Usually they ended up arguing over the money Sam insisted was still paid to her from her father's share of the business. It was deposited in a bank and she had not touched a penny of it. Sam would turn up with two theatre tickets or coerce her to dine with him and throughout he would tease her as if she was a younger sister.

Unaccountably that had irked her of late and she had begun to dread that he would meet someone and marry them. When she teased him about other women friends, he always laughed and said that he was too busy for romance.

'What about Polly?' she persisted. 'She cares for you and would make you a good wife.'

He had looked at her strangely. 'Is that what you've been thinking? I suppose she was grateful for the little I did for her at the beginning, but that was all. She knows what her sister went through before she got over what happened to her. It made her wary about starting a new relationship for fear of how it would affect Sal.'

'She never told me.' Tanya felt hurt, believing that she and Polly were close.

'She probably thought you had enough worries rebuilding your life after the fire. I took Polly and Sal out for a few drives, that was all. Sal trusts me and is beginning to trust men. She even has a young man she sees once a week. But you haven't, have you? You've built a wall round your emotions which I'd give anything to break down. But you resist.'

That night she had wept for the first time since leaving the hospital. Why couldn't she stop loving Sam? Sometimes in her dreams she could recall the joy she had felt in Sam's arms that night in the conservatory, then suddenly his face would change to become Archie's and she would wake up trembling, her body cold, her flesh crawling from the horror of his touch.

As she stared at the moon, the ancient symbol of love and fertility, an emptiness smote her.

Throughout the last year Clare had been determined that Tanya's life should not be all work and whenever Tanya visited she had a house full of guests. It was her way of matchmaking, but none of the men interested Tanya. If she was held too tightly during a dance her body would tense and panic would well up in her, and she would make an excuse to break away.

'Not dancing, Tanya?' Sam's voice teased from behind her. 'It's not done for the guest of honour at her own birthday ball to be alone.'

She smiled wanly. 'Clare means well but there is a rigid formality about these dances. I was remembering the night we went to Earl's Court. They suddenly struck up a waltz...'

'And I grabbed you like this.' He reached for her and spun her round and round. 'And we danced through the trees with people staring at us as though we were mad.'

Instantly Tanya tensed but Sam disregarded it and whirled her faster and faster.

'Stop, Sam,' she began but her protest was drowned by his laughter as he spun her across the lawn away from the brightly lit terrace. Suddenly he stopped dancing but continued to hold her. Every pore of her body was aware of him, each nerve resisting the feel of his arms round her.

'Let me go, Sam,' she said stiffly.

He released her with a heavy sigh. 'It's no good, Tanya. I can't go on like this. I've tried to be patient, but you keep shutting me out.'

'I value your friendship, Sam.'

He eyed her sternly. 'I told you once that I did

not believe that a man and a woman can be friends. I was right about us. I've tried to stand by my promise to the brigadier and even that is no longer important.'

Tanya's heart scudded as she stared at him. 'What else can there be between us? I can't shake free of the nightmares. I'm scared. I don't ever want you to touch me and I react with horror.'

'Do you really think that would be so?' his voice was low.

Before she realised his intention he took her face in his hands and gazed down at her. 'I'm going to kiss you, Tanya. That is all. I cannot believe that the loving, sensual woman I once held in my arms has been destroyed. Trust me. I'm not going to hurt you.'

As he finished speaking his mouth descended to cover hers. Immediately her body became rigid. Her lips clamped shut and her teeth were gritted. Her hands were open claws pushing against his hard chest.

The pressure of his mouth was light and infinitely tender. It moved with unhurried, caressing precision, thorough, loving but without the urgency of passion. When he drew back, he stared into her eyes. 'Did that repel you?'

A faint shake of her head was the only answer she was capable of, but the tension within her remained. This time when he kissed her, his arms slid lightly about her shoulders, the movements of his mouth subtly persuasive until the stiffness in her limbs drained away and slowly her fingers uncurled to lie relaxed upon his jacket. There was no horror evoked by the kiss. The play of Sam's fingers as they travelled down her spine were those of a lover. Archie had never touched her except to humiliate and degrade. Sam venerated, revered. Her eyes were open and fastened on the moon above them, the moon which had wrapped them in its magic in the conservatory. And its magic was working again now.

Her eyes closed, there was the faintest tingling in the pit of her stomach and as Sam's lips moved from her mouth to nuzzle her ear, he whispered, 'I love you, Tanya. Let me make you whole again.'

His hand slid the length of her spine and a ripple of pleasure followed in its wake. Her lips parted, hesitant at first, then as his tongue teased the softness of her mouth, her arms went round him.

There was no fear, no horror, only peace, exhilaration and anticipation of a heaven yet to be experienced. Time and Sam's special tenderness had enabled her to conquer her terrors.

'Marry me, Tanya.'

'You are not asking me out of pity or loyalty to my father?' she asked, breathless from his kiss.

He kissed her again, this time allowing his passion full reign. It was several long moments before they broke apart and both were breathing heavily and trembling with longing. His voice was gruff with desire. 'Does that answer you?'

'It's the only answer I've ever wanted from you.'

The publishers hope that this book has given you enjoyable reading. Large Print Books are especially designed to be as easy to see and hold as possible. If you wish a complete list of our books please ask at your local library or write directly to:

Magna Large Print Books
Magna House, Long Preston,
Skipton, North Yorkshire.
BD23 4ND